OPERATION RAVEN

OPERATION RAVEN

A Novel

Stuart White

BEAUFORT BOOKS
Publishers
New York

No character in this book is intended to represent any actual person; all the incidents of the story are entirely fictional in nature.

Library of Congress Cataloging-in-Publication Data

White, Stuart, 1947—
    Operation Raven.

    I. Title.
PR6073.H52706   1986   823'.914   85-26721
ISBN 0-8253-0348-6

Published in the United States by Beaufort Books Publishers, New York.

Printed in the U.S.A. First American Edition, 1986

10 9 8 7 6 5 4 3 2 1

To my brothers Owen and Christopher,
to Anne and to Monika.

'In Britain the prospect of a royal kidnap—Lord Hailsham was particularly concerned about the fate of the "Little Princesses"—was taken seriously. It would be an excellent engine of blackmail.'

The King Over the Water—The Windsors in the Bahamas 1940-45 Michael Pye

'In Britain alone some thirty German agents were executed by hanging. Others died mysteriously, like Ulrich von der Osten, a senior Abwehr agent. Osten landed at Los Angeles in March 1941 in the name of Don Julio Lopez Lido, and checked into the Taft Hotel in New York on 16th March. Two weeks later he was dead. His movements were shadowed by the FBI and British Security Co-ordination, the M16 organisation in North America with its HQ in the Rockefeller Center, and when he left the hotel to dine at Child's Restaurant in Times Square, he was hit and fatally injured by a taxicab.

'Another equally mysterious death involved Jan Villen Ter Braak, a man whose true identity was never established. He was found shot to death on the grimy concrete floor of an air raid shelter in Cambridge, England, his suitcase wireless set beside him. Whether it was suicide or murder would never be known.'

Bodyguard of Lies Anthony Cave Brown

Chapter One

28th May, 1940

THERE WERE two of them, Hawker Hurricanes, easily distinguishable by their stubby wings from the more graceful Spitfire.

They roared in at illegal, treetop height over Windsor Great Park sending the deer scattering, terrified, in all directions.

Two young girls watched from a distance, off near the Royal Lodge where the public was forbidden. The elder of the two could just make out the bulky, hunched figures of the pilots before the planes veered sharply off.

The girls watched them go, across the lazy Thames, over Eton college where the schoolboys strained necks encased in starched white collars to see them.

The pilots would get a rocket back at Northolt. Low-flying was one thing, low-flying over the home of the royal family quite another.

But the girls had loved it, thrilling to the martial display, reassuring in its power. For off to the south was the deep rumbling of the guns from France, growing louder by the day. Rumour had it the British Expeditionary Force was leaving France from Dunkirk, and after what the Germans had done to Holland, Belgium and now France, could a strip of water stop them?

That night as the girls prepared for bed, the elder of the two seemed anxious and more subdued than normal, for she was a

9

carefree child, despite the war. But tonight she bit at her lip, a sure sign that she was worried.

She had made her nightly telephone call to her parents in London, and after listening to the BBC news bulletin with her sister and their governess, the girls pushed their tiny paper flags into a battle map of Europe on which they had been following the course of the war. The Germans seemed to be everywhere, and the French and British were not a continuous line any more. At length the elder girl said: 'Crawfie . . . they wouldn't ever come here, would they, out of the sky in parachutes, like they did in Holland?'

'Come here in parachutes, Lillibet, why?'

'To take us away, they wouldn't would they, Crawfie?'

Marion Crawford cooed reassuringly. It was absolutely unthinkable; or was it? If not, why the crack troops of the Coates Mission geared up for quick flight in the event of invasion? Why the anti-aircraft guns and the anti-parachute defences?

And why did she scan the night skies herself, anxiously looking for the ghostly white parachute shrouds?

But she took hold of Elizabeth's hand firmly: 'Lillibet, you are to be the next Queen of England. Believe me, they would not dare.'

Dunkirk, 31st May

Three kilometres from Bray-dunes, east along the beach from Dunkirk, a six-man patrol of British soldiers squirmed forward on their bellies and elbows through the sandy soil and pine-needles, towards a small wood. The men were dog-tired from days without proper sleep. Tired and considerably scared. For they had been ordered to check a report of tanks in the copse ahead of them. For reasons no one could yet fathom, but for which everyone was wondrously grateful, the German panzer columns which had been wreaking such havoc among the British and French armies had suddenly stopped at the grimly-held Dunkirk perimeter.

But if the report was true and tanks were coming, there was nothing but a handful of tired infantry, and little heavier than one anti-tank gun to stop them. They'd go through the line like a bowling ball through skittles; down the beach, in among the knackered troops queueing for the boats.

It was a nightmare in a landscape of them. But if the tanks could be confirmed, perhaps the so far invisible Brylcreemed warriors of the Royal Air Force could come over and try to shoot the Panzers up. It was a slim hope, the whole of the Western Front had gone to hell anyway, so it was worth a try.

And while the rest of the British Expeditionary Force moved backwards as fast as it could, Lieutenant Harry Prendergast, Sergeant Albert Fothergill and four men went in the opposite direction. Fothergill thought the whole thing was crazy. If there were tanks, and if the patrol found them, they would get killed before they could get the news back, he felt sure of that. Either the support Panzer Grenadiers would scatter them like rabbits with the spandaus and stick grenades before they got close. Or if they did get *that* close, close enough to see the big, black terrifying metal bastards, then they would just roll out and squash the patrol flat like khaki bugs. Then they'd be off to Bray-dunes and Dunkirk, and probably Dover after that. It seemed there was nowhere those Jerry bastards couldn't go when they had a mind to do it.

Crack! Crack!

He had the Bren up on its bipod in four seconds flat, and by then everyone was opening up in panic. The thud-thud of Lee Enfields, and God knew what they were firing at, there was nothing to see. Even the chinless wonder Prendergast was firing his Webley, God give us strength.

Fothergill aimed at the base of the treeline and gave it two quick bursts, *zzzzzppp, zzzzzppp.*

They were dead now, it was a matter of time only. Out in the open, no cover within fifty yards, just the wood, and the wood was where the Germans were. Soon the spandaus would open up, and then the deadly stick grenades trailing their ribbons.

11

Thud-thud! Thud! Thud! Silence. *Thud!*

'Cease firing. Casualties?' The reedy voice of Lieutenant Prendergast trilled falsetto with fear. 'Call out.'

No one was hurt. Fothergill wondered why. He ripped out the curved magazine, now empty, and fitted another. He put the back of his hand as close to the barrel of the Bren as he could and felt the heat from it. He swore. Soon it would be red hot and useless and there was no spare. So no Bren, not that it mattered now.

And then there was a rag being waved from the copse. Perhaps he was hallucinating, none of them had had any proper sleep in over forty-eight hours. He rubbed his eyes, the white flag was still there.

'White flag, sir!'

'I *see* it, Sergeant.'

'Sir!' Six sets of eyes were riveted on a dirty white cloth fluttering from what looked like a tree branch.

'It could be a trick.' Prendergast's voice was still trembling.

Trick? thought the sergeant. Why would they bother, they've got us, they don't have to play cowboys and indians with us.

'I wish to surrender.' The voice from the copse had almost no trace of accent, it was as neutral as a hospital room, and had the same quality of cynicism, pain and death.

It was the first German they had ever heard, apart from Hitler's ranting on the newsreels, and that was mumbo-jumbo. 'Do you hear me? I wish to surrender.'

Prendergast cast an anxious glance to his sergeant. The look said 'What do I do'?

The sergeant went eyes-front. Do it yourself mate, you've got the pips on your shoulder, you're the one who went to frigging Sandhurst. The lieutenant hissed: 'I'm going to make him come out with his hands up. If he makes one false move, let him have it.'

'Sir.' Fothergill suppressed a sneer. False move? Let him have it? Prendergast must have sneaked out of boarding school and down to the Regal to spend his pocket money.

The lieutenant cupped his hands and shouted: 'Put down

12

any weapon you have, put your hands high above your head and walk forward slowly. If you make any hostile move my men will open fire.'

Fothergill levelled the Bren, and thought: It was the British and French who surrendered, not the Germans. What was up with this one?

There was a movement of bushes and the men tensed. Four .303 Lee Enfield rifles, one Bren gun and a Webley .38 revolver (the revolver would have missed, though the others would not) trained on a tall, hatless man in an unbuttoned tunic, who came into view. His hands were held as high as he could get them. He had no wish to have a .303 round from a trigger-happy Tommy crashing through his guts, not at this stage of the game. He walked forward slowly but deliberately towards the prone khaki figures.

The sergeant had his finger on the Bren's trigger, eyes squinting round the curved magazine, the German squarely in his foresight. So this was the master race, the bloody supermen was it? The sergeant had been strafed, dive-bombed, shelled and machine-gunned all the way from Arras, and the only glimpse of the Germans he had seen was a distant blur of feldgrau and coal-scuttle helmets. Now here was one up close, hands in the air, crapping his pants, packing it in, God knew why but who cared. Fothergill felt a visceral urge to squeeze the trigger, to let the Bren kick and buck, to see a stream of bullets hose into the Jerry and knock him backwards, stone bloody dead, all the way into the trees.

Later, all concerned would wish the Geneva Convention ruling on the treatment of captured enemy soldiers had been breached on this occasion. But the sergeant was a Regular, and he restrained himself. He wasn't blond, this German, not like the ones they'd seen on Movietone. He was tall, but not anything like six foot. Fothergill reckoned the Jerry was a tough bugger, and resolved to give him one or two with a rifle butt if he caused any nonsense.

Prendergast climbed to his feet, feeling very naked. Perhaps it was some devilish German trick to get them all to stand up and show themselves. He expected a bullet to smack into him

13

any moment. They said you never heard the one that got you. It hadn't been like this at Sandhurst; not at all.

'Come forward.'

The German took steps forward obediently. He saluted, not the Hitler salute of the Nazi party, but the military salute of the Wehrmacht, similar to that of the British army, except that there, to salute hatless was forbidden.

Lieutenant Prendergast snapped up his very best British longest-way-up-shortest-way-down-and-a-slight-quiver-at-the-top salute.

The German said: 'Colonel Hans Keiller, 2nd Panzer Grenadiers. I surrender to you.'

'Lieutenant Prendergast . . . ' the officer stopped himself, he was about to give the name of his regiment. 'I accept your surrender. You are not armed?' The German shook his head. His eyes seemed to be boring into the young British officer. Prendergast felt chilled by it.

'I have your word as an officer?'

'As an officer—and a gentleman.' There was deep irony in the German's voice.

'Your men also wish to surrender?' Prendergast gestured towards the copse.

'My men are dead, Lieutenant, and I have brought you a tank.'

'Your men are dead?'

'I killed them.'

One of the private soldiers giggled nervously, on the edge of hysteria from fear and fatigue. 'Taylor!'

'Sorry, Sergeant.' The nervous laughter died.

Prendergast turned to his sergeant: 'Check out what he says. Go into the wood . . . ' One of the privates swore under his breath. What was the point of getting killed now? The officer turned to his captive: 'If my men don't come back I promise you I'll shoot you where you stand, is that clear?'

'Perfectly,' said the German. Of the lot of them he seemed the least frightened.

The three soldiers ran to the treeline, zig-zagging. They were out of breath when they reached the copse, and

14

Fothergill could feel his heart pounding against his rib-cage, from fear, exertion and lack of sleep. Sod this for a game of bloody soldiers. I'm thirty-five, too old for mucking about, let the kids have it, it's their war not mine. When I get back to Blighty I'll shoot myself in the foot, let them stick me in the glasshouse and see if I care.

'Come on.' They pushed through the bushes, as carefully as they could, ears straining for a hostile sound: a clank of equipment or the snap of a rifle bolt.

Taylor, the one who had giggled, saw a mound of grey next to a tree at the opposite edge of the wood. He flung himself to the ground and took cover, watching the mound for a long time. When it still failed to move he became bolder and began to edge forward. The grey was field-grey, and it *was* a German soldier. Even though it was immobile it still frightened him, all Germans did. As he got closer he could see that the German was humped over, one arm struck out, the hand curled, almost like a baby asleep. Taylor stood up and prodded the grey with the fixed bayonet on his Lee Enfield. He was holding his breath, waiting for the inert form to leap up at him. It didn't so he turned it over with his bayonet like a bale of hay.

The German was dead, that much was obvious, and so Taylor wasn't frightened any more. He'd been a farm labourer before 3rd September, 1939, and the next day had rushed down to the recruiting office in a flush of patriotism he now wished someone had curbed. It was life and death all the time there, decapitating chickens, shooting the pork pig with a .22 at Christmas. He knelt down and looked at the corpse. There was a red mark on the neck, like a deep weal which went all the way around until it was out of sight behind the head. In the forehead was a hole, turning blue, a dab of blood, and little else. Taylor shoved the corpse a little with his bayonet to look at the back of the head. There was a sort of squashy mess, mostly red but with dabs of grey, like papiermâché pellets. He grimaced, remembering what their arms instructor had told them about bullets. 'They go in small and come out big.'

15

Then he found two other corpses in an almost identical state, and began to shout for the sergeant, proud of his discovery. But he could hear the sergeant, and Welland and the other private shouting too. They'd got three bodies of their own, lying face down side by side. One man had a weal mark around his neck, but naturally it was the bullet wounds that attracted the gruesome attention.

When they put it all together, Fothergill said: 'Well bugger me gently, and I'm damned if I know what's going on.'

There was more to come. Sixty yards away was a barn, and parked behind it, only partially hidden, a tank. Suppose the Jerry was lying, and the tank was still manned?

The sergeant was taking no chances. He dropped to the ground and wriggled into cover like a demented earthworm. Privates Taylor and Welland followed suit.

They all watched the tank, fascinated. It sat squat, black and menacing. Tanks had a particular horror for infantrymen. This was *one*. Imagine hundreds of them coming down on your position? No wonder the French had broken and run at Sedan, and our lads too on many an occasion, 'though we kept a bit quiet about all that,' the sergeant thought. No wonder they are beating the living shit out of us.

They waited two full minutes and still nothing moved, except a big, black crow which settled on the tank. Welland had a liking for horror stories, and he didn't like that. He thought it was a bad omen . . . that was the word . . . *omen*.

At last Taylor said: 'Sarge, those bodies, they're tank crew, aren't they? They've got those leather helmets on, and overalls. That's tank crew. There's only one tank, if the Jerry has killed them. . .'

The sergeant looked at Taylor. 'If you want to win the Victoria Cross lad, get on with it.'

Taylor, nettled, said, 'All right, Sarge, I will.' He stood up and cradled his rifle. He started to walk, waiting for the crack! Waiting to go crumpling over. Waiting for the kick of a starter motor, the bark of an exhaust, and the terrifying clank and creak of tracks as the Panzer came for them all like a prehistoric creature. Nothing happened and he reached the tank. Wait until he told his Mum and Dad about this.

Prendergast said, 'I can't believe it.'

'Intact and undamaged, sir. Crew and Panzer Grenadiers all dead sir.' The British soldiers were sitting at the edge of the wood. The German had been made to squat, cross-legged, his hands clasped behind his neck. He was guarded by a private named Albright who was so tired he could feel his eyelids shutting and opening like an Aldis signal lamp.

'How were they killed, Sergeant?'

'Shot, sir.'

Prendergast wheeled on the German: 'You shot your own comrades?'

'They are your enemies, Lieutenant, you should rejoice.'

The sergeant could fight above his weight and would back off from no man, but something in the German's eyes frightened him.

Prendergast's mouth worked angrily: 'I promise you, Colonel, when we get you back to England you'll be tried for this . . . it's . . . it's criminal.'

The sergeant looked uneasily at the young officer. The man's eyes were red-rimmed from lack of sleep and battle fatigue. He was on the edge.

The sergeant said firmly: 'Sir, the tank. We'll have to destroy it, we can't take it back with us. And we'll have to let GHQ know it's not an attack.'

The officer whipped round: 'I'm aware of what has to be done, Sergeant. Check it for documents, drain the oil, then start the engine; eventually it will seize up.'

'Yes, sir.' They'd all had enough practice this last couple of weeks in that particular method of ruining vehicles abandoned to the enemy. 'And I'll put a couple of grenades down the gun barrel, sir.'

'Yes, quite. I want two men out on picquet at each end of the copse. I'll come with you to the tank, we'll take Private Taylor; Private Albright can guard . . . Albright! Albright!'

Private James Albright jerked awake. He'd been at

17

Goodison Park cheering on Everton, packed among the crowds at his favourite Gwladys Street end. Dixie Dean had just scored, as ever with his head, but instead of the crowd roaring for the immortal Dixie they were shouting, Albright! Albright!

'Sair.' The soldier's Liverpool accent was harsh and guttural.

'Don't close your eyes man, we're all tired.'

'Sorry, sair.'

'Stay guard over this prisoner, and be careful. If he tries to escape, shoot him.'

'Yes, sair.' Albright fixed his bayonet and worked the bolt of his rifle, putting a round up the spout. He gave the German a ferocious look. The German smiled back. Albright felt frightened by that smile.

The German said lazily: 'Aren't you forgetting that I have just surrendered? Why should I wish to escape?'

The lieutenant looked at the German with contempt: 'A man who would kill his own comrades is capable of anything.'

The German smiled. How typically British. The man suspects all is not well, yet does not translate his thoughts into any action. In his place I would shoot the prisoner out of hand. Instead he goes off to immobilise one tank and leaves one man, a man virtually out on his feet, to guard me. You are committing suicide, Lieutenant.

How he hated the British. How could anyone who had seen them up close as he had done, as a growing boy, have anything but contempt for them, their poor diet, their absurdly inadequate housing, their silly humour and pompous prejudice. Years of childhood among the British, suffering their xenophobia, their hatred of his race and his nation, had left a deep scar. Nothing he had seen, heard, or read since had changed his loathing for this mongrel bunch, this divided people of stunted, tubercular proletarians and simpering aristocrats.

'You heard me, Private Albright. Watch him carefully.'

'Like an 'awk, sair.'

18

The sergeant posted the two remaining soldiers on piquet duty at the western and eastern ends of the wood, then moved off with the officer and Private Taylor. The sergeant was a little happier. He was not dead or captured, and if the cards were played right they could all end up with something on their records. Make the officer see sense, which was that they had *captured* the Jerry (the Jerry himself would soon learn to fall in with that one), add five dead Jerries and a burned out tank—once again old Prendy would have to accept the new version of events—and it was a mention in dispatches for the NCO, an officers-only-variety medal for Prendy and sod the privates. Could get made up to sergeant major, land an instructor's job somewhere, leave the rest of this bloody nonsense to the young 'uns. Fothergill had a feeling the war could go on for a long time, unless Jerry came barging over the Channel and then it wouldn't matter a sod anyway.

Maybe he wouldn't shoot his big toe off, after all. That Jerry had done Albert Fothergill a good turn.

The laissez-passer was signed by SS General Reinhard Heydrich, chief of the SS security arm, the Sicherheitsdienst.

It took SD agent Uwe Eilders from Berlin to the Western Front in less than twenty hours. It also gave him the rank and uniform of a colonel in the Panzer Grenadiers. And now Heydrich's own pass was being questioned by a similar Panzer colonel, a grey-haired man of around sixty. Eilders could scarcely contain his fury. He had an urge to take the man's grey cropped skull between his hands and crunch it like a pomegranate. The man was a Junker, he knew the breed and hated them, they had more in common with the English upper classes than he cared for. They were all snot and sabre scars, from good Prussian universities. They were the ones who, as young officers, had given up in 1918 and marched back to Berlin, still shouldering their arms as if they were the victors and not the vanquished.

'The purpose of your reconnaissance . . . Colonel?' The man said the last word with a sneer. The man opposite . . .

Keiller . . . that would be a pseudonym no doubt . . . was no Wehrmacht officer. More likely Gestapo or SD, they had the mark of Cain on them, around the eyes. The Panzer Colonel hated the Nazis and their police scum; the dregs of the Munich beer cellars; drunkards, gangsters and homosexuals, elevated by Hitler who wrapped black uniforms around them and laughingly called them an élite force.

'To capture a British prisoner.'

The colonel smiled and waved an arm towards the window of the small hut in which they sat. Outside was a packed field of bareheaded men in khaki uniforms, worn-out, dusty, bowed and beaten.

'Take your pick, Colonel *Keiller*, look. Tommies by the metre, I have every type, Grenadier Guards. . . '

The colonel went white. Eilders' Walther pistol was pressing into the colonel's forehead.

Eilders was on the point of a killing rage. He had work to do, deadly work, and it bothered him not if this old Junker was the first. He would enjoy seeing that look of stunned surprise as the bullet struck home; the glazing of the eyes in death, the sight of the brains and tissue splattered across the far wall.

'Simply, Colonel. You have thirty seconds to comply with General Heydrich's orders. Your alternative is your brains blown out. Understand?'

The colonel nodded dumbly. He had not survived the Poland and France campaigns to die at the hands of some Nazi thug. The man holding the pistol was a psychopath, he could see it deep in the eyes. There was no one at hand to help; the man would get away with it.

Within fifteen minutes 'Colonel Keiller' was riding on the back of a PzKW Mark Two tank, with two Panzer Grenadiers beside him, heading out towards the British lines. If, as he suspected, the British sent out a patrol to investigate the engine noise, he could then get captured by the British. The tank crew and Grenadiers would easily kill such a British patrol, so he would have to deal with them first.

He ordered the small tank parked in cover of a barn, and

told the three-man crew to close themselves in. He moved up to the treeline with the two Grenadiers. Yards from the wood, he slowed, turned, and with his drawn pistol shot both men quickly in the head. In the split second before they died their faces registered only a kind of brief bewilderment as though they were victims of some silly practical joke.

He walked back to the tank and rapped on the hatch. It opened, and the worried face of the tank commander appeared. He had heard the shots.

'Trouble?'

'A Tommy straggler who saw the tank; we killed him.'

'I thought you wished a prisoner, Colonel?'

'A prisoner with information, not a dwarf Scotsman who can hardly speak his own language. Leave one man in the tank, and then bring your other man up to the wood.'

The man's face showed uncertainty: 'Colonel, we are supposed to remain with the tank.'

Eilders locked his eyes on the man: 'Obey my order.'

The tank commander hesitated only a fraction before obedience, discipline and training took over. He and a crewman walked with Eilders up to the copse. He shot the first tank crewman quickly, but the commander turned, and as he did so the Walther jammed.

'Colonel?' The man's face was a mask of disbelief.

Eilders went for his garrotte, a thin loop of steel wire secured to a tab inside his shirt collar. In an instant it was out . . . just as the tankman rushed at him, trying to take his pistol out of its holster at the same time.

Eilders kicked at the man's legs, and he stumbled. Eilders was on him from behind, the garrotte around the man's neck, choking him quickly. Desperate hands flew uselessly to his neck, trying to prise away the deadly metal snake which was biting into his throat. The man arched his feet up, almost reflexively, trying to escape from the deadly attack, but Eilders was expecting it. He had done this before, and was enjoying it.

He dropped to his knees maintaining the pressure, and the Panzer commander's heels began to drum on the sandy soil.

21

The man's tongue was protruding horribly; his eyes started to bulge from their sockets, then he lost consciousness.

Eilders tightened his grip and held it for one minute until the man was dead. Then Eilders took out his pistol, turned the man over and shot him in the forehead. He remembered the fictional English detective, the one with the deerstalker hat and the Meerschaum pipe, the one played by that Hollywood actor, Basil Rathbone was it . . . ? Eilders liked those movies. Sherlock Holmes would no doubt have looked at the gunshot, then at the neck wound, and realised that perhaps one had been put there to mask the other. Holmes was a fictional Englishman—also an absurd one—but the rest were a little more stupid.

He went back to the tank. It was time for enjoyment. He opened the tank hatch and slid down into the claustrophobic interior. It smelled of oil, leather and heat.

'Kapitan, is that you?'

The boy was young, perhaps just eighteen. He had taken off his leather helmet and his face was smeared with oil. He looked a kid, a fat kid; he had jowls despite his youth. He would be a Mummy's boy, fat on Sachertorte and apfelstrudel.

Eilders took out the garrotte and held it out, a hangman showing the victim the noose.

The boy couldn't understand but he was terrified.

Eilders moved in the cramped interior and the boy yelped with fright; suddenly he knew what was going to happen. He had heard the shots . . . now he knew . . . and it was all the worse because . . . he couldn't understand why. There was nowhere for him to go . . . except the escape hatch! He fumbled with the hatch cover and Eilders was on him. The boy farted in terror. The stench was terrible; it disgusted and excited Eilders in the way that all olfactory responses did.

The boy's legs became jammed behind the track brake levers and it made Eilders' job easier, there was no leverage away from the deadly snare.

He could smell the boy, his sweat, his sphincter odour, feel

22

the dying tension of the muscles. There was the sheer moment of elation, like an orgasm, then exhaustion.

He rested for a few minutes then pushed the dead boy out through the escape hatch and dragged the body up to the wood. He put a bullet into the head of the corpse and laid it with two of the others.

He crawled through the wood to its opposite side, put a fresh magazine in his pistol, unbuttoned his tunic, threw away his hat, and settled down to wait.

An hour later he saw the Tommies crawl like soldiers on exercise across the open ground. They really were pathetic, these British. He could have killed the lot with one rifle.

He took out his pistol and fired two shots into the air. Then he lay down, tying an oily handkerchief around a piece of branch as the inevitable fusillade flew over him. Then he waved the white flag, hoping that the British didn't kill their prisoners. Surely they were much too 'civilised' for that?

Scotland Road, Liverpool—Scottie Road to the initiated—is a grim, violent place of rough drinking houses, all spit and sawdust, where the beer comes rich and lustrous with a thick creamy head and served in tall, straight glasses which can always be used as a weapon if the occasion arises. Jimmy Albright was enjoying his pint. It was good to be home and the beer was going down a treat. They always did a good pint in the Caledonian Arms; but suddenly the beer was choking him, choking, couldn't breath, choking . . . then blackness for ever.

The soldier died before he was fully awake. Eilders removed the garrotte and rolled the man over, checking him for size. Dammit but the man was a midget, all these Englishmen were stunted from poor food.

It would have to be the sergeant, the nasty looking one with the light machine-gun, he was about the right size.

Eilders took the dead man's rifle and moved into the wood. At the eastern end of the wood he found the second Tommy asleep against a tree. He thought it strange that a man should

23

die because he was too tired to keep awake. Then he killed him.

The third was not so easy, and Eilders wondered, as he had wondered before, whether he preferred it this way. The Tommy heard some noise, the breaking of a twig or the rustle of a leaf, and turned, bringing up his Lee Enfield, his mouth opening to form a shout. Eilders kicked him in the teeth and heard the crunch of bone and splintering of teeth.

The shout died and blood gushed from his mouth. He dropped his rifle, but recovered his wits and began to scrabble for it. Eilders dived at him with the garrotte, but the Tommy was clambering to his feet and the two men met in a collision of bone. Eilders grunted from the shock of the meeting. The Englishman was flailing wildly with his fists, whimpering in fear and pain. Eilders chopped at the Tommy's neck with a rabbit punch, and as the man's hands went up to his neck, Eilders grabbed at the bayonet in the scabbard at the man's waist. The Englishman saw the bayonet come out and tried to scream through the blood and mucus in his mouth. Eilders thrust the bayonet with all his might in a short, sword-like thrust to the stomach. It went in deep, choking off the cry.

The soldier's hands went to his stomach. Eilders rooted in the dirt, found the garrotte which he had dropped in the struggle, and strangled the man quickly.

There was no time to waste now. If the other Tommies had heard the man's cry they would be rushing back from the tank to help him.

He grabbed the soldier's rifle, checked the magazine and worked a round into the chamber. He moved quickly to the edge of the wood. He could hear an engine racing, the tortured sound of a motor screaming for oil, churning in its death throes. Then a *whoof-whoof* as two grenades exploded in the gun barrel. Seconds later the officer, sergeant and soldier came into view, running. The engine noise had drowned the dead private's death cries.

Eilders made a loop of the canvas rifle sling, steadied the rifle, slowing his breathing. He tracked and fired once, worked the bolt in a second and fired again, rolling away from

24

his position a split-second later. He did not see Lieutenant Prendergast flung backwards into the dirt, nor Private Taylor's legs collapse from under him. Eilders was moving, fast along and back from the edge of the treeline. The sergeant would have to be a head shot. No holes must mar that uniform. It had a purpose to serve.

Eilders heard the *zzzppp . . . zzzppp* of the Bren, and the crashing of foliage and squawk of birds as the bullets lashed into the wood. When he judged he was at least thirty metres from his last position, he edged forward until he could see out of the trees. The Tommy sergeant was worming his way backwards, furiously, towards the barn and the shelter it provided, but he was at an angle as Eilders wished.

He could see the man's face, his ears, half his head, the ridiculously exposed neck all beneath the helmet. What use were they, these British helmets? They did not offer even the most rudimentary protection, nor the illusion of it.

He aimed carefully, breath held. He fired once. The backward scrabbling stopped.

It wasn't a perfect fit, and the British Army serge battledress itched like hell. But it would do. Eilders took off the dead man's identity tags. Fothergill A.R. 2593066. He retied them around his own neck, then checked that the soldier's pay-book was in the top breast pocket of the battledress blouse. He grabbed the Bren and began to walk at an acute angle from whence he guessed the patrol had come.

It had been Heydrich's idea for getting him to England. The British were absurdly conscious of spies, and any stranger was at risk. One sentry who had seen a particular dock worker every night for a week at Chatham shot the man when he failed to respond to a challenge. One Abwehr spy had killed himself with his cyanide pill after being handed over to the British, ironically by the Irish Republican Army. It was crazy. The spy had been carrying his war medals in an old army beret, and had a torch marked 'Made in Dresden'. Heydrich knew that the Abwehr, and for that matter the SD,

25

did not have enough information to simply parachute Eilders into England or put him ashore by submarine. His plan was for Eilders to insinuate himself into the British lines and kill a British soldier, and having done that, to assume his identity.

Heydrich knew only Eilders could possibly get away with it. His English was fluent and idiomatic. He had learned the language as a child by the best possible method, hearing it spoken on its native ground and having to speak it to live. Over the years, thanks to the SD, that skill had been refined, honed, sharpened, until Eilders' language skills were second to none.

His impersonation of a drunken Scotsman was the hit of the SD language school.

Heydrich knew the British army was disintegrating fast. In the confusion, Eilders could get back to England with other soldiers, disappear and assume his next identity, that of a Dutch seaman.

London was already a cauldron of nationalities. Poles, Czechs, Frenchmen, Belgians, expatriate German Jews, Austrian Jews, Danes, Norwegians . . . and Dutchmen. Papers could be forged, but the details of papers could easily be checked. If Eilders was to be an Englishman, the danger was acute. The address on his papers would be checked, and the truth revealed. The most cursory of interrogations would tear holes in any cover story. It was easy for someone like Eilders to speak like an Englishman. But what was his school, his university, his father's job, his uncle's hair colouring? As a Dutchman he would have alien papers, but Holland was under German occupation, so nothing could be checked.

As soon as Uwe Eilders could get to England and divest himself of his army uniform, he would become Jan Villen Ter Braak, a seaman from Scheveningen. The English had a soft spot for the Dutch, particularly since the carnage at Rotterdam.

The method used to get to England involved hazard, and Heydrich knew Eilders, knew the kind of man he was. He had resigned himself to the fact that German as well as British casualties might result.

Eilders walked on towards the British lines. The sergeant had been from London, the accent was like a familiar refrain from childhood.

Unless he met someone from the sergeant's regiment who knew the man personally, in which case he would be shot out of hand, he would be all right. The Tommies seemed too tired to know what day it was, so any slips he made should go unnoticed amid the panic, fatigue and fear, the mad scramble to get away from the all-conquering Germans.

Ten minutes later there was a nervous shout: 'Who goes there, friend or foe?'

'Leave it out, a bloody friend, who else?'

'Advance friend and be recognised. Today's password.'

'Shove your password up your arse. I've been out there two frigging days and I've lost some mates.'

A head appeared round a stone wall, white and frightened, then the body, arms holding the rifle out. The sentry saw the uniform and the stripes. 'Sorry, Sarge, can't be too careful. Come on, we'll get you a brew.'

Chapter Two

IT HAD always amused the Marquis of Blackington to know that if ever he was to be hanged by the neck until dead, even in death he would remain privileged. As they marched him to the scaffold, arms pinioned with a leather strap, and then placed the hessian hood over his head, the noose which they would put around his neck, with its carefully positioned knot, would be made from silk, not hemp. At least, as a Peer of the Realm he had that privilege in law, though whether it had ever been taken up he did not know.

Silk or hemp, the efficiency of the spine-breaking knot and the plummeting drop would be the same, of course. But he thought of it now as his chauffeur-driven Rolls-Royce purred down the treelined Mall, that avenue which leads to Buckingham Palace.

For one capital offence punishable by hanging was treason. And the fourteenth Marquis of Blackington, William Trevellic, was in the process of committing just that. He intended to go on committing treason until the final act which would be the unseating of his royal sovereign the King of England.

The prize was great, to become the ruler of a new and resurgent nation with a new King; a nation that could take its place in the Europe of the New Order.

The penalty for failure was sure. A speedy trial, in camera, the triangular black cap over the judge's faded wig, and the ritual words that he be taken from the court to a place of execution, and that on a given date he be hanged by the neck until he was dead. And may God have mercy on his soul. But since a German shell had blown the then Captain, The Honourable, William Trevellic into a shell-hole at Passchendaele twenty-three years before, death had ceased to hold any great terror for him.

The splinters from the shell blew out his left eye and mangled his right arm. As he'd lain there in the mud, without pain, listening to the din around him, assuming that he must surely die from loss of blood or eventual gangrene if he didn't drown in the rising water of the shell-hole first, he had realised that the prospect of death did not really bother him.

Perhaps death was the only logical way out of the madness around him.

But he made a resolve, slipping in and out of consciousness, that if he *did* survive this three-year bloody shambles, he would do everything in his power to ensure nothing of the like ever happened again. It was sheer insanity, the flower of German, British and French manhood slaughtering each other in the mud, the frost, the snow . . . and then the summer heat like some seasonal and tragic circle. Perhaps war had retained some glamour in his father's day, with cavalry, muskets, sword, chivalry, the rock-like squares of red and white uniforms. Now it means high explosive, scything shell splinters from howitzers, trying to run through barbed wire with fifty pounds on your back and machine guns firing enfilading streams of bullets.

He did not die. Stretcher-bearers pulled him out of the mud, and the next few weeks were a blur of pain and ether. The eye was gone, the arm mangled like some blasted tree branch, hand curled into a claw.

When his father died in 1926 he took his red-cushioned seat in the House of Lords. He was still a bachelor, and all the girls wished to nurse and mother their crippled hero who managed to look somehow piratical in the black eyepatch and leather glove.

The Marquis of Blackington had no wish to be mothered, or married, or nursed. He had a secret life and it left no room for women.

In the demi-monde he was in the outer limits. There were those who knew, and those who suspected. For those who did not, the reasons for his continued bachelorhood could be encapsulated in a meaningful glance at his disability. How could any woman be expected . . . And the matrons would murmur their sympathy.

He had his full-time charity work. The East End was a cess-pit of poverty, and he worked tirelessly helping to provide hostels for the young homeless. There were rich pickings for the likes of Lord Blackington there.

But when he made his maiden speech in the Lords, half the country would happily have lynched him. He urged the end of reparations by Germany. Such theft, as he called it, could only enfeeble Europe and strengthen the arm of extremists within Germany, and Bolsheviks without.

He went further. He said that the men alongside whom he had fought, the venerated Tommy Atkins of popular legend, had not come home to the 'land fit for heroes' Lloyd George had promised them. On the contrary they had been shabbily treated. Lord Blackington urged a comprehensive health care system, a massive housing programme, an all-round increase in wages. Great Britain, he warned, was not immune to the germ of Bolshevism.

The *Daily Express* called him a traitor. *The Times* said his speech was unwise and unfounded, and hinted that the aristo-crat might be a closet Bolshevik himself. Only the *News Chronicle* reported his speech and commented on it without going into paroxysms of printed fury.

Lord Blackington found himself no longer invited to society parties. He felt sure his main crime had been to be nice to the Germans. No one could do that—not yet—the Germans were devils incarnate.

He did not think so. Without a strong Germany, Bolshe-vism would triumph, and he did not wish that. It would mean the destruction of his class, and like all aristocrats he was dedicated to its preservation.

He went to Germany several times in 1930 and 1931, staying at the homes of Prussian aristocrats, at last resuming pre-World War friendships. They mentioned a chap called Hitler who certainly seemed to have the right idea about the Bolsheviks within Germany.

This man Hitler became Chancellor of Germany, and Blackington returned. He noted the resurgence of German national pride, the elimination of the plague of Communism. He checked the statistics, and it was all good news. Unemployment down, production up, new homes and roads being built, the German people in better health, the Jews put in their place. The Bolshevik menace might brood in the East, but Hitler had scoured it from Germany, at the same time giving the German worker enough to eat and a pride in his land. Could it work in Britain too?

He met Hitler at a private party. The man was warm and humorous; he seemed to like the British too, respecting them as former adversaries and wishing them as future partners in a strong Europe.

Back in Britain, Blackington saw only gloom. Unemployment, dreary towns of mean streets, houses without bathrooms or adequate heating, poor, ragged under-nourished children, cloth-capped faces of men without hope.

He toyed with the idea of joining Mosley's British Union of Fascists. He admired Mosley, but occasionally when Blackington looked into a mirror he imagined what effect he would have in a black shirt under spotlights. An eye-patch, a clawed leather glove. He would certainly frighten the horses as well as the man on the Clapham omnibus without whose approval no political advance was possible. And Mosley was too honest, too outspoken, he was offending too many people with his outspoken anti-Semitism.

His was not the way to power. Blackington waited. One man, in his opinion, could harness public opinion, and lead Britain out of its malaise. That man was his former wartime friend, David, Prince of Wales, the son of the King of England. In March, 1918 he was responsible for having the Prince invited to a party in Belgrave Square at which David met the wife of a Liberal MP, Mrs Dudley Ward. The two started a passionate and long affair, and David was ever grateful to Blackington. A prince had to be dicreet about whom he slept with. Later Blackington arranged for the heir apparent to meet several married women (always the safest) who wished to sleep with the Prince of Wales. One of those women, Lady Furness, ironically was the person who introduced the prince to an American, Wallis Simpson.

Blackington knew instantly that this was to be the big love of his friend's life.

And meanwhile the heir began to take more and more notice of Blackington's political views, and shared his admiration for the dictators Mussolini and Hitler. Later the Prince of Wales was to make a speech urging ex-servicemen from the Great War to go to Germany and meet in friendship the men they had fought. It was an extremely unpopular speech.

Blackington knew that the politicians of the day did not like David, and that British Intelligence suspected the heir of having fascist tendencies. But none of that would matter a jot once the old King was dead and David was on the throne. There were problems. The man was besotted with Wallis, he was also weak and easily lead, and he drank too much. Blackington could handle Wallis, and with her help he could handle David too.

When the King was dead, long live David!

He had spoken seriously with David only days after the King's death. David had no intention of being a figurehead king; he would *push* the politicians into doing something, both on the domestic front and abroad. This sabre-rattling between Britain and Germany must cease. It was unthinkable that the horror of war between Britain and Germany could ever be repeated. He was attracted to Blackington's idea, an alliance of steel between Britain, Germany, France and Italy, an alliance so strong the Bolsheviks would never dare try and export their barbarian revolution.

Then the nightmare started, and Lord Blackington's hopes began to be torn into shreds. As the news of the King's friendship with Wallis, a divorced woman, began to leak out, there was a hysterical reaction from newspapers and the establishment. These same cabinet ministers and newspaper editors who took mistresses and whored it in Mayfair and even Paddington, the less fussy ones, *they* dared criticise their King. For the first and last time in unholy alliance with that Hitler-hater, Winston Churchill, Blackington and the King's Party, as it was dubbed, fought to let their King keep his throne and the woman he loved. Blackington felt sure the public was for David, but they were being poisoned by the newspapers and bishops.

It was all slipping away, the dream of power and influence, slipping away on a rising tide of spurious morality. David made the speech of Abdication and slunk away like a thief in the night from his own land. Such was the humiliation that the sentry at the dock gates even challenged the man who had been his sovereign only hours before.

Now the throne went to King George the Sixth, David's younger brother. His cruel nickname was 'stuttering Bertie'. His father had treated him so harshly that now the man could hardly produce a coherent sentence. The night David went into exile, for such it was whatever the hypocrites chose to call it, Blackington did two things.

He took his Rolls-Royce to the East End and picked up a youth of his acquaintance, losing himself in the particular misery and erotica of his chosen proclivity. He also made a decision. If England would not save itself from the petty politicians and the warmongers, he would save it for them. This useless figurehead King would go, and David would be returned in triumph. The redundant system of Parliamentary democracy would go too.

He went to visit David and Wallis in France, telling them nothing of his plans, but talking urgently of the deteriorating political situation. Both David and Wallis had met Hitler, and liked him.

'This silly alliance we have with the Poles,' David said, 'it will just get us into trouble. Stalin will have them eventually, they're hardly worth us fighting Germany over.'

But war came and inevitably the defeats. Blackington wept; it was tragedy. Now Britain had the most Germanophobe

Prime Minister ever in Winston Churchill. He would never make peace, this man, and in the meantime there would be more crazy Churchill adventures like Gallipoli, more deaths, more widows, more blood, barbed wire and horror. Dunkirk was just a taste. And now rumour had it the PM was planning a defiant speech. Was he stark, staring, raving mad?

Once Hitler unleashed the Luftwaffe and Britain's cities were razed, the paratroops and sea-barges would come from France with the Panzers. Once they got ashore nothing could stop them, nothing. Certainly not tired Regulars with rifles and a few imported Thompson guns; certainly not conscripts with five rounds apiece for their World War One rifles, nor old men with pitchforks and twelve-bore shotguns. Nor all the oratory of a prime minister famous for little else.

But at times of crisis in a nation's history, great men rose to the occasion, and he, Lord Blackington, was ready. He had been preparing for this moment, committing treason all the while.

In January of that year, with movement across France possible and Italy not yet in the war, he had gone to his winter home in San Remo. There he received a personal letter from Count Ciano, Mussolini's son-in-law and Italy's foreign minister. It asked if Lord Blackington would receive a personal emissary from German Foreign Minister Herr Joachim von Ribbentrop.

Such a meeting was forbidden in time of war, and Britain and Germany were at war. Lord Blackington should have said no. He said yes. He had once met the former champagne salesman Ribbentrop and been impressed by the man's mind. Ribbentrop seemed to see clearly that the problem for Germany and Britain was not each other but the Soviet Union.

So the emissary came, smoked cheroots and talked, while Blackington listened, entranced. He thought his chance may have gone with David's abdication, but now it looked as though his wildest dreams could come true after all. But first he had listened. The German Reich, the emissary said, intended to inflict a military defeat on the French. The defeat would be crushing and total, a revenge for the humiliation of Versailles visited on Germany in 1919.

The British Expeditionary Force in France would be destroyed. Blackington held his breath. And afterwards? After the defeat Britain would be at the mercy of Germany, but would be spared invasion under certain circumstances.

The English Lord sipped as calmly as he could at his whisky and soda. 'Which are?'

The German calmly stubbed out his cheroot.

'The Royal Navy must be scaled down to a size which does not pose a threat to the Reich. You can sell the ships for all we care. Your government will give an undertaking that your navy, army and air force will not make any hostile preparations or actions against Reich forces in any part of the world.'

Blackington said: 'Churchill will never do it.'

The German smiled: 'I'm coming to that. You will cede to the German Reich various colonies taken from us under the iniquitous Versailles agreement, Tanganyika for example. We would also like Kenya, but that is negotiable. Egypt will remain yours but we must have agreed right of passage through the Suez Canal. In the event of hostilities between Germany and the Soviet Union . . . ' Blackington felt his blood race, Germany and the Soviet Union had a Non-Aggression Pact and had carved Poland like a turkey between them . . . 'the British would be required to contribute £300 million sterling and an army of 120,000 men as evidence of her desire to eliminate Bolshevism.'

The German lit another cheroot and inhaled. Blackington raised the decanter; the German shook his head; Blackington refilled his own glass and added soda.

'You ask a great deal.'

'I haven't finished. We seek the removal of King George the Sixth and his replacement with the former King, now Duke of Windsor. And the formation of a government friendly towards the Reich, with you as its Prime Minister.'

Blackington spilled his drink.

The German smiled easily: 'And I forgot, the repatriation

to the Reich of all Reich Jews and subversives who have alien status in the United Kingdom.'

Blackington didn't hear it. David back on the throne! He prime minister! He steadied himself. 'What is the alternative?'

The easy smile vanished: 'We shall obliterate your cities, land our troops in England and march into London ourselves. Do you really wish to see England have a Gauleiter, Lord Blackington, your soldiers in camps, your people starving like the Poles?'

Blackington said: 'Has the Duke of Windsor had these proposals put to him?'

The German shook his head. 'He has, however, spoken with both the Fuehrer and Herr von Ribbentrop on separate occasions. We believe he will be sympathetic to these proposals. He will be contacted in due course.'

'You realise that under our constitution it is not possible for a King who has once abdicated, to regain his throne?' Blackington held his breath once again. There was only one answer. The German gave it.

'Under certain circumstances, my lord, even the constitution of England can be changed. We shall tell the Duke of Windsor as much.'

Lord Blackington was reeling. The re-birth, the moment he had dreamed of and waited for. 'Tell *me* more.'

The German talked until the first light of dawn was fingering the hillsides rose-pink. There was a mountain of cheroot butts in the ash-tray, and Lord Blackington felt drunk on whisky and the heady scent of power. He said, 'But really, until such a time comes . . . *if* it comes . . . there is stalemate in France at this moment, you are asking me to be a German agent, a spy, a traitor to my country.'

The German viewed him calmly: 'We know you, Lord Blackington. Everything about you, *everything*. You are a man of vision, a man who does not concern himself with petty morals. You know where the future of Britain lies, in the New Order. You have spoken out for Germany, you did everything you could to prevent this pointless war between us. If you fail to seize this chance now, you will regret it all your life.'

'It is treason. They hang people for treason.'

'It has been in your mind long before my visit, my lord.'

Blackington bit his lip.

The German said: 'You could have died in 1917. You have lived longer than you ever expected. What is it they say, "a coward dies many deaths, but a brave man . . . "? '

The Marquis of Blackington brought back an extra suitcase in the Rolls-Royce, all the way through France. His chauffeur was an ex-serviceman who had served with him on the Western Front. Blackington had rescued him from unemployment, debt and possibly starvation. He did not share his employer's proclivities, but made no judgement on them, and helped in the procuring. He was utterly loyal. He loaded the suitcase realising it was both heavy and additional to the luggage which had made the outward journey.

The Marquis was well-known at the French/Italian borders, and no one would have checked the luggage of an English milord. At Dover the Customs man saluted obsequiously and waved the Rolls out onto the London road. It had all gone without hitch, as he had expected. But nevertheless the Marquis of Blackington was surprised at the level of fear.

His insouciance about death was beginning to drip away, drop by drop, so slowly he would not notice until the moment his reservoir of courage was empty.

He lived in a five-storey house in Belgravia designed by John Nash. At the very top of the house was an attic room which would normally have housed a maidservant; Blackington used it as an extra room for housing his considerable library. It was always kept locked, as private papers were stored there, and only he had the key, the rest of his household forbidden to enter.

He set up the suitcase radio-transmitter there. In April, after months of regular tuning in at the given time, he received a one-word message from Berlin. He deciphered it. It said: 'Wait.'

The Royal Standard was flying from the flag-pole above Buckingham Palace. It puzzled visitors. The Union Jack was the British flag, wasn't it . . . or did the country have two flags? And Blackington would patiently explain. The Union Flag . . . 'jack' was slang . . . was the flag of the British union, the Royal Standard was the family's personal flag.

Its blaze of blue, red and orange, its harp, lions and unicorn showed that the monarch was in residence wherever it flew. Blackington looked at it again. How long would it fly for this present king?

The Rolls-Royce turned into the roundabout in front of the Palace. The Guards were in khaki now, gone their scarlet tunics and shaggy bearskins, battledress and steel helmets for the duration. The Palace itself was sand-bagged, the windows taped to avoid blast damage from flying glass. The monument to Queen Victoria in the centre of the traffic island was boarded up.

As the car nosed into Constitution Hill, he could see the office workers eating their picnic lunches under the trees in Green Park. Their little cardboard boxes with the string carrying strap were close by them.

'Got your gas mask?' It was as familiar now as 'Got your coat?'

Since the outbreak of war it had been an offence not to have your gas mask with you, even for women and children. Though when the bombers failed to come, many had begun to disregard the regulations. Dunkirk had changed all that. Would the Germans use poison gas as they had in the first war?

Blackington looked out at the picnickers. A man and woman were whispering endearments, or so it seemed, the man's face close to the woman's ear. Everyone seemed content, even jovial, as though Dunkirk had been a victory and not a crushing defeat. Didn't they understand their world

38

had fallen apart, that their country was in mortal danger, and that it would take a man of courage and vision to save them? That man was Lord Blackington, not the pompous, adjective-happy Winston Churchill and his absurd posturings.

Last night there had been a message: 'Expect a visitor from the sea.'

Chapter Three

EILDERS WAS lucky. He got off the beach almost immediately. He didn't even have to queue in the water like so many of the others. The men were tired and scared; few spoke, most just smoked and waited with a kind of weary resolution which, despite his hatred of all things British, he respected.

He looked the part, acted it and thought it. He knew everything about the British Army from its command structure to its slang. When he'd first met the sentry he'd known it was the moment of truth, but the speech came naturally, the accent, the inflexions, and within minutes it was as though he was back in the East End of London all those years ago.

Anyway, the British Army in France was hardly a coherent organisation: units, even regiments were mixed; he saw officers' orders sullenly ignored, and occasionally acts which bordered on mutiny. No one was on the lookout for spies.

Once they had been bombed by Stukas. The dive-bombers had whistles on their wings and made a banshee wail when they dived, but luckily the sand of the beach absorbed the shock of the bombs and there were few casualties. A plane came down several hundred yards away, but it was impossible to tell if it was Luftwaffe or Royal Air Force. It did not seem to matter to the men on the beach; they had been machine-gunned and bombed for too long to have any love for air forces, even their own, which they felt had failed to protect them. The luckless pilot was colandered by hundreds of rifle bullets as he clambered from his downed plane.

Eventually a beached whaleboat and a hearty Royal Navy crew got him and a dozen others out to a destroyer.

He checked the cologne he always carried with him. It was his vanity, perhaps his only weakness; he could not bear the smell of sweat from his own body. It had been a gift from Ilse—that amused him—and if any of the Tommies questioned it, then it was looted. It had no other identifying marks than the words 'Eau de Cologne' and not even the British could be stupid enough to think *that* was German. He was tempted to splash some on his face now, to drive out the stench of the unwashed soldiers around him. He immediately stifled the desire. A Tommy sergeant might steal a bottle of some weird French perfume for his wife, but he would not put scent on himself.

Halfway across the Channel the boat was attacked by two Messerschmitt 109s, and several men amidships were killed. Eilders could hear the screams of the wounded, and cursed the Luftwaffe fluently like the rest. They could have killed him!

At Folkestone, Eilders was invited to deposit his Bren gun. Every man with a weapon was being treated as a hero, which wasn't surprising. The British had left virtually every piece of equipment they had in France, and some men were minus their trousers.

He was given a meal of soup and a thick white bread sandwich, plus a mug of very sweet tea, and then told to board a special train for London. He was informed that he must go home and await instructions to rejoin his unit. Eilders looked around him. It was absolute chaos. Exhausted men littered the quaysides or climbed into the special trains provided.

He laughed to himself. My mission is almost redundant. The Wehrmacht could come tomorrow and nothing would stop them, not this beaten rabble.

A military policeman checked his pay-book, but it was no more than a cursory glance. Soon Eilders was on a non-corridor train specially recruited from Southern Railways. It huffed and puffed through the hop fields of Kent, often stopping for long periods without explanation. He could see oasthouses, vine trellises. The garden of England.

41

To relieve themselves men urinated out of the window, but most were too tired to do anything but sleep. The train went through two large towns, but the station signs were painted out; and so, he noticed carefully, were the location names on merchants' walls. The British were taking this very seriously. He wondered if they realised that the German Army, when they came, would have maps, and would not need to take directions from advertising hoardings and railway stations.

After three hours the train began to slide into the grimy suburbs of what obviously was London. Twenty minutes later Eilders saw a glimpse of the famous Tower Bridge. Within a minute the train had pulled in to a station and stopped.

The station was empty, no other trains and no passengers. He wondered if they had cleared it for the arriving soldiers: it would hardly be good for British morale to see their troops return like this.

Someone in the compartment woke up with a start.

'Where the hell are we?'

A distinctly Cockney voice said: 'Facking London Bridge station, innit?' Eilders checked his mental map.

Someone shouted an order and the men climbed out, stretching themselves and swearing. He noticed that they profaned a great deal, particularly using one four-letter word. He resolved to use it a lot until he dispensed with his present identity.

The men began to shuffle into a funnelling slope which led to a subterranean passage under the railway tracks. They looked what they were, which was a tired, beaten shambles hanging on to the last vestiges of discipline. The passage split right and left, and the pack moved left, presumably from an order at the front. When he reached the turn, he pushed through the crowd and headed right, across to the other side of the station. Someone shouted: ''Ere, where you going, this is the bloody way?'

Eilders froze and turned. He was being addressed by a soldier with just one stripe on his arm—a Lance-Corporal—next rank up from Private. A 'Lance-Jack', but to be

42

addressed as 'Corporal'. The man could not have seen Eilders' stripes.

'On your feet, Corporal.'

The soldier got up, laces untied. He could see now that the man he had shouted after was a sergeant.

'Sorry, Sergeant.'

'So you should be. But since you ask, I am going for a crap which I have been holding back since bloody Folkestone, the Flying Scotsman there having no bog, and the khasi is that way. When I get back I'll consider putting you on a charge. Do yourself a favour and lose yourself.'

'Yes, Sergeant.'

Eilders could feel himself sweating. He wished he had put on some cologne. He walked on. When he reached the other platform, he could see across the station, above the milling heads, two red-banded peaked caps. Military policemen.

He walked quickly to the exit barrier. A bored-looking man in a blue waistcoat and blue peaked cap was reading a *Daily Sketch*. He had an unhealthy, pitted face, and there was a pinched cigarette behind one ear.

He looked up at the uniform with a kind of jealous hostility. 'Other side for you lot.'

'What?'

'Other side, you heard me. No one comes out this side, that's me orders. More than my job's worth.'

At the opposite side of the station the milling mob was thinning. If he didn't get out soon the Redcaps would see him. He didn't want his pay-book checked again and the strain was beginning to tell. He wanted to become a Dutchman—quickly.

Eilders pushed his face close to the railwayman's: 'Listen, you little squirt. I've been fucking bombed and shot at till I'm up to here with it . . . ' he put a flattened hand to his forehead. Mr Archer used to do that after a hard day being bossed about . . . 'up to fucking here.' He saw a public house down the incline which led from the station.

'Now I'm going for a pint, any objections?'

The ticket collector shrank back. He looked a nasty bit of

work, that sergeant. 'OK mate, please yourself. Can't all be in the frigging army, some of us got to keep the trains running, you know.'

Eilders could smell his guilt and his two-day-old sweat.

He pushed past the man, walking purposefully towards The Railway Arms. He did not want a drink, he wanted to get away . . . from the uniforms.

He heard a shout, and froze. ' 'Ere Hitler, Sergeant storm-trooper.'

He turned. The ticket collector had cupped his hands: 'Railway's your best bet.'

Eilders turned reluctantly back and headed for the pub. Damn the man, he could feel his eyes boring into him. Eilders saw two cars, then a woman pushing a pram, and another woman with two toddlers. Obviously the British still had petrol, and not everyone had been evacuated.

He remembered the first time he had arrived in England. He had got off a train at such a station, and the English couple had greeted him in their incomprehensible language. They went into an eating house, restaurant was too fine a word. He couldn't understand what they asked him, so he took what he was given. It was eggs fried in heavy lard, and chipped potatoes. Afterwards he had vomited. The English seemed to eat a lot of food like that, fried in the same cheap and heavy fat, and it always made him want to vomit. Now he could smell it again in these streets. To Eilders it would always be the fragrance of England.

He clip-clopped on, the steel tips on his British Army boots ringing on the pavement. They sounded like jackboots to him. On the corner of the station approach was a small wooden kiosk, outside which a man was selling newspapers. Eilders took out a sixpence and picked up a *Daily Sketch*, the same newspaper that he had seen the ticket collector reading. The stubbled, toothless news vendor handed Eilders five copper pennies in change.

He took the newspaper and folded it, the way he had been taught, until it was like a baton. Then he tucked it under his arm, the way the English did. From the corner of his eye he could see that the ticket collector was still watching him. He would have to go into the pub. He opened the half-glassed doors with the engraved legend 'Railway Arms' and a stench of beer and male sweat hit him.

He forced his way through a throng of drinkers to the bar. 'Pint, please.'

'Bitter?' The landlord wore a waistcoat which bulged around a pot belly, and his arm was poised over a gaily-decorated beer pump handle.

'Bitter?'

Bitte?

For a fraction of a second Eilders was on the point of repeating his order. Bitter? Bitte? They could train you as much as they liked, but could they eliminate the small things? And it was the small things which caught you out. He nodded quickly.

'You just made it then, son.' Eilders glanced at the round wall clock with its Roman numerals. It was two twenty-eight. Of course. In two minutes he would have been unable to buy a drink. These Englishmen made arbitrary rules about what hour a man should slake his thirst. But he had forgotten. Damn! No wonder the railwayman had watched him so closely, to see if he would get into the pub on time. Why would a man hurrying for a pint, a pint he has been waiting for for months, stop and buy a newspaper? Eilders could feel the hairs on his neck standing on end, and fought to control a rising sense of panic. You spent three years of your life here, you know the language like any native. You know the English, the way they think, feel, *smell*! Once you have shed this uniform you will at least have the excuse of being a foreigner, a friendly one, but one who can be forgiven for not knowing every social more.

The uniform felt like fancy dress, now, among the civilians. Before it felt as though it fitted perfectly, British uniforms were hardly tailored after all, but now it seemed grotesque. It seemed to scream: 'I am a German agent'.

The landlord handed him a large glass of caramel-coloured beer and he handed over another sixpence, hoping that at least

45

that was right, and that the price had not risen since the SD interrogators had extracted it from a puzzled Tommy from South London now sitting in a POW cage in France.

The landlord pushed his hand away: 'Have this on the house, guvnor, you lads have been through hell in France.' Eilders thanked him.

The landlord raised a smaller glass of the same beer. ' 'Ere's to 'Itler, hope he chokes.'

Eilders drank to the instant demise of his Fuehrer by choking.

He took his newspaper quickly to a small, marble-topped table with wrought-iron legs, and sat down. The pub was beginning to thin a little. He would wait for the last drinkers to urinate before going to the lavatory and taking the false papers from his boot.

He passed the minutes reading the newspaper. P.I.H. Naylor's horoscope said Eilders must be strong and resolute and not let little things upset him. Tasks he had set himself would eventually be accomplished. His health prospects were good. Eilders noted that Piccadilly cigarettes were sixpence for ten, and that a Miss Florence Wood of Acton promised to remove superfluous hair from ladies' faces permanently. He felt you learned a lot about a nation from its newspapers, particularly the advertisements.

There was a picture of a woman with her hands over a man's eyes. The caption read: *Did you Maclean your teeth today?* Eilders read it again, and puzzled; then it dawned. Mac-clean. It was a pun, the English were fond of those. He turned to the news pages with stories of what to do in case of invasion or paratroop attack. He expected blood-curdling exhortations to kill and maim; instead he saw a photograph of a woman hiding some tinned food under the stairs. The caption urged: *Do not give any German anything. Hide your food.* It amused him, and eased the tension he felt. The British secret anti-invasion weapon, starvation.

He felt hungry, went to the bar and bought a pork pie which proved to be stale. He ate it nonetheless: English soldiers were not fussy about their food. He finished his beer

46

and looked at the clock. It was fifteen minutes to three, legally past the time when he should have finished his drink, and presumably left.

He went to the lavatory and removed a set of alien registration papers in the name of Jan Villen Ter Braak from one boot. From his gaiters he took out a squashed roll of five pound notes, and replaced the roll. He had a further roll in the other gaiter. The SD had not left him short of money.

He went out of the pub with a final knot of departing drinkers, eyes searching for the ticket inspector. But the man had obviously had no real suspicion, just idle curiosity, and he had gone back into his cubbyhole. Eilders walked west. He passed one policeman, and felt the growing tension as he approached the blue uniform, the big man who strode with a slow gait, hands behind his back, towards him. The policeman saluted, and Eilders, surprised, saluted back. If this was the reception they gave the defeated, what would they give to the victors?

Within a mile he found a pawnbroker's shop. It was off the main road, in a quiet and dingy street, and there was no one in the customer area. Eilders went in. The pawnbroker was a Jew, that much was obvious, and looked worried, which was understandable. Judging from his strange English accent, and his very un-English mannerisms, Eilders judged he was from Austria. The nightmare he thought he had woken from when he reached England was now just twenty-one miles from Dover.

Eilders said he had a week to kill before returning to his unit, and was sick of walking round in uniform. The man hardly seemed to hear. He sold him a collarless shirt, a navy blue rough serge workman's jacket, and heavy black shoes with thick soles. The man seemed mildly surprised when Eilders asked for underwear and socks as well, but was glad of the sale.

He allowed his customer to change in the back room, and even gave him two brown carrier bags with string handles in which to put his uniform and boots.

Later, Eilders visited a public convenience—how delicate a

47

term, he felt—put a penny in the slot of a cubicle and slid the bolt home. Ignoring the crude graffiti and homosexual invitations, he took out the uniform, and carefully removed every badge, button and stripe. He wrapped them in toilet tissue and put them in his jacket pocket with his dog tags. Then he shredded his pay-book into tiny pieces and flushed them down the toilet bowl. It took three pulls on the ancient chain before the last shred of paper disappeared.

He left the public lavatories, and at the nearest drainage grid, he bent down as though to tie a shoelace and let the small parcel of toilet tissue and contents drop into the scummy water, where it made a small 'plop' then vanished.

If it *was* ever removed, and if it ever was handed to the authorities, all it would reveal was that Sergeant Albert Fothergill went on patrol in France, disappeared, and was listed Missing in Action . . . but that somehow he wasn't, but had managed to get back to England and deserted.

Eilders walked on until he reached a narrow canal which ran between a series of warehouses, not far from the river. He walked along the footpath, heading for a small, hump-backed brick bridge.

The day was hot, and the jacket was making him sweat. When he reached the darkness beneath the bridge, he found a broken piece of brick and pushed it into the carrier bag containing the uniform. He eased the weighted bag into the water, pushing it beneath the mossy green surface, until it sank of its own accord. He took out the boots from the remaining carrier bag, and dropped them one after the other in two small splashes. He took the empty carrier bag and pushed that into the water, holding it there until it was water-logged and began to sink.

He wiped his hand, which felt greasy, on the arm of the thick coat, then came out into the sunlight and looked down at his image reflected up at him from the murky water. Now he was a Dutch seaman who, according to his papers, had been in England for well over a month. That would be a great deal less difficult than trying to impersonate a British Army sergeant, with all that entailed.

Correspondingly, of course, the British might be initially more suspicious. A foreigner! How the British could be suspicious of foreigners! But his story and his papers were water-tight, and, better still, uncheckable.

The first time he had landed in England he had been a scared, confused boy, not knowing a word of the language of the nation that had conquered and then humiliated Germany. Now he was a man, a man with a mission that would help Germany wreak revenge on the country he hated. Of course, when he had first arrived he had been fed egg and chips.

This time, if they caught him, they might do the same. And then hang him.

Despite the warm sunlight, he felt the chill of death.

Chapter Four

EILDERS PICKED up the heavy black telephone receiver and slid four copper pennies into the slot. Each coin made a hollow 'ding' sound as it dropped. He dialled the letters B-E-L, and then four digits, a sequence he had memorised. There was a *brr-brr* sound in the earpiece, and after three of those a woman's voice said: 'Lord Blackington's residence.'

The accent was not English. He noted the fact.

'Lord Blackington.'

'Hello, Lord Blackington's residence.' Eilders remembered, and hurriedly pushed the silver button near the letter 'A' on the metal box beneath and to the right of the telephone handset. He heard a clanging of dropping coins, and was connected. 'Lord Blackington, please.'

'Who is calling, please?' The accent was Mediterranean, probably Spanish. It was a language he spoke fluently, having spent eight months in Burgos with Franco.

'Jan.'

'Just a moment, sir.'

Eilders waited. At length what he thought was another receiver was picked up, the first replaced, and a voice said: 'Blackington.'

' 'I've come from the sea.' Eilders thought it was stupid and melodramatic, but it was also orders.

'Where are you?' Eilders read out the printed address on the white label which was fixed under a glass panel in the telephone kiosk. 'Wait outside the kiosk. My driver will be there in ten minutes.' The receiver was replaced.

* * *

50

Eilders did not like Lord Blackington. He hated Englishmen, aristocrats and homosexuals, and Blackington was all three. But it was the man's security he disliked most. 'At least two servants saw me come into the house dressed like this.' He swept a hand down to the rough clothes. 'I know you English. A man like me would not visit such a house.'

Blackington was lounging against the long mantelshelf, a cut-glass tumbler of whisky and soda in his hand. He wore a dark-red quilted smoking jacket. He looked at ease, but he wasn't. What he was doing was beginning to frighten him. Eilders certainly did.

'Perhaps you would feel more secure if I told you that from time to time I have, shall we say, guests at this house. Some are your age, some even younger. You are . . . ?'

'Twenty-seven.'

'Much younger. Many dress in rougher fashion than yourself. Sometimes they stay one night, sometimes they stay longer. My staff have become accustomed to such interludes.'

'They will assume I am that type?'

'Naturally. And don't look so worried, Jan, you don't interest me. I am a rich man, I can do as I wish, and in this city there are only too many willing to do anything in return for just a hot meal, friendship, a little money.'

Eilders looked at the greedy, traitorous, weak, debauched man who stood in front of him. If it came to killing Blackington, *when* it came to killing him, it would afford Eilders great pleasure. 'You don't worry me, my lord.' The tone of the young man's voice left Blackington in no doubt that the formal address was meant as an insult.

The aristocrat ignored it: 'I'm so glad. Now let me tell you what I have organised. Tomorrow my chauffeur will take you to Clapham. He will drop you at the north side. Cross the common to an address on the south side. They do not yet know who you are but they have on occasions lodged friends of mine . . . '

Blackington put his own inverted commas around the word 'friends' by the inflexion of his voice.

'They will have a room for you. You will have to give your name, I am afraid the regulations require it now, but I assume your papers are all in order?'

Eilders nodded.

'The chauffeur has done this before, and knows the address, but I do not think it would be fitting for you to be dropped at the door by a chauffeur-driven Bentley, do you?'

'Can you trust the chauffeur?'

'Completely. The man once made an understandable if regrettable lapse of honesty. If I made certain disclosures he would end his days breaking rocks on Dartmoor.' Blackington smiled lazily: 'Of course, he could do the same for me . . . but then, I am an aristocrat and would be believed, while he . . . ?'

'Then?'

'Then you will telephone me every forty-eight hours. Now, what do you need?'

'A small suitcase, something worn and used, as a sailor would carry, perhaps a kitbag if you have one.'

'I shall arrange it.' Blackington moved away from the mantelshelf.

'Now, Jan, seeing that I am to be your provider, perhaps you would be good enough to tell me exactly what you are here to do, and what part in it your masters require me to play.'

So Eilders told him, leaving out just one very important fact.

The Germans planned to kidnap the 'Little Princesses', Elizabeth and Margaret. They would do it in a combined parachute and glider-borne assault, using Kurt Student's fighting paras and the combat engineers, the Fallschirm-Pioniere. The princesses would then be used to break the morale of the British and make them sue for peace.

The plan was that of Reinhard Heydrich, head of the Sicherheitsdienst, and so far it was a close secret. His plan was to go ahead with the operation without the knowledge of Adolf Hitler, and to present the princesses as a prize. That way he would curry favour with the Fuehrer, a notorious

52

player of favourites. When the British made peace, as they must, without invasion, then Hitler would surely make him deputy Fuehrer in place of the strutting Hess. It was the job Heydrich had always coveted, to be second in the Reich only to Adolf Hitler. And when Hitler died or stepped down, he, Heydrich would be the leader of all Germany!

Heydrich was convinced his plan was the easiest way of taking Britain out of the war. He did not share Goering's assuredness that the Luftwaffe would sweep the RAF from the skies, leaving Britain ripe for invasion. The absence of the Royal Air Force over Dunkirk led Heydrich to believe the planes were being saved for a future battle.

Heydrich had had two careers, and was a survivor. Kicked out of the navy in disgrace after flaunting his loose morals, he had found himself as a small-time clerk in a fledgling National Socialist German Workers Party. Now he was in complete charge of the Third Reich's security police . . . that within ten years. His reasoning was as sound as his ambition. Something would be needed to bring the British to their senses. That something would have to be stunning in its execution, and enfeebling to the enemy in its result.

It had to be a blow which struck at the heart of everything the British loved and held dear. Something reverent and central to their way of life.

He had considered first the kidnapping of King George or Queen Elizabeth or both. But that was a blow from which a nation could recover. A King could be a warrior. He could be defiant, preferring death to dishonour, even bringing about the latter himself if careful watch was not kept. He could urge his nation to continue the fight, offering himself and his queen as symbolic sacrifice for his nation's struggle.

He had considered kidnapping Winston Churchill, then instantly dismissed it. A prime minister was expendable, the English parliamentary system and its continuity saw to that. A prime minister was not a fuehrer in the German sense, and this prime minister would be particularly expendable. Half the British nation would probably have applauded after what Churchill had done to the miners in South Wales, and his

53

military adventure at Gallipoli in the First World War. Then it struck Heydrich with staggering simplicity. The little princesses! If you took two young girls, two beloved princesses, then imagine it. Imagine the girls pleading over Berlin Radio, begging the King and Queen, Churchill, Parliament, to make peace. (And beg they would once the head doctors had finished with them.) How could the British demand defiance, heroism or suicide from two young girls who had spent their lives in the sheltered, deferential atmosphere of the royal court? A girl of fourteen, and one barely ten. It would wring the heart of every Briton.

And what country could feel secure from an enemy which had pushed its troops into the sea, then weeks later swooped from the skies over London, disdained to take its King and Queen, but plucked away instead its darling princesses? Heads would roll in England; the public clamour for peace would be overwhelming.

Heydrich's idea of an ultimatum would be much as Ribbentrop's. The abdication of King George, with safe passage to Canada for him and the princesses (once the Reich could be sure the perfidious British were not to renege on the deal), his replacement by the Duke of Windsor, and a new government sympathetic to the Reich. He knew Ribbentrop had Blackington in mind as that government's head. Heydrich had other plans for Lord Blackington.

And if the British refused at first to consider peace, they were a stubborn people after all, then there would be no martyrdom, no Berlin version of the princes in the Bloody Tower for these two modern royal personages. Instead, humiliation. The girls would continue their broadcasts. They would tell of how they were re-discovering their German ancestry, the British were sensitive about that. They would tell how many friends they had made, of how agreeable life could be in the Third Reich. It mattered not if the British believed it; what *would* matter was that no censor on earth could keep the British from knowing their princesses were in the hands of the enemy and appeared to like it. Actresses, spliced tapes and other devices could be used to augment what

54

would be a natural reluctance (even with psychological help) on the girls' part.

The princesses would have their picture taken with the Fuehrer, perhaps sitting on his knee, or playing with his dog Blondi. With Reichminister Goebbels and his children. The propaganda ministry would send them out to every country in the world—particularly the United States. They would be sensational.

Naturally the British would ban them, but copies would filter in as contraband, and the effect would be devastating.

And each night, the steady drip-drip of their princesses, begging them to make peace; begging their own father to step down in favour of the Duke of Windsor; begging their subjects to spare the country the horrors of air bombardment by Germany. The British would crack, Heydrich was sure of that, and sooner or later, in Geneva, Lisbon, Dublin, or Washington perhaps, the peace feelers would come out, the emissaries would make contact.

But how to kidnap the princesses in the first place?

The British had been told that the princesses Elizabeth and Margaret were at a house 'somewhere in the country'. German intelligence knew better. The girls were at Windsor, either at the Royal Lodge or in the castle itself, probably the latter since Dunkirk.

A team under Kurt Student had made a feasibility study of an attack on the castle, and concluded that it stood a strong chance of failure. The area was large, well-defended, and spread out. The *exact* location of the princesses within the area was not known, thus it would be relatively easy for the men of the Coates Mission to rush the girls away at the sight of the first parachute, or take them to specially prepared strong points and tenaciously defend them against capture until troops with heavy weapons could be brought in to crush the lightly-armed paratroops.

Student concluded that the assault had to be at a place and at a time where the airborne commandos could hit suddenly and with the minimum of warning to the defenders; then the combat engineers had to blast their way into the building in the minimum time possible, allowing the snatch squad to get to the princesses' location as quickly as possible. From landing to take-off (the girls would be flown off in a fighter plane) no more than forty-five minutes could elapse. Anything more and the paratroops could find their mission impossible.

The vital need was for a strip of land or road, clear and long enough to allow gliders and a fighter plane to land, and for the fighter plane to take off from again. The landing area must also have an area that could easily be sealed from unwitting civilian traffic, and with defined exit and entrance roads along which military traffic would be expected to arrive. In addition, the site was to offer the minimum possible distance between the glider landing points and the defence line to be breached by the engineers.

Buckingham Palace fitted all those requirements. The raiding party would consist of six troop-carrying Junker 52s and two towed gliders of the DFS 230 type which had successfully landed on the Belgian fort of Eban Emael. That capture by the paratroops only weeks before had given Student and his men the fillip and the sense of belief they needed.

Goering's help would be enlisted, he was an ambitious man, and the commando would fly at the centre of a mock bombing formation, well protected from any marauding British fighter planes.

Once over the City of London, the commando echelon would break off, the JU 52s first, dropping their paratroop sticks to land in a curve from Admiralty Arch, Hyde Park Corner, Victoria Railway Station. Their job would be to attack the Guards' barracks in Birdcage Walk and block off all access to the Mall, Constitution Hill, Birdcage Walk and Buckingham Palace Road. Student thought these men had little chance of surviving to be prisoners of war.

The gliders would be released three thousand feet over the City of London, and slowly swoop down over St Paul's cathedral and the newspaper bastion of Fleet Street, down the Strand, across Trafalgar Square past Nelson's column, skim

Admiralty Arch, and land along the Mall, crashing if possible into the very iron railings of Buckingham Palace itself. The Fallschirm-Pioniere would deal with those railings and any other obstacle.

The commandos would then storm the Palace and find the royal family. If possible, photographs were to be taken of the complete royal family held captive. Then the girls would be drugged and taken to the Mall. A converted and supercharged fighter plane would by this time have landed in the Mall, the combat engineers having cleared the gliders and any other obstructions. The princesses would be loaded into the space behind the pilot, along with the containers of film. The pilot would then take his plane off over Admiralty Arch or the Palace, depending on the wind, and head for France.

Once airborne, the pilot would fly fast and at treetop height. Over an open frequency he would announce the identity of his passengers, and threaten that any attempt to force him to land would result in his crashing the plane. He had orders, if a serious attempt *was* made to force him down, to bale out, leaving his plane and his charges to crash. He had a cyanide capsule with which to take his own life before the enraged British tore him limb from limb.

The rest of the German troops would then fight on until death or capture.

Student and his men had practised the exercise, using Wehrmacht troops as the British, in a schloss in East Prussia which roughly fitted the dimensions of Buckingham Palace and its environs. Live ammunition had been used for realism and two men had been seriously injured. The conclusion was that it could work. It had all been done in thirty-five minutes, from glider-landing to take-off of retrieval plane.

But Student knew that firing live bullets over soldiers' heads was one thing, firing them *at* their heads, quite another. Nevertheless he believed they could do it in forty-five minutes, an hour at the outside, and he knew his devoted, fanatically-fit paras could hold off the British for that long. Only one tiny but vital piece of the jigsaw remained. When would the princesses visit Buckingham Palace, as they must?

It was obvious that such a move would be carried out on a spontaneous basis, and in the utmost secrecy.

Student needed just twenty-four hours notice, and as it was almost summer, weather conditions were not expected to present any problems. The vital factor was the man in London.

Heydrich knew that all the agents in Great Britain were run by the Abwehr: the SD had no one there—yet. The Abwehr and SD were rivals, naturally, as all competing intelligence services are, even when they work for the same side.

The SD monitored all the incoming messages, but there was one which came in on a different frequency, and some quiet investigation had revealed that its destination was not Abwehr head Admiral Canaris, but Ribbentrop at the Foreign Office.

Heydrich knew Ribbentrop had ambitions of his own, and that feelers had been put out both before and since the declaration of war to various high-ranking Britons. Within days Heydrich had the file on Ribbentrop's man: the Marquis of Blackington, ex-officer, war cripple, peer, homosexual—and more importantly, a friend of the Duke of Windsor, at present languishing in Portugal. Ribbentrop was no doubt using the man as an inside track to the British government, an élite fifth columnist. But he, Heydrich, decided that Blackington should serve a more immediate and practical purpose. Afterwards there would be more of the Blackington ilk only too willing to curry favour with the Reich.

It helped that the British lord knew nothing of the deep rivalries between the Foreign Office, the SD and the Abwehr. The FO code cipher was simple, so when the message came from Berlin, the man would not think to question its validity.

Perhaps Blackington would not wish to harbour a German agent, but he would have no choice, he was too far in now and must know it. Heydrich doubted if the peer would question the fact that his cipher and wavelength were being changed, an act that without his knowledge would put him in touch with the SD and not the Foreign Office. Any Foreign Office messages would be in the old cipher and would therefore be ignored. Ribbentrop would think his man had gone cold.

In fact, Blackington could thank his lucky stars he was not dealing with the Abwehr at that stage. Had any of *their* men contacted him, the lord would have ended up in Wandsworth being hanged for treason. The British double-cross system run by MI5 had captured every Abwehr agent, and turned them all. Those who refused, or who were considered unsuitable, were hanged or imprisoned. Blackington's task was simple. He would discover when the princesses were to come to the Palace, and exactly where they would be at a given time.

Heydrich had no doubts that Blackington could do it. His files showed he had friends among the highest and lowest of the royal circle. His lovers had included a much removed cousin of the royal family, a fellow peer, now a court circle confidante, and several servants of the household. He had also taken part in homosexual acts with junior ranks Guardsmen, some of whom might still be on royal duties.

'He'll find out eventually from the top or the bottom!' Heydrich laughed uproariously at his own joke, and his staff thought it prudent to laugh with him.

The plan needed one more man. A man in London to make sure Blackington did it. If he refused, Eilders would threaten to expose him. Treason was treason, and it was impossible for Blackington to explain away what he had done. Eilders would get the information, check as far as possible that it was accurate, and then relay it without delay to Berlin.

Then, of course, the agent's job would be to kill Lord Blackington. Personally, Heydrich never trusted for long a man prepared to betray his own country for power or profit.

He thought his old friend Uwe Eilders would be perfect for the job. The man would especially enjoy killing an English aristocrat.

Chapter Five

THE SMALL, rather hunched man looked out of the window of his office in the Tirpitz Ufer, hands clasped typically, behind his back. The junior officer waited. At length Admiral Wilhelm Canaris turned, those piercing blue eyes unblinking.

'Why Operation Raven, Franz?'

'Heydrich's idea, I understand, Herr Admiral. His agent acquired the name while serving in Burgos. He had a penchant for dressing in black. We understand he rather liked its sinister implications and he made no effort to disclaim the soubriquet.'

'Edgar Allan Poe,' said Canaris almost to himself, 'not the most light-hearted of writers.'

'Poe, Herr Admiral? I don't believe I know the writer . . . ' the aide was puzzled.

'An American, Franz, a disturbed personality, possibly insane, obsessed with terror and fear. He wrote of the dark side of man. Among his works is a poem called *The Raven*, a sombre work. He died in the gutter—literally. I wonder if this agent is familiar with Poe? But enough. How far advanced are these plans?'

'They can go in twelve hours after the signal from London. They have had at least one full-scale dress rehearsal. The rest is for chance and providence.'

'And why did this information take so long to reach us? Parachute troops come under the Luftwaffe, not the SS, and Wehrmacht troops were used also, so you tell me.'

'It was the extraordinary tight security, Herr Admiral.

Student's men didn't breath a word. It seems that before the assault on Eban Emael two of them were sentenced to death for trifling lapses of security over the plan. Naturally no-one would risk the firing squad talking about this. Our leak eventually came from the Wehrmacht. Actually I think they are a little jealous. A raid on Buckingham Palace could net a bagful of Iron Crosses.'

Canaris waved his subordinate into a chair and sat down himself. 'This man the SD have put into London, this . . . Raven?'

'His name is Uwe Eilders. He was close to Heydrich in the early days; they share the same tastes.'

Canaris swallowed and blinked. He knew what Heydrich's tastes could run to.

'The agent's parents are both dead. He had lived in England, then came back to Germany; had pretensions to being an actor, then joined the SS.'

Canaris narrowed his eyes. 'He *lived* in England? He has English blood, the Raven?'

The aide shook his head: 'His ties were by marriage. His grandfather's sister married an Englishman in 1891. Eventually she went to England and became a naturalised British subject in 1904. The couple had three daughters. One of them was very religious and when the orphanage to which Eilders had been sent somehow traced her, she felt it her duty to take the child to England.'

'How old was he then?'

'Thirteen . . . seventeen when he returned.'

'So his English is fluent then; they are formative years and the best for learning a language. In which part of England did he live?'

'London, the working class area of the East.' The aide refreshed his memory from the paper in front of him. 'Because of his language skills he was eventually seconded to the SD. His English is considered fluent and idiomatic. He also took an intensive Spanish course so he could liase with the Nationalists during the Civil War. That was where he became Raven. He can speak French too, and some Italian.'

'Raven . . . ' Canaris rolled the word . . . 'a talented man.'
He thought for a moment . . . 'Why did he return from
England?'

'Sent home, Herr Admiral. An unfortunate incident with a
boy of the family . . . '

'Sexual?' Canaris raised his eyebrows.

'No, Admiral. He stabbed the boy in the chest with a penknife. The family packed his bags and sent him back to the
orphanage. He was too old, of course; after that he
wandered.'

'Why did he stab the boy?' Canaris was intrigued. Everything about Eilders could be important, he had a premonition
about it.

'I don't know, Admiral, but from what we know of him I
think he probably enjoyed it.'

Canaris nodded to the file: 'Read it.'

The aide said: 'Before he went to Burgos he married a clerk
from the Foreign Office, Ilse Koburg. A month after his
return she fell down the stairs at their apartment, damaged her
spine and lost the use of one eye.'

'And Eilders did that?'

'We are sure he did. It seems that in Spain he made several
trips to the line in Zaragoza. One night he went out with a
reconnaissance patrol and strangled a Republican sentry with a
garrotte. The Nationalists complained to our Intelligence
liaison officer. They didn't mind our Condor Legions doing
the dirty work for them but they objected to our spies as well.
There was an incident in a bar with a Moorish soldier . . . '

'Muslims do not drink, Franz . . . '

'A military police patrol, Herr Admiral . . . Eilders
provoked the man, then injured him severely.'

'You are saying he likes inflicting pain . . . likes killing . . .
for the sake of it . . . ?'

'Yes, sir.'

'And it was after he got back from Spain that his wife
was injured? As though once he had started he could not
stop?'

The aide nodded his silent assent.

62

'And this is the man the SD have put into London, a psychopath who knows the British as few do. But a childhood in the East part of London does not befit you to wander around Buckingham Palace. His job is to frighten the English lord, and once his usefulness is over to kill him. My God, we are becoming like Chicago gangsters.' Canaris got up and began to pace. 'We are sure that there is an Englishman there, a lord, and that he is helping in this insane plan?'

'That is what we have learned from our SD sources. They say it was one of Ribbentrop's men, and that somehow the SD have taken him over.'

Canaris fixed the junior officer with his deep blue eyes. Some said Canaris was homosexual, though his wife Erika for one would deny that, and the aide shifted uneasily.

'So, let us hypothesise, Franz. This English lord betrays his country and gives information to Eilders who gives it to Ribbentrop. If the Englishman refuses to cooperate, Eilders terrifies him by torture or threat of betrayal. So . . . then Eilders kills the man when he has passed over the information on when the princesses will come to the Palace.'

'We believe that to be the outline, Admiral.'

'Then let us hypothesise further. Let us say that the British are obliging enough to let two gliders float down the Mall . . . if they haven't already shot down the whole formation over Dover . . . Let us say that the gliders do not hit any trees, of which there are many on either side, and then that those same gliders crash into the very gates of Buckingham Palace.'

The aide kept silent.

'And then, Franz, let us imagine that these fellows from the Coates Mission, royal guardsmen, probably the finest troops in the British Army, that they obligingly lie down like the Wehrmacht did at that schloss in Neustrelitz. And then say that the princesses sit tight with the King and Queen until Student's men come to get them, and that they surrender without a fight; you know they say that both the King and Queen have practised regularly with pistols and Thompson guns . . . '

'I did not know that, Admiral . . . '

'But, everything is going well, the King hands over his revolver. The photographer take his absurd pictures, the princesses are drugged, and then the fighter plane gets off the ground without demolishing the Palace or Admiralty Arch, and the RAF lets it fly back to France.' Canaris pushed a hand through his snow-white hair.

'We allow Heydrich all that. He has the princesses, he dances a jig. Then what?'

'I don't know, Admiral.'

'Then disaster! Disaster! I sometimes think there is a conspiracy of madness to bring Germany to ruin, and that the chancellery is where the madness starts.' The junior officer started to sweat, and felt his collar tighten. Canaris' views were common knowledge in the Abwehr, and they were dangerous. Many thought they would lead their chief, and perhaps them with it, into serious, possibly fatal trouble.

'Can you imagine the opprobrium heaped upon Germany? The sheer revulsion in the neutral countries? You can level a city, Franz, and people think you strong. Steal a princess—an English princess—and they will think you a monster.'

If there were hidden Gestapo microphones in the Tirpitz Ufer headquarters, as many believed, the subordinate wished to make sure the transcript had some balance that would save him from the executioner's axe. The Nazis had added a sadistic refinement even to that cruel enough execution. They made the victim put his head face up on the block, so he saw the axe coming down!

'Admiral, I hardly think the Fuehrer need worry about the Swiss, I . . . '

'Damn the Swiss, you idiot, it is the Americans I am talking about. Roosevelt is just itching to declare war on Germany. He is a sick man, and I believe a weak and sentimental one. Such a trio of faults is dangerous in a man at the helm of so powerful a country; he likes to bluster and bully. Imagine the effect on United States public opinion. King George and Queen Elizabeth went there before this war, they were adored, mobbed, Roosevelt received them in his own home. Good Christ, doesn't Heydrich read the papers . . . ?'

The aide had never seen Canaris so worked up; normally he was a man of ice-cold temperament.

'He is honestly suggesting we kidnap the daughters of the King of England?' Canaris sat down again and shook his head, hardly believing the folly of such an act.

The aide ventured: 'The isolationist lobby in America is strong, Admiral.'

'It would be swept away on a tide of revulsion in an afternoon. Roosevelt would get his declaration of war in twenty-four hours. Who in Congress would oppose him? He's pushing them into war with Japan, and Tokyo directly threatens American interests. He is so thick with Churchill they could be brothers. My God, war with America, is that what Heydrich wants? They would say that a Germany capable of taking such an action was no longer civilised. They could very well be correct.'

'Admiral, the intelligence estimates are that America has virtually no army. With Britain over-run soon, what could they do? They could not launch an army across the Atlantic. We are the masters of Europe.'

'You jump the gun, Franz. The British are not *yet* over-run. If we took on the Americans we would be taking on the world's greatest industrial nation, with a vast reservoir of manpower. Armies can be built. Then if the Fuehrer decides to invade Russia, a subject always close to his heart, what a trio to conjure with for enemies, the world's biggest factory, the world's biggest navy . . . and then the world's biggest army. And do you believe the British would sue for peace even *if* we took these girls? On the contrary, Churchill has a streak of gangster in him from his American side. He would hit back. Who would *they* take or kill, Heydrich? Me? the Fuehrer himself?'

'Reprisals?'

'Why not? These British are ruthless, they'd get some lunatic Czech or Pole to gun down God knows who. We could forget the rules of war. And do you know why Heydrich is doing this?'

'No, Admiral.'

'Because he wants Hess's job. He must be in thick with Goering, and I'll wager the Fuehrer has not been told.'

The subordinate permitted himself a small smile. After all, what he was about to say could only be considered complimentary to his Fuehrer.

'I would have thought being deputy to Adolf Hitler compares to being Vice-President of the United States, Herr Admiral, very little real power and almost no chance of the top job.'

Canaris said: 'Even Caesar died eventually.'

The junior officer wished the conversation would end . . .

' . . . and anyway, perhaps the Fuehrer will one day decide to retire, and then we would have Heydrich as Fuehrer.'

'At least his wife would get a larger housekeeping allowance, sir.'

Normally Canaris' features were sad, almost melancholy, but for the second time that day he smiled. He knew that Heydrich's wife Lina had a reputation for meanness. Heydrich himself had an insatiable appetite for Berlin bar girls, and Canaris tried to imagine him as Fuehrer of Germany if Hitler died or stepped down. It was absurd.

'What do we do, Admiral, approach Heydrich?' The aide hoped not.

Canaris shook his head: 'They have a saying in England, this man Eilders will no doubt know it. "I wish to talk to the organ grinder, and not to the monkey." ' He translated it from the English for his subordinate, who thought: Then if Heydrich is the ape, Canaris will talk to the master barrel-organ grinder himself. Adolf Hitler.

Hitler said: 'Your proof, Canaris.'

The head of the Abwehr handed the Fuehrer a file, and Hitler sat down in a leather armchair, crossed one leg over the other, and began to read. It took him four minutes. He put the file down and looked evenly at Canaris. 'The name of this operation, "Raven", why did they use it . . . because they are coming from the sky?'

'No, mein Fuehrer. The man Eilders acquired the soubriquet in Spain during the war against the Bolsheviks there. He dressed in black. The operation is named for him.'

Hitler said, almost to himself: 'Not a bird I care for . . .' He put down the file. 'Operation Raven is cancelled. Heydrich was wrong to pursue it. I should have been informed and consulted on a military operation so delicate in its implications. Frankly, I have no wish to unduly antagonise the British, nor the Americans, and this insane plan would do both even if it failed. Soon I shall speak to the Reichstag offering the British peace terms. The French are finished and shall get the terms we dictate, but I would prefer to be at peace with Britain. When they have had a little time to consider their position they should be only too glad to come to terms.' Hitler clasped his hands over his genitals. 'You may go, Canaris. It was an act of courage, ingenuity and the utmost loyalty to the Reich to have discovered this foolish plan, and to have informed me.'

Canaris saluted and left, wondering why the leader of Greater Germany did not look more angry.

Adolf Hitler had saved up all his anger for Heydrich. Heydrich was feared by millions of Germans, Austrians, Czechs and Poles. He very soon would be by millions of Frenchmen, Belgians, Luxembourgers, Dutch, Norwegians, Danes, Yugoslavs, Greeks and Russians: anyone whose territory felt the heel of German occupation.

Heydrich controlled the Reich Security Main Office, the RHSA to give it its German initials. Under the RHSA came the Geheimestaatspolizei, the Gestapo by common usage, which was Section Four; then the criminal police, Section Five, and the SS Security Police, the Sicherheitsdienst, or SD, which got two sections to itself, three and six.

Heydrich was a violinist of concert standard; he was also a psychopath. He'd once congratulated his men for their reputation, one he said of 'brutality, an almost sadistic inhumanity.'

Now this man with rank of SS Obergruppenfuhrer trembled before the person in whose hands his immediate future lay. It need take only one word from Adolf Hitler, and the Fuehrer's personal SS guards would take out their own general and shoot him.

A speckle of foam bubbled at the corner of the Fuehrer's mouth; a dangerous sign. 'I should have you beheaded Heydrich, like the common criminal you are.'

Heydrich stammered: 'Mein Fuehrer, I assure you of my undying loyalty to the Reich and to your person.'

Hitler stamped his foot in rage, and Heydrich cowered physically. 'Silence! Your concern was not for the Reich or for my person, it was for your own glory. These parachutists would have flown without my knowledge, then you would have rolled two princesses at my feet like Cleopatra at the feet of Mark Antony.'

Heydrich wisely stayed silent as Hitler raged on, hoping the storm would blow itself out. At last Hitler sat down, his eyes bloodshot from the exertion of temper.

'You will recall your agent, Heydrich. Immediately!'

'Immediately, mein Fuehrer.'

'I sincerely hope you have not compromised Ribbentrop's man in London. He is to be of much use to us in the days ahead. He is a friend of the Duke of Windsor. The Duke is at present in Portugal, or soon will be so Canaris tells me.'

Heydrich tasted bile at the name of his rival.

'Your deputy, Brigadefuhrer Schellenberg?'

'Fuehrer?'

'I wish to see him. If events follow as we foresee, then he will be our emissary to the Duke in Portugal.' Heydrich brightened. Not a man from the Foreign Office or from the Abwehr, but the SD. He still had a future.

Hitler said: 'Do you realise what your insane plan would have meant? The end of our plan to get Windsor on the throne of a sympathetic Britain, and possibly a declaration of war by the Americans. *We* dictate the course of this war, Heydrich, not our enemies.'

'Yes, mein Fuehrer.'

Hitler was leaning back in his chair, eyes closed. The earlier outburst seemed to have exhausted him. 'Thank your stars no harm came to the princesses. You may go.'

Heydrich clicked his heels and flung out his right arm, ramrod stiff: 'Heil Hitler.' Hitler made the suggestion of a return salute.

Heyrich left.

Adolf Hitler felt sure this had been an aberration on Heydrich's part, albeit a dangerous one. Heydrich's work was too good to remove him altogether, but he needed something to keep his mind fully occupied. Later that year, or early next, a man would be needed to control what had been Czechoslovakia. The Protectorate of Bohemia and Moravia was to get a Reichsprotektor. Prague was sufficiently far enough away from the mainstream—and the workload enough—to keep Heydrich out of mischief.

Hitler made an *aide-mémoire* on a small notepad, and thanked God for his own wisdom in ensuring that all the spies kept an eye on one another.

Chapter Six

EILDERS TOOK a London Transport red double-decker bus, number 137, which he boarded at Clapham Common Underground station, and alighted at Sloane Square. He walked the rest of the way to Lord Blackington's house. When he rang the front door bell he was worried for two reasons. When he had telephoned, Blackington was agitated. He said there was an urgent message which had to be delivered personally and that Eilders must come to the house. The whole tenor of the conversation worried him.

So did knocking on the front door of such an obviously grand house in this part of London, dressed as he was in such rough clothes. That would not be normal, a man dressed as he was would be a workman or deliveryman and would use the side door with the hand-painted sign; 'Tradesman's entrance'. But he had tried that door and it was locked. Either Blackington was getting careless or he was making sure as many entrances into the house as possible were locked. Blackington was frightened.

The door opened and Blackington ushered him in. The Marquis was wearing a double-breasted grey suit. His withered arm and its black leather claw seemed even more sinister, and the man's good eye flickered and darted in fear.

Eilders said: 'The servants?'

'They are all out of the house, I got rid of them except one, Maria; there is always one servant in the house, anything else would appear suspicious. But she is downstairs in the scullery, and I have orders not to be disturbed. Come to the top of the house.'

Eilders followed him until they reached the yellow-painted door, where Blackington took out a bunch of keys, selected one from the ring, and let them into the attic room.

The Klamotte was in its suitcase, but Eilders recognised it for what it was immediately. Blackington slumped down on the chaise-longue, seemingly exhausted, and Eilders kept his back to the door, suspicion burning into him.

'Well?'

'It's cancelled.'

'What!'

'It's cancelled I tell you. The message came last night. You're to leave . . . here . . . ' He took out a folded slip of paper from his jacket pocket. Eilders read it and handed it back.

He felt a wave of giddiness, and steadied himself secretly against the door. He did not wish to show weakness in front of the Englishman.

'You're lying. You have invented this because you are frightened.'

'No, I swear.'

Eilders moved to the suitcase, opened it and began to set up the radio.

'No! In the name of God, please.'

He was on his feet, the dead arm swaying from the movement. 'It is too dangerous. MI5 have listening devices, locating machines. I was told to use the radio sparingly. Please!'

Eilders ignored him and began to send expertly.

Blackington watched in fear. Overnight the terror had become complete, the reservoir of courage and ambition suddenly empty. His cyclops face now showed the enormity of what he was doing. Now he wanted the German to go, to disappear. When he had gone, Blackington could take the radio in the Bentley to some marsh in Essex and heave it to the bottom.

He did not want to be leader of Britain any more . . . he just wanted to *live*. Death seemed near to him, he could smell it in his nostrils, the perfume of execution, a compound of the

71

urine and disinfectant of a prison cell. He could feel the pinioning straps . . . the horror of the bag over his head . . . the brisk, breathless walk to the scaffold . . . it was horror . . . horror . . .

'It's finished.' He looked up to see Eilders facing him. The man's face had a chilling ashen-paste complexion.

It seemed hardly credible, but Heydrich himself had cancelled the operation. The agent was to take a train to Liverpool, a boat to Belfast, then a bus to Armagh. There he would be met and guided through the scrub of South Armagh into the Irish Free State. In Dublin he was to make contact with the German Embassy who would arrange for his return to Germany. It was all over.

Eilders became aware that the English aristocrat was speaking. 'You must get away as soon as possible. There is a train to Liverpool tonight, it connects with a ferry to Belfast. You *must* leave!'

Why? Why? Why had Heydrich cancelled the operation? Eilders could not understand it. It would have been the greatest *coup* in the history of warfare, and he would have been the key to it. He would have been Uwe Eilders, the man who coordinated Operation Raven, the man who went into the citadel of the enemy and masterminded the stealing of the King's children. And now it was over. Eilders was desolate; but inside, conflicting forces and emotions were tearing at him like rip tides. Forces of loyalty, emotions of revenge on the English.

It was hard to put into words what the National Socialist German Workers Party, the Schutzstaffeln and the Sicherheitsdienst meant to someone like Uwe Eilders.

He was Nazi Germany incarnate. Before he had joined the Nazi party he had been close to starvation, unable to find a regular job, scraping a living as a would-be actor in flea-bitten theatres all over Germany. He had lived in an alien land, a land he hated, for three years, and could hardly speak his own language when he first returned. He hated that heritage.

The Nazi party, in the shape of the SS and later the SD, had given him an identity and made him proud to be German once

72

more. It had put clothes on his back and food in his belly. It had taken that knowledge he secretly despised, his ability to speak fluent English, and nurtured it, making him understand how useful it could be to the Reich. It made him realise that he was a natural linguist and mimic, and transformed him into someone hard and proud, an élite policeman and intelligence operative.

And better. In the SS he found others who shared his dark joys; others who liked to inflict pain for the joy it gave. In the SS such activities were sanctioned and rationalised.

He had been taught instant obedience. *Befehl ist befehl.* An order is an order. In the SS Training School he saw a young recruit ordered to jump in a canal in full kit. The youth did it, instantly, knowing that unless he was considered too valuable to die, he must surely drown from the weight of his kit alone. But he jumped, and the instructors waited fifteen long seconds before two men, lightly clad, were ordered in to pull the drowning man from the bottom.

When Heydrich had told him of the mission, Eilders knew he risked death, but did not hesitate for a fraction. His name would be in the history books, a German hero along with Frederick the Great, Bismarck, the Fuehrer himself.

And now they said take a train to Liverpool. *Befehl ist befehl.*

He wiped a hand over his face, realising he was perspiring heavily.

'This train, what time does it leave?'

Relief shone like a beacon on Blackington's face: 'Seven. You get into Liverpool about eleven and connect with the midnight ferry to Belfast . . . Northern Ireland is part of the United Kingdon so there are no passport checks. Your cover is that you are to join a ship in Belfast Lough, if your papers are checked.'

Eilders looked at his watch, it was two o'clock.

'I'll wait here. If the mission is cancelled it means we have been betrayed. Tomorrow when I have gone, send your man to the lodging house at Clapham to retrieve my things. Burn them.'

Blackington opened his mouth to speak, but it was as

though his vocal chords were paralysed by fear, and only a dark, croaking sound emerged. He licked his lips nervously. At last he said: 'The radio?'

Eilders looked at him dangerously: 'If they had located the radio they would be here already. But someone has betrayed us. You would be wise to flee before your part in this is discovered. Have the maid make me up some food, then drive me to the station . . . how long from here . . . ?'

'Thirty minutes at the most, allowing time for you to buy your ticket.'

'I will need another case of some sort, a seaman would not join a ship without belongings.'

'Yes, I'll see to it,' Blackington stammered nervously.

'Now leave me. I need time to rest and think.'

Blackington left, the relief beginning to show in his relaxing frame. Once the German was gone he could get rid of the radio, and without the radio no one could prove anything, surely?

After he had left, Eilders locked the door. Then he checked the escape route through the skylight. The house was joined to a row of others, stretching over fifty metres. In an emergency he could get through the skylight, shin along the roof, and hope to climb down a drainpipe or leap to an adjoining row of houses.

He did not honestly believe it would come to that. As he had earlier said to the Englishman, if the spy catchers had located the radio they would have been at the house by now. Telling the aristocrat to flee was simply to terrorise him further.

Eilders lay down on the bed, and began to think. Operation Raven had been cancelled because of treachery, he was sure of that. But whose treachery, and where. Here—or in Germany?

It had started with insects and butterflies, at an age Uwe Eilders could scarcely remember. First he would catch them, then impale them on some surface with a pin. Then he would pull at their wings slowly, watching the delicate fabric tear.

74

There had been a mangy cat in the block where he lived, a pitiful creature, its ribs showing through, always anxious for food or drink. It would mew piteously and push against you for the merest scrap. The young Eilders had a brilliant idea. He took a cupful of drained sump oil from a small motor-car garage, poured the remains of a cabbage soup into a bowl, then added the oil. Then he placed the starving cat before it. The cat took hungry licks, gulping down as much as it could. Suddenly it backed away, puzzled at the conflicting tastes. It walked several paces before lying down slowly. Seconds later it contorted in agony, and made a sort of high-pitched screaming sound like a baby in agony. Uwe watched it die with interest.

At school, as at all schools, bullying and unsophisticated torture in the guise of initiation was common. Young Uwe entered into it with more than the normal gusto. As early as the age of ten he had begun to understand two strangely contradictory facts about himself. He hated the smell humans gave off: whether body odour and stale sweat from the changing rooms, the farts of boys, or the scents of girls and that heady, musky odour they imparted.

And yet; when he was up close, *hurting*, twisting, squeezing, pulling, gouging; male or female, it didn't matter, then there was an *excitement*, a power there, that satisfied something deep within him.

His had been a typical German childhood of the time. His mother had died early, he hardly remembered her. His father told him it was from the effects of starvation owing to the British blockade. She had given young Uwe food she should have been eating herself. His father had been in the army, but was so badly gassed that he was unfit for the post-war Reichswehr, and soon the army pension became worthless because of raging inflation. But there was always money for cheap brandy, and Herr Eilders consumed it in whatever quantities he could lay his hands on.

When he was drunk he veered between maudlin sentimentality, and fits of violence which he took out on his young son. One night, after his father had beaten him, young Uwe

75

took a feather pillow and pushed it over the face of the sleeping man. He had killed a rabbit that way once.

His father was very drunk, and deeply asleep. Uwe felt him struggle a little, his arms waving feebly, but he simply pushed harder with the pillow, and soon the struggling stopped. When he took the pillow away his father's face was deeply red, and there were explosions of red like grapevines where the tiny veins had burst. A small dribble of vomit was coming from his father's mouth. Uwe took the pillow and held it there firmly for several more minutes. After that he could not hear his father's breathing.

At the cheap funeral he sang a hymn, but he found it hard to restrain the joy he felt as dark-clad women wept and tried to comfort him. And beneath it all the sensuality of the power at having taken a human life. There was no family, or none who would acknowledge him, and he went to an orphanage. It was paradise. The Lutheran sisters were strict, but he was fed regularly. And best of all, at night they locked the dormitory doors, and then he became the poacher in his own game reserve, hunting down the human child animals for his personal pleasure.

But then he was called to the big office and told to pack a suitcase. He was going to England. *Gott strafe* England, his father had always said. The English and the French had ruined his country. Why was he going? Where was this England? He was terrified.

The sister said they were to be his new 'family' and explained, but it went over him, he was far away, frightened and confused. He was thirteen years old, the orphanage was his territory, he knew it and understood it. Tacitly he had been accepted as its leader, the others were frightened of him. Now he was being sent away to the land of the people who did these terrible things to Germany.

He was given a small suitcase and a label was tied to his collar. He was pushed on to a train, and then a boat . . . and suddenly terror as he had never known. People towered above him and babbled in a strange language. Mr and Mrs Archer met him at the station and took him for the meal that made him vomit, and then on the long journey by bus to East Ham where he was to live. There were two other boys who stared at him strangely and said things he could not understand.

Uwe Eilders had never known such misery or fear.

The red-faced man worked in a shop, his wife had a shiny, well-scrubbed face, a tight, mean mouth, and hair pulled back into a bun. She read the Bible a great deal, and insisted that her children and her 'special' child, as Uwe was to learn later he was called, read it with her. He could not understand the words she spoke, and when he tried to say the strange words on the page the boys laughed. It instilled a loathing of the Christian religion in him.

The first six months were sheer misery. He was isolated like a deaf person, unable to understand anything that was going on around him. He could not speak to anyone, nor understand what was being said to him.

Mrs Archer bought books with pictures in them, trying to make Uwe repeat words, but he could never seem to get it right, and her shiny face used to screw up in annoyance. Mr Archer pointed to objects and said: 'A fork', 'A plate', 'A chair'. So Uwe said 'fock' . . . the boys sniggered . . . and Mr Archer slapped Uwe and shouted at him in the words the boy could not understand. At length he knew that the object being shown to him was 'fork' or 'plate' or 'chair'. But then someone would speak to him, quickly, and they didn't say fork, or plate or chair, they just babbled, and he shook his head.

The brothers hated him and made no pretence of it. They called him a Boche and a Hun, he could understand those insults. They played war games, thrusting a stick into his hand for a rifle and charged at him, throwing him to the ground. They were both older, bigger and stronger, and he always came off worst.

Suddenly and without realising it, as much as dawn can break imperceptibly, he began to understand what was being said to him, and could form replies. Week built upon week like a rapidly completing jigsaw, and there it was, he could speak and understand this strange language. Within another few months he spoke with the accent of his 'brothers' and would dream fitfully in the argot of his new land.

But he never lost the hate he had first felt. The hate of the bullying, the meanness, the petty jibes and above all the dislike of Germany he heard everywhere. Some teatimes he was forced to sit in a tight collar while Mrs Archer and her husband entertained friends. As they sipped their tea they would talk of the dreadful Huns, the Great War and the atrocities. They would discuss him as though he were not present.

Once Mrs Archer pointed at Uwe and told her friends he was becoming English, just like his great-aunt, thanks to the love of the Lord Jesus Christ.

Uwe was sent to a secondary school where he was taunted and bullied repeatedly for being a Hun. During a geography lesson, the teacher was pointing to all parts of the world Britain 'owned'. The boy next to Uwe stood up and said: 'Why ain't Germany in red, we own it don't we, sir?'

Eilders struck out at the boy and they went down in a whirl of fists. It was Eilders who was caned six times on the buttocks.

The fights diminished as the other boys got bored. There was a young Jew in the class now, and they took out their spite on him. But the hate never diluted.

At fifteen he was made to leave the school and go to work in his 'father's' store, carrying boxes and delivering groceries. He came to know the East End intimately. He lost his virginity to a pale-faced storegirl in a darkened alley-way, but he squeezed her breast so hard she cried. He knew the habits of the boys with whom he shared a room, he could hear them at nights, the grunts, the squeaking of the ancient beds. One night the older boy tried to persuade Uwe to join in. Uwe refused. The boy persisted, getting Uwe in a neck hold, trying to disarrange his pyjamas. Uwe freed a hand and reached for the tiny penknife with which he had earlier sharpened a pencil. He grabbed the handle and plunged the blade into the boy's chest . . .

The brother recovered, but the Archers realised that their Christian experiment with this distant relative had failed. It was obvious that all Germans were beyond redemption, even the children. So Uwe was put on a boat back to his own country, with a loathing in his heart for the British that nothing could ever erase.

At first, if spoken to, he would automatically answer in English, and had difficulties with many German words. He was too old for any orphanage, but yet hardly a man. He was trained for nothing, and had no skills save his knowledge of English. In desperation he attached himself to a small group of touring theatricals who played to tiny audiences. He understudied, shifted scenery, loaded the aging van in which they travelled, and occasionally played small parts. The group barely survived, so there was no pay, just food—whatever could be afforded or scrounged. After a year he was forced to leave the group. There had been an incident with a girl, a minor injury; it would have meant policemen, enquiries, perhaps gaol, so Eilders had fled. He drifted through Germany living rough, taking religious charity or stealing to survive. One night he was savagely beaten by two policemen who caught him stealing a side of ham.

It was on the morning of that encounter as he roamed the streets of Munich with an empty belly and bruised jaw that he saw a poster outside the local HQ of the National Socialist German Workers Party. A firm, sturdy youth with a swastika armband stared resolutely out at him, and the message urged Uwe to join the Nazi party's élite guard, the Schutzstaffeln. For Uwe, like so many Germans of that era, there was no real choice; he walked in the door and volunteered. The SS quickly became his spiritual home. He took to the discipline, the physical fitness, the purpose and the fierce love of Germany, with the enthusiasm of a man who has been exiled from his land, and wandered in the demi-monde of theatrical 'sophistication'.

Once his natural language skills—and that fluent, idiomatic and colloquial knowledge of English—were discovered his promotion was assured, and eventually also gained him a transfer to the Sicherheitsdienst.

When he met Ilse she was a clerk at the Foreign Office, a

79

deeply attractive girl actively pursued by several admirers, one of them an officer in the Abwehr with pretentions to aristocracy.

He proved no match for Eilders. Uwe was startlingly handsome, an accomplished liar and totally committed to whatever he set out to do.

Heydrich was Uwe's best man at the wedding, and the couple drove to the Baltic Coast for their honeymoon in a black official Mercedes.

Ilse was not shy; she understood what Uwe needed and provided it. Occasionally she would urge him not to be so robust, but he knew that she understood the rules of their behaviour and went along with them.

After a year, however, she began to change. No longer was she willing and cooperative; rather, she made excuses to avoid the bedroom with him, even on one occasion telling him that he was sick and should seek help. He hit her very hard that night.

Then one evening she simply told him she was leaving, and stood defiantly at the bedroom door with her two packed suitcases.

He struck her. Once, twice . . . a third time. If his wife would not give him what it was his right to take, then he would enjoy himself without her consent. Ilse reeled onto the landing of the house under the impact of the blows, the suitcase she had held in one hand flying from her grip. Uwe followed, striking her again with the back of his hand, feeling the familiar excitement coursing through him.

She slipped sideways, then tripped on the suitcase, teetered, flailed her arms trying to recover balance and cartwheeled down the stairs with a series of harsh thuds and a sickening crack as her leg struck the banister. Uwe later told the police it was an accident, and Ilse was in no position, unconscious as she was, to contradict him. He was SS anyway, so he could get away with murder, even if it was his own wife. And Ilse was not dead, simply crippled for life, her spine damaged. She was disfigured too. The fall had damaged one of her eyes, rendering it sightless, and it had been removed. In a few moments a healthy, beautiful woman had been turned into an ugly cripple. Eilders arranged for the quickest possible divorce.

His plaything gone, Eilders began to get bored with the SD and thought of a transfer to Section Four of the RHSA. In the Gestapo there would be other playthings, other human guinea pigs for his sadistic games.

Then Heydrich outlined Operation Raven—and accorded him the enormous privilege of naming it after him—and all thoughts of leaving the SD vanished.

This would be the ultimate revenge on the English . . . the *ultimate*. Mrs Archer had kept a portrait of the old King and Queen on her sideboard, and the family prayers had included one for the Royal family. No doubt the old woman would now dote on the little princesses Elizabeth and Margaret.

How sweet it would be, Eilders thought, to carry away those little princesses.

It would be *his* triumph, and when he returned to Germany, no doubt the Fuehrer would allow him to meet them, face to face, to put his hands in theirs. The most famous faces in England, admired, looked up to, and he, Uwe Eilders, a *German*, would meet them as equals.

It was a dream.

And now it was over. Denied him. Eilders hoisted himself up from the chaise-longue, up from the memories, up to reality.

The question was why, and it was not resolved. It could only be, then, that someone had double-crossed Heydrich and put pressure on the Fuehrer . . . It was probably the SD's deadly rivals, the Abwehr, headed by that lisping queer, Canaris. Damn the man for twisting the Fuehrer round his little finger. They would ruin Germany unless the Fuehrer understood that the only people loyal to him were in the SS. He wished Heydrich had disobeyed and told him to go ahead alone, without Student's paratroops or Goering's Luftwaffe. If he could only kidnap the princesses himself, take them to Germany and deposit them triumphantly at Hitler's feet in the Reichs-kanzlerei.

But that was stupid and pointless thinking, for it needed paratroops and gliders, an escape plane, all the things Heydrich had so carefully organised. One man could get near the princesses, an assassin perhaps, but no one man could get them out of the Palace and back to Germany.

Assassin.

He was powerless to do anything but scuttle back to Germany like a coward, leaving these British unaware of what might have befallen them.

Assassin.

Would Canaris have changed Hitler's mind alone? Or was the Fuehrer poisoned against the plan too, by the upper-class generals who thought they knew better than he what was good for Germany? They were like the English, like the man Blackington, they'd run Europe for too long. Hitler's was a National *Socialist* revolution, it had no time for aristocrats. Damn and blast them all, the blue-bloods, they should be gassed and shot, eradicated like rats. Wiped out as the Bolsheviks had wiped out the Tsar and his family and their hangers-on.

Assassin.

Where was Heydrich's guts. Why didn't he make the Fuehrer see sense? The Wehrmacht would never dare challenge Hitler and the party now, the time for that was long gone. They had had their chance and let it pass. Damn the Fuehrer too! Eilders was overcome by dizziness . . . the Nazi party is bigger even than he! The Party and Germany are bigger than any one man. We could take these damn princesses and let the England-ers beg for peace, then what would the Fuehrer say? We could take the girls, or dash them away, kill them, then let the English wail. Take them or kill them!

Assassin.

Assassin!

The dizziness passed, and a wave of unnatural warmth started from his toes, and swept upwards until his groin and scalp prickled with it.

Kill them! Kill them both. Walk into the very lair of the enemy's King and put to death his children. Strike at the very heart of the enemy's morale. It was medieval in its concept. By striking at the standard, the enemy would falter. It would not need a detachment of gliders or parachute troops, just one man, a determined man, with information and a loop of wire. The audacity of it! The sheer sensuality of killing two princesses!

But they had told him to go back, an express order from Heydrich himself. He felt like a man bowed by a great weight, in this case the weight of obedience. *Befehl ist befehl.*

That, or to kill for Germany, the *real* Germany, the Germany of the Party and the Fuehrer, not the traitors who poisoned Hitler's mind and worked against their country.

And when the deed was done, Germany would rejoice, and he, Uwe Eilders, would be at the peak of his life, a hero greater than Germany had ever known. And if he had to die in the process, which was probable, what would that count after so memorable a feat? He had long known that the so-called sanctity of human life meant nothing to him. Now he realised with astonishing clarity that in the long run he cared little for his own life either.

He unlocked the door, and started down the stairs, as he did so, feeling inside his right hand pocket for the looped piece of wire.

Lord Blackington was in his study, sitting at his desk when the door opened. He moved his hand to the top drawer of the desk, and eased it open a fraction more. He said, as calmly as he could: 'It isn't time yet.' Eilders moved in to the room.

'You had a plan of Buckingham Palace, a map with details of the layout, and the different rooms.' The good eye blinked nervously: 'But you have no need of it now.'

Eilders moved a step nearer the desk, every sense alive and tingling, totally alert. Blackington was on the point of betraying him, he felt sure of it. He would allow him to get on the train, then ditch the radio, and somehow tip off the authorities so that Eilders was arrested at Liverpool or on landing at Belfast. Without the radio, Eilders would be unable to prove Blackington's treachery, and the aristocrat would somehow be able to explain away his actions. Eilders decided that as soon as he had the plan he would kill Lord Blackington.

'The plan is no longer here.'

'Then where?'

'I do not see the necessity any longer: tomorrow you will be in Ireland.'

Eilders moved a step closer to the desk, and as he did so, Lord Blackington took out a large World War One military revolver and pointed it across the desk.

'Please don't take another step. I know how to use this, and I've killed Germans with it before.'

Eilders smiled. 'Another change of allegiance, my lord?'

'My God man, this business has to stop, it's sheer madness, even your people in Berlin have realised that.'

'Ah . . . ' Eilders smiled easily, 'there has been another radio message, my lord. We do not kidnap the princesses now . . . we *kill* them!'

Blackington's hand wobbled under the weight of the revolver, his face flushing from the shock of what Eilders had said. Eilders could see the strain on the man's face as he began to pull the heavy trigger. He dived to his right, Blackington's blind side, and the gun went off with a deafening bang and swirl of smoke.

Blackington swivelled, trying to find Eilders. The German had his hand on a big red heavy volume, and threw it at Blackington. It was *Burke's Peerage*.

The book hit Blackington in the face, and the shock made him pull the trigger of the revolver again, and the gun went off with a report that set both men's ears singing.

Then Eilders had the garrotte and was on him. The Englishman choked, kicked, and the chair he was on went backwards. Both men were in a heap on the floor, the garrotte tightening, Blackington's legs kicking and drumming on the sides of the desk, scarring the wood in their tattoo. Blackington went limp and the kicking stopped.

Then a door opened. Eilders saw a woman, young, pretty, Mediterranean features, a maid's uniform, her mouth forming into an O shape. It was the Spanish maid, Maria. She screamed.

Eilders swore and pulled the garrotte away, struggling to his feet to go after her.

In her terror the girl stumbled on the stairs, shouted in Spanish, then regained her feet and dragged herself, limping and crying in fright, to the next flight. Eilders took three steps at a time, risking a broken ankle if he put a foot wrong. If she got to the front door, opened it and ran into the street, then he was dead and not she.

He caught her in the hallway. She knew he was close and had turned, kneeling, her hands clasped together, tears streaming down her face, pleading with him in Spanish not to harm her, and calling on the Virgin Mary and all the saints to save her.

Eilders killed her. Then he dragged her easily—she was light—back upstairs to the second-floor study. He rummaged among the bookshelves, throwing out the books one by one until he came to what he was looking for.

The pages had been torn from a book on Buckingham Palace. It was a complete floor plan of the Palace, with names of the various rooms, their functions, and the nearest exit points to different floors from them. Eilders put it inside his shirt.

Among the books on the floor he found a thick, leather bound volume with a lock on it, which he took to be an address book. He took a metal paper knife and snapped off the lock which was there only to deter casual readers.

Eilders swore. There were hundreds of names and addresses. He wanted only those that might be useful to him, palace confidantes or servants, preferably men who were part of that dark, London homosexual circle. He thumbed through some of the male names. God, it was impossible. He hurled the book down and tried to think. Homosexuality was illegal in

England, those practising it could be sent to prison. Even a lord was not immune from prosecution if he was careless. But he would have to write down names, addresses, telephone numbers, he could not possibly keep them all in his head. He would have a secret list somewhere.

Eilders began to ransack the room, but without success. He ripped out all the drawers of the desk and searched them, finding nothing.

In the empty drawer spaces he inserted his arm, running his fingertips along the heavy wood which marked the front of the desk. The left-hand of the desk yielded nothing, but on the second drawer down on the right he found it. A small lever, virtually invisible even peering into the empty drawer space. Eilders hooked his finger on it, pulled first one way, then the next. There was a click, and a panel swung out. Eilders put in his hand and extracted a slim volume.

In the light of the desk lamp he examined it. There were thirty names and addresses, thirty-five at most, some with telephone numbers, the vast majority of them in London. In an emergency he could memorise them, it would not be too difficult, just like learning lines. He put the book into his pocket, not realising how vital the information it contained would be to him. Remembering, he kneeled down and closed the secret panel.

Information was a weapon. Blackington could no longer get him into Windsor Castle or Buckingham Palace, but it was possible the late lord's associates could.

He debated whether or not to take the gun, then decided against it. If he was caught with it he would be imprisoned, even if his arrestors remained unaware that he was a German agent. And he had the garrotte. Most people were unaware of what they were, it was not an English weapon despite the fact that it had been used on them first by the Thuggees of Bombay. And a sailor could always explain away a piece of wire.

Eilders looked dispassionately at the two bodies, then left the room.

He was alone now. There were no friends anymore, no

86

radio links with Germany, and he was acting against orders. He was just one man, and he had to get into one of the two most closely guarded establishments in Europe. Without knowledge of when the princesses would come to Buckingham Palace, it would probably have to be Windsor, but for the moment he would have to solve the problem of his landlady, and then find somewhere to lie low. After that he could kill the princesses. It did not occur to him for one moment that he would not do it.

A red scorching sun, the heat clawing at his throat, tortured by the thirst, an agony of heat searing him. But he clambered on as by some instinct, pushing desperately upwards, upwards towards consciousness.

Blackington's face was buried in the thick pile carpet, and when his eyes flickered open, he saw first the long tufts like a miniature forest before him. His hand went instinctively to his throat, and when he touched, the pain arched him. He dragged himself up from the carpet and immediately saw the maid's body. He heaved, tried to vomit, but only bile issued, and the pain in his throat was intense. He righted his chair and sat in it for a long time, looking at the debris around him. He got up unsteadily, went to his bathroom and surveyed himself in the mirror. There was a sickening, deep cut under his larynx from which blood still oozed. He tried to form words and couldn't. He coughed up some blood and phlegm.

It was all over now, he knew that. He went back to his desk, found some crumpled notepaper and began to write. He put everything in, it was a complete document of his treachery with as much detail as he could give to help catch the monster, Eilders. He put the paper into an envelope and addressed it to a diplomat of his acquaintance at a neutral embassy, with instructions in the letter to forward it to Masterman at MI5.

That would take at least a day, he had no intention of giving MI5 the time to get to him. He thought of the gallows. No, he wouldn't go that way.

At length he dressed and wrapped a white silk scarf around his neck to hide the wound. He took a cab the short distance, told the man to wait, and dropped the envelope. He tipped the cabbie a sixpence and the man recognised him, saying cheerfully: 'Winnie should call for you, sir. Get you in his War cabinet.'

Blackington could only grunt painfully.

Back in the house the maid's body was stiffening with the onset of rigor mortis, and her face was horribly contorted. She had saved his life by her untimely intervention, at the cost of her own. Blackington felt suddenly very sorry for her, and covered her in his overcoat.

He sat down at the desk after picking up the discarded revolver, and checked the chamber. There were four bullets left.

He had never married, for obvious reasons, and there would be no fifteenth Marquis of Blackington. Nor, for the same reasons, had he sired any illegitimate children as so many of his ilk had done. It was the end of a once-noble line, now terminated in treachery and tragedy. The fourteenth Marquis made sure of that.

He picked up the revolver, cocked the hammer, placed the barrel to his temple, closed his one good eye, and blew out his brains.

Chapter Seven

THE WANNSEE was a sheet of blue flecked with the tiny patches of white sails, and dotted with the blobs of rowboats and pink heads of swimmers who splashed streaks of silver across the water's surface.

Ilse sat on the grass, her legs stretched out covered by the checked blanket. The day was hot and she had no need of covering, but even now she did not like Ulrich to gaze upon her wasted legs which had once been so beautiful.

She put a hand on her forehead, gazing out across the lake looking for Ulrich. He swam so far out she feared for him, but he was a strong swimmer, it was a calm day, and he always returned.

Strong Ulrich, strong, good Ulrich, who had wanted her so much, who had pursued her so gallantly, and whom she had rejected for a man who was little more than a wild animal. Why had she not known then? Why had she not seen that the one was bringing love, the other incapable of it?

But it was far too late now. At the time Ulrich had seemed stolid, so very typically German, polite, a little lacking in humour, very serious and very honourable . . . while Uwe . . . ? She hated to admit to it now, but he had been so very different. Undeniably handsome, fun, witty . . . eloquent, he could quote Shakespeare in English, while Ulrich, whose English was by all accounts almost as good, said he considered it bad manners to address someone in a language they could not understand. Ulrich could be somewhat over-polite, Uwe the opposite, and it was obvious his rank and status were impressive. Fully-booked restaurants had a habit of suddenly discovering a table when she had arrived with Uwe.

Uwe knew the best people in the Party, she had been introduced to Heydrich, Kaltenbrunner, even Himmler on one occasion.

Ulrich blankly refused to join the Party, knowing the harm that must do to his social status and his promotional prospects. Life with Uwe had been champagne, parties, and . . . she shuddered to think of it now . . . sex.

She had known for the first time she went to bed with him, what excited him, and the kind of man he was. But even that was exciting, like a dangerous, crazy game, and she had gone along with it, even instituted variations. It seemed like danger somehow made safe, controlled. Pain for pleasure, a contrast she could never before have imagined, a relief and liberation from her strict Bavarian Catholic upbringing where sex was a sin, and perversion an invitation to eternal hellfire!

The marriage was grand, Heydrich resplendent, a coterie of top Party officials present, more champagne, a Mercedes limousine to drive them to Sylt.

But as the months had passed, she had become more and more frightened. The game didn't seem that any more. Suddenly the pain was no longer pleasurable. It hurt her, and there was no frisson, just pain and fear. And the look in Uwe's eye when he did those things, began to chill her. One night, when he was very drunk, he had placed his pistol against her nipple and pressed very hard. He had said that the ultimate sexual sacrifice a woman could make was to let her man kill her.

She had made the decision to leave, and when Uwe left the house she packed her bags. If he had not returned unexpectedly she would be a free woman now, with her looks, her legs . . . and perhaps even Ulrich as a proper man for her. If . . . if . . . if . . . in the event Uwe returned. He refused to let her leave, and humiliatingly tried to get her into the bedroom with him once more, despite her protestations.

He had hit her once, twice . . . she could remember little more. Only the slow awakening, the pain, the treatment, the dawning of the fact that she would never walk again, would never again be a beautiful woman.

And the burning knowledge that she hated Uwe Eilders.

She had moved to a small room in the Charlottenburg district, and found she could get about in her wheelchair. The Foreign Office paid her a small disability pension, and occasionally Uwe would send her some marks. At least, they came from his office, but Ilse believed it was a colleague.

At first, the only thing that helped make her plight bearable was schnapps. After three she felt the mental torment recede temporarily like the tide; after six she could bear to look at her now blurred reflection in the bar-room mirrors, at the ghastly eye-patch that made her resemble some ludicrous pirate from a children's story book.

Then, one morning she had looked up from her schnapps at the man who sat down opposite her, as the newcomer said: 'Hello, Ilse, it has been a very long time.'

The man was Ulrich von der Osten.

She lied about the accident and about Uwe Eilders. She said they had separated, and then she had been hit by an automobile on the Unter den Linden.

They met several more times after that, nothing romantic or sexual was possible between them now, that was unspoken but understood. Yet Ulrich obviously retained a deep affection for her, and she, wiser after the event, saw the qualities she had overlooked before.

Eventually he prevailed upon her to move to a house he owned on the edge of the Wannsee. He spent most of his time in Berlin at a flat rented by the 'firm'. His housekeeper Titti would welcome someone to look after, and he would visit at weekends. She was too weary of the life she was living to protest.

She knew Ulrich had a private income from his landowning parents, and that money was not a problem. Reluctantly she accepted the stream of doctors who came to see her at Ulrich's request, and stoically accepted the news she had long ago resigned herself to. Her spine was dead, and she would never walk again.

91

She sensed that Ulrich knew more about her 'accident' than he was prepared to admit, but she never broached the subject, and neither did he.

When the days grew warmer, he would lay her down on the grass by the lake, then sprint off in his swimming trunks to plunge into the lake, tearing through the water leaving a wake behind him.

Once he had persuaded her to let Titti dress her in a bathing costume, then carried her protesting into the delicious, ice-cold water, until she was deep enough to float. The effort to keep herself above the water, unless she was lying on her back, was immense, denied as she was the use of her legs, but for the first time she was in an element that allowed her a mobility denied elsewhere.

It was that day, as he carried her back out of the water, her heart alive with happiness, as he laid her down on the grass and covered her with a towel, that day that he said: 'You didn't hurt yourself in an automobile accident, Ilse. Uwe Eilders struck you and you fell down the stairs.'

She had pushed herself upright on her arms. 'You knew?'

'I suspected. I found out properly about three months ago. I went on the language refresher course, English, remember?'

She nodded, her heart full.

'Eilders was there. He made a remark, a half joke and I only partly heard it, but it concerned you. I was suspicious. When I returned to Berlin, I checked. It is hardly a secret, Eilders boasts of it. If I was not the most stupid, short-sighted man in the whole Abwehr I would have known.'

She could swear his eyes were wet with tears, or was it simply globules of water falling from his hair?

'You should have told me.'

'To what purpose? To hurt you, so that you would have done something foolish to Uwe, and found yourself in Dachau?'

Ulrich was looking out over the Wannsee, afraid to let her see his face.

He said: 'I want to kill him. I have never wanted to kill a human being before.'

She put a hand out to touch him, then almost lost her balance and had to steady herself.

'I would like to kill him too, but there's enough killing now. It's over.'

'Yes . . . it's over now. Let's go in, it's getting cold.'

It was still very warm.

That night, after the wine and the cognac, he had kissed her on the lips before she wheeled herself to her room.

As she had lain there, listening to the wind off the lake, she had hoped he might come to her. That he might walk in through the door, climb into the big bed and go through the pretence that she was still a woman. But he did not, and she fell asleep, dreaming, as she always did, that she was running, running along the shores of the Wannsee.

Ulrich was dreaming too. Of revenge.

Now she watched him come churning into the shallow water in a fast crawl, until he stood up, streaming water, his muscular body gleaming and glistening in the sun. He padded up to her, shaking water from himself, snorting with delight. Then his face became anxious. He was never sure if the sight of someone using his legs so vigorously and with so much delight, could upset her.

'Good swim?'

'Marvellous. Are you warm enough?'

'Mmmmmm . . . it is so beautiful today.'

There was a shout from the house, and Ulrich cupped his hand to his ear. 'What?'

'Telephone . . . ' his housekeeper shouted, miming a telephone to her ear . . . 'your office . . . Berlin . . . '

Ulrich got up and ran to the house, still dripping water as he strode across the carpet and took up the receiver.

When he eventually replaced it, there was a frown on his face.

Admiral Canaris wished to see Ulrich von der Osten in his office at four p.m.

Ulrich walked out into the sunlight to tell Ilse, wondering what he could possibly have done wrong.

Canaris looked ill. His skin was sallow, and Ulrich noticed how he constantly suppressed a shiver. He knew that during the First World War, Canaris had escaped from internment in Chile following a naval encounter with the British. He had trekked through the poor villages of the Andes in midwinter until he reached Argentina, then taken a Dutch steamer from Buenos Aires to Germany. The experience had left him with enteritis and recurring malaria. Ulrich suspected the man was suffering a bout of it now.

Canaris said: 'Luckily the attaché felt we would prefer to know before Masterman, so the letter went out in the diplomatic pouch. Blackington should have chosen his friends more carefully. Anyway, our people in Lisbon paid a hundred thousand escudos for the information. I believe it was the cheapest buy of the war.'

'Can we be sure the British do not know, Herr Admiral?'

'As sure as we can be. I think if they knew the diplomatic wires would be humming, or Churchill would have launched into one of his speeches. Besides, the attaché believes Germany will win the war, and he wishes to back the winner.'

And you, Admiral, thought Ulrich; who do *you* believe will win?

He said, 'Do we believe this SD man will try and carry out his threat? It could have been an idle boast?'

'I believe it, so does Heydrich, more importantly the Fuehrer does. Heydrich is terrified. Because it was his idea in the first place, if this lunatic succeeds it is Heydrich's neck, and he knows it. The Fuehrer's famous intuition says this man just might succeed unless we do something to stop him.'

Ulrich took a deep breath: 'We could *tell* the British, Herr Admiral.'

Canaris fought a shiver and lost. It racked his whole body, and he had to steady himself.

Taking Ulrich by surprise, he replied: 'Of course, that goes without saying, and we must make it absolutely clear to them *and* have our version ready for the Americans should the worst occur, that this man is a rogue, a psychopath, who has made his way to England without our permission. The Fuehrer does not wish the Americans to enter the war at this stage. It would wreck everything he has set his heart on, peace with the British on terms which leave them as no threat— especially the Royal Navy—then six months or so respite, and a quick campaign against the Russians to take Moscow before the winter of forty-one.'

Ulrich suppressed a whistle.

'So we will offer the British our fullest cooperation in tracking down this man and capturing him before any harm comes to these royal personages. Our action is unprecedented in time of war, but so are these events.'

Ulrich said: 'What chance does one man have, sir, in a foreign country, using a foreign language, trying to penetrate security which must be as tight as that which surrounds the Fuehrer himself?'

Canaris beat another shiver before he answered: 'None. No chance whatsoever. But would you bet the possible outcome of the war on it, Colonel? The Fuehrer would not. Your English is still good?'

'Yes, sir, though a private in the Gordon Highlanders made me think otherwise recently, during a prisoner interrogation.' Ulrich smiled. 'You are not suggesting I parachute into England and track down this man, are you sir?'

Canaris shook his head: 'No, Colonel, not parachute. If all goes well you will land in England by aeroplane with the full cooperation of the British, as a regular German officer, not a spy. *Then* you will help them to find this man.'

Ulrich was momentarily stunned. When he recovered his wits and let the information sink in, he said: 'Herr Admiral, with respect, we are at war with the British. To tell them is sensible, of course, it is in keeping with the honour of Germany . . . but to *help* them, in *England*?'

'It was the Fuehrer's idea, and a good one if I may say. We

95

think Winston Churchill will agree. He has made a career out of doing the unorthodox. He and the Fuehrer have much in common. No one will be told, of course . . . ' he narrowed his eyes a little. 'You will mention it to *no one*, not even those closest to you.'

'Of course, Herr Admiral.'

'If Churchill refuses our help, if this man succeeds and if we told the Americans the British had refused our help, well, it would go very badly with Mr Churchill.'

'Why am *I* being sent, sir? Why not someone from the Sicherheitsdienst, someone who knows the man?'

'At this moment, Colonel, the Fuehrer does not count the SD among his favourites. We have been given the task of pulling their chestnuts from the fire.'

Ulrich felt there was more.

'But why *me*, sir?'

'The man is dedicated and ruthless, I suspect he has psychopathic tendencies He has lived in England, and he speaks the language fluently as well as having a detailed knowledge of the capital city. He has been an actor, he can impersonate, he knows how to disguise himself, he . . . '

Ulrich got up from his chair.

'Uwe Eilders.'

'Yes, of course. We think your motivation will be very strong.'

'Sir, I must protest, my private life . . . '

'Don't be foolish, Colonel, and sit down. Your private life is not private, you are a spy, spies have no private life, it is our job to know everything about one another. What you have done for the girl is very noble, few would have been so compassionate after the way she threw you over for this other man.'

'And you believe that because of Ilse, I will want very much to stop Eilders?'

'I *know* you will. Am I wrong, then?'

Ulrich stared at the carpet.

'No, Admiral.'

'Because, naturally, you must volunteer, you could not be

forced to undertake this. What you are to do is extremely distasteful, working with the enemy in this manner.'

'I volunteer, Admiral.'

'Good man.'

Canaris was suddenly lost in thought, peering out from his fourth-floor window, across to the Tiergarten.

Ulrich took in the room; an old but very valuable Persian carpet covered the floor, and the desk was nineteenth century, ornately bound in bronze. The gossip was that Canaris refused to let it be cleaned or polished for fear of ruining it, and there was a thick layer of dust on the outer edge.

Ulrich could see that Canaris was gripping the window ledge as he fought yet another shiver.

On the desk was a letterpress with an Abwehr insignia, and the three famous monkeys, hearing, speaking and seeing no evil.

On one wall was a photograph of the Fuehrer boarding a battleship, *Schlesien*, which Canaris had once commanded. On another wall a portrait of the devil, a gift to Canaris from the Japanese ambassador.

It seemed to stare straight at Ulrich.

Seppl, Canaris' dachshund, roused himself from sleep on a pile of blankets atop the old army cot in one corner of the room, jumped down and waddled across to his master, as though sensing the man was unwell. His presence seemed to snap Canaris back from his malarial trance.

'Forgive me, Colonel, I was just admiring the Tiergarten, so beautiful at this time of year. I ride there, a habit our friend Heydrich has now got into.'

Ulrich knew the matter had to be raised.

He said, 'Sir, in the business of Eilders, what are my instructions?'

'Ah yes, Eilders. You will make sure that he is not captured alive by the British. We do not trust Winston Churchill; once the threat has passed he might try and make use of Eilders, the beastly Hun who eats babies.'

Kill Eilders! 'I understand, sir.'

'And Colonel, one thing. I was in two minds about using

97

you. Sometimes the desire for revenge can make a man lose his head, thus nullifying what is gained in motivation.'

'I will not lose my head, Admiral.'

'Good. Remember too that the man you are hunting is dangerous. He *likes* to kill.'

'Where Eilders is concerned, sir, I can be dangerous too.' Ulrich stood up and saluted.

'Sir . . . how will we tell the British, I imagine it would have to be at the highest level?'

Canaris said, 'Leave that to the Fuehrer, Colonel, I think he will make a simple telephone call.'

Chapter Eight

As FAR as the man from MI6 was concerned, Winston Churchill drank far too much brandy at absolutely the wrong time of day for someone with so much responsibility resting on his shoulders.

It was just after noon, but the prime minister already had a balloon crystal glass of the stuff tucked between his fingers.

Still, the MI6 man had to concede that the alcohol never seemed to cloud the man's mind or render him inarticulate or muddle-witted.

The prime minister said: 'Why do they not communicate with us in the normal way, through the language of the broadcast, an interview with a neutral newspaper correspondent through Lisbon or Berne? Why this?' He stabbed a stubby forefinger at the document before him.

'I really don't know, Prime Minister. We can only conclude that whatever the German Chancellor wishes to tell you is of such import and of such secrecy that it cannot receive wider dissemination.'

Churchill scowled: 'Communicating with the enemy in time of war is treason. I wonder what view the House of Commons would take of my action if I consented?'

The man from MI6 put on his blank face. 'Time of war, Prime Minister, special case, sometimes necessary to take bold steps?'

'Perhaps?' Churchill sipped his brandy and studied the

document again, as though it might give some clue to Hitler's motivation.

'Besides, Prime Minister, the German Chancellor is laying himself open to the very same charge.'

Churchill laid down his brandy glass: 'The German Chancellor, my friend, has no electorate, no Parliament and no higher law of God to concern him. He has made himself by treachery, trickery, sleight of hand and sheer gangsterism, the very embodiment of Germany. Each German soldier, from the lowliest private to the highest Feldmarschall, swears his oath not to Germany . . . but to the *Fuehrer*! The Fahneneid, an oath of blood to one man, Adolf Hitler himself. The German people are *his* servant, *I* am the servant of mine. We must never forget that fact.'

'Never, Prime Minister,' said the man from MI6, suitably chastened.

'Now then, to practicalities. How secretly can this be done? There must be no trace, no transcript, no recording of this event, so that future historians not disposed to myself or the British people can distort what I did in an hour of grave peril.'

'A handful of people, sir, all covered by the Official Secrets Act, extremely dire penalties, etcetera. We believe we can put an electronic signal on to the line which would make it impossible for the conversation to be recorded.'

'Good. You know, it is possible the German Chancellor is offering some kind of respite, a temporary armistice. That could be useful to us.'

'Make peace, Prime Minister?'

'Never! A pause, to draw our breath, fill our arsenals and gird our loins for the coming battle.'

'Of course, sir.'

'And I am curious, very curious. The event has a historic feel to it, the German Chancellor and the British Prime Minister speaking together at a time when their two countries are locked in mortal combat.'

The man from MI6 stayed silent. He could almost hear Winston Churchill thinking, weighing the dangers and the possible rewards—even survival?—for the people he held most

100

dear; the burden of responsibility for leading Britain from its most perilous hour, and yet the possibly damning judgement of history if ever the event was made public.

The man's face had a certain cherubic quality, far from the bulldog image he was later to represent in the minds of so many. 'Arrange it,' Churchill said. 'I will speak with Chancellor Hitler.'

The Germans kept records of everything, a fact which was to send many war criminals to the gallows after Nuremberg, convicted on their own meticulous paperwork. One copy of the transcript of Hitler's conversation with Churchill, taken from the Luftwaffe stenographer's shorthand note, was put into a Most Secret archive. The stenographer was killed in a Flying Fortress raid in 1943, and the document itself destroyed when a drunken Soviet infantryman looted the office and set fire to it on 3rd May, 1945.

The transcript was relatively brief.

Chancellor: 'Good morning, Prime Minister.'

Premier: 'Good morning, Mister Chancellor.'

Chancellor: 'I shall waste no time. What I have to say is a matter of the greatest urgency.'

Premier: 'The urgency is welcomed.'

Chancellor: 'A matter of the utmost gravity has arisen in the relations between our two countries.'

Premier: 'Mr Chancellor, our two countries are at war, that is the ultimate crisis between us . . . *that* is of the utmost gravity.'

Chancellor: 'I will not trade words with you, Prime Minister. A German national has insinuated himself into Great Britain . . . '

Premier's interruption: 'He will be dealt with, never fear . . . '

Chancellor: ' . . . this man is a traitor to the Reich, a renegade from the Schutzstaffeln, with neither authority nor status from or within any branch of the Reich government or its forces. However, the man has had military training, and is skilled in the art of espionage . . . '

Premier's interruption: ' . . . he will be dealt with; the British government . . . '

Chancellor's interruption: 'Prime Minister, I said this matter was of the utmost gravity! We have received reliable information that the man in his un-German insanity, plans to assassinate Princess Elizabeth and Princess Margaret.'

The transcript records a long pause, then a request by the British interpreter for a repetition of the previous sentence. The request is complied with by the German interpreter, Herr Schmidt.

Premier: 'Mr Chancellor, what you tell me is indeed of the utmost gravity. Let me stress, most strongly, that if one hair of the head of either of our beloved royal princesses, or indeed *any* member of our Royal family was harmed, then the most dire and calamitous retribution would be Germany's fate for this act of infamy.'

Chancellor: 'The German Reich has no ill-wishes to the personages of your Royal family whose connections with Germany are so very strong and enduring. I have instituted this historic call, at a time when our two nations are at war, because we wish to offer the government of Great Britain every assistance in staying the hand of this renegade.'

Premier: 'If the circumstances were not so grave I might express my appreciation for the Reich's proper concern in this matter. But what assistance can Germany offer? We wish to know everything of the man, what papers he carries if any, his identity, how he landed in our islands.'

Chancellor: 'You shall have it, and more.'

Premier: 'What is the more?'

Chancellor: 'I propose to offer the services of Colonel Ulrich von der Osten of the Wehrmacht's Abwehr service to assist your police forces and intelligence services to track down and apprehend this man.'

The transcript records the next words as 'Unintelligible', and London is asked for repetition.

Premier: 'Impossible!'

102

Chancellor: 'Do not spurn our assistance too easily, Prime Minister. Colonel von der Osten knows this man, of how he works and thinks. We feel his assistance can prove invaluable. Additionally, the Reich wishes it to be known that by offering this help it is putting out the hand of friendship between our two great Anglo-Saxon nations.'

Premier: 'I repeat, impossible!'

Chancellor: 'Then so be it. The Reich washes its hands of this matter. Germany, in my person, has taken an unprecedented step of honour in the midst of war. We have sought to alleviate what would be a terrible tragedy, and His Majesty's government, in your person, has decided to spurn Germany's assistance. Be aware, Prime Minister, that our propaganda ministry will be instantly ready to tell the world, should this ghastly tragedy occur, that Great Britain was prepared to let its Royal princesses die rather than accept German help.'

The transcript records London asking Berlin for a brief pause. Transcript records a break of forty-seven seconds.

Premier: 'Mr Chancellor, are you still there?'

Transcript records an affirmative from Herr Schmidt.

Premier: 'With a heavy heart, I reluctantly agree to the entrance into Great Britain of your colonel. I will have your solemn assurance that he will not, under any circumstances whatsoever, at any time, or to any person, communicate or attempt to communicate, anything he sees or hears during his stay in the United Kingdom. If he were to do so, his special status would be nullified, and he would be a common spy, liable to the fate which befalls spies in any country.'

Chancellor: 'You have the assurance of me, Chancellor of the German Reich, Fuehrer of the German people.'

Premier: 'How soon could your colonel be in Lisbon?'

Berlin asks for a pause. It lasts twenty-three seconds.

Chancellor: 'Within thirty-six hours.'

Premier: 'I shall instruct our embassy to receive him.'

Chancellor: 'It is done.'

Premier: 'There is nothing further?'

Chancellor: 'I admire you for the courage of your decision, Prime Minister. It grieves me that our two countries should be at war when our mutual enemies lie elsewhere. Your view of Bolshevism is well known.'

Premier: 'Mr Chancellor, I and the British people will not rest nor flag until you and your evil regime are no more. The years shall be the test, and we grow stronger by the hour.'

Chancellor: 'Since you choose to spurn the hand of friendship, I will remind you that we are the masters of Europe, and soon our bombers will darken the skies above your cities. Think on that, Prime Minister.'

Premier: 'Herr Hitler, God grant me that I live to dance upon your grave. If the princesses are harmed, the wrath of our nation shall fall upon your head, directly and savagely.'

The connection is cut from the German end.

Transcript finishes.

Chapter Nine

EILDERS FOUND the old woman in her foul-smelling kitchen and killed her. There was a store cupboard beneath the stairs, where she evidently had been hoarding tinned food. He placed her body behind a shield of corned beef, custard and marrow-fat peas.

Then he found the grimy ledger in which she kept a register of her guests' names, and burned it. He had had to kill her because she was the only other person, with the exception of the dead lord, who knew his identity and had seen him up close. The maid Maria had, and she was dead too. The chauffeur had glimpsed him, but the Bentley was not equipped with an interior rear-view mirror, so Eilders was confident he could not give a good description.

However, when the bodies in Belgravia were discovered, the chauffeur would inevitably tell the police about the visitor he had taken to Clapham Common. Perhaps, even, Blackington had the lodging house address written down somewhere. The woman had obviously lodged the lord's homosexual pick-ups before, and would have immediately suspected her present assigned lodger. She had to die.

Some other servants had glimpsed him, as well as the chauffeur, but he knew as a policeman of sorts how rarely any description matched that of the person it was supposed to fit.

Soon he would change his appearance as much as he could, and London was the biggest city in the world: no one would find him.

When the bodies were discovered, it would not be long

afterwards that the police found the suitcase radio in the attic room. It had been too heavy and cumbersome for him to try and dispose of, and to have carried it out of the house would have been sheer insanity. The police would conclude, rightly, that either the late Lord Blackington had been a spy, or he had been host to one.

The body in Clapham would be found quickly, probably as soon as the lodgers got home; it was hardly well-hidden. After the chauffeur had been questioned, and the murders linked, the British spy-catchers would come to the conclusion all three were linked. They would assume that their enemy agent was desperate and running for his life. Logically, Eilders concluded, they must believe he was making a break for home, either to the Irish Free State or by trying to steal a boat from one of the Channel ports and heading for France. But they would have no name, and only a very rough description. And instead of breaking cover and running like a terrified fox along the escape routes the British could monitor, he was going to ground.

He needed a lair, a den, a place to lie low, take stock of the devastating events of the last twenty-four hours, and plan. His lair had to be in a jungle where he was camouflaged, where if the enemy came looking, he could fight or run with some chance of success. He knew such a place.

He walked to Clapham Common Underground station, and took a dirty, airless Northern line tube train to Charing Cross.

A hot, unhealthy wind roared through the narrow pedestrian tunnels, whipping up scraps of litter and discarded sheets of newspaper as he made his way upwards to the District Line. The indicator said the first train terminated at Aldgate East, the entry point to the East End of London. It was his jungle, the district in which he had spent those unhappy childhood and early adolescent days. The East End was more than just a geographical connotation, it was a state of mind and a cultural, almost ethnic, identity. Here the rough proletariat of London lived in housing that was uniformly squalid. Few homes had bathrooms, and lavatories were usually at the end of the postage-stamp yards. The houses were damp, small and set back to back, separated by narrow passageways that ran between them. Few starved, but the food was poor of quality and meagre in quantity. Uwe remembered a time when some local industry failed, workers could not pay their bills, business was slow and Mr Archer was forced to give continual credit to his regular customers. The family became desperately short of money, but even they never descended to what Uwe knew the neighbours lived on as a staple diet: bread with a scrape of margarine or pork fat, once a week a 'treat' of fried potatoes and fish concealed in crisped fat and flour, all bought from a corner shop. And the constant cups of harsh tea, sweetened with the syrupy condensed milk from tins. He remembered the pathetic funerals with the tiny coffins of the child diphtheria victims, the women who simply died because they could not afford the operation that might have made them well, and the haunting sight of the ubiquitous bowed men with cheeks sunken from tuberculosis, coughing up their lives into their handkerchiefs, doomed eyes artificially brightened by the illness that consumed them. And yet, for all that, there was a strange and fierce pride there, a grim acceptance of a common lot that bound them together like cement. Crime was accepted, criminals welcome, police hated. It was the face of England the world hardly knew or understood, the dirty underside of the Imperial coin from the shiny face of Union Flags, pomp and pageantry.

Here too lived the aliens, the non-British who had fled to escape whatever persecution threatened them. Some had been here for centuries, like the descendants of the Huguenots, some for just a few years like the Jews of Germany, Austria and Czechoslovakia. There were Italians and Greeks, sailors who had settled; Syrians, Turks, Levantines, Chinese who ran laundries, black people from Africa and the West Indies.

In few other places in Britain would they have been allowed to live out their lives with their strange customs undisturbed.

And like the beads on the mosaic, the transient population of foreign seamen, living in the seamen's missions and cheap lodging houses, dulling their misery and loneliness in the public houses and seedy brothels.

It was a rough land, dangerous for the unwary, the unwelcome or the stranger who did not belong. But Eilders knew it. He could swim in it like a friendly sea.

The train thundered in at last, and the red doors slid open. He took a seat opposite an old woman, her legs bowed out as a result of childhood rickets. He had seen many such women during his East End years, they were hardly an object of curiosity, so common was the condition.

He remembered the smells and faces that he had left behind ten years before. The poor markets, with their cheap tin kitchen implements, second-hand clothes, and the stalls that served a green concoction in chipped enamel bowls. Pie mash! An eel dish, East Enders were fond of eels, they jellied eels and made up songs about them. The incredible slang they had, a patois which even few Britons could penetrate.

Eilders had tried to explain it once at SD language school, but it had met with blank looks. You took a pair of words, the last rhyming with the one you wished to imply. Thus 'up the apples and pears' meant 'up the stairs'. Once you understood the rhyme it was easy, but then the East Enders would leave out the second word . . . they would just say 'up the apples'. If you were not aware what the second word was, or could not guess, the meaning was impossible.

One had puzzled him because at first he had thought it had sexual connotations. The East Enders frequently referred to a woman's breast as a 'tit'. But they called a hat 'titfer'. Tit for tat—hat!

The East End had its own rules and its own moral and sexual mores which, thanks to his years there, he understood. His understanding of it did not prevent him hating it with all his being. But for now it was a place in which he could hide. And when he judged it was time, he would venture out once more. He would go back to the sweet-smelling places, the bright lights in the land of full bellies and complacency.

There he would seek out the Palace of the enemy's King.

And kill his children.

Chapter Ten

THE GENERAL feeling at the Yard was that Harry Jones had never been quite the same since he received the telegram. It informed him with the deep regret of the War Office that his son Gareth was missing believed killed at Narvik. Meg having died in 1934, Gareth was all he really had left, and he'd adored his son to the point of hero-worship. The lad was a fly-half of great potential, and both Harry and London Welsh had great hopes that he would one day play for Wales. But those hopes vanished with the telegram; the young Welshman had been sacrificed in the snowy shambles of the Norway campaign.

So now Supt. Harry Jones had nothing except the small flat in Kennington, and life at Scotland Yard. The force had come to play a larger and larger part in his life after Meg had died, but at least at the end of the days or nights, there was young Gareth to come home to, a bright-eyed boy obsessed with rugby. When you left the stiff corpses at the mortuary, when you had sought out the pathetic wretches responsible, and set in motion the remorseless procedure which would end in their own death or long incarceration, at the end of all that, there was home.

Instead of stale cigarette smoke, cynicism and the cheap, bitter, policemen's jokes, there was youth, hope and an innocent belief that the world could be made better.

But Gareth had joined up, been sent to Norway and had never come back.

Some parents clung to the belief that 'missing, believed killed' held hope; that one day the son would walk up the garden path, bright and breezy, moaning about another military foul-up. Harry didn't fall for that, he'd been in the first lot. It meant there was not enough left of the body to identify. His son was dead, obliterated. He had long weeks ago swallowed that hard fact.

Now there was only memories and work, later a pension and work as a store detective, perhaps. Or the last chance to go back to Wales, buy a little terrace house and struggle to grow roses amid the coal dust. Then die.

Until that time he would do what he had always done so efficiently. Catch villains. He had joined the police force in 1920 after eight months of unemployment following his demobilisation from the Royal Navy. Four years of pounding the Pontyprydd pavements left him bored, and he applied to join the Metropolitan police in London. He courted Meg by letter and two-monthly visits, and married her exactly one month after his transfer to the Criminal Investigation Department. In 1930 he joined the Murder Squad, and at last found his niche. Murder was the simplest of crimes, murderers more often than not the simplest, even most stupid, of criminals. Murder usually had simple motives, greed, jealousy, instant anger or the slow building of repressed hate suddenly surfaced. Harry had seen humans done to death in more ways than he previously would have thought possible. But once you got used to seeing murder victims on a regular basis, the job wasn't too bad. A body like that was beyond your help, neither to be feared or pitied, simply part of a problem you had to solve.

Three men whose crimes he had personally detected ended up on the gallows. He reminded himself at the time that he did not make the law or its punishments, but nevertheless he got very drunk the night before each hanging.

When war came he was a superintendent, doing vital work, and far too old to be considered for active service. The pay was reasonable, a pension at the end of it, and the work was secure. That was one of the reasons he had chosen the police in the first place; the importance of food in your belly was never lost on a kid who'd seen the hungry faces of a South Wales pit village.

110

Meg had begun to recede like a fading photograph left for too long in the sunlight, and there was young Gareth; sometimes, when the lad smiled, Harry could see that unmistakable look of her. Even the outbreak of war didn't upset him too much. They had beaten the Germans before, they could do it again, and the war would keep him busier. It produced more murderers because they had more opportunity and more motive.

And then suddenly the War Office deeply regretted, and there was no Gareth anymore, the world a bleak landscape with only his job to hang on to for support, like a solitary tree. Harry Jones had never been a jovial type, the bardic Welshman of popular myth, but he didn't mind a joke, a few drinks now and then, and the blue eyes could twinkle when he had a mind to.

That was gone now. In the weeks since his son's death he had worked maniacally, never away from the office. There was a single-mindedness to him, a ruthlessness his colleagues had barely witnessed before.

And when the work was finally done he would slip away back to Kennington, refusing offers of drink or solace. One night a colleague called, hoping to persuade Jones to come out for a pint. When he rang the doorbell at the ground floor flat, there was no reply. Eventually he peeped in through the window. The curtains were undrawn, and the flat was in darkness. But there in the deep gloom was Harry, still in mackintosh, hunched in the chair, peering straight ahead as if seeing and hearing nothing.

The general feeling at the Yard was that Harry had never been quite the same since the telegram. Or would be again. The cynics said it would make him an even better copper.

His office was in one of the castle-style turrets that flanked the entrance to Scotland Yard. Out of the window down to the right you could see the statue of the English warrior queen, Boadicea, frozen in martial splendour at the edge of Westminster Bridge. Boadicea had fought the Romans and

111

lost. But the Romans had brought roads, drainage, law and currency. In 1066 King Harold had fought the Norman invaders, and he had lost. But the Normans had brought culture, art and an enriching language.

But if the new invaders came, if we fought *them* and lost, what would they bring? Prison camps, thumbscrews . . . wholesale murder and starvation, the dawn of a new Dark Age?

Jones shivered, and as he did the telephone rang. Would he make his way to the commissioner's office as soon as possible.

It was only the second time he had met the country's top policeman, and on that occasion the commissioner had called him Superintendent Jones. Now he was calling him Harry, and that bothered Harry very much. The nicer they spoke to you in the police force, the dirtier the job they were about to hand you.

The document the commissioner pushed across to him, and asked him to read and sign, further fuelled the suspicion that he was about to be lumbered. It was a kind of super-duper Official Secrets Act pledge, with the meatier parts of the Defence of the Realm Act stirred in. It threatened dire penalties if the signatory revealed anything of what was to follow. Jones read it and signed it.

The commissioner got straight to the point. 'MI5 wants to borrow you.'

'That'll be the Belgravia business then, sir?'

'Yes,' the commissioner looked surprised, 'that's all they've told me, how did you know?'

'I guessed, sir. As soon as we found the radio at Lord Blackington's, we called in Special Branch, naturally, and in no time at all the place was swarming with the mystery men, and Murder Squad wasn't welcome. But I felt that sooner or later they might just call on our expertise. Whatever else was going on there, it was *still* a murder.'

'And you have your theories about the "whatever else"?'

'Yes, sir.'

'And they are?'

'I think the place was a nest of spies, sir. The spies fell out

112

and murder and mayhem resulted. A very strange business all in all, because Blackington topped himself, no doubt about that, but someone *had* tried to kill him. Then we had the old biddy over at Clapham, killed in exactly the same way as the maid, and neck wounds similar to those on her *and* Blackington. A garrotte of some kind, not the usual weapon a murderer might choose.'

'And it is the same person?'

'I would think so, sir, but suddenly we were told to pull out and mind our own business, that *would* be the case if a spy was involved, MI5's department. Perhaps now he's just another murderer on the run they think we can help again.'

The commissioner rubbed the bridge of his nose. Jones was very astute. 'Yes, well, that's as much as I know. This is all very hush-hush.'

And what would they tell me, Jones wondered, that they would not tell the country's top policeman whose shoulders had been touched by His Majesty's sword? 'Why all that, sir?' Jones nodded towards the document he had just signed.

'Well, you'll be going to meet some people who will tell you things—things *I* do not know—which are vital to the security of this nation. Shot at dawn if you so much as breathe a word, and so on.'

The commissioner coughed awkwardly: 'By the way, I was so very sorry to hear about your son. Terrible business . . . you got my letter of condolence?'

'Yes sir, thank you, sir, very comforting.' Jones said it without a trace of sincerity.

'You will be at this address at twelve noon sharp. You can walk it from your office.' Jones looked at the piece of paper, realising that he was going to mix with the spy-catchers.

At 11.45 he locked the door of his office and strode briskly into Whitehall. It would not do to keep a legend waiting.

The legend said, 'Lord Blackington was a spy for the Germans, he was harbouring an agent sent here on a special mission. That agent has killed two people, and is now on the run. We

113

wish to catch him, and we believe you can help us. I shall tell you why we want to use an ordinary—I hope you'll forgive the term, Superintendent—policeman, rather than someone from here.' The legend started to explain, and Jones instantly realised why he had had to sign a document that could put him in the Tower of London if he broke its undertaking.

When he had finished, Jones said: 'So I will be hunting a murderer, not a spy. That way it will not raise any awkward questions. But working alone, sir, that could be difficult, my sergeant and . . .'

'Not exactly alone, Superintendent, but I'll come to that later . . . have you heard of Tyler Kent?' Jones shook his head.

'Kent is an American, he worked at their embassy, and he is now in prison. The Americans agreed to waive his diplomatic immunity so we could arrest him. He had been copying telegrams sent between the Prime Minister and President Roosevelt. He intended to publish the contents, and that would have embarrassed both men.

'Kent was in touch with a group of people called the "Right Club" whose emblem is an eagle clutching a snake. They all have fascist sympathies, and several hundred have been arrested and are off for an extended holiday on the Isle of Man. We do not *really* know how many more there might be. What is clear to us is that many of them are rich and influential. Now let us say the German agent succeeded in assassinating Princess Elizabeth and Princess Margaret. It is unthinkable, of course, but in war one must anticipate the unthinkable.'

Jones nodded, fascinated. He felt he did not need to be told so much, and *was* being, so that he dare not whisper anything.

'Two possible events could result. The United States might declare war on Germany. The Prime Minister would welcome such a declaration, but not at such a tragic cost. Or . . . and this is our fear, the Right Club could use the event to unseat the Prime Minister, to launch what I believe is termed a *coup d'état.*'

'In Britain, sir?' Jones was genuinely astounded. Such things happened only in other countries.

114

'Yes, Superintendent, we are not immune. The new leaders would then try and install a government friendly to Germany and Italy.'

Jones was puzzled: 'But the Germans told us, sir, they don't want their man to succeed either.'

The legend said: 'They believe an American declaration of war is more likely. *We simply do not want the man to succeed!*'

'I'll catch him, sir,' Jones said quietly.

'Yes, you will. Now . . . ' the man stood up. 'I would like you to meet the person with whom you shall be working. And Superintendent,' the man winked, incongruously, 'try not to be too shocked.'

He pressed a buzzer on his desk, an aide opened the polished door, and a tall, well-dressed man came in and sat down. Everything about him spelled 'foreigner' to Jones, the cut of his hair, his face, his clothes and shoes, the smell of his cologne and the fact that he wore any at all.

After what he had heard that morning, Jones felt nothing else could shock him. A German agent was in London and had boasted that he wished to kill the King's daughters; the Nazis themselves were so put out by the thought of what their renegade might do that they had informed their enemy and betrayed their own man by giving information about his alias. No one must know that there had been communication between the two sides, or that the agent was in Britain; it would spread alarm and despondency. He was to tell his colleagues that he was hunting the Belgravia murderer, when in fact he was hunting a crazed German assassin. And he couldn't tell a soul, not even Gar . . . Jones remembered. Of course, no Gareth any more to tell or not tell.

But there was nothing else that could shock him, not now. Until the MI5 head said: 'Superintendent Jones, may I introduce Colonel Ulrich von der Osten of the German Abwehr service.'

The man was extending his hand, and Jones shook it automatically, his brain hardly registering what was going on.

'Colonel von der Osten will be working with you to catch

115

this man we seek. We have agreed to this rather remarkable arrangement, because . . . ' the voice droned on. Jones felt a sensation of nausea, and for a moment thought he might black out. Then the blood began to pound in his ears and temples. It wasn't possible . . . a Nazi! He was to work with a bloody Jerry, after what they'd done to Gareth?! Christ, weren't we supposed to be at war with the bastards? They'd raped half of Europe, bombing, burning and killing, them and their bloody swastikas and jackboots. Then they dispatched a lunatic to kill our Royal family, and instead of just sticking it on the front page of the *Daily Express* it had to be all hush-hush, and lick Hitler's boots, yes Adolf, no Adolf, thank you for telling us, Adolf, please send your man over, we'll have a car waiting, we've got just the bloke to work with him, son's lying at the bottom of Narvik harbour, your Stukas put him there, but don't worry about that . . . have a cup of tea old boy, meet Superintendent Taffy Jones, the daft boy from the valleys . . . and him sitting there bold as brass, stinking like a cheap brothel, bloody Gestapo man, it wasn't . . .

'Are you all right, Superintendent?'

Jones blinked: 'Yes, sir.'

'Good. I'll continue, Colonel Osten worked with . . . ' It was a sick bloody joke, that's all, a sick obscene joke; the Jerries kill Gareth and six weeks later I sit down with some Heinie, a square-headed stormtrooper, and it'll be cup-of-tea-Heinie? Sugar Heinie? One-lump-or-bloody-two-Heinie?, three-bags-full, kiss-my-arse. He should tell them, tell them to stuff it, it wasn't on, find your own assassin, boyos, and find him without Harry Jones.

Give me the bullet? No need, here's my warrant card, stick it wherever it suits, if you don't like it do the other thing, see if I care, stick the bloody job . . . and all that goes with it, pension, flat, security . . . and . . . and, of course, he knew instantly he would never do it.

He had been chosen for the most important job he would ever be asked to do in his life. He was a copper and he always would be, and when it came to the crunch, if they asked you to go out and catch a villain, you went. He hated them for it, more because he knew they'd judged him correctly. They knew he'd do it.

The faintness had passed now, but he still felt warm and clammy.

He would obey the orders then, work with the Jerry, catch the assassin . . . and then get back to catching proper villains, once he'd had a damn good bath to scrub away the smell of this German. But he wouldn't like it, and that was one thing they couldn't force you to do, like it.

He looked bitterly at the man from MI5, hating him more than the seated German at that moment. Anyway even if I *wanted* to chuck it in, I couldn't. Think they'd let me bugger off and grow roses after what I've been privy to? No chance. They wouldn't risk me blabbing my mouth over a few pints, and in their place I wouldn't risk it either. They'd dream up some nonsense and I'd be in Pentonville for as long as it took to catch chummy. Then my career really *would* be over.

They had me by the balls from the word go, and knew it.

'So . . . ' the man from MI5 finished, 'you both have a vital task. This man must be caught, and caught soon. He must not even get *near* the little princesses. And no one must under any circumstances realise why you are really hunting him.'

He gave Jones a small, hard look. 'I am aware of the recent loss of your son, Superintendent, and the potential problem of that. I felt, however, that your loss might be eased somewhat if you were totally involved in a task of such great national importance.'

Lying bastard, thought Jones bitterly, motivated is what you thought I might be. My own personal little Nazi hunt. Well, I would have been; more, if you hadn't turned the pill bitter by sticking a Nazi alongside me. Working with one to catch one. God help me, and forgive me, Gareth.

'Sir.'

'I take it there will be no difficulty in your working with Colonel Osten—under the circumstances?'

The German's face remained neutral. Jones felt he hated it more than any face he had ever seen.

'We all have to make sacrifices, sir, don't we . . . ' then, he

117

couldn't stop himself . . . 'but you'll forgive me if I don't whistle *Deutschland Über Alles.'*

The legend from MI5 felt that under the special circumstances he would forgive the policeman that one minor insubordination.

Chapter Eleven

CLOSE TO the Mile End Road, in Whitechapel, Eilders found a crumbling terraced house with a cardboard sign in the window. On it was scrawled in thick pencil 'Rooms to rent'.

The rooms were damp, there was mould where the ceiling met the walls, and the furnishings were sparse and old. There was a single bed made of tubular metal, such as one might find in a military hospital, a rickety chair and a wardrobe of cheap wood, nailed not jointed. The window was covered in a thick layer of grime inside and out. There was no heat source in the room, the curtain was thin and frayed, and the floor covered only by pitted oilcloth.

In winter it would be unbearable, but for now it was anonymous, and above all Eilders wanted anonymity. He rubbed some dirt off the window and looked up into the sky over towards the dock area. Barrage balloons like sullen grey fish floated on their cables.

The landlady was a toothless old hag interested only in money. She had not asked his name, nor his nationality, nor made him write them down in her register as the law required. She had taken two pounds for a week's rent, and a further pound as deposit on the room's contents. Eilders doubted if anything in the room was worth more than an English florin.

He had been told that breakfast was included, but he had seen the kitchen, smelt the familiar odour of old frying, and decided not to eat any food produced in there.

After locking his room door with one of the two keys the woman had given him—the other was for the front door—he walked along the bare boards of the landing to the bathroom. He noticed a door open a couple of inches, and saw a glimpse of an Oriental face. That pleased him. The neighbours would be used to foreigners far more exotic than a Dutchman. He went into the bathroom and locked the door. After urinating in the closet, he flushed it by pulling at the ancient chain. The whole place was filthy, it disgusted him: the enamel bath and basin were encrusted with grime, neither could have been cleaned properly for months. There was no question of taking a bath, it would leave him dirtier than before. He filled the basin with cold water from what was an obviously redundant tap marked with an 'H' for hot. Then he stripped naked and washed himself vigorously using a flannel and a piece of soap. He took his cologne and splashed the perfume onto himself liberally.

Back in his room he changed his clothes, putting on an open-necked shirt, grey flannel trousers and sandals. He put his coins and identity cards into a small leather wallet, and secured it in his back pocket. He took his usual precautions with his leftover coins, and made sure the vast roll of notes was safely hidden. Then he went out to look for a public house and a woman. It was neither sex nor alcohol he needed, it was far more important than that. He was searching for a real refuge.

The night was warm, and the soft air and gentle light was as kind as possible to the harsh streets. Ragged children, many boys with the seats of their trousers hanging loose, their feet in rough working boots, played games in the cobbled street. They pushed the rusty metal of discarded bicycle wheels with lengths of wood.

Several more played the incomprehensible summer game of the English. Eilders had never quite understood it, despite his years there. But he knew that someone ran up, threw a ball, and a man with a wooden bat tried to defend a short fence of sticks by striking the ball away. The urchin children were grouped around the brick wall that marked the last house in the street, chalk marks stood for the fence they must defend, and a jagged piece of wood for the bat. The ball was a dirty, discoloured thing. Eilders thought of German children hiking through the forests, their faces tanned, singing lustily.

The houses were little more than boxes, their owners or renters obviously poor, you could tell that from the cut of their clothes and their shoddy footwear. But it was obvious there was some pride in their dwellings; several had recently been painted on the woodwork, and the step at the front door had been whitened on most. One prematurely aged woman, her hair crimped and pinned beneath a mesh net, was down on her knees before the altar of her front door, scrubbing her step vigorously with a coarse brush which she frequently immersed in water with her red hands.

This had been the territory of Jack the Ripper in the previous century. Here he had roamed, down the damp, foggy streets and foetid back alleys, looking for prostitutes to murder and mutilate. It was summer and so it looked better. In winter it would hardly have changed from the days of Jack the Ripper.

He went into a pub called The Ranelagh Arms and ordered a whisky. The landlord said: 'You'll be lucky chum.'

It was an excuse. There was no shortage of Scotch whisky, not at that time, but the landlord was hoarding it against a time he thought it would be hard to procure. Until then only his favourite customers would be served the drink. Eilders was a stranger.

He shrugged: 'Rum please, a large measure.'

He affected a small accent. It would help, if he was going to spend time in the area, to establish who he was, and that he was safe, not a threat, not a police informant, and although a foreigner, what the British would call 'one of our sort'.

The landlord noted the accent, and the seaman's clothes: 'Off the boat, mate?'

'Yes, I am from Holland, I cannot go back now. My family are still there. Mother, father, two brothers, one sister.' He did not want to portray himself as a married man in case he eventually picked up a girl in that pub. The English had

121

strange views on morality, views that were mostly hypo-critical.

The landlord said: 'You poor sod. Don't worry, we'll sort out Jerry eventually, just give us time.'

Eilders took the rum and his change, and sat down. There were several women in the pub, the majority old, sitting in groups, arthritic hands wrapped around glasses of dark beer with a thick, creamy head. There were others who drank short drinks and glanced around them, occasionally casting a glance in his direction and smiling. He took them to be prostitutes. None of the women present would do for his purposes.

He left after he had finished his rum, and walked up the Mile End Road, that central thoroughfare of the East End. There was some traffic, mostly lorries, a car painted olive green with some insignia on it containing men in British Army uniform.

He saw two policemen carrying their gas masks in khaki bags slung across their shoulder, and with steel helmets in place of their usual headgear. Neither gave him more than a passing glance. There were plenty of strollers; it was a warm night. One or two of the men had put suits on, but their collars were open, and the detachable piece itself discarded. Several wore floppy caps despite the warmth of the night. The women on their arms looked pinched and undernourished as everyone seemed to in the East End, but they were dressed surprisingly well for their promenading. Almost the 'Sunday best' of which the British spoke . . . and he realised that it was, in fact, Sunday, the day for East Enders to put a brave face on their poverty and dress up.

He branched north and saw a pub called The Gunsmith. Inside he purchased a half of bitter beer, then drank it quickly and left. It was obvious from the mincing walk of the barman and the mannerisms of some of the clientele that the public house was a haunt of homosexuals who might draw regular attention from the police. And anyway, it was a pub with women in it, young women, that Eilders wanted.

Several streets away he found the Frog and Toad. He

122

ordered a dark rum and surveyed the place. There was a small section at one end of the bar on which he leaned, and it was partitioned off with a wall of wood and frosted glass. Engraved in the glass was the word 'Snug'.

The partition ended at the wooden bar itself, and as he drank he edged his way along until he could look round the edge of the wall.

There was a girl sitting at a small table reading a magazine called *Woman's Weekly*. He took his rum into the small, partitioned room and sat down at a similar table. The girl was vaguely pretty, rather thin, and her skin was very white as if she rarely saw sunlight. She wore a French-style black beret from which blonde hair peeped. He suspected the hair was dyed; the colour seemed unnatural. She had on a belted red mackintosh, cheap shoes, and no stockings. On her face was rather too much make-up.

She was not a prostitute, there wasn't the guile in her face for that, but she was trying to be what she imagined was a *femme fatale*. Perhaps she thought she resembled Marlene Dietrich. The poor girl just didn't have the legs for it.

He watched her hand carefully as she flicked the pages of the magazine. In England women wore their wedding and engagement rings on the third finger of the *left* hand, not the right as in Germany. He saw with a surge of disappointment that on that finger was a gold band with a pearl inset. But he thought it might not necessarily signal a liaison. Wedding rings were usually plain gold or silver, or imitations of the same. An engagement ring would have a diamond, fake or otherwise. He judged the girl to be twenty-five or over. She was not married but she wished to be. She would not want to put off any potential admirer, but a bare finger at her age would be an encouragement to any man who might think she was a prostitute, or willing to have sex.

Someone attractive and yet discreet would clear that hurdle. She wished to meet someone, that was obvious, or she would not have come into a public house. But she wanted to be sought out and *wooed*, so she sat away in this corner hoping a knight in armour would ride in and carry her off.

She read silly magazines, full of absurd ideas of romance. Even Mrs Archer, God-fearing Mrs Archer had read *Woman's Weekly*. It was a bland diet of home hints, recipes and ludicrous romantic fiction. At this girl's age she would be feeling a hint of desperation about finding a man who would marry her. Eilders knew he was handsome, and that if he was not too forward, the girl would eventually be his.

He took his drink and walked the couple of places to her table. She looked up from her magazine, startled, but she was instantly attracted; he could see the pupils of her eyes widen, a sure sign.

'Excuse me, Miss, please do not think me rude, but may I be permitted to buy you a drink? My ship has been in dock for two weeks, and I have hardly spoken to a soul. I like to practise my English.'

'You foreign then?'

'Yes, from Holland. Have you been to Holland?'

'Oh no, I've never been abroad, but I know what it's like, it's got windmills, they told us at school.'

'Yes, many windmills, you would like it. May I buy you a drink?'

'Well, I don't know. I shouldn't really . . .'

'Just one drink, and you will help me improve my English.'

'Go on then, if you're insisting, a gin-and-it.' He turned to the bar, and the warning sounded. It is not something I should know. He turned back.

'Gin and . . . it?'

'Gin and it, oh you're foreign of course. It . . . Italian vermouth . . .' she pronounced the word vermoof, she was definitely local . . . 'Gin-and-it . . . get it.'

'Yes, I see.'

He bought her a gin and Italian vermouth, and another sickly, warm rum for himself. He did not care for it, but sailors drank rum. He put the drinks down and said: 'My name is Jan . . . what is yours?'

'Tilly . . . Tilly Butler, well it's Mathilda, like Waltzing Mathilda, that's a song, only everybody calls me Tilly.'

'That is a very pretty name.' He put out his hand: 'How do you do, Tilly.'

She took it: 'Pleased to meet you.' She withdrew her hand quickly: 'I shouldn't be doing this, you know, taking drinks from a strange man, I wouldn't normally.'

'I am *strange*?'

'I don't mean *strange* strange, I mean that you're a stranger like.' She giggled.

'Well, Tilly, we're introduced now, so I am no longer a stranger, yes?'

'I suppose so.' She sipped her drink. God but he was ever so good looking, he was like something off the pictures. And that way he had of speaking, it was continental, a bit like Charles Boyer, he was Dutch or something, well French, it was almost the same. It had been a long time since Tilly Butler had felt the touch of a man, and she felt a giddy sensation at the prospect that it could happen soon, if she wished it. She thought: I'm a disgrace even thinking about it. I'm a good girl, and I certainly don't let myself get picked up, he'll soon learn that.

But she felt it must be Fate, him walking in like that, Fate ordained by the stars. Tilly Butler believed in Fate, and in the stars and their portents. Only last week that gypsy had said she was going to meet a tall, handsome stranger.

Eilders encouraged her, let her talk about herself; it was obvious that few men did that, and the Tilly Butlers of the world rarely get an audience for their life story. He listened carefully, spotting the clues for her weaknesses and her strengths, if she had any, but most important of all he had to know if she lived alone. If she did not, all this was in vain, and he would have to move on and go through the whole business again.

He asked about her parents, and saw the momentary hesitation before she answered: 'My mum's sort of in and out of hospital, you know, on account of her nerves, the war's been a great strain on her . . .'

Mother a psychiatric case.

'Your father, he is in the army perhaps?'

'Well . . . no, he's away at the moment.'

'Away', in the East End, meant prison. Mother a lunatic, father a convict, no wonder the girl lived on pulp magazine fictional dreams.

'It must be hard living alone.' He held his breath.

'Oh, it's not so bad. I've got rooms over a newsagent's shop, matter of fact he's got a soft spot for me. I pay ten and six a week, and I've got me own kitchen and toilet.'

Eilders realised the landlady at his lodgings was robbing him because he was a foreigner.

'Do you work nearby?'

She shook her head: 'I've got a job up at Enfield in the ordnance factory, we make Bren guns . . . oh . . . ' she put a hand up to her mouth, 'Careless talk costs lives, that's what they told us. You're not a spy are you?'

He laughed heartily, and she felt her heart race a little. She had never seen a man so good looking, his teeth were all white and even. 'No, Tilly, I'm not a spy.'

'Well, you can't be too careful, look what them Germans done in Holland, your *own* country, they dressed 'em up as nuns.'

Ludicrous, Eilders thought, these people will believe anything their government tells them. 'Yes . . . I will ask no more.'

They had several drinks, and she knew he would ask to walk her home, and then he would try and come into the house, and expect her to kiss him and let him touch her. It was always like that, never like in *Woman's Weekly*.

She said: 'Well I'd better be off now, I'm on the earlies tomorrow, the bus picks us up at half-past five.'

'It has been a pleasure, Tilly, a great pleasure.'

She shook his hand: 'Thank you for the drink.' He's not going to ask. I'll never see him again. 'Good night then, Jan.'

'Good night, Tilly.'

She got up. 'Tilly?'

'Yes?' She said it too quickly.

'I thought of going to see a film tomorrow night, and

126

calling into a café on the way back. I am not one for drinking. I wondered if you would like to come with me?'

She was flushing and she knew it. 'Well . . . I don't know . . .'

'Because I'm *strange*?' he pulled a funny face.

'No, I didn't mean, strange, like that, I meant . . . oh, all right, I'll come.'

'Good, here at 6 p.m?'

'Yes.'

'I shall look forward to it, Tilly.' He took her hand and kissed it.

She walked home on a cloud. That French nobleman had done that in *The Lady of the Chateau* Chapter Nine, but she had never seen a *real* man do it. She lay in her narrow bed and hugged the pillow. What if he didn't turn up? If he didn't, she'd die, she just knew it.

Eilders stayed in his room for most of the day, as the vile smells from the kitchen seeped up through the floorboards. He must seduce the girl if possible tonight. Then she would have to invite him to share her rooms. The newsagent who had the 'soft spot' for Tilly, would he be a problem? It took all Eilders' self-control to stop him feeling that the whole business was hopeless. He was miles from the Palace, the Castle at Windsor was even further away. He had a map of one, vague information about the other, but no knowledge of the whereabouts of his targets.

He would do it! Nothing could stop him. First the girl would give him refuge. Then he would use her somehow to get to Windsor, perhaps he could propose that they take a trip by Green Line bus, he remembered even the poorest families doing that when he had lived in London. Somehow he could contrive to take her to a lonely spot, dispose of her, then enter the castle at night.

Or maybe the British were foolish enough to put an announcement in the newspaper, an indication that the princesses were going to Buckingham Palace. Then he could simply take a tube train into the heart of London, alight at Victoria railway station, and the Palace was just a few hundred yards away. No building was impregnable to the determined man.

And in the meantime, there was the girl. He felt a faint stirring of perverted attraction for her. She was so weak, and so attracted to him, she had almost died of fright when she thought she was not going to see him again. He could enjoy that weakness, enjoy seeing her beg and whimper when he hurt her. He doubted if an English girl of that class had played such games as that before. He would enjoy teaching her. But first he must go through the charade of chocolate box romance she seemed to need so much. He lay down again to wait for the evening.

They went to the Hippodrome in Whitechapel, and the cinema was full although it was Monday night. East Enders, like all the English working class, loved the cinema. Here they could escape from the dreary drudgery of their day to day lives into the dream worlds of Hollywood, Ealing and Pinewood. He bought her a bag of boiled sweets and she sucked at them through the first feature about a middle-aged but very wise Scotland Yard detective solving a murder at an English country house. When he finally unmasked the killer, the audience cheered.

There was a short interval during which the lights went up and girls came round with trays of ices and confectionery. Then the lights dimmed and a Movietone newsreel, full of pompous bluster, explained that Germany would soon be starved out of the war thanks to the Royal Navy blockade. The cheering erupted again. Eilders suppressed a smile; when he'd been in Berlin the shops were packed with imported coffee, wines, even Havana cigars.

There was a stale smell of body odour in the cinema, but all Tilly could smell was the wonderful perfume of the man next to her. She'd noticed how his leg had brushed hers, and hoped he'd noticed that she'd not shied away. The main feature started, and she let her hand trail between the seats. His hand brushed hers, she tensed; but he took it in his, intertwining his fingers. She noticed that his hand felt very soft and cool, and so . . . smooth. George Formby was shouting . . . 'oooh . . . mu-th-er . . . ' and Tilly tingled all over. He'd squeezed her hand, and now he was stroking it softly with his other.

Afterwards they had plaice and chips at a café on the Mile End Road. She had seen it before, but never really dared to go in, it was so posh. It had white tableclothes and vases with flowers, and the waitresses wore little black dresses and white pinafores. A lot of the better-off merchants went there for lunch or supper.

Afterwards they went to the Frog and Toad again, and she drank four gin-and-its. He asked her if he could escort her home. 'Escort', that's what he'd said, not walk. The French nobleman in *Woman's Weekly* talked like that.

At her door she paused. 'Would you like to come in for a cup of tea before you go home?'

He followed her up the steep stairs, and sat in the small, airless room on the single bed while she brewed some tea in the ante-room that served as kitchen. They sipped the tea for a while, she sitting on the one stiff-backed chair, not speaking. She was looking down vacantly at the threadbare rug. He knew it was time. He leaned across, took the cup and saucer from her and put it on the floor. Then he took her in his arms and kissed her expertly for a long time. He broke for breath and said: 'We'd both be more comfortable sitting here.' She did not protest as he sat her beside him on the bed.

He started to kiss her again, between kisses telling her that she was the most beautiful girl he had ever known. No one had ever said that to Tilly Butler before. He let his hands stroke her neck and caress her shoulders through the thin cotton dress, then tentatively touched her small breasts, feeling her stir slightly as he did.

He pulled her closer to him, and he heard her give forth with a small moan as she felt the hardness of him press against her thin body. He started to kiss her ears and throat, whispering endearments. He hated it, but it was business.

129

He undid the cloth buttons on the front of her dress and slipped his hand inside, and under the cup of her brassiere. Her breast was small and very soft, yet the nipple seemed gigantic and was very hard. He took it between his fingers, stroking it, pulling gently, rasping it this way and that with the front and then back of his hand. He heard her mutter something inaudible, yet the low passion was unmistakable. Eilders had been right, of course. Tilly Butler had never been spoken to so kindly or romantically, or treated so well, nor led into a seduction so gently. Her soldier boyfriend had just grunted a lot, had smelled of beer, cigarettes and sweat, and when he had finally done it, it was over in minutes. Then he had walked out on *her*. This was how she had always imagined it could be, but she was still terribly frightened.

'Tilly I want you . . . '

'No Jan I mustn't . . . '

'Tilly darling, please . . . '

'I can't . . . I hardly know you . . . '

'Please . . . '

It went on. He hated the whole ghastly charade, but continued it, knowing it was part of the necessary ritual for a girl such as this. She must not be thought 'easy'. He waited a little while, kissing her vigorously, whispering into her ear, then he put his hand onto her bare leg above the knee.

She moaned a little and he moved the hand upwards. She put her hand on his and said, 'No, Jan, please . . . ' But it was just a pretence, no more. He waited some seconds, then moved his hand upwards, taking hers with it, until it fell away of its own accord.

He slid his fingers beneath the elastic of her knickers and she started to give small cries. She was wet there, and he worked on her expertly, using his free hand to unbutton the flies of his trousers. Tilly could hardly believe what was happening. His fingers seemed like quicksilver . . . and he knew the spot! He knew it! Something was building up deep inside her.

Then she felt the hard flesh of him on her own wet skin, and experienced a moment of panic. 'Jan . . . wait a sec, please.'

'Of course,' he stroked her face, moving his body away slightly, not wishing to terrify her. She just needed reassurance. It worked. Billy would have just gone ahead and done it; this man was a gentleman.

She said: 'I've only ever done it once . . . I mean, been all the way with one man, honest. You do believe me, don't you?'

'I do, my darling.' Stupid bitch, stupid little bitch!

'And you love me, don't you, I can't . . . unless you love me?'

She was being absurd, he had known her for just forty-eight hours, but it was obviously the last act in the ritual before intercourse. So he told her he loved her very much, and she urged him, as she lay back, to be careful. Yet ignored the fact that he did not use a rubber contraceptive.

He had intercourse with her, prolonging it, bored by it, but trying to do all the things he knew that women themselves liked. He felt her tremble and hold on to him tightly.

Her mouth tasted of sticky sweets, and she smelled of sweat and cheap perfume, it made Eilders want to throw up, but he hung on grimly. Perhaps it was a climax, perhaps she was just pretending, he didn't really care, as long as the whole act had fulfilled something for her, and she saw in him the embodiment of some romantic dream.

He felt her body go limp. He withdrew without climaxing himself, and she made no effort to relieve him. He needed that to be done with, so he guided her hand, and though he felt her tense with surprise, she made no objection.

Tilly Butler was hardly able to take in her own physical happiness. *It* had happened, just like some of the girls had told her. And within minutes, she could hardly believe this, he wanted to do it again, and did . . . and it lasted for *ages*!

He left her at four a.m. promising to return the following evening, and she lay on her bed hugging her pillow and reliving the magical night.

Uwe Eilders alias Jan Villen Ter Braak trudged carefully home through the pitch black streets, stumbling on uneven pavements, inwardly cursing the blackout yet thankful the

131

British had not imposed a curfew.

'Out late, sir?' Eilders started from the shock. Out of the darkness, a tall figure in a steel helmet. God, it was a policeman.

'Girlfriend,' said Eilders, hoping it was both non-committal yet explanatory.

Would the man ask for his papers? Would they pass?

'Well at least there's no sign of Jerry again.'

Eilders could just make out a large white letter on the steel helmet, it was a 'W' . . . the man was an air-raid warden not a policeman. Thank God.

'Well, mind how you go mate, no good to your ladyfriend with a broken leg, eh?'

Eilders agreed, thanked him, and walked on carefully.

Back at his lodging house he collected his toilet things and went to the filthy bathroom. The landlady had removed the light bulb, she said to comply with blackout regulations, but that was nonsense, it was because she was miserly, and the blackout had given her an excuse to save electricity.

But he had to wash, even in this cess-pit. He felt dirty and dissatisfied after that parody of sex with the girl. He would like to have gripped her hard, to have squeezed and hurt, to have taken that white flesh and pinched it whiter, and nipped until the blood came. Then to have beaten her until she screamed, and . . .

He steadied himself against the sink, turned the tap, filled the basin and sluiced lukewarm water over his body, feeling the calming effect.

Back in his room he splashed on more of the precious cologne and lay down to sleep, the scent of himself drowning the evil smell of England.

Chapter Twelve

THERE WAS a certain uneasiness between Winston Churchill and the King of England and both men realised it.

The King felt that the previous Prime Minister Neville Chamberlain had been unfairly treated, but that if he had to be replaced it should have been with Lord Halifax, a man the King knew well and trusted. He was not entirely happy with Churchill, the man was unpredictable, a political maverick, of unsure loyalties to his colleagues. Quite frankly the King did not trust him. He remembered Churchill's role in the Abdication affair, when the man had formed the 'King's party' in a last-ditch effort to let David keep his throne *and* Wallis Simpson.

So the few audiences up to now had been stilted affairs, not helped by the King's stutter, an impediment he felt most strongly when in the presence of such a natural and gifted orator as Winston Churchill. The Prime Minister had deliberately not asked for a special audience as court circles were notoriously gossip-ridden, and if he had gone to the Palace for other than his normal weekly audience, the whispers would start; he wished none of that, there were too many traitors in high places.

But as soon as he was alone with the King he came straight to the point, and felt that his sovereign took the news with amazing calmness. 'This is extremely grave and disquieting news.'

'Indeed, Your Majesty. I believe the danger is acute. Their royal highnesses are guarded by able and dedicated men who would lay down their lives for the safety of their charges. But history tells us an assassin without thought for his own safety can defeat even the bravest of guards and penetrate the strongest of screens.'

'And so what do you propose, Prime Minister?'

'It is my firm suggestion, Your Majesty, that their royal highnesses be removed instantly from the British Isles. At this moment a cruiser and escort is in readiness in the Clyde. Their royal highnesses could be taken to Halifax, Nova Scotia in total secrecy. There they would be lodged until this danger has passed, then they would be returned safely to you.'

'Would the Canadian Prime Minister be informed of the reason for their stay?'

'No one must know, Your Majesty. The Canadians would simply be told it is a temporary expediency.'

'And the British people would not be told at all?'

'We believe that wisest, Your Majesty.'

The King gave a wry smile: 'But the news would leak out eventually and my subjects would think that I took the view that while it was all right for *their* children to risk air bombardment or invasion, it was not right for mine. The answer is no, Prime Minister.'

'Sir, their highnesses' danger is acute and personal. None of your subjects would reproach you for a second.'

The King's stammer was fully controlled: 'But of course, they would never know the reason, not even when hostilities have ceased, so you tell me. They would *never* understand. You will remember what the Queen said on this subject?'

'Yes, Your Majesty.'

In a sentence that endeared her to everyone in the country Queen Elizabeth, dismissing any thought of sending her daughters to safety in Canada, had said: 'The children won't leave without me, I won't leave without the King, and the King will never leave.'

'So you see it is impossible. Princess Margaret and Princess Elizabeth will stay.'

'I am your servant, Your Majesty.'

'Prime Minister, I love my daughters beyond words, they

134

are closest and precious to my heart. Let no harm come to them.'

'Your Majesty, I shall lay down my own life if necessary, in their defence.'

When the audience was over, the King quickly lit a cigarette and inhaled deeply, trying to steady his nerves, waiting for the nicotine to calm him.

Until then he could not trust himself to form words.

When Jones had sat down, Ulrich said: 'Well, Superintendent? are they to leave?' He searched the Welshman's face, waiting for a reply. 'Well?'

Jones chewed at his lip: 'This goes against the bloody grain, right against it. I don't see why we have to tell you anything that's not absolutely necessary.'

'It is not your decision. Your orders were that I be told everything, and I would like to know that the princesses are going to be safely out of the country while we hunt Eilders.'

Jones exhaled breath fiercely: 'They're staying.'

'What!?!'

'You heard me, they're staying. God knows why, I don't . . . ours not to reason why . . . '

There was a knock on the door. Jones shouted: 'Come in.'

A plain-clothed constable with two mugs held by the handles in one hand, came in.

'Tea, Super, usual for you, milk and two sugars.' He plonked the big white mug down on Jones' desk.

'Ta.'

'I rustled up some coffee for you, Mr Osten, best we can do under the circumstances, but it won't be up to Dutch standards, I'll bet. Still, it's hot and wet.'

Ulrich took the mug: 'I'm sure it will be fine.'

Jones coughed uneasily, and Ulrich gave him a hard look as the young detective went out, closing the door behind him. That was Osten's cover: he was a detective of the Amsterdam police force who had fled before the German occupation. Now he was on temporary attachment to Mr Jones' office, observing and helping on the Belgravia business.

London was full of refugees of all nationalities, and government-in-exile offices were springing up all over the place. The pubs were full of exotic uniforms and strange accents, and no one thought Osten moving into Jones' office strange in the least. He had been issued with credentials, and the fact that his name was not, to British eyes, typically German, helped.

Jones had arrived at his own attitude towards Ulrich. He would be correct, no point in being bloody rude. And anyway, you couldn't keep that up all day long: it just gave you a sore head.

He would be correct, polite when it was called for, and tell the Jerry no more than he had to. In turn he would pick Ulrich's brain for whatever he could about this loony, and the sooner they got him caught the sooner they could pack the one off to the gallows and the other to the Fatherland.

Ulrich said: 'Do you believe your colleagues are convinced of my identity as a Hollander?'

Jones did not look up, but said: 'Yes. I think it would stretch even their fevered imaginations to think I was sharing my office with a Gestapo man.'

Ulrich flushed: 'Actually, Superintendent, I am from Abwehr, not Geheimestaatspolizei.'

Jones shrugged, face still down: 'Beg your pardon . . . a Nazi then.'

Ulrich choked down his anger. 'And I am not a member of the National Socialist German Workers Party, neither am I a Nazi . . . I am a German officer, and it gives me no pleasure to be working with my enemy. Can we have that understood at the outset.'

Jones looked up innocently: 'Right, now we've got all that established, can we get down to business. He's posing as a Dutchman, right . . . just like you . . . '

Ulrich glared.

' . . . posing as a Dutchman, Jan Villen Ter Braak, and you have a reasonably up to date picture of him?'

136

Ulrich fumbled in his briefcase: 'Six years old, the latest we could get from SD files.'

A man can change a lot in six years, Jones thought.

Ulrich pushed the picture across the table.

So this was chummy was it? The lad with the wire, the lad who thought he was just going to knock off the junior branch of the royal family. He was handsome, no doubt about that, women would go for him, but not a man's man, liked himself a bit too much for that, judging by that little smirk on his face. Harry looked at the eyes, and it was as though he was looking at a different man. The eyes seemed to have been put in there as an afterthought; they were cold and forbidding. They put a chill into Harry Jones and he searched his memory for where he had seen eyes like that before.

The Bayswater Butcher. 1931. Only a kid, eighteen, killed three women with a meat cleaver, just climbed the drainpipe, in the window, walked into the room where they were drinking tea and turned the place into an abattoir.

Mad as a March hare, and when Jones had asked him why he'd done it, he'd just said, 'I felt like it'. And he had, he'd *enjoyed* it. They'd topped him, nutty as he was, and someone up Pentonville said he was whistling when they put him on the trap.

Same eyes. A psychopath, oh yes, thought Jones, he loves it does this boy.

Ulrich said: 'Now we have his identity, what chance does he have of remaining undetected?'

'Not a cat in hell's. Wherever he stays he has to produce either a National Registration Identity Card or his ration book to the hotel keeper or landlady. He's a seaman, and you say his mob gave him the right documents, so he'll stand out, seamen get a colour all to themselves. Unfortunately seamen are exempt from registering their ration books at particular shops like everyone else, otherwise we could pin him down when the ration slips come in. But he's got to eat, and if he's out morning, noon and night flashing big white fivers, he's going to stick out like a sore thumb.'

'What is our first move, publish the picture?'

137

'Hold your horses and listen, I've been doing this for years, don't tell your grandmother how to suck eggs.'

Ulrich didn't know whether to bridle or add this to his vocabulary of colloquial English, 'sore thumbs' 'grandmothers sucking eggs' . . . even the accent was hard.

'We have an advantage over him. He must assume that *we* think he's heading for home, probably via the Free State. He can't know his mates have shopped him. You say he's got a fictional address in Cambridge on his cards?'

Ulrich nodded.

'So that's one place we can eliminate . . . right, he'll take a room somewhere, presumably in London, he'll register under his false name, and eventually he'll draw rations. We will circulate every police force in the country, just to be on the safe side, and they'll go round checking every hotel, guest house, boarding house, Sally Army hostel, seamen's mission, any place a man lays his head for money. Sooner or later that name is going to surface.'

'Suppose he rented an apartment or a house?'

'We'll cover that, we'll do estate agents, private lessors, councils, everyone. The police will go back three months through the property columns of their local newspapers. Then they'll check out each property that has been sold or rented, and visit the new tenant.'

Ulrich forgot, and took another sip of the awful coffee. 'Suppose he acts now!'

Jones shook his head. 'I gather you know this already: the girls are at Windsor, it's a big place and I don't propose to tell you exactly where' (because I don't know it myself either, Jones thought) 'but the place has been sealed off as tight as a Grenadier's drumskin. No one but no one gets within half a mile of the princesses who has not been known to them for a hundred and fifty years. The local bobbies are geared up to go through Windsor town, Eton, Slough and every other town within a twenty-mile radius like a dose of Epsom salts. He *cannot* move, not now. He is outside, they are inside, and that is the way it's going to stay.'

'A *cordon sanitaire?*'

'Quite. So now we can work, slowly and methodically, without panic, and one sunny morning he walks into our net.'

'He is a clever man, there are ways . . .'

'Like living rough, I've thought of that. London isn't rural, the parks are policed regularly, and people are on the lookout for spies. You spend a few nights in a field, summer or no summer, and you'll stick out a mile.'

Ulrich felt Jones was too complacent. 'Suppose . . .' he stroked his chin . . . 'suppose Eilders inveigled . . . yes, inveigled himself into a woman's heart. He could live with her, use her rations, not show his face, not have to present his identity . . . then he could wait until we think it is safe again . . .'

'Aha . . .' Jones had been waiting for that. 'That is why we don't issue the picture first off. If we haven't got him in a couple of weeks we know he's up to something dodgy . . . not that our girls shack up like that with foreigners . . . anyway, we don't normally flap about individual enemy agents, and if possible we want to get him without that kind of fuss. The boys in blue down at Windsor know something's up, we don't want the rumours floating around if we issue a picture straight away. We do it like this. Two weeks, and we issue a picture . . . the Belgravia Murderer. It'll be all over the papers. Fleet Street will do anything for a story that's not about the war.'

Ulrich pushed away the cold coffee. 'Superintendent Jones, isn't there a much simpler way to end all this?'

'Is there?' Jones looked up innocently.

'Yes. Call all the newspapers to Scotland Yard and have some pictures ready for them. In the meantime print 10,000 posters of Uwe Eilders. Tell the editors that a man called Jan Villen Ter Braak has come here from Germany on forged papers to kill Princess Elizabeth and Princess Margaret. Ask the public to hunt this dangerous German . . .' he bit on the word with irony . . . 'and hand him over to you. I believe you call it a hue and cry. Wouldn't that be simpler?'

Jones had never met a German before, and this one discon-

139

certed him. He hated him, of course, but the German wouldn't be what Jones wanted. He wasn't arrogant, on the contrary he acted in a rather modest manner, he didn't shout and bluster, he didn't even look, well, the way everyone *knew* Germans looked. He was very direct too. Jones didn't know if that was a German trait or not, but it was certainly an uncomfortable one.

'And suppose the word gets out? We're not all bloody daft you know. Suppose the word gets out about how we knew that he was here, about his identity? Some bright sod in Fleet Street will want to know how we got his picture.'

'Tell them.'

Jones snorted in disbelief: 'Tell them! That we were in touch with the Nazis . . . are you right in the head? Tell them that a bloody German . . . ' Jones lowered his voice . . . 'a German intelligence man came over here on the flying boat from Lisbon to help us . . . ' his voice rose again.

'I thought England was a democracy, that was what your propaganda always told us. That we were not told the truth, while your people had the "right to know" . . . ah yes . . . the right to know. What happened to that?'

Jones was rattled. It was true, every word of it. They were deliberately risking the lives of the princesses because no one dared say they had taken help from the Germans. One sign of weakness at this crucial time, one hint that all was not one hundred per cent dogged defiance, and the whole façade of continued resistance to the all-conquering Nazis might crumble. He knew from his mates in Special Branch that they were locking up hundreds, anyone who dared talk in public of coming to terms with Hitler.

'It's been suspended for the duration, Colonel. It seems we have to fight fire with fire and be a little ruthless.'

Ulrich von der Osten had lost two members of his family to the Allied blockade of World War One. He said, with more than a hint of bitterness, 'We have never doubted that you can be ruthless.'

He got up and left the office.

Chapter Thirteen

EILDERS SPENT Tuesday, Wednesday and Thursday nights with the girl, and eventually she asked him if he would like to come and stay for the weekend. He told her he would have to leave his lodgings, retrieve his deposit and bring a suitcase. She readily agreed, so readily that he knew that 'to stay' was just her way of making it seem more respectable. When the weekend was up she might suggest an extra day and it would become permanent. He was delighted with the way events were going.

But so far he had been sneaking in to her flat because of the landlord, the man who had the 'thing' for her. What would the man say when he came to stay?

'I'll tell him you're my cousin from Southampton, and he'll believe me. I'm not supposed to have men friends staying here, but a cousin will be all right.'

Eilders consented to the fiction; he found a time when the man took a lunchtime nap and planned to enter the flat at that time. He did not want to get into conversation with the man. If he were attracted to Tilly, and if he didn't believe her story, he might turn awkward.

He had one more day and night to fill, and decided to buy some real food. The fare the girl got on her ration books was appalling. He knew that illegal trading always went on when goods were forbidden, as in America during alcohol prohibition, or when they were restricted. He visited several public houses during the lunch hour, listening carefully to conversations.

He had tried earlier to buy silk stockings at a hosiery shop, knowing the girl had none, but he had been met with an incredulous stare.

'Silk stockings?' the girl behind the counter said. 'You must be joking. Don't you know there's a war on?'

He decided to buy the stockings where he bought the food, from the man he had heard referred to simply as 'Dave'. Dave came into the pub carrying a battered suitcase, and immediately headed for one of the private rooms at the rear. Customers went in and out, carrying bundles wrapped in newspaper.

Eilders went to the door, knocked and went in. Dave was sitting at a table, a bottle of Scotch in front of him, the suitcase closed. Eilders told him he wanted to buy silk stockings and various items of food. The man shook his head and said he did not have the faintest idea what Eilders was talking about. Eilders produced a thick roll of fivers.

The man said, 'Close the door.' Eilders did, and the man said: 'How do I know you're not a copper's nark?'

Eilders said nothing; there was nothing to say. The man looked at the money again. His face was bloodless, but his eyes were greedy. He pushed back the thinning hair and said: 'It'll cost you. I'm running big risks.'

Within four hours Eilders had every item he wished, paid for at an extremely exorbitant price. His first roll of fivers was getting thinner.

Tilly said: 'Silk stockings, Jan, they're wonderful . . . and the food . . . her eyes widened . . . how did you get such food?' He remembered an East End habit and pulled the skin down below one eye: 'No questions, please.'

He got up and drew the curtains, returning to her in a kinder gloom. The room was stuffy and smelled of cabbage. He was very hungry but he decided to get the sex over with first. He had been too ardent too soon, and she seemed to expect it whenever he arrived.

'Jan, it's only tea-time, you're . . . awful.'

It happened *again* . . . and silk stockings, and the wonderful food. She felt she must wake up very soon.

The sergeant said: 'Hello Ma, are you keeping well?'

'Mustn't grumble, who's he?' she jerked a thumb at the new constable.

'New; can we come in, Ma?' She moved aside to let them pass.

'And what's all this about, pray tell?'

'Routine check for German spies. Let's have your register.'

'German spies indeed, this is a respectable household.' She bustled off to the front parlour.

The ledger was dog-eared and covered in a thin film of dust: 'I can't vouch it's up to date.'

'You're telling me,' said the constable, as he brushed the dust off it and handed it to his sergeant. 'March? You haven't had any guests since March?'

'One or two,' said the woman, sullenly.

'Then they should be in. You're supposed to check their identity cards or ration books, and put their names and addresses in your book.'

'I haven't been well.'

'Who've you got now?'

'Two Chinamen, they're sharing, second floor back. First is empty, a traveller from Glasgow top, and some seaman second floor front.'

'What's his nationality, British?'

'Haven't the foggiest. Foreign I think, got that funny smell about him.'

'Dutch? Is he from Holland?'

'Search me, all look the same.'

The constable consulted his notebook: 'Jan Villen Ter Braak, that him?'

'I *told* you, I don't know!'

'Should we take a gander at his room, Sarge?'

'Good idea. Key, Ma.'

The old woman unhooked a key from the ring tied on a

sash around her waist. 'I'm not coming up with you, I can't be climbing stairs all day long.'

The policemen let themselves into the room which was tidy, with the bed made. That seemed in order: seamen were known to be tidy individuals. There was a small suitcase and the constable checked the label: 'Empire Made'. There were some rough clothes suitable for ship life, a change of underwear, no foreign labels, the constable checked. On the small chair coins were littered on the seat. He checked to see if there were any German Pfennigs, but no, just pennies and halfpennies. He tossed them back, and one fell onto the floor.

Beneath the chair was a bag, waterproofed on the outside. The sergeant opened it and found a toothbrush, made in England, Macleans toothpaste, a shaving brush with well-worn bristles, a cut-throat razor of Sheffield steel, and a stick of Erasmic shaving soap, half way through.

And a bottle with a screw top and a quarter of the contents remaining. He opened it and put his nose to the neck. 'Phew! Get a whiff of that, that's a bit nancy-boy all right, wonder if we've got a bit of a fruit here?'

The constable had a sniff and grimaced: 'Imagine wearing that down the nick? Wouldn't catch an Englishman wearing that.'

The sergeant took back the bottle and read the lettering, his heart started to beat faster. 'Well, will you look at that. German, flaming German writing.'

'Can I have a gander, Sarge?'

The constable took the bottle, looked, coughed, and said respectfully: 'That's not German, Sarge, it's French. "Eau de Cologne", that's French.'

'Cologne's in Germany, don't tell me it isn't.'

'I know *that*, Sarge, but eau de cologne's French, it's a sort of perfume. Eau is water in French, my old man told me that, he was in France during the first lot.'

'You sure?'

'Positive, Sarge. I've seen it in some of them posh shops up West.'

144

'Oh.' The sergeant gave a sheepish grin, screwed the top back on the bottle, and replaced it in the bag.

'Thought I'd caught a German spy then.'

'Never mind, Sarge. He travels bloody light though, doesn't he, and nothing to identify him.'

'Got to keep them with him, that and his gas mask, that's the law.'

'Is he really a German spy, this Jan Whatjamacallim?'

'Well . . . there's a flap on, that's all I know, and he's foreign too. They wouldn't go to all this trouble for just anyone.'

'How many more?'

The sergeant sighed and took off his helmet, scratching his bald head: 'Three more down Victoria Street, one in Raglan, look in at the Sailor's Rest and that's yer lot for us.'

'She in trouble, her not filling in the register and everything?'

The sergeant put his helmet back on: 'I should report her, but she's daft as a brush anyway, never been the same since her old man ran off with the barmaid from the Swan. She can get all their names tonight, we'll nip round first thing tomorrow and Bob's your uncle. It'll save us a lot of work.'

'Right, Sarge.' The constable wrinkled his nose: 'Distinctive that cologne stuff, isn't it?'

'It is that. Why not get the wife to buy you some next Christmas?'

The constable flushed. He hadn't even got a girlfriend, and the sergeant knew that.

In her candlewick dressing gown she went into the kitchen and prepared some of the food he had bought illegally. She felt terribly *wicked*. Making love, then eating afterwards, and she with not a *stitch* on underneath the dressing gown, and him still half-naked. Wicked.

'This is a real treat. It's blooming ridiculous what they allow you on the ration.'

'My friend was very generous, apparently the ship's larder is overflowing.'

She had hardly heard him: 'Four ounces of butter a week, and four of ham or bacon . . . *and* they say tea's going on the ration next month. Now that's one thing I *can't* manage without, me cuppa! Where are you registered?' she said idly. 'Your friend's ship isn't always going to be in port.'

'I'm not. I was told when I came to England that seamen don't have to register.'

She ate some illegal pork: 'Blooming regulations, I lose track. Half the shopkeepers behave like flaming 'Itler already, not to mention the wardens.'

'The wardens for air raids you mean?'

'Yeah them . . .' she had not tasted meat like this for ages.

'Why . . . what is wrong with the wardens?' He was genuinely curious, if there were stirrings of civil discontent between the British populace and their officials, all to the good.

'Well . . . they boss everyone around, or *try* to. You daren't show a chink of light, or you're up the police court.'

'But the bombing . . . the black-out is to stop the bombers seeing light, isn't it?'

She wiped her hand across her mouth, and a smear of grease was deposited on it. He suppressed his revulsion. 'Oh the *bombing* . . . we've heard all about that, haven't we. Soon as the war started we were all going to be blown to smithereens, all the poor kids sent out to the country, poor little blighters, Mums crying their eyes out, and us all taking shelter like maniacs everytime there was a warning. Only we didn't get bombed did we?'

He noticed her wipe her hand surreptitiously on the dressing gown: 'The bleeding Germans never came did they, and you know why, cause they're scared to, that's why.'

'Aren't you a little bit frightened, Tilly . . . in the blackout?' He wanted to frighten this girl, to frighten and hurt her. Her stupid complacency made him want to take her and slap her until she bled.

'Well . . . a bit, some girls have been, you know . . .'

146

'Raped?'

'Yes . . . that, and there's been some stabbings, too.' She pushed back her plate: 'That was smashing . . . shall we listen to the radio, ITMA's on . . . you'll like Tommy Handley.'

'It—ma?'

'Silly . . . ITMA . . . It's That Man Again . . . it's a comedy.'

They listened together in the gathering gloom. The show featured a cleaning woman called, unsubtly, Mrs Mopp, and a German spy called Funf. Eilders didn't like the show one bit, and wondered why they would choose to call a spy 'Five' and omit the Umlaut.

He let himself back into his room, and immediately the hair on his scalp began to prickle. He switched on the sickly light.

Someone had been in the room! His case was moved. He checked the coins. They were not where he had left them, positioned carefully so they formed a parallelogram . . . and one was on the floor.

He began to pack urgently; surely if they had known, they would have waited for him and arrested him as he closed the front door behind him?

He put down the filled suitcase . . . Good God if it was just a sneak thief and if he'd taken . . . he lifted the leg of the wardrobe, and peeled up the oilcloth. The notes were still there, and he put the whole lot down the side of one sock. A careless thief? Just the nosy landlady? Nothing taken, which made it so much worse.

Two knocks on the door. He froze. Moved to the window, eased back the curtains. He knew the stringent black-out regulations, that he could be arrested or at least cautioned for what he was doing, but he had to check the street, and if he switched off the light now, whoever was at the ill-fitting door would see that he had done so, and it would be even more suspicious.

The street was empty, no cars and no people, no one

147

leaning 'casually' in a doorway reading a paper he couldn't possibly hope to see in the darkness. But there was no means of escape via the window, just a long, ankle-breaking drop.

Three knocks. Irritable.

'Who is it?' They cannot know. They *cannot* know.

'Mrs Millington.' He opened the door and was greeted by a waft of gin fumes.

'The police have been here.' She said it triumphantly, her arms folded, a smug grin on her face.

'The police?'

'Yes, the *police*. Checking my lodgers, you should have registered and you never.' Police checking lodgers. Why?

'You didn't ask me to register, and I had not known it was required.'

'Well, I'm asking now . . . you're a foreigner ain't you?'

'Yes.' There was nothing else to say. He was going cold. A lodging house as obscure as this: *Why*?

'You from Holland then, that's who they was looking for, a man from Holland?' Cold, now burning hot, sweating, heart palpitating, and she must see it all, everything.

'Poland . . . I am from Poland.'

'Poland eh, what's your name, then?'

The man from Danzig with the Polish name, the one he had trained with, gone into the Algemeine SS, tall, beak nose, almost like . . . 'Devrewski. My name is Felix Devrewski.' They were looking for a man from Holland. Why?

'That'll be all right then, it was a Dutchman they was interested in . . . ' She unfolded a scrap of paper, she had been keeping in one fist . . . 'Jan Villen . . . ' she peered down . . . 'Ter Braak. You ain't him then?' She grew smaller in his vision and there was a great roaring in his ears.

'You all right, you look ill? Here, have you been drinking. I don't allow drinking in my establishment . . . '

He made a massive mental effort and steadied himself. 'No . . . a little tired. I am Felix Devrewski. What has he done, this Dutchman?'

His world was reeling, spinning, threatening to go out of control, to pull him into a whirlpool and drown him.

'I dunno flower, coppers came round this morning, they had a look in here.' It was the *police* who had examined his room!

She had her hand out. 'So I'll have to take your ration books and your identity card, then put your name in the book all above board like.' She saw the suitcase.

'Oh yes, and what might all this be . . . doing a moonlight was you?'

'I have paid you, Mrs Millington, remember . . . I can leave when I wish.'

'But I still need your cards.'

'They are on the boat. I only returned for my things, my ship sails on the tide . . . an emergency convoy . . . ' he was saying too much. Desperate.

'Well . . . this is a fine state of affairs. Things have got to be regular, can't be falling out with the police.'

He was an inch from killing her, and realised it was panic and desire. He must *think*. If the police returned in the morning, as she said they would, then they would find her body and start a massive hunt. If they had the name Jan Villen Ter Braak, a body could only confirm that he was here, in the district. They would scour it, searching every house, every hiding place . . . his refuge at Tilly's that he had worked so hard to find would be useless. But if somehow . . .

He turned and took out two big £5 notes from his sock, in such a way that she could not see the two rolls . . . one almost gone, the other thick and fat. She was a venal woman, greedy and dirty, if he could appeal to her vanity, put it in such a way that it would not *seem* like a bribe, then perhaps? The English were as corrupt as any nation, they just *felt* they were honest. But the fear was biting at him . . . they know my name . . . how?

He opened his palm to show the big white notes: 'I am causing you such problems, the police visiting your respectable house, and me failing to write down all the particulars. I am so sorry for that, Mrs Millington.' She was looking at the notes.

'But if I stay behind to present my papers, I shall miss the

149

sailing of the ship and my bonus. That will cost me money
. . . but I do not want you to lose . . . '

'I could be fined,' she said solemnly, 'it's against the law.'

'So . . . ' he continued, 'if I was to leave ten pounds with
you, you could tell the police that you have established my
name, and my country, that I am *not* from Holland, but
Poland . . . that perhaps you *saw* my papers . . . '

Her eyes did not flicker, but gleamed wetly at the promise
of the two notes . . . 'You could do that?'

She took the money from his palm, her hand darting
quickly like a striking animal. 'I shouldn't, but this once, for
convenience sake.'

He followed her down to the parlour and made her write
down the name, then thanked her and left quickly.

How could they know? How *could* they? Had
Blackington's chauffeur been told, or discovered it, and had *he*
told the police? Only one other man and one other woman
had known the name properly, seen it written down, and they
were dead. He should have made sure and killed the chauffeur
too, but that would have meant waiting round the Blackington household for hours.

But everything was changed now, everything. He was
being hunted, and all his papers were useless. If he was
stopped at any time by a policeman and his papers examined,
he would be arrested.

And hanged.

The streets were dark and deserted, the black-out total. The
next time a figure loomed out of the darkness it might be a
policeman, not a warden, and that policeman might ask for
proof of identity. He *had* to get to Tilly's apartment and stay,
so he began to think desperately of an excuse to arrive early
clutching a suitcase. She must not panic and forbid him to
stay, if she did he would have to kill her.

He found an area of waste land at the end of a row of
terraced cottages, and began to search for a piece of timber, his
suitcase tucked under one arm, both hands clutching and

150

shielding a lighted match. Even that speck of light could draw a warden, the men were paranoid about guiding the non-existent bombers.

At last he found a piece of wood and extinguished the match. He put down the suitcase, carefully, so he would be able to find it again, and like a blind man he ran his hands over the wood looking for protruding nails or large splinters.

Satisfied that there were none, he braced himself, took a firm grip of the wood by one end, closed his eyes and clubbed himself fiercely across the forehead.

He saw stars and there was a vicious stab of pain. His body seemed to welcome it like a narcotic against the fever of panic. He struck again and felt the stickiness of blood. Again and again he struck until he felt it would be dangerous to continue, then he dropped the timber and ran his hand gingerly over the front of his head. The hand came away wet. He groped for his suitcase and began to walk to Tilly's apartment, ears strained for the sound of other footfalls. By the time he rapped urgently on her door the pain had done its work. The courage and the confidence were back.

'Jan! God what's happened to you?'

He slumped through the doorway, and she helped him up the stairs. She fetched a cold flannel from the kitchen, and as he lay on the bed, she wiped away the excess blood. 'What happened?'

'I was on my way home, two men bumped into me, they were drunk. You warned me about the blackout, remember? They attacked me with a piece of wood and stole my documents . . . *everything* Tilly . . . they took everything.'

'They took your money . . . oh Jan?'

'No, I had hidden some money, they didn't look.'

Her eyes flickered to the suitcase, and she was puzzled, momentarily. 'But your suitcase, you said you were on your way home?'

'I went back to my lodgings, but my landlady refused to help me. She accused me of being drunk, she wouldn't give me help. When I told her I had lost my papers she went for the police. Without my papers I will be arrested and sent back to Holland . . . to the *Germans*.' Nothing quite so exciting had ever happened to Tilly Butler before.

'I packed my suitcase, ran . . . came here . . . there was nowhere else I could go. Don't make me go, Tilly.'

She stroked his head, careful of the wound. 'No Jan. No, of course I won't, you can stay here as long as you want, it's all right, honest.'

'Thank you, darling Tilly.'

'You can go down the Food Office, get new ration books, then I'll come down the cop shop with you, explain to them, they'll understand . . . '

'No!' He had her arm in a vice-like grip, feeling the bone through the thin flesh. He could have snapped it like a twig. 'No! If you tell the police, they'll deport me.'

'But what about food, you can't get food without ration books, mine isn't enough for two, unless your friend would . . . ?' She tried to release her arm, but it was like being in a lock. 'Jan . . . you're hurting, please, my *arm*.'

Reluctantly he let her go, and she began to rub her arm, a hurt look on her face. 'You don't know your own strength, sometimes.'

'Tilly, I can always get food, there are ways . . . '

'The black market . . . ?' her eyes were wide with adventure again, sore arm forgotten . . . 'That's illegal.'

'Just for a little while. Later, when the fuss is over I will contact officials of the Netherlands government here, they will intercede on my behalf.'

'Yes, that's the best thing then. Now let me put a bandage on that.'

'You'll tell Mr Donaldson I am your cousin, the one from . . . the port?'

'Southampton . . . I'll tell him. Best if you don't go out for a couple of days.'

'Very well . . . ' he pulled her towards him, she would need her reward now.

'Ooh Jan, you shouldn't when you've been hurt like

152

that . . . you let me go this minute so I can get you that bandage.' She made no real effort to pull away.

Her dressing gown was partially unbuttoned, and he could see the soft outline of her tiny breasts through the flimsy nightdress.

He put his hand inside the gown and began to stroke; her nipple became hard almost instantly. He could feel her breath on his face, and turned slightly.

'Oh Jan, yes, please.' The French nobleman had done that in *Woman's Weekly*, come home wounded from the wars, seeking refuge from his enemies, and the heroine had bathed his wounds and sheltered him, just like she was doing for Jan.

She felt a wet urgency. 'Do it . . . *please*.'

And he did. Hating the act, hating her. But at least he was safe now, for a little while.

Chapter Fourteen

'WE'VE GOT him, sure as eggs are eggs.'

Jones' voice was high and exultant, and Ulrich had to hold the telephone receiver away from his ear.

'Are you sure?'

Just forty-eight hours since they had issued the name of Jan Villen Ter Braak to the police forces of Great Britain, and Eilders was caught? Ulrich could hardly believe it; he didn't know which was stronger in him, the feeling of exultation, or that of doubt that it had *really* been accomplished.

'Are you sure?'

'Well, I can't be *sure* . . . Colonel . . . ' Jones' voice was mocking, 'until I actually set eyes on him and compare him with the photograph, and of course until he coughs all.'

'Then how do you know?' Jones had not wanted to make the call at all. Ulrich had been out of the office when the news came in, and he had been tempted to just sort it out and leave the German in the dark until it was over. But that same morning he had had a terse memo from a VHU . . . a Very High Up, and it had said, leaving out the Whitehall officialese . . . *'cooperate with the Jerry a bit more or find yourself in deep trouble'*.

But it was fortuitous that Colonel von der Osten was at his hotel still. Harry reckoned he could get over to this nick, get meladdo's name on the statement, have him cautioned and charged before the Jerry could arrive. And if there *were* any waves from across Whitehall, well, he had rung him, sir, he was not actually in the office, sir, matter of great urgency, sir.

'A girl came into Cannon Row police station last night . . . well, early hours, actually. She's living with her boyfriend, right? He's Dutch, hear me, Dutch. Jan something-or-other, she never got his full name, wasn't too keen on spilling it. He's got no papers, no ration books, nothing. He's buying on the black market, everything she wants, whisky, chocolates, sides of beef, silk stockings.'

'Why did she go to the police?' Ulrich was suspicious.

'He started cutting up a bit rough. When money ran short he put her out on the streets to earn a few extra bob. She found a pistol in his luggage . . . the lads down at Cannon Row tell me it is a German pistol . . . Luger . . . ring any bells?'

Ulrich said that a Luger was certainly a German pistol. He also knew that Eilders was not issued with a Luger but a Walther, and he would not bring such a gun to England with him.

'He caught her having a peep so he threatened her, said if she mentioned it to anyone, he'd kill her. She waits until he is asleep, then sneaks out. Our lads went round there mob-handed and found him stark, bollock naked. As per instructions, him being Dutch and having no papers, they thought he could be our man and gave us a tinkle.'

'Does he fit our description, from what they told you?'

'Same build, same height, same features, bit of a good-looker to all accounts. His hair is a different colour, but you said yourself that picture was six years old, he could have dyed his hair. Anyway, I'm on my way there now . . . I'll send a car for you.' Jones put down the receiver before Ulrich could reply.

The hotel was in Kensington, so the car would take some time. Ulrich assumed the hotel was run and probably staffed by one of the British secret services. He had been asked for no papers and presented with no bills, and anyone he met in the corridors simply averted their eyes. The German secret services had similar places, and Ulrich began to realise for the first time that the secret services of all nations had more in

155

common than they realised. He went to the lobby to wait for the car from Scotland Yard. Although it was another fine day outside, it did not lift his spirits.

Jones' hostility apart, and he had expected that, Ulrich did not have total confidence in the man. He seemed to think that if he wished Eilders' capture enough, it would happen. The policeman had been hamstrung by the restrictions placed upon him, but because of his hostility, he had to pretend that he was totally confident.

This man could be Eilders, and he hoped to God it was. But why had Eilders brought a German gun to England with him? Surely that would have made him more vulnerable to arrest and betrayal? Going to ground with a girl was sensible, but why then risk all that by ill-treating her and threatening her life? Eilders was a sadist, but in something *this* important, where his life was at stake, surely he could control it? But worse, Ulrich knew Eilders. He would not have threatened the girl. If she had made a threat to betray him, he would simply have killed her.

But if it *was* Eilders in that police station, then Ulrich had to fulfil Admiral Canaris' order. Eilders had to die before the British could put him on trial or try to use him for propaganda purposes. Ulrich did not have a weapon. He would have to do the job with bare hands, but he knew that when he tried, Superintendent Harry Jones would be doing everything possible to stop him.

Harry Jones stopped at the heavy, green-painted iron door, slid back the small cover and peeped through the Judas hole. The prisoner was sitting on his bed, head in hands.

'Open up.'

The constable turned a key in the massive lock, and swung the door open. The prisoner did not move.

Harry said: 'OK, lock the door behind you and make yourself scarce.'

The policeman pulled an embarrassed face: 'I can't do that, sir, I've got to stay with you, that's the regulations.'

Jones said: 'I told you to make yourself bloody scarce, now *piss off*!'

The constable, young as he was, held his ground: 'Sir, I'm custody officer, and I'm responsible for the prisoner. Any interrogating officer has to have a witness with him, that's form, sir. It's for our protection, not his. In case of allegations.'

The prisoner looked up through splayed fingers at the two policemen. Jones could feel the blood rising in his face. 'What's your name, Constable?'

'Entwistle, sir.'

'Well, look, *Entwistle* . . . you know who I am, and I am taking personal responsibility for this prisoner as a matter of urgent national security. Do you understand?'

'Yes, sir.'

'Good. If you are not out of that door within ten seconds I will make it my *personal responsibility* to see that you are out of blue uniform and into khaki in one month, and in bloody Cairo three months after that. Do you read me?'

'Yes sir.' The constable went out and locked the door.

'Right.' Jones faced the prisoner. 'On your feet you. Hands to your side.'

The prisoner got up sullenly. It was hard to tell, bloody hard. The face was very similar, that kind of Continental look they all had, foreigners, the way they cut their hair. And his eyes were hard and cruel. It *must* be him, how many Dutchmen were there walking round London with Lugers? 'Jan Villen Ter Braak?'

The prisoner looked blankly ahead. 'Is your name Jan Villen Ter Braak?'

'My name is Jan Van Der Elst.'

'You're a liar.'

'My name is Jan Van Der Elst.'

'I said you are a *liar*.'

The man turned his back contemptuously on Harry Jones, tossing the words over his shoulder: 'Oh why would I lie, I'm under arrest, aren't I? I came in the country illegally, I have a pistol, I am going to prison.'

157

'Turn around when you talk to me, scum.'

The man turned around. The German was an actor and an accomplished one, he seemed not to care, but prison as another man for a firearms offence would be better than the gallows as a spy. 'Can I call you by your German name then, Herr Eilders?'

The prisoner gave a nervous smile: 'I really don't know what you're talking about.'

Jones moved closer, but he could see from the eyes that the man was not afraid. 'Your girl turned you in? Why?'

'She wanted to be top girl, but she didn't work hard enough. She wished me to be hers alone, and she got jealous. I should have killed her, not threatened to, then I wouldn't be here.'

'You're a pimp are you? Very good.'

'There are worse things than pimps, policemen for example.'

'You're in trouble, my old son.'

'I'll survive, I always have, no doubt your prisons are better than the Nazis'.'

'You'd know?'

The prisoner shook his head in resignation, bored by the silly questions.

'But now that you're in here the princesses will survive too, won't they?'

'You're talking in riddles.'

'Am I just?' Jones took a step closer, an arm's reach from the man. There was only one sure way, he didn't like it, but under the circumstances it seemed the way, you couldn't talk this little sonny boy into coughing, that much was obvious.

Jones brought out the blackjack from his raincoat pocket and hit the prisoner hard across the top of his shoulder, avoiding the collar bone.

The man grunted with pain and fell to his knees. 'You fockink English bastard.' The Dutch accent was pronounced now. He's an actor, remember, Jones told himself.

He hit him again across the right arm, on the flesh of the

158

muscle. 'Your name is Uwe Eilders and you're a German agent, aren't you, you little bastard?'

'You're fockink crazy man.' Jones hit him again across the fingers nursing the points of the first blows.

The prisoner grunted but made no cry. A tough one eh, that the way they make him in Jerryland, well try this for size. Jones struck him hard on the upper leg.

'Why the luger?' That for Gareth, you German bastard, that for all the poor sods you've put six feet under.

'Protection.'

'You're an agent aren't you, you're in the SD and you were sent here to attack the Royal family.'

'You're crazy . . . crazy . . .'

Everything was up in Jones now, his hatred of the Germans for taking away his son, his sorrow, his frustration at the restrictions put upon him, his tiredness from the long hours, his loneliness, all of it was welling into one great volcano of eruption. 'You're Dutch then are you . . . where from?'

The prisoner spat some phlegm: 'Rotterdam.'

'You're a liar.' Jones swung the blackjack and it struck the man across the bridge of the nose, and there was a crack. The man cried out.

This time it was blood he spat, and then dived at Jones trying to tackle him to the ground.

Jones was too quick, stepping back and kicking the man hard in the torso.

'You're a German . . . *aren't you*?' His voice was almost a scream now, he *wanted* this man to be Uwe Eilders.

'I came here in thirty-eight, from Rotterdam, it's the truth . . . ask the girls. I've been running them for eighteen months . . . ask the girls . . . please . . .'

Jones felt a fluttering of unease. It was too easy to check, why would he tell a lie so easy to check?

'Your name is Uwe Eilders!' He raised his blackjack, and as he did the door opened.

'That's enough.' It was the station sergeant, and he had Ulrich von der Osten with him.

Jones turned, and his face frightened Ulrich, it was suffused with blood and hate. 'You keep out of it, Sergeant, it's none of your bloody business . . . and get *him* out of my sight until this prisoner has confessed.'

'Oh no, Super, not in my station. I don't care who you are, *I* say what goes on in here . . . he's my responsibility.'

Jones came forward clutching the blackjack. 'We need to know who this man is, Sergeant, and we need to know fast.'

'Using that, sir?' the sergeant waved a hand at the blackjack. 'We the Gestapo now?'

'You know the score pal, how many have you roughed up down here on a Saturday night?'

'Plenty, those who asked for it, but we didn't use that . . . and chummy here has been as quiet as a mouse. I've got to put him in the dock in the morning, how do I explain this little lot?'

'Say he fell down the stairs, that's what you usually say . . . now fuck off and take him with you.'

The sergeant was a big man, and he stepped forward: 'No, sir, I can't do that. You're out of order. Either give me that cosh or I'll take it from you.'

Jones squared-up, eyes red and demented. 'Try it you flat-footed cunt and I'll take your head off.'

Ulrich said softly: 'Harry . . . ' It was the first time he had used the man's first name. 'Harry . . . let me take a proper look at him, I know . . . ' he stopped himself . . . 'the man we want.'

Without waiting for an answer he pushed gently past the sergeant, past Jones and lifted the prisoner up from the floor. The man raised his bloodstained face, waiting with resignation for the next blow.

'I'm sorry, Harry, but it's the wrong man. That's not him, on the name of God it is not him.'

Jones was swaying on his feet: 'It's him I tell you. It's *him*!'

Ulrich took the blackjack gently from Jones' hand. 'No, Harry, you're wrong. You only had to wait five minutes, that's all, five minutes. I know him, and this is not the man.'

160

Harry Jones put his head slowly into his hands: 'Oh my God what have I done?'

Ulrich put his arm around the man's shoulders, and Harry could not bring himself to stop it.

'Mornin', Ma.'

'Morning, Ernie, I got it all, just what you wanted.' She handed the sergeant a list, and he put it in his tunic pocket without reading it.

'Let you into a secret, Ma, we got him, that bloke we were looking for. The lads up at Cannon Row nicked him, shacked up with a tart he was.'

'See . . . ' Mrs Millington was triumphant. 'I told you there was no hankey-pankey in *this* house. German spies indeed . . . I never did in all my life.'

'Just mind you do it properly in future, Ma, or I'll be down on you like a ton of bricks.'

'I will, Ernie, I promise.'

As the sergeant went away, Mrs Millington patted her ample if sagging bust where the two £5 notes were tucked safely away. All was well that ended well, and it was an ill wind that blew nobody any good. She believed in the proverbs, did Mrs Millington.

The worst part for Tilly Butler was not being able to tell anyone, because Jan had made her promise. One night when she was feeling a little funny about him being there all the time, it was what the neighbours might think more than anything, he had said that they must get married. He had *proposed* . . . down on one knee like on the pictures. She was his fiancée now, so it was more respectable. Once all his papers were in order they would get married, and after the war they were going to Holland. Holland was smashing, he'd told her all about it. She was going to have lots of kids and live in a big house with a garden, the sort only posh people had here. Oh, if only the war would hurry up and be over.

161

They'd celebrated with some whisky, and her favourite, gin-and-it . . . she'd got all squiffy. His new beard he was growing made him look even better, like a pirate, or an artist. They made love all the time, even when they were squiffy, it never seemed to affect him . . . he was always, well . . . capable.

Sometimes he frightened her a little bit, some of the things he wanted to do. He said that everybody on the Continent did those things, that it was quite normal, more of a game than anything. But he gripped so hard sometimes, and once he'd slapped her because he said she was hysterical, but she wasn't, she'd only been laughing, ordinary like. Still, they were different, foreigners.

Tilly Butler worked at her lathe skilfully if robotically, and wondered what Holland was like.

Neither Ulrich nor Harry Jones spoke of the incident again, and the station sergeant agreed to make no mention of what had happened.

Jones seemed embarrassed at having broken down in front of Ulrich, and at having taken comfort from him. Once he recovered, he resumed his polite, formal distance, but Ulrich noted moments when he seemed to forget that Ulrich was a German and an enemy, and bordered on being warm. Then Harry would seem to remember, and consciously stop himself.

Both men were working solidly now following up details on arrested Dutchmen. It seemed hardly possible that the United Kingdom possessed so many citizens of Holland who had violated the laws of their host country. The Dutch were a law-abiding people; it was simply that the British had been infected with spy phobia, and the police had the bug along with everyone else.

Dutchmen were arrested in Liverpool, Leeds, Plymouth, Reading, Dover, Glasgow, Dundee and Londonderry. None bore the name of Jan Villen Ter Braak, but the police of each town assured Scotland Yard that each had some irregularity of papers that merited their being seen.

162

Reading seemed the most likely because of its proximity to Windsor, so Jones and Ulrich went there first by car along the A4. Ulrich glimpsed the turrets of Windsor Castle from their route. The prisoner turned out to be a Belgian, a Fleming from Antwerp with a Dutch sounding name. He'd had his papers stolen in a pub and gone into Reading police station to report them, and been promptly arrested. He was fifty-five.

Jones was not pleased and made that clear to the officer who had made the arrest.

Jones then went by train to Liverpool, on to Glasgow, across to Dundee and back to London via Leeds. None of the men were Jan Villen Ter Braak.

Ulrich did Plymouth, back to London, then down to Dover. Plymouth was negative—the man was actually French, God knows why the British police thought he was Dutch. Dover was a blanket and a corpse beneath it. The man had been seventy-two and he had died of a heart attack two hours after his arrest. Both men were now extremely weary, and Jones decided that before either of them made the arduous journey to Londonderry he would check further with the Royal Ulster Constabulary. Close questioning revealed that the Dutchman had lived in the town for twenty years and was married to an Irish girl. He had been arrested after coming out of a pub in the Bogside shouting: 'Up the IRA.' He also had a wooden leg.

Jones swore at the inspector from Londonderry, and slammed the telephone down. 'A spy with a wooden leg, can you believe it.' Jones shook his head in dismay. 'Back in Napoleon's day a monkey got washed up from a shipwreck in Cornwall. The locals hanged it because they thought it was a French spy. I thought we were all modern and sophisticated; it is the nineteen-forties after all.'

Jones subsided into silence, and Ulrich watched his face. The man was very, very tired, but he must know what had to be done, surely.

'It has been two weeks since we issued the name, and he has not been found. That is two weeks in which he could have been changing his papers, planning, creating a new identity.'

163

Jones looked up sharply: 'You think I've ballsed it don't you . . . well let me tell you, if it'd been up to me we'd have had him on the front pages from the word go. But it *wasn't* up to me.'

'He should have been found, Harry, why hasn't he been?' He noticed that Jones seemed too tired to protest at the informality of being addressed by his new name, but Ulrich was equally tired of sitting in an office with a man all day and calling him 'Superintendent'.

'I don't know.'

'You said a man could not live without papers here.'

'I said a lot of things . . . but don't worry, I'm going to have him if it's the last thing I do.'

'You'll issue the picture now?'

In answer Jones picked up the telephone, asked for an outside line then dialled the letters F-L-E and four digits. He put his hand over the mouthpiece: 'By this time tomorrow our Dutchman is going to be so well known that if he so much as pops his head out of doors he'll have crowds asking for his autograph. He doesn't know it yet but he's about to become The Belgravia Strangler.'

Chapter Fifteen

'EVENING, REG.'

'Evening, Tilly, *Woman's Weekly* and the usual?'

'Ta, Reg.'

He rooted under the counter for the magazine and handed it to her. 'You got a lodger now then?' His tone was peeved and hurt, and she could feel herself going red.

'Only my cousin, the one from Southampton, I told you about him.'

'Oh yes, your *cousin*, you going to bring him down and introduce him to me, then, haven't seen much of your cousin? And why not tell him to pick his feet up, he clomps round that room all day like a bloody stormtrooper.'

'I'm sorry, Reg, honest. I'll tell him to be quiet.'

Mr Donaldson put his hand over the counter to touch Tilly's, and she was terrified of moving it. 'Maybe it's your cousin and maybe it's not, Tilly, I just don't want you to make a fool of yourself, that's all.'

'You're a love, Reg.'

'I could be more than that, Tilly, you mind on what I said to you last month.'

'I'm still thinking it over, honest.' She was getting redder. Sooner or later she would have to tell him that Jan and she were getting married and then he'd probably kick her out of the flat.

'Well mind you do, it's a good offer. Little gold mine this shop is, and I'd look after you champion. I might not look like a film star, but you'd have food in your belly.'

'I'll think about it, Reg, promise I will.' She turned, anxious to be out of the shop.

'Here . . . you've forgotten your *Evening News*.' She took the folded paper and put it under her arm with *Woman's Weekly.*

'I'm home, darling.' It was ridiculous really, the door opened into the bedsitting room, and he was lying on the bed looking at her. But in the films, the wife always came through the front door and shouted: 'I'm home, darling.'

It made her feel important and of course when she was in Holland, the house would be big enough to do it properly.

He got off the bed and kissed her, taking her into his arms. She let the magazine and newspaper fall to the floor and flung both her arms round his neck.

'I've been waiting for that all day,' she giggled coquettishly. It was silly, but she felt in the mood for love at the strangest times of day now.

'Did you make a lot of Bren guns today?'

'Two million, all by myself, they'll kill lots of Jerries, and the war will be over next week.'

'Of course, the more Germans we kill, the sooner we can go to Holland.'

She pressed closer to him and he smelled the familiar cheap scent, the sweat from working in the hot factory and that odour of metal and oil.

'Why don't you get out of those things.' She knew now what that meant.

'Oh, Jan, you make me go all funny, it's like being squiffy.'

'Then let's squiff.'

She giggled. He repeated the whole dreary routine.

He lay on the bed in his underpants, total nakedness still seemed to embarrass her, so he had abandoned it. She was in the kitchen whistling tunelessly: 'We're gonna hang out our

166

washing on the Siegfried Line, if the Siegfried Line's still there.'

Eilders ground his teeth in frustration. He was safe for the time being, but he was stuck. The princesses were at Windsor, almost thirty miles away, guarded by élite troops, while he sat in a dingy apartment with an infatuated brainless girl who could be of no practical use to him beyond providing a refuge. His papers were now useless, and he had to live with the knowledge that somehow they had discovered his alias. All he had was the money, his wits and his determination. That and a diagram of the layout of Buckingham Palace, and not even an idea if or when the girls would ever go there.

He let his hand trail over the side of the bed, and it touched paper. He scooped up the magazine and newspaper from where the girl had discarded them.

Her irritating voice came from the kitchen: 'Do you want carrots? Our pilots eat lots of carrots.'

'Yes, carrots.'

He glanced at the magazine and tossed it away. He unfolded the newspaper and found himself looking into a mirror.

It was him! He sat bolt upright, his heart pounding. The girl was still singing some stupid ditty but he could hardly hear for the blood thumping at his ears. A photograph! A younger Uwe Eilders, and clean shaven, but him! The picture was from SD files, he knew that because there was only that one left in existence. He had ruthlessly hunted down and destroyed every picture ever taken of him, however distant and blurred. A photograph! Just one photograph left in existence and it was here, staring out at him from a British newspaper like a haunting doppelganger.

He read the words quickly. He was a dangerous murderer who had killed Lord Blackington, the Spanish maid and an old Clapham landlady. There was a reward of £1,000—a massive sum—for his capture.

Eilders' skin was on fire. He had been betrayed: there was no other explanation. Germany, his heartbeat, his religion, his very soul, Germany had betrayed him. He lowered the newspaper and pushed it under the bed. Now everyone in

England would be hunting him, they knew his face! His name was useless, his papers too. He was just a body now, a husk, he could go nowhere, just wait until they came for him.

He had disobeyed orders, yes, but *betrayal* and to the British, it was unthinkable.

The girl was singing again: 'Run rabbit, run rabbit, run, run, run . . . '

He closed his eyes and felt himself spinning like a drunken man. Betrayed. Betrayed. He opened his eyes again. But betrayed by whom?

Someone did not wish him to succeed, some group, some faction, or just one person, a traitor to the Reich? ' . . . here comes the farmer with his gun, gun, gun . . . '

Germany was riddled with traitors: communists, army officers, Junkers, Jews. When he had not returned from the mission, some traitor had learned, and had plundered the files to give his picture to the British. And they must believe he was now delivered to the British hangman.

But they were wrong. There was one more refuge, one more place, a risky place, but there was no other choice. He would go there, get more papers, let his beard grow, and change his appearance as much as possible. Tomorrow everyone in Britain would be looking for him . . . in a week the edge of curiosity would be gone. He would wait here for one week, and then find his new refuge.

But for now there was the matter of the girl.

He doubted if she had seen the newspaper picture; the paper itself had been rolled up, and if she had seen it she would certainly have recognised him. Neither could the picture have been in that morning's newspapers, or she would have seen it at the ordnance factory. She had told him she read a paper called the *Daily Mirror*, he remembered it from his youth. It had a picture strip about a girl called Jane which she liked. So the morning newspapers would use the photograph the next day. If he let her go to the factory she would see the picture and call the police.

He thought about keeping her prisoner here for a week, but dismissed it as impracticable.

168

He got up from the bed and hunted out his loop of wire from beneath the mattress, next to the springs. He went into the kitchen with his hands behind his back.

She looked up from the small stove: 'Now you put something warm on, you'll catch your death dressed like that.' He could feel his breath coming a little faster, his skin clammy with anticipation. It had to happen, it was just sooner rather than later, but he had waited for this moment.

She put her hands on her hips: 'And what *are* you doing in my kitchen anyway? Go on, shoo.' She felt like a proper little housewife.

'I have a surprise gift for you.'

'A surprise, oh, I love surprises, what is it?' She stood on tiptoes, trying to see what was behind his back.

'If I told you, it wouldn't be a surprise. Turn around and close your eyes, and keep well away from the stove, I don't want you to scald yourself with shock.'

She did as she was bidden, eyes screwed firmly shut, and she heard him come up behind her, and then the movement of his hands.

'Your eyes are properly shut?'

'Cross my heart and hope to die.' Oh yes, dear Tilly.

She could hear his breathing, it seemed heavier than normal, then something touched the front of her neck, something cold and metallic. He had bought her a necklace, she just knew it.

Tilly Butler opened her eyes, but did not have the chance to scream.

Chapter Sixteen

AN ACCOUNTANT from Weybridge was arrested on his way to catch the 8.21 commuter train to Waterloo. A seaman in Grimsby was dragged out of bed and his wife's arms at 5 a.m. by police acting on an anonymous call.

Two Local Defence Volunteers riding bicycles and armed with pickaxe handles hauled a fellow cyclist off his machine in Somerset, and dragged him roughly to the local police station.

In Doncaster one man actually gave himself up to a policeman on point duty and confessed.

In all there were forty-three suspected Belgravia Stranglers arrested the day the picture appeared in the national morning newspapers. There were seventy further sightings which came to naught.

The man who gave himself up was eliminated right away, as he had confessed to every publicised murder ever committed in England, Scotland, Ireland and Wales for the past fifteen years. He was also five feet one, bald and toothless.

An extremely indignant accountant was released after Jones and Ulrich had seen him. The seaman spent twenty-four hours in a cell but was finally allowed to go when his wife, with five kids in tow, vouched that he had been bobbing on the North Sea when the murders occurred.

There were others to eliminate personally, and the two men travelled hundreds of miles doing it. Who knew, perhaps Eilders *was* posing as an accountant, *or* a fisherman. He had eluded them this far, and who could say what he was now, or where?

By the end of the week the arrests and sightings began to

tail off as public interest waned. It was said that each person had a double, and it was clear that a lot of men looked like Uwe Eilders, young, clean-shaven, good-looking with a healthy head of hair.

If you knew the man as Ulrich did, then it was obvious the suspects were not he; but to a passer-by, or a keen police-man, the suspects had looked enough like the grainy newspaper picture to alert suspicion. There was simply nothing distinguishing about Eilders, a crooked nose, uneven teeth, a facial blemish, nothing that made him different from lots of other men his age, not if he made himself look English, and Eilders could do that, Ulrich had no doubt.

When his name had been issued, he had not been found. Suppose he knew, suppose he realised that his papers were useless, perhaps he had seen a check being carried out? He would go to ground then, cease pretending to be a Dutch-man, try and get new papers and become English. His picture had been in the newspapers for over a week, and still he was free.

Ulrich was very worried, despite Jones' assurances that no one could get into Windsor Castle, and that the princesses would not budge from there until Eilders was behind bars. He had been allowed to travel freely, with a uniformed officer to 'guide' him, but no one could prevent him seeing a great deal. He had looked out of the car or train carriage window and watched England at war. Men drilling with pickaxe handles in place of rifles, and only an armband for uniform. Clearly the British were in a bad way.

In southern England, pits for anti-aircraft guns were being dug, and there was fiendish activity on the railways, with train after trainload of troops heading for the coast around Dover and Folkestone. Obviously they were to man coastal defences against invasion. In the countryside he saw pinch-faced undernourished children with accents different from the locals. One boy had approached him at a railway station, begging money, and had been reprimanded by a stern woman in a hat. Clearly there was friction between the evacuees and the people on whom they had been dumped.

But the more he saw, the more worried he became. How could the British let him return to Germany with the knowledge he had gained? He was an agent of the Abwehr, they must know that whatever he felt personally about his word would mean nothing once he was home; he would be de-briefed exhaustively. Just the positions of the anti-aircraft pits alone would make it worthwhile.

They were ruthless these British, and Ulrich did not think they would hesitate to kill him once Eilders was discovered. Ulrich realised he was in an absurd and dangerous position. The sooner Eilders was found, and killed by Ulrich before the British could use him, the sooner the British would dispose of him, Ulrich von der Osten.

Yet Eilders *had* to be found, and then had to die. Ulrich felt it was more vital for Germany and her honour than for England. How ironical that when he found and disposed of Eilders he would be signing his own death warrant.

The strain was beginning to tell. Jones had deep, dark bags under his eyes, and had started to smoke heavily. Ulrich couldn't remember the detective smoking at all when he'd first met him. Jones had set up a camp bed in the office and was staying there at night. After midnight and beyond when Ulrich could take no more of the peering at files, taking calls, telephoning, arguing, theorising, prognosticating and worrying, then he could whistle up the black Humber and go back to Kensington, a hot bath and clean sheets.

But Harry Jones never budged. And in the morning at eight when Ulrich arrived, Harry was there, eyes red, clothes rumpled, and the office with a sour, sleep smell to it to add to the stale tobacco.

Ulrich himself was going paler and more drawn by the day. He drank incessant cups of black, bitter coffee, and his hands seemed to have developed a slight tremor. He was clearly living on his nerves. Jones couldn't even begin to work out what the Germans might do to the Abwehr man if he failed.

As he lay there at night in his vest and underpants beneath

the thin blanket, trying to get comfortable on the canvas camp bed, Harry Jones tried to put himself in the German's position.

Suppose we had some looney of ours on the loose in Berlin threatening to knock off Hitler, and we wanted him stopped though God knows why we would, how would I feel if they sent me there to help? Me, helping the Nazis to track down one of our side. How would I feel, especially after what happened to Gareth, helping the Germans, walking round Berlin, taking trains and cars all over the country. Don't even think I could do it, not unless I had something personal against him.

Something the MI5 man had said, about Ulrich knowing what Eilders was capable of . . . suppose it *was* something personal.

'Ulrich . . . ' he said it without thinking, he'd always called him colonel before, but it just came out. It didn't mean anything, it was only his name, and it was shorter anyway, Jones rationalised.

'Yes?'

'This Eilders, he done you some harm at any time?' Jones saw a dangerous look on the German's face.

'He hurt someone I loved.'

'Hurt?'

Ulrich got up and went to the window, looking down at the grey Thames. The Wannsee would be blue now, perhaps Ilse was out on the grass, looking at the sailboats and the swimmers as she had done when he had been there.

Ulrich turned round briskly. 'We were both escorting the same girl. I loved her and wished to marry her, she chose to marry Eilders instead . . . '

A door opened and a young detective said: 'Super, can I have a minute . . . ?'

Jones roared: 'Out!' The door slammed quickly.

'You were saying.'

'She refused to play his filthy perverted games, so he knocked her down a stairway. Now she is blinded in one eye, and is confined to a wheelchair.'

They've played us both like toy soldiers, Jones thought, I want to get him because the Nazis killed Gareth, you want him because he crippled your girl. Personal motivation.

But Harry Jones had a feeling it might be a tad too personal in the German's case. He said with apparent casualness, 'You weren't thinking of taking the law into your own hands . . . when we catch him like?'

The German's eyes met his, and Jones got his answer.

'Well forget it, boyo, this is Britain not the bloody Fatherland . . . the courts dispense justice, not you.'

Ulrich forced a smile: 'I remember a man dispensing justice with a cosh . . . '

Jones went red. 'It's a warning, and a promise. When we catch him we'll hang him. If you kill him we'll bloody hang you!'

The telephone rang, and Jones left it for three long rings as he stared at Ulrich. The German was going to mess this up; if he did he, Superintendent Harry Jones might become Police Constable Jones very quickly.

'Yes . . ' he snatched at the phone.

'Yes, sir, sorry, sir.' He sat bolt upright in his chair, as though to attention.

'I'm on my way over right away, sir.'

He replaced the receiver and let out breath through his teeth. He straightened his tie, stood up and put on his jacket, standing on first one leg then the other as he brushed the black toecaps of his shoes on his trousers to polish them. 'I'm going out. I've got to see someone.'

'Who?'

Jones couldn't resist it: 'As a matter of fact, Winston Churchill.'

He wondered how deep below ground they were. There was a faint touch of damp in the air despite the humming generators.

The Prime Minister was wearing a heavy pin-striped suit and a spotted bow tie, and he was smoking a cigar. So this,

174

thought Harry Jones, as a way of trying to damp down his nerves, this is the scourge of the Sidney Street anarchists, the man who buggered up Gallipoli, the warrior who sent troops against unarmed villagers in Tonypandy. Nobody in South Wales cared much for Winston Churchill, and Harry Jones was no exception. He just hoped the man wouldn't make a bloody mess of the job he'd got now. *Everything* depended on it.

'Superintendent, I have no wish to direct or control your enquiries, or to interfere with your ways of working. However, I thought it, ah . . . wise . . . ' Churchill smiled coldly . . . 'to tell you at this point of my deep concern and moreover of His Majesty's deep concern, at your failure to apprehend this German agent.' Churchill sat back and inhaled Havana.

This was it then, the first pressure, and right from the bloody top. Jones cleared his throat: 'I can assure you, Prime Minister that we are pursuing every possible line of enquiry, and we confidently expect an early arrest.'

Winston Churchill released a cloud of blue smoke and barked through it: 'I am not the British public, Superintendent, and you are not issuing a police communiqué. Why is he not caught, this vile would-be assassin?'

Jones trembled: 'Frankly, sir, I don't know. He has no papers that we are aware of that can be of any use to him, his photograph is on railway station walls . . . '

'He cannot be allowed to get near their Royal Highnesses.'

'Prime Minister, I do not believe, in the present state of security surrounding their Highnesses' domicile, that the German agent can possibly penetrate it.'

Churchill glowered but Jones plunged on: 'He is free, sir, and that is something we are doing everything we can to change, but he is powerless to carry out his threat. It *must* be a matter of time before he is caught.'

Jones realised, properly, for the first time, just how much this all meant. It was not just his career, being put back on the beat, or the tragic death of two girls the country loved, it was more. Perhaps the whole outcome of the war might hinge on

175

it, and that was on his shoulders and a German's. A Welshman and a German trying to find another German who wants to kill two English princesses.

Churchill picked up a buff-coloured envelope from his desk, and handed it to Harry Jones.

'That makes you the most powerful policeman in the United Kingdom. Under the Emergency Powers Act there is no peacetime law, save that of murder, that you cannot break. You can requisition what you wish from ships to aeroplanes. A sum of £10,000 will be made available to you to pay informers.'

Jones could feel his chest tightening and his breath leaving him. Money, ships, aeroplanes . . . Jesus, they were pulling out all the stops.

'If you wish the use of any officers you will tell the commissioner to release them, *tell*, mind you, Superintendent, not ask. You can cordon off towns, stop traffic, tear down doors, put people in prison, anything you wish. As long as your Naaaazzi friend is in your company he can share those powers, but *you* control them, not he.

'And beware, Superintendent—beware of the German. When his usefulness ends he will be a danger to England.'

'Yes sir, thank you, sir.'

'Find him, Superintendent, find this odious man, this threat to our beloved princesses. Find him and let him hang—quietly. The fate of our nation could depend upon it.'

'You have my word, Prime Minister.'

But how, how!?

Chapter Seventeen

EILDERS REMOVED the girl's clothes, wrapped her in a sheet and trussed the body with twine he found beneath the kitchen sink. He left the corpse in the narrow kitchen and lay down on the bed to think.

She would be missed tomorrow at Enfield, that was certain. It was clear from her conversations that she could not simply miss a day or more without a valid reason. If she just failed to appear, it was possible someone would come to the apartment.

He needed a week. A week and then he would head across East London to what he prayed could be his bolthole.

That night he walked hurriedly to a telephone kiosk on the Mile End Road. In the darkness he doubted if anyone would recognise him, but he turned his coat collar up to shield his jaw, and kept his face down. After finding the number of the factory through a bored-sounding woman—Enfield was not listed as a London number in the tattered telephone directories —he called the ordnance factory and left a message that Miss Mathilda Butler had been injured in a blackout car crash. She had a broken leg, the leg had been set, and she had gone to stay with a relative to recuperate.

Sooner or later, someone would check when the girl failed to send a note of explanation, but he doubted if that would happen within a week as the British were notoriously tardy.

The days were warm and the nights little cooler, and after three days he detected that faint and unmistakable odour from beneath the bed where he had hidden the girl's body. He drank some of the whisky and stayed in the kitchen with the windows open.

Jones did the rounds with a bigger bundle of money in his pocket than he'd ever seen before. He did the grasses in their usual pubs and dives, and they thought Christmas had come early. He doled out fivers like sweets, and eyes popped like corks.

He didn't even want a promise, nothing on their mother's life Mr Jones, just a few minutes of their time, the bloke, what he looks like, and the fact that he was wanted, very, very badly.

They knew it was the Belgravia Strangler, of course, and knew there was a grand reward in it, so why this special visit from Mr Jones and the offer of a hundred quid just for a telephone call if they thought the right man was around? It had to be important to someone, but money was money so if they set eyes on the geezer they promised Mr Jones he'd get a bell.

Then Harry Jones went up West to the land of the big villains. Money they had aplenty; Harry was offering them something money couldn't buy, future goodwill. They could run the girls and the games for all he cared, as long as they kept their eyes open for chummy, and if they thought he was about, just *one* phone call, and in the event of future mishaps he'd personally intercede on their behalf. Eyebrows were raised. What was so special about the Belgravia Strangler just because he'd topped a lord?

At the end of it all, Harry felt soiled. Every detective mixed with villains, drank with them, exchanged information with them, bartered with them, that was the essence of detection work. They gave, you took; you promised, they gave a bit more; you cheated them, they lied to you. But in the end you came up on the plus side of the deal, and it was important they understood that fact.

Today, to his eternal disgust, he knew that he'd been out

begging, scattering money like confetti, and pleading . . .
Worst of all he knew they'd realised that.

Eilders had been right, Tilly Butler's hair colour was not
natural. He found the dye and used it himself on hair and
beard. Then he rummaged around among her possessions until
he found a black and white photograph of a young man in
uniform, presumably her soldier boyfriend. The hair was very
short, but Eilders noted the way it was parted, very severely
down the right side. He'd noticed a lot of the English young
men with similar partings, and he re-combed his hair until it
was the same. He had already experimented with soaked
cotton-wool pressed next to his gums, and it had served to
make him look far fatter in the face. That and the beard gave
him a bloated look.

It was superficial, but it would have to do. Tonight, when
darkness fell, he would leave for Plaistow, just a few miles
away. Luckily the weather had cooled considerably, but the
smell in the small apartment was becoming intolerable.

He lay quietly, waiting for the night.

He awoke to a noise on the stairs, a footfall.

He stiffened. It was dusk and in a few minutes would be
dark enough for him to leave, but who was on the stairs and
why?

The doorbell rang. He cursed, got up and moved silently to
the kitchen. The doorbell rang again, and he heard a man's
voice shout: 'Tilly? You home? It's Reg.' There was another
ring, and another. Then silence. And more silence, he must
have gone away. Then slowly and unmistakably, the sound
of a key turning in the lock. Damn the man, what did he
want?

The door opened, and the man said: 'You home, Tilly?'

The room light went on, and Eilders moved further back
into the darkness of the kitchen. He could hear the man
muttering something and complaining, then his footsteps

179

coming closer, and the kitchen light came on. 'Jesus!' the man literally jumped from the shock of seeing Eilders there.

'Who the hell are you, you nearly gave me a bloody heart attack lurking in the dark like that.'

'I am Tilly's cousin—from Southampton.'

'Oh yes, her cousin. Well, where's Tilly, and what the bloody hell have you been cooking up here? The smell's bloody awful.' The man wrinkled his nose in distaste.

The smell! Of course, Eilders had grown, if not accustomed to it, at least somewhat inured, but it must be strong now, and have penetrated to the man's apartments below.

'It was something that died—a rodent.' An English rodent.

'Well, you should find it and get rid of it, stinking the bloody place out like this. And where's Tilly? I haven't seen her for days. She never misses her *Evening News*.'

'Gone away, to friends.'

'Friends, where?'

'Essex . . .'

'She never mentioned no friends in Essex to me, and she tells me everything.'

Eilders gritted his teeth: 'Maybe it was her family, I don't know, but she has gone away.'

'Where in Essex?'

He tried desperately to think of a town in Essex. Ipswich, that was in Essex, surely.

'Ipswich.'

'Ipswich is not in bloody . . . ' the man cocked his head to one side and squinted. 'Hang on a bit, your face looks familiar.'

Eilders killed him.

He left the apartment carefully, putting the newsagent's body with the girl's beneath the bed. In death at least, Mr Donaldson had achieved his wish.

Now Eilders had to get to Plaistow. There was an Underground train which would have taken him there in three stops, but he did not dare risk recognition at this point, so he decided to make the long walk. It was mid-evening, warm and there were plenty of strollers. Now that the fear of air-raids had diminished, more people were coming out even though the black-out was in force.

Eilders walked down the Bow Road, past the poor shops, the ubiquitous pawnbrokers, up the long High Street and into Stratford, then swung south down West Ham Lane and into the Plaistow Road. Just a couple of miles away he could see the stark silhouettes of the cranes from the Royal Victoria and Royal Albert Docks, a familiar sight from his childhood, against the night sky. He found the Barking Road and then began to tick off the streets from memory.

Most of this area was poor tenements, three-storey affairs, meagre apartments, often overcrowded, the families forced to share communal lavatories and kitchens on each landing.

But there were proper houses too, small, two-up, two-down affairs built for journeymen in the last century. They were crude affairs with plaster walls, no internal heating save for small coal-burning fires, and they had no bathrooms or hot water. The lavatory was an earth closet in a brick cubicle at the end of the small brick-enclosed yard.

It was in such a house that the Archers had lived, paying for its eventual purchase at four shillings a week through a local friendly society. This had made the Archers a cut above their neighbours, most of whom rented from a local Jewish landlord.

Though cheek by jowl with the tenements, the houses were considered vastly superior, because they had privacy, the English dream, and the people who lived in them considered themselves a social degree higher than the tenement dwellers. Families rarely moved from their homes in the East End, and as the Archers had actually been buying their house, Eilders felt sure they would still be there, unless, of course, they had died in the meantime. Their death might mean his too.

At the fourth street on the right he stopped and peered through the gloom at the street name plate. Olive Road.

A strange sense of past overwhelmed him. This was the

street in which he had played football with a bunch of rags tied with string, kicking and being kicked, grazing his knees on the cobbles. The cobbles had gone now, in their place a stretch of rough concrete, but the street looked much the same; the stunted remains of trees which had given up the unequal struggle against factory pollution and motor-car exhaust fumes; the same matchbox houses, nestled to each other as if for comfort in their less than genteel poverty.

Eilders turned into the street and began to count. He heard the cry of a baby, or was it a cat? Both sounds were hauntingly alike. At the tenth house down he stopped. From inside he could hear the faint murmur of a distorted voice from a wireless.

He knocked twice. A light came on down the narrow hall, then it disappeared. Someone had opened and closed the inner door to keep the blackout. A woman opened the door.

'Mrs Archer?'

'Yes.' Her face was still the same, shining in the darkness, the hair in the familiar bun, but she was more rounded now like a well-baked loaf.

'My name is Terence Smith. The local mission said you might have a room for the night.'

She peered into the dark. 'A room? There must be some mistake, I don't take in lodgers, never have.'

'They said perhaps for one night, they said you were a good Christian family who would put up a stranger in need of a decent home.'

'Well . . . ' she was pondering, 'you'd better come in for a start and have a cup of tea. Wandering out in the blackout like that, you could break your leg.'

They walked down the hall in the darkness, together, then she opened the door into the living room. It had hardly changed. A wooden mantelshelf dressed with tiny china ornaments topped an open coal grate, unlit but littered with scraps of paper. An old Bush radio sat on the sideboard, the programme tuned to the Home Service. There was a round dining table with one leaf lowered, laid with a white tablecloth and a vase of flowers at its centre. Three plaster geese flew across one brown-painted wall. The leather-bound Bible was on the sideboard, open.

Eilders remembered it all, instantly. There was some fresh paint, different knick-knacks, and the sideboard was new (he remembered that the Archers paid regular small sums of money to a furniture agent who 'put away' items for them). It was all the same as he remembered, and yet somehow smaller, like a doll's house.

A voice came from the front room, a plaintive cry with the whine of the invalid in it. 'Who is it, Ada, who's calling at this time of night?' The voice of Mr Archer, but the strength gone. 'Just a visitor, Dad, I'll pop in in a minute.' She said to Eilders by way of explanation: 'My husband is bedridden, he broke his hip three years ago. He has his bed in the front room now.'

'I'm sorry.'

'We do the best we can with the Lord's help.'

She motioned Eilders into one of the chairs which flanked the empty grate. 'Now, you say it's a room you want.'

He told her he was a commercial traveller from Leeds, a newly committed Christian who did not want to be put to the temptations of a commercial hotel or lodging house, watching as he did for any signs of recognition in her face.

It came suddenly and without drama.

When he had stopped speaking, she said slowly: 'You came back to us . . . after all these years you came back. Young Uwe . . . young Uwe . . . why . . . there's a war . . . I don't understand?'

He took hold of her hand, this woman he hated, who had made his childhood such a misery. 'I want to be English, Mrs Archer, just like you wanted me to be. I want to fight for England, so I came here. Will you let me stay, just for a few days? Then I will go and join the British Army . . . God is against Germany.'

She stroked his hand. She was old now, but she had never forgotten her failure with her special son. She had often regretted packing him off to Germany so quickly and without chance of reprieve.

183

But the police had come only two weeks ago and said that if Uwe turned up she was to tell them, that he was a German and had no right to be in England now the war was on. And he had come, just like they said, at first with this silly story about being from Leeds, but she had recognised him as soon as he sat by the fireplace. Now he said he wanted to join the British Army; who should she believe, him or the police? The radio said there were spies, and that everyone should report them, but if the police knew Uwe might come he could hardly be a spy.

Her memories were all rose-tinted now, she forgot the violent, unyielding, stubborn boy. She saw instead a hapless foreign youth, struggling to come to terms with his new life. Had they been too harsh with him? Mr Archer was very strict in those days.

'The police came here, you know.' Eilders stiffened. He had suspected they would, but would they return?

'They said if you came, I was to call them . . . that you shouldn't be here.'

'That is because they don't know I want to join the Army. Once I have joined they will know I am loyal to the King, and they will let me stay. I came here at great risk to myself from Germany.'

'Oh Uwe, you're all I have left now. Our youngest Ian died of pneumonia, and Tommy . . . well, Tommy went off with a harlot and he is dead to us now.' Eilders remembered, Ian, the quiet sickly child, and Tommy, the eldest, a wild lad, now broken away from his repressive childhood.

He stroked the old woman's hand, feeling the old hatred, and yet a surge of something he could hardly recognise. She had been the only 'mother' he could remember.

'I'll be your special child again, Mrs Archer.'

Uwe did not visit the invalid Mr Archer, and persuaded the man's wife that it was better he did not know that his once-adopted son had returned.

The moment of danger came when Mrs Archer went

shopping. Uwe knew he could not keep her confined to the house, but suppose she realised, when she was out, just exactly what she was doing. So as she had made her way to the front door he had said, softly: 'While you are away I will make sure Mr Archer comes to no harm.'

And old woman as she was, she seemed to understand the hint of menace in that. If Uwe *was* still bad, as the police said, then her invalid husband was his hostage.

While she was out, Uwe rummaged through drawers until he found Mr Archer's National Registration Identity Card. Before he left he would kill them both, and the identity card would be good until the murders were discovered. His beard was growing, he was putting on weight, eating as much as he could. Mrs Archer cooked large meals considering the ration limitations. Within forty-eight hours he could venture out again.

He was ready to leave. Everything was packed, he had the stolen identity card, and planned to head West, at last getting nearer to the princesses.

There was just the question of disposing of Mr and Mrs Archer.

The old woman was in the kitchen, making sandwiches for Uwe to take with him and was singing a small hymn to herself. Eilders took out the garrotte and moved as quickly as he could into the kitchen, but there was a creak of linoleum, and she turned, a strange look in her eyes.

She opened her hand, and in it was a small silver crucifix on a chain. 'I got you this, at the market today, I don't like crucifixes normally, far too Roman, but I thought you'd like this, that it would help keep you safe.'

Eilders had the garrotte behind his back, and could feel it biting into his hands.

The woman held out the crucifix, and Eilders released one hand and took it. She said calmly: 'Harm me if you want, if it's God's time for me, I'm ready, but please don't hurt Mr Archer.'

Almost without realising it he said: 'I won't harm you, Mrs Archer, or your husband, just promise me you will not tell the police I was here.'

'On the word of God.'

He left without killing them, and not really knowing why.

After two days someone called the police when Mr Donaldson failed to open his shop. The policemen rang at the flat upstairs, but got no reply. Then they noticed the sweet, cloying smell that touched the back of the throat. They had smelled it before, and knew what it was, so they broke down the door and discovered the bodies.

The first detective to take a close look at the corpses called Scotland Yard, and Jones and Ulrich came rushing down in a patrol car with the bells going and the headlights full on. Without a word spoken they knew it was Eilders, and Ulrich particularly seemed shocked at the man's total ruthlessness. Harry Jones seemed deflated by it, as though it was another prick at whatever confidence he still possessed.

Back at Scotland Yard he sat, flopped like a collapsed marionette, in his chair. Pushing a hand wearily through his hair he said: 'After all that you were right, he shacked up with a bird. The landlord finds him, he tops 'em both. What a bastard.'

Ulrich was pacing anxiously: 'But *now*, Harry, now! What can he do now? Where can he go, he's got no papers, the man Donaldson's were still in his lock-up safe . . . if he steals papers they will be reported and we'll have a record of it.'

'Every missing ration book or identity card in the whole of the United Kingdom is being reported back here . . . ' Jones lifted a sheaf of papers, and let them flutter down like falling leaves. 'Lots of careless people in merry England, one hundred and twenty-three missing cards this week. We've put them all on a Missing list, and if anyone attempts to register one of those cards or ration books we get told. So far we've had fifty-five duds, mostly people whose papers turned up eventually.'

'So he could have papers?'

'He could have, but if he has they'll show on our list. He'll surface, eventually.'

Ulrich sat down and put his face in his hands, thinking desperately. He looked up suddenly. It was crazy surely, but he didn't have great confidence in the English police.

'Harry, this family Eilders lived with in England, they were checked out . . . surely?'

There was a hint of anger in Jones' voice: 'I was doing this job while you were wet behind the ears, boyo . . . of course we checked them, it's the first bloody place we went . . . I mean he wouldn't be as daft as to turn up there, but I went there myself. The old man is bedridden, and the wife is a religious nut, daft as a bloody brush. We told them that if he showed his face to give us a tinkle . . . *and* we asked the local bobbies to pop round there occasionally to keep an eye on things. Forget the Archers.'

Ulrich said: 'Look, we're not doing anything else . . . we were out that way this morning and we could have called, why don't we drive out there now? We'll feel better if we check it ourselves. Anyway, we can talk to the old couple, maybe they can tell us more about him, about his English habits, it might help.'

Jones hauled himself out of his chair: 'Why not, as you say we're doing bugger all else.'

The Bible was open, the woman had clearly been reading it. Jones said: 'You may remember me, I called in a couple of weeks ago, about the German boy you fostered.'

'Yes, I remember you.'

'I wondered if he had been here to see you, Uwe Eilders?'

'Of course not.' The woman's eyes flashed uneasily to Ulrich: 'He's German, he can't come here, there's a war on.'

'We thought he may have paid you a visit.'

'Like I said, no one's been here.'

Ulrich said: 'Excuse me . . . ' and backed out of the living room.

187

In the front room Mr Archer was propped up on pillows, his face brightened as the door opened.

He said: 'And who might you be?'

Ulrich said: 'A policeman, I'd like to talk to you.'

Jones was sipping tea when Ulrich returned, and the woman was chatting more easily.

Ulrich said without preamble: 'Who was your visitor, Mrs Archer?'

Jones looked up sharply, and Mrs Archer spilled her tea. 'Visitor?'

'Your husband said you told him you had someone staying. He left this morning. Why didn't you tell us you had a visitor?'

She went deep red. 'He was from the mission, a Christian boy.'

Jones got up. 'I'll check the bedrooms. Get everything you can out of her.'

Harry dragged his aching frame two at a time up the narrow stairs. He checked the woman's bedroom, then the back room. The bed was stripped and there was no sign it had been slept in or the room otherwise used. Then he detected a sweet odour and wrinkled his nose. He dashed back down the stairs again.

He took Ulrich aside. 'Have you been upstairs?'

Ulrich shook his head. 'Just the front room with the old man, why?'

'You're sure?'

'*Yes*, what is it?'

'That cologne you wear sometimes, you bought it in Germany?'

'Yes?'

'Does Eilders ever wear it?'

'It's possible, it is a popular brand . . . why?'

'He's been here . . . ' Jones said flatly. 'The back room reeks of it . . . her bloody visitor *was* Eilders.'

He turned to the woman, who was trembling now. 'Mrs

188

Archer you are in serious trouble. You have harboured for the last two days, knowingly, a German agent called Uwe Eilders. That's true, isn't it?'

The woman nodded, dreamily: 'He was my special son . . . he's come back to join the British Army, he wants to fight for King and Country.'

Jones said under his breath: 'God give me strength.'

He took the woman firmly by the shoulders. 'Unless you tell me everything you know about this man, *everything*, you are going to die in prison, Mrs Archer, and that's a promise. Lives may depend on what you tell me.'

She was crying now, softly, little weeps that made her shoulders lift: 'I always felt I'd wronged him.'

Jones shook her roughly: 'First, find your husband's identity cards and ration books, and I don't care if you have to ransack the house.'

The woman left the living room, and Ulrich looked Jones in the eye: 'He was here, and we were three miles away, if we'd come this morning we might have got him.'

'I know,' said Jones bitterly, 'but we didn't, and we haven't. But by God we're going to, and I don't care if this old bag gets fifteen years in Holloway in the process.'

Chapter Eighteen

THE METROPOLITAN Police Commissioner was angry. This Superintendent was getting quite above himself.

'Now look here, what you're asking is out of the question. I know this is all hush-hush, but your request is simply not on, and that's final.'

Jones produced the buff-coloured envelope and the document signed by the Prime Minister.

'I am afraid this says I can do it, sir.'

The Commissioner read the paper and glowered. He handed it back to Jones.

'That's disgraceful. I have never seen anything like it in my life, I just hope nobody gets wind of the powers you have there, they'll be calling *us* the Gestapo.'

'I don't intend to use a quarter of what is in there, sir, but I do need men, and I need them tonight.'

'How many men?'

'Everyone in uniform, sir, rest days cancelled, double shifts if necessary, no leave . . . every man-jack uniformed officer out on the streets checking papers, a saturation job.'

'What about CID?' said the Commissioner, bitterly. 'You're sure you can spare them?'

'It's bodies we need, sir, CID already have their standing instructions. Sir, I'm convinced this man is in the centre of London, and that he has an identity card in the name of Frederick Archer. I am further convinced that he does not know we have that information. If we swamp the city with spot checks there is a good chance we'll net him.'

'Very well, I'll call a meeting of assistant commissioners, divisional chiefs and station officers for three o'clock. At least with CID we'll have someone left to cover the rest of the crime.' The Commissioner looked long and hard at Jones. 'I don't suppose you're allowed to tell me what is so important about this man you're looking for.'

'I'm afraid I'm not, sir.'

'Well you can expect questions in the House after an operation of this sort, you know, a lot of people are going to be put to a lot of inconvenience.'

So are the princesses, Jones thought, if Eilders get into Windsor Castle, and imagine the questions in the House then.

Eilders left his suitcase at the Charing Cross station left-luggage office, then strolled up to Soho, watched a bad film, drank equally bad coffee and waited for the dusk. Even with the blackout this was by far the most lively area of London, always teeming with a polyglot mass of humanity. Here he could lose himself for the early night hours among the cosmopolitan crowds in the sleazy back streets, in the strip joints, drinking dives and brothels. After midnight when it quietened, he would slip down to Waterloo, south of the river, and sleep rough with the derelicts under the railway arches. He doubted he would be challenged if he kept that company. Tomorrow he would retrieve his suitcase, take a Green Line bus to Windsor, find himself a lair in the countryside and steal some food. He would live rough, wait for the right moment, and then when a moonless night fell he would climb the castle walls, kill any guards, find the princesses and despatch them.

He knew it was the last desperate throw of a gambler almost broke, but there was nothing left to do. He intended to use Mr Archer's papers for tonight and tomorrow only, in case the old woman did go to the police, or the police themselves made another check.

The British were too close, too clever, they hounded him at

every turn, so he would make that last desperate effort and if he failed, then no man could have done more.

Derek Morris was a respectable man who did not have dealings with the police. Tonight, however, he had been stopped twice and asked for his identity card, once in Whitehall and again in Shaftesbury Avenue. And damn him if the process was not about to be repeated. Mr Morris would have felt less agitated had he not been a married man with two children, and a civil servant in the Ministry of Pensions, and if he had not been in Soho to keep a regular assignation of which his wife had no knowledge. As he turned into Frith Street he came up behind a line of police, he could have gone around, but it would have meant a long detour and he was late as it was. He paid by the hour.

He tapped the nearest policeman on the shoulder. 'May I come through?'

'Identity card.' The policeman said brusquely.

'I've shown it *twice* tonight, my name is Morris.'

'I have to see your card.'

Mr Morris produced it reluctantly, the policeman flashed his hooded torch across it.

'What's all the fuss anyway, half the police force is out?'

'*All* of it actually, sir, and we're looking for a Mr Frederick Archer, so as you're Mr Morris I won't detain you further. Off you pop.'

'There's no need for sarcasm, Officer.'

'So sorry you've been troubled, Mr Morris.' The policeman gave the hint of a salute.

Eilders turned right into Frith Street from Old Compton Street and saw the whores lining the pavement and the steps leading to the houses. He was conscious of his wad of money: it would not do to have it stolen by a prostitute, though he would have liked a woman, a professional, one who would understand and cater for his needs. These looked pathetic wretches, not like the big, buxom girls in Berlin.

He began to walk towards Bateman Street and Soho Square. Something shone momentarily in the darkness beyond, then again a few feet from the same point. He stopped and peered into the gloom, and saw yet another glimmer of light go on, then off again. Like disturbed animals sensing a hostile presence the whores began to shift uneasily and start huddled conversations.

Then Eilders saw the source of the light. It was the police, a line of them moving shoulder to shoulder down the street, checking anyone who passed them from either side. They were checking papers, that was the only explanation, and Eilders cursed his luck, but it must be a random check, the sort any city police force would carry out in wartime, checking deserters, aliens and the like. He turned to make his way back down Old Compton Street, and as he did two blue vans pulled up and policemen began to tumble out of the back doors. They quickly formed a line and began moving towards him. He felt a moment of panic, and put his hand into his inside pocket, running his fingers along the stiff edge of the green identity card.

It was just a routine check, it had to be, even if Mrs Archer had gone out straight away and telephoned the police—something he doubted—they would have had to discover the card was missing and launch a check like this in less than half a day. He doubted it was possible. But he was beginning to sweat.

The line moved closer as he stood in a shop doorway, and several of the girls sidled off the street, closing doors behind them.

He saw a man allowed through the cordon from the direction of Bateman Street and as he drew level Eilders stepped out.

Mr Morris jumped, startled.

'Excuse me, I want to go to Soho Square.'

Derek Morris jerked a thumb back towards the police: 'The one after Bateman Street, once you've got past those ignorant beggars.'

193

'Yes, what is that commotion?'

'Search me, they're looking for some bloke called Archer. I've been stopped *three* times tonight, I'll be writing a strong letter I can tell you.' Mr Morris raised his hat, anxious to be off to his appointment. 'G'night.'

Eilders felt that all too familiar wave of faintness. It was him they were hunting. Damn his weakness, he should have killed the old lady; what on earth had stopped him? Now they had his name again. He thought of the Jack London story, of the man who sat by his campfire in the snowy wilderness, battling sleep and throwing log after log onto the fire to keep the encroaching wolves at bay. The British were like wolves, whatever he did they came closer and closer. He wiped a hand across his forehead, and took deep breaths, trying to clear his mind. Across the street, a thin figure wrapped in a shawl was leaning against a railing at the foot of a set of stone steps.

Eilders strolled across the road, as casually as he could.

The girl looked up, her eyes vacant, her face thin and sad. 'You looking for a good time?' She said it mechanically, without pretence at allure.

'Yes, I would like to go inside with you.'

The girl shifted her waif-like body. 'It'll cost you thirty bob.'

'I agree.'

'Come on then.'

She went into the doorway, and he followed. As she shut the door behind him he could hear the sound of the policemen's boots dim. He knew he was sweating badly. The whore seemed not to notice. She led him up two flights of rickety stairs and into a small room lit with a single, naked red bulb. The room, which was surprisingly clean, contained two single beds each covered in a purple eiderdown, and there was a washbasin against one wall. He noticed bubbles of damp under the flowered wallpaper.

She looked very young and undernourished, like the girl Tilly, a face that had never seen sunlight. She had put on too much make-up, but applied it inexpertly so she looked like a child playing grown-up games. Only her eyes betrayed the cruelty she had seen.

She put out her hand: 'We'll settle up first so there's no shenanigans afterwards.'

Eilders was forced to use his second, so far untouched roll of fivers. He peeled one off, the roll in his pocket so she could not see it.

'A fiver! I 'aven't got change for that, mate.'

'It doesn't matter, keep it all.'

He could hear the policeman talking, laughing and joking beneath the window.

'Thanks . . . thanks a lot.' Some fire seemed to burn in the girl's eyes.

She started to take off her sweater, and Eilders realised he would have to go through with it. It would be like doing it to a child.

The whore apologised: 'I'm sorry . . . you know . . . if you didn't enjoy it . . . after the fiver and all.'

Eilders was fastening his shirt, the whole thing had been ludicrous.

'It doesn't matter.'

He could still hear the police. Getting his shirt he had peered out of the window, and he could see them gathered in a knot outside a Greek café. Someone had given them mugs of tea and they were drinking and talking among themselves. Damn them, why didn't they go?

The girl put on her coat, and cast a look of impatience at him.

He said suddenly: 'Could I stay all night?'

The girl seemed shocked. She hadn't thought this client was attracted to her, but if there were more fivers . . .

'All night . . . you're sure you want all night?'

The thought was abhorrent to him. 'No, not sex, can I stay here? I have no hotel.'

The girl bit her nails. 'Well, I don't know, where would I bring my men friends?' Her affected gentility sickened him.

'Look, I'll pay you twenty pounds.'

'Twenty quid!' Once more the fire of greed flashed in her eyes.

Mavis was only nineteen years old, and she'd been a prostitute for less than a year, but she knew the oldest maxim of the oldest profession. Milk the punter for all he's got if he's daft enough to let you.

'I couldn't, I mean . . . '

Eilders was desperate, and it was shattering his caution and his instinct. 'Twenty-five.' He took the money out, big white five pound notes, five of them. The girl knew just how long it would take to earn that, how much pawing, grabbing, huffing, puffing and degradation. And this way she could keep it all. Eddie need never see a penny if she played her cards right.

'All right then, love, just while it's you, but you mustn't tell no one.' She took the money and put it somewhere beneath the shawl she had once more wrapped around herself.

'You'll say nothing about me being here?' He had to buy her silence. A prostitute would have a pimp, perhaps a husband or boyfriend, she would be missed too quickly.

'Mum's the word, love. Now you make sure you keep the place clean and lock the door after you when you go in the morning and push the key under the door. I've got a spare.'

She left. Eilders sat down heavily. He had escaped the police for the time being, but things were disintegrating around him. He had failed to kill the old woman and she had betrayed him, he was bribing people to keep silent, spending large sums which must attract attention.

He put his head in his hands wearily, then looked up, determined not to fall victim to defeatism.

There were things to be done. He went to the sink. The old woman must have given them a description, so the beard must go. He rummaged in a toilet bag hanging from a tap, and found a battered razor which he concluded the whore must use to shave her legs. He put carbolic soap on his face and tried to work it into a lather. Then he shaved slowly and carefully, anxious not to cut himself. Then he cleaned the sink, tore the useless identity card into tiny pieces and washed them down the sink.

Then he lay down on the bed fully-clothed, and slept. Uwe Eilders was exhausted.

The fat man in the camel-haired overcoat stepped out of the shadows, and the thin girl jumped.

'Good God, Eddie, you nearly gave me a heart attack.'

'Early night, Mavis, I thought it was all blood, toil, tears and sweat, what happened to your contribution?'

'I've done my quota.'

'It's only eleven, Mavis.'

The girl delved into her shawl and produced some notes which the man took and counted.

'I'm impressed, you must have been going at it like a bloody rabbit? How much did you keep yourself?'

'Just the usual, Eddie, honest.'

The fat man smiled at her, and she shivered. Last week he'd cut one of the girls who held out on him and they said she'd never work again.

Quickly, she said: 'Oh, I forgot.' She delved and produced more notes.

He took them, counted, and handed her one back. 'Next time don't tell fibs.'

'Sorry, Eddie. I've been so busy, sometimes you lose track.'

The man was engrossed in one of the notes, peering at it under the thin glow from a basement club.

'You get these fivers from different punters?'

'Yes,' she lied quickly.

He took another one, and walked down several steps to get more light.

When he came back up his voice was dangerous.

'Are you sure about that?'

Her voice shook: 'Oh, all right, where's the harm. A bloke give me twenty quid to doss down in the flat, no harm in it.

197

The bobbies was out in force tonight and I think he didn't want to bump into them.'

'I'll bet he didn't. Open your mouth, Mavis.'

'What?'

'Open your bloody mouth before I carve an extra couple of inches onto it.'

The girl opened her mouth. The man crumpled one five pound note into a ball and pushed it between her teeth. With both hands he viciously clamped her jaw shut.

'Now chew.' The girl chewed.

'I'm not surprised he's dodging the bobbies. These fivers are forgeries. They're not even good ones. I was in the business once and I know. Look at Britannia, that's always the hard bit, and on this she looks like the bloody Mona Lisa.'

She said thickly: 'I didn't know, Eddie, honest to God. What are you going to do?'

'He's at the gaff, definite?'

She nodded, not daring to spit out the note.

'Well, I don't mind a bit of law-breaking, just as long as I'm not on the losing side. What do you do when you need a policeman urgently, Mavis?'

'Dial Nine-Nine-Nine.' The girl said through a mouthful of currency.

'Exactly.'

Eilders was dreaming that he was tied to a rack in a torture chamber. His torturers were leaning over him, he could even smell their foul breath. They were shouting to him in English. 'On your bloody feet. Move!' The nightmare became reality. He came plummeting upwards from the depths of exhaustion staring into two faces both of whom wore trilby hats.

'Police officers, come on, sunshine, on your feet, wakey-wakey. Identity card, ration book.'

He stood up shakily, the reality finally permeating through the shock of the sudden awakening. He was caught, after everything, he was caught!

'I . . . I lost my papers . . . I was going to report it to the police.'

'Lost 'em did you . . . ?' The smaller, weasel-like man smiled hideously. 'It's a bit early in the morning for fairy stories, son.'

First rule of escape from capture. The first few moments are vital, after that it becomes practically and psychologically more difficult to make the break.

'It's true, I was going to report . . . ' he lunged at the bigger man, crashing the side of his hand into the man's solar plexus. The man gasped and began to crumple. The smaller one grabbed his arm, but Eilders chopped him, and went for the door handle. He pulled at it but the door refused to open. There was a big metal key and Eilders scrabbled at it, trying to unlock the door. Then something hit him very hard on the back of his neck and he felt his legs buckle. Then there was another blow on the same spot and the pain lanced through him. A voice from very far away said between gasps for breath: 'You're under arrest . . . don't have to say anything . . . 'less you wish to do so . . . anything you do say may be taken down and used in evidence against you.' Then the small weasel-like man swore and kicked Eilders in the ribs.

There was a hollow ringing in his ears, and as he looked up, the two men began to recede like figures at the wrong end of a telescope. His last thought before unconsciousness was: I failed.

Weasel squinted, reaching forward to type with two fingers: his arm hurt like hell and now he had to write up all this bumf, what a waste of bloody time.

At last he finished and slid the flimsy out of the battered black Imperial: 'Why this on top of the normal skip? We don't normally send copies down to the Yard.'

The sergeant stubbed out his cigarette and took the flimsy, scanning it: 'New rules, anyone without proper identity we have to send a description and details of arrest up to Murder Squad at the Yard, bugger me why, I think they've got a big job on . . . that Belgravia business perhaps, God only knows.'

He grunted satisfaction with the information on the sheet, lifted a heavy lead Buddha paperweight off a pile of papers in the 'Out' tray and put the sheet on top of the pile.

He toyed with the Buddha, as though it might help his reflective mood. 'It's the war; it is, it's the bloody war, paperwork, paperwork, you can't catch villains now until your paperwork's up-to-date.'

Weasel nodded at the flimsy in the 'Out' tray. 'This Yard business anything to do with all bloody uniform being on the streets tonight?'

The sergeant shook his head: 'Naw . . . some bloody bloke called Archer . . . ' He laughed. 'Wonder what he did, fiddle his ration books?'

Weasel laughed. He always laughed at the sergeant's jokes. 'We having a look at chummy again tonight, Sarge?'

'Naw . . . ' he scratched a thumbnail down the Lord God Buddha's ample stomach . . . 'Let him stew in his own juice. He'll cough tomorrow. Fancy a drink down Nick the Greek's?'

Weasel's eyes brightened. There was a new girl in at Nick's, from Bristol she was. Weasel fancied his chances there, and he wasn't paying for it, that was for certain sure.

'If you like, Sarge,' he said, casually as he could.

'Right then . . . ' the sergeant looked at his watch. It was 2.15 a.m. He tossed the paperweight carelessly in the direction of the 'Out' tray, and it rolled off onto the desk with an initial dull thud. The two men went out, weasel slamming the office door hard behind him. The draught lifted the flimsy and it fluttered slowly to the floor like a falling autumn leaf.

In the next three and three-quarter hours it was tramped on by at least four night-shift detectives who left big boot print marks on the blank side which faced upwards.

When the cleaning lady came in at 6 a.m. she cleared it with the rest of the debris into a large sack. The first detective on the day shift cleared the 'Out' tray and put the Buddha back on top of the now empty tray.

Chapter Nineteen

THE ARRESTED man was punched, kicked, spat at, reviled, insulted, his flesh gouged, pinched, then he was kicked and punched again. There was never a moment's rest. He was pushed into a stark, empty cell and told to strip. If he hesitated his clothes were ripped from him until he stood naked, shivering before his captors. There was no hard man and soft man, no carrot and stick, just stick.

Questions were hurled at him with verbal ferocity. Why had he committed the crime, he need not deny it, they knew he was guilty. Come on, answer! The prisoner's head would spin, but any hesitation or discrepancy in whatever he chose to say was punished by a beating and the promise of unspeakable tortures if he continued to lie.

The bestiality was not casual, it was designed to remove the prisoner totally from civilisation and hurl him into a primeval world of terror. Its total aim was to strip him of any dignity or belief he might have in justice or fair play. He was deliberately reduced to a naked, helpless animal whose life was worthless and with whom his captors could do what they wished. His existence had ceased to be of consequence and he was made to realise that. Once he did, then he said whatever his captors wished him to say. If they wished information he gave it, if he was stubborn then he was tortured, and that rarely failed, and only with the death of the prisoner, for there was apparatus against which a man could not hold out.

As he lay on his cell bunk, warm and adequately fed, Eilders reflected that the British had learned no lessons from German police methods of the past seven years.

They simply failed to even try to terrorise their prisoners, and therein lay their biggest mistake. The first detective had hit him with a cosh twice to stop him escaping, and the thin, rodent-like one had kicked him in anger. But from then on, no one had treated him other than correctly. He had been charged on his arrival at the police station with uttering a false document, namely a Bank of England five pound note, and he was listed as 'A.N. Other' and 'of no fixed abode'.

Then he had been pushed into a cell after being made to surrender his tie and shoelaces (presumably in case he tried to hang himself) and then he had been left alone.

He could scarcely believe his good luck for he realised that his captors did not know who they had taken prisoner. He had been arrested as a passer of forged currency. And for that he cursed to damnation his paymasters in Germany. Eilders knew, as anyone in Germany's secret services did, that experiments in counterfeiting British pounds sterling were taking place at Sachsenhausen concentration camp under Major Bernhard Kruger. The project was named Operation Bernhard, and used prisoners who had been printers and engravers in civilian life. The aim was to perfect notes for use in paying agents in neutral countries. There was wild talk of one day flooding Britain with the notes to collapse the economy, but that was way off in the future. It was obvious that accidentally or by design his paymasters had included a batch of forged five pound notes in his supply of money.

He could not believe that Heydrich or anyone from the SD would deliberately prejudice his mission by including forged notes. However, the money would initially have to be drawn from the Reichsbank. As foreign currency was so precious, it was possible that an ambitious official had used this opportunity both to save the Reich currency and test the efficiency of the forged notes from Sachsenhausen.

The other alternative was that whatever traitor had later sabotaged his mission with the Fuehrer had deliberately made sure he was issued with easily identifiable forgeries.

That was all academic now. He was a prisoner of the British—who did not know, yet, that he was the man for whom they had been hunting. The longer he was held, the less likely that fortuitous state of affairs was to last. Time was therefore vital. He understood the British police had to present a suspect to a court of law within forty-eight hours of his arrest, otherwise a lawyer could apply for a writ of habeus corpus. The wartime regulations could have changed all that, and if the detectives decided to bend the rules there was little he could do.

But assuming he was taken to a court, that was the moment he must try and escape. For after that he would be remanded to a prison and brought back periodically to the court. While in prison he would almost certainly be interrogated, perhaps even by intelligence officers because of his lack of identity papers. That fact might be referred to some central bureau which was hunting Jan Villen Ter Braak and 'Mr Archer'.

Eilders did not think he would last very long with the spy-catchers. If there was the slightest suspicion that he was their man, then they might torture him. The British were not known to torture, at least scientifically, but in Eilders' view special secret service departments made up their own rules. After that, of course, he was finished. No one could stand up to torture, they could only die. The British would win and he would lose.

But that was in the future: for now, as far as he knew he was unknown and must escape as soon as it was feasible.

He had checked outside the tiny window at the top of his cell. The window was barred from the outside, and beyond it was a cobbled courtyard bounded by buildings on three sides and a large green double gate, twice the height of a man, at the third. There was no way out of the cell by the window, and the door was heavy steel. Inside the cell was a flat jug with two handles which he was supposed to use for all his toilet requirements, so there were not even visits to the lavatory during which he could make a break for it. His food—such as it was—was brought into the cell on a tray.

While one officer set the tray down, another guarded the door. Escape was impossible there too. Soon the detectives would be back and he must stick to his story, or lack of it, just long enough to be taken to court. Only then could there be any hope of escape.

The cell door opened and a uniformed officer let in the two detectives who had arrested Eilders.

'Hello, mystery man.'

Eilders remained silent. He noticed that the weasel-like detective was still rubbing his arm where Eilders had chopped at it with the flattened ridge of his hand.

One man sat on the bunk, Weasel put his back against the door. 'Want to talk?' It was the sergeant.

Eilders remained silent.

'You're in deep lumber, my old son, you've sussed that, have you?'

Weasel said: 'Now where would a nice lad like you get his hands on over a hundred quids' worth of forged fivers?'

Eilders said: 'I won them gambling.'

The sergeant raised his eyebrows: 'It walks, it talks, it even pees.'

Weasel grimaced: 'Stone me, son, you won't learn will you?'

The sergeant came up and put an arm around Eilders' shoulders, the man smelled of stale sweat and last night's whisky.

'Look son, do you really want to do a five stretch? Cause that's where you're heading, on my mother's life. You give that tart twenty-five quid . . . *twenty-five quid* just to doss down for the night. Blimey O'Reilly, you could have had a suite at the Ritz for that. But of course, they don't like funny money there, do they?' He pressed his face inches from Eilders' eyes, unblinking.

'Maybe he likes dossing in whores' boudoirs,' Weasel laughed.

'I would say, from my long, exciting experience with the criminal classes, that you was running my son, running like a rabbit with a banger up its arse. And now you're going to tell

204

us where you picked up these forged fivers,' the sergeant grimaced, 'assuming naturally that you're not making them yourself.'

Weasel came away from the door: 'Running, with no ration books, no identity card, with a bankroll Hitler himself could've forged, and nothing to tell us you couldn't even be a bloody German spy. Oh dear, oh dear,' Weasel shook his head: 'And lo and behold when we disturb your beauty sleep, you turn all Joe Louis.'

'You'd agree, that those facts as related by my colleague do not, under any circumstances, make you Snow White who won a bundle off the Seven Dwarfs, now do they?'

Eilders kept silence.

'That could be it, Sarge,' Weasel said, 'he could be a German spy.'

His colleague said: 'That's very possible . . . you know what we do with German spies, mystery man, we hang 'em, don't we, Eric?'

Weasel lifted his tie until it was a hangman's rope, and made his tongue protrude.

Eilders spoke, carefully in practised argot.

'You're not fitting me up for that bleeding nonsense. Do I look like a bleeding German spy? It's like I said when I first got in here, I went up West for a poker game. I won a bundle, and then I had this tart, I wasn't to know it was dodgy stuff. Maybe it was the tart who nicked me papers, I had 'em when I went up West.'

Weasel said sarcastically: 'Well, it's talking again, Sarge, that's an improvement.' He looked scathingly at Eilders. 'It wasn't the tart who nicked your papers, sunshine, because it was *her* who bloody told us you was passing funny money. And if she did, how come she didn't nick all your money?'

His colleague prodded Eilders in the chest. Maybe now the rough stuff would start.

'And anyway, you didn't *have* the tart, did you, she told us that, you couldn't even get a bleeding hard on.'

Both men laughed, enjoying it. 'Not exactly Rudolf Valentino is he, Eric?' Both men guffawed.

205

Eilders was happy, despite the insults. The men thought they had him, but they did not know what or who they had, and they did not have him.

The word came up, deep from his subconscious. 'When do I go up before the beak?' It was the slang word for magistrate.

The sergeant said: 'I shouldn't worry if I was you, you won't be getting bail, that's for sure, but as it happens, you'll make a first appearance and remand in custody, mark my words, tomorrow morning.'

Eilders smiled inwardly, that was good news.

The sergeant went on: 'After that you'll be banged up in Brixton for a week or two while we have a look at your Mickey Mouse money. It's far too comfy here; a couple of weeks in Brixton you'll develop verbal diarrhoea, am I right, Eric?'

'We'll have difficulty shutting you up, son.'

'And if the Jerry bombers come you'll have nowhere to run. Just wait until that poison gas comes floating in your cell, and you start choking and throwing your lungs up. Cor blimey you'll be in a state.'

The sergeant got up: 'You think on what we've said, son. You could save yourself an awful lot of trouble.'

The two men left the cell.

Eilders was astonished. It was hardly credible, but they had made no serious attempt to either threaten or use violence against him.

A beating up would not have sufficed, he could withstand that, but a little knowledge of testicle shock applied skilfully would have worked. He had seen it done, and knew that under normal circumstances it could not be resisted for very long. The British were really very strange; weak, sentimental, randomly cruel and yet not prepared to use their capacity for cruelty in any organised or scientific way.

It would certainly lose them the war, and it would help him, Uwe Eilders, to escape and kill the princesses. Once more he was full of confidence and hope. Tomorrow he would escape from either the courtroom or the vehicle taking him to prison. He lay down on the hard bunk mattress to plan.

He was handcuffed with his hands in front of him, another mistake; to really restrict freedom of movement the hands should be *behind* the body as Eilders knew the American police forces put them.

He was taken in a police car flanked by the two arresting officers and deposited in a cell beneath the courtroom. Then he was re-handcuffed and led up a stone stairway into the dock. Two men and one woman, in civilian clothes with no trappings of office, sat behind a long, raised polished-wood bench. Behind them there was a coat of arms and a motto in French *Dieu et mon droit*—God and my right. Amusing, Eilders thought, that the British should use French to justify their legal system.

A uniformed officer in the well of the court told the civilian magistrates the circumstances of the arrest, the general nature of the charge, and the information that many more enquiries had to be made. The officer asked that the prisoner be remanded in custody. The woman sitting between the two men asked Eilders if he wished to make any statement or to apply for bail. Eilders simply shook his head, and the detectives on either side of him tried to suppress their smiles.

The woman with the upper-class voice then told Eilders he would be remanded in custody for seven days when he would re-appear at that court. He was then taken back down the stone steps.

A man sitting at a long desk facing the magistrates got up, made the suggestion of a bow, shoved a notebook in his pocket and left the courtroom.

He found a small cubicle which smelled of tobacco, and picked up the receiver of the black telephone which sat on a small stand beneath a sign saying 'Press Only'.

Weasel said: 'We'll be saying goodbye for a while.' He

207

turned a key and released the handcuffs. Eilders rubbed his wrists gingerly. Immediately a man in dark blue uniform with the gold letters HMP on the epaulettes came up and produced another set of handcuffs.

'Aw,' Weasel said, 'such a short period of freedom.'

The prison officer put the fresh handcuffs on Eilders and the detectives went away.

'You'll be off in a couple of minutes,' the gaoler told him, 'just got to get the mad blackout rapist down from upstairs and we'll have you both in the van and banged up in an hour.'

It was time to start. Eilders said: 'Can I go to the lavatory?'

The man's eyes flickered suspiciously: 'Yeah, but no funny tricks. The bars on the bog here are an inch thick.'

He led the handcuffed prisoner down a small corridor and into a room marked 'Gentlemen'. He pointed to a urinal. 'Help yourself.'

Eilders thrust his handcuffed hands in the direction of a cubicle: 'It's a big job.'

The officer shrugged. 'Be my guest—but don't be all day.'

'Aren't you going to take these off?'

The prison officer laughed heartily: 'You must be joking. If you need any help unbuttoning your trousers I'll oblige, after that you're on your own. If you can't wipe your arse, don't fret, you'll be having a good bath when you get to Brixton, *and* a haircut.' Eilders went into the cubicle.

The prison officer said: 'You can push the door to, but don't try and lock it, and that's the last bit of privacy you'll be getting for a few years, my lad.'

Eilders pushed the door closed. He lowered the toilet seat with a bang, waited a few seconds, then made a series of grunting noises, followed by a loud sigh. He could hear the gaoler's footsteps. The cistern was lofted high, but luckily the cubicle door was tall too. He could see that a linked chain with a pull-ring handle operated the flush system. Eilders reached up and felt the link where it joined with the flush lever protruding from the cistern tank. As he suspected, the metal was extremely soft. With his handcuffed hands he stretched up and pulled at the link, trying, at the same time,

208

to keep the flush lever steady so it did not flush prematurely.

The gaoler's footsteps stopped. 'Come on, don't be all bloody day in there. Get on with it.'

'All right.'

The link parted. Eilders pushed with both thumbs and index fingers, desperately trying to enlarge the gap so he could slip the chain from the flush lever.

He heard the footsteps start up again and move closer to the door. 'I said don't make a bloody meal of it, now move yourself.'

The chain came away, almost slipped from Eilders' grasp, but he held on, and at the same time pushed down with both hands on the flush lever.

Carefully he eased the chain link by link into his cupped hands, and then stretched across to tuck it into the right hand pocket of his trousers. He pulled his jacket across and fastened it on both buttons, desperately hoping it would hide the bulge.

He left the cubicle as quickly as he could, hoping the officer would not check it.

The man said: 'Done?' Eilders nodded.

'Well about bloody time. I think your travelling companion will be just about ready.'

Ulrich answered the telephone and said: 'No, but I'll get him.' He called through the open door and Jones came in, holding a cup of tea in one hand and a half-smoked Senior Service in the other. His eyes were haggard and bloodshot.

'Who is it?'

'Algy? That's all he said.'

Jones grimaced and said almost to himself: 'Pain in the bloody arse.' He picked up the receiver and exclaimed gaily: 'Hello Algy old son, how's tricks in Fleet Street?'

He listened for a while, and at length said, 'I'm obliged to you, Algy. Of course we'll take a look, it's very public spirited of you. The chances are against it, naturally, but—'
He listened again, pulling his face into a grimace: 'Of course,

mate, you *are* a member of the public, even if you are a reporter too. If it *is* him you'll get the reward: don't fret.'

He replaced the receiver: 'Avaricious little muck-raking bastard.' Ulrich gave Harry Jones a quizzical look.

'A court reporter, I've used him a few times when I needed press coverage. He's just covered a case, a remand in custody, some bloke nicked in the early hours of yesterday morning with a bundle of forged fivers on him.'

Ulrich went icy cold. Forged money! Surely it was not possible? He knew what was going on in Sachsenhausen, and what the money was for, but surely no one would have been so stupid as to give an SD agent forged money . . . to bring to England! The money just wasn't good enough. He tried to make himself relax. Every country had its counterfeiters; Britain would be no exception. And the arrested man's papers would have been checked, unless . . . ?

'Did he have papers, Harry?'

'No, nothing. They found him in some tart's bedroom . . . ' Harry Jones nodded towards the latest arrest reports which had been sent up to the office. 'I don't recall anything about anyone caught passing forged money and with no papers. Do you?'

Ulrich ran a hand through the latest sheets. 'No, nothing.'

Harry Jones scratched his head. 'Strange that. Wonder why we didn't get a report.'

'Does he fit our description?'

Jones stubbed out the half-smoked cigarette: 'Algy's not so hot on descriptions for a man who spends his life describing things. It's not promising, no one of Eilders' calibre is going to carry around a bundle of funny money. Germany's not short of cash is it, Ulrich? Not printing your own now are you?'

Ulrich smiled weakly. He could not tell Jones about Operation Bernhard, but it made him anxious to see the man of whom the court reporter spoke.

'Let's check him out, Harry,' he said as casually as he could.

'Why not, he's not going anywhere, that's for sure. Grab your coat and let's pop up to Marlborough Street Mags.'

'Mags?' Ulrich was puzzled.

'Magistrates . . . mags . . . Magistrates . . . get it?'

Ulrich said he got it. But what a strange language English was.

The uniformed prison officer said: 'What's his name?'

'Identity not established, no papers.'

The officer looked down his list: 'Here he is, A.N. Other. Van left about five minutes ago. Brixton.'

Jones swore.

'Which route does the van normally take?'

The officer shook his head: 'I don't give out that kind of information, mate, not even to you.'

Jones produced his buff-coloured envelope and showed the officer the contents. The man went white. 'And I promise you it'll go badly with you if you mess me about.'

'Down to Chelsea Bridge via Belgravia, up through Battersea past the park, up to Clapham Common, along the High Street, through to Brixton Hill, turn right and then Bob's your uncle.'

'Ta . . . you've been a great help.' Jones laid the sarcasm on with a trowel.

The officer said peevishly, anxious to regain his lost pride: 'You can wave that paper all you like, he'll not stop for you, not on a public road.'

Jones turned to Ulrich: 'That's how we're winning the war —all pulling together, one united effort of teamwork.'

Chapter Twenty

INSIDE THE blue prison van, four compartments which were little more than cupboards had been installed to take prisoners. Each was fitted with its own metal door which had a grille and a lock.

The alleged rapist was put in the compartment nearest the partition which separated the driver and his mate, and Eilders got the next but one towards the back doors.

The officers left both prisoners handcuffed and locked each in his cell.

Two got into the front of the van and one stayed in the narrow corridor outside the 'cells'.

Eilders felt a jerk, and the van moved off.

There was a tiny window on the outside of each compartment—too small to climb through—and he tried to keep track of the journey.

He recognised Belgravia, then what he thought was probably Sloane Square, with a small fountain playing in the sunshine.

Marching soldiers on a parade ground, a man in red drilling them, his voice reaching even into the moving van. Then a bridge, water below them, the Thames obviously, and across on the opposite bank trees, greenery, a park of some kind. Eilders estimated they must be almost halfway to the prison, and he must act soon.

He put his back to the compartment door, so that no view would be presented to the guard if he chose to peer through the grille at that moment. He pulled out the lavatory chain, and wrapped the ends around both hands.

His freedom of movement with the garrotte was restricted because of the handcuffs, and you needed both hands free to use it properly, but there was no choice. He would have to work swiftly. There would be one chance to get the chain around the man's neck and if he failed it would be his last chance of escape.

He lay down, doubled up, face downwards in the cramped compartment and gave a loud cry of anguish, then another. He started to make choking noises.

The muffled voice of the guard: 'What's wrong?'

'My heart, God . . . I'm dying.' He heard the bite of the key in the lock, and a scraping noise as the door opened.

'Come on, chum, what's the bloody game?'

Eilders twisted his face up, contorted in make-believe agony. 'I'm having an attack, you've got to get me to hospital.'

The guard's response was to kick him viciously in the leg: 'Pull the other one, son, it's got bloody bells on.'

Eilders ignored the searing pain. 'Please . . . I'm dying . . . aaahh . . . '

He slumped forward, prone and seemingly unconscious.

'Come on, this is not a panto, on your feet.' The prison officer kicked him again, hard, in the leg. Eilders remained motionless.

'If you're playing silly buggers, mate, you'll be for it.'

He kneeled over Eilders and tried to turn him over. Eilders let himself be turned, then struck out with two fists in a short, fast and vicious blow to the man's face.

The man reeled. Eilders pivoted his body like a wrestler and threw the man sideways, trying to get him face down. The man put an arm down instinctively to take his weight, but Eilders saw an opening, and jabbed his knee sideways into the man's groin and he crumpled.

In a flash Eilders had the short length of chain around his neck and strangled him.

He put his two hands under the man's body, feeling for the

213

bunch of keys attached to a gold-coloured chain fastened to the belt. He found it and gave a sharp tug. There was a tearing sound but the chain wouldn't come, so he pulled again and felt it rip free. He grabbed the bunch of keys . . . twelve or more! What would he need all those for, and which was the one that would fit the rear doors of the van?

But first he had to get out of the handcuffs. He found three of the same type, the type he felt sure had been used to lock him into the handcuffs.

He tried the first, but it didn't work.

The van was slowing.

He tried the second. It didn't work either.

The van stopped.

Eilders held his breath. Had they heard the commotion up front?

He tried the third key quietly, and as one bracelet came free, he quickly unleashed the other.

The van jerked forward, and he fell off balance. The van was gathering speed.

He went cold as he heard a voice. It was the prisoner from the other cell. 'Come on, mate, I know what's going on. Unlock me, I want out too.'

Eilders hissed: 'Be quiet!'

The prisoner lowered his voice, but only to say: 'Oh I'll be quiet, mate, just as long as you open this door in two seconds flat. If you don't I'm gonna yell so hard they'll hear me in Brighton.'

Eilders cursed, and moved to the cell door. He searched through the keys, fitting them into the lock one after the other.

If the man called out, the prison officers in the front of the van would discover him before he could get the back doors open.

At last the compartment door swung open. The man had a pencil-thin moustache and looked the type the English called a lounge lizard. Why had he found it necessary to rape?

Eilders smiled at him: 'Come on, we have no time to lose.'

The man pushed past Eilders, eager to be free.

In a second he was choking, the metal biting into his windpipe. In thirty seconds he was dead. Eilders climbed over his body. Damn the man for eating up precious seconds.

He could feel the van slowing, as though on an incline, and moved quickly to the van's rear doors. He checked the remaining keys, careful to use none he had already eliminated. He poked one after the other into the back door lock, and none of the damn keys worked! The van was slowing even more. Eilders slowed his actions, patiently trying the keys again, one after the other, inserting them gently in the lock. If one snapped off he was finished. At last he felt the springs give, and the door opened. The van was doing just a few kilometres an hour.

Eilders saw a blur of things, a tarmac road, a van behind them, a man's surprised face behind the steering wheel. Then Eilders leaped, rolling away from the pursuing van's wheels, and then he was up, onto his feet and running, running.

The black Wolseley driven by Harry Jones crossed Chelsea Bridge and went on past Battersea Park. He was driving fast, and there was a slight squeal of tyres as he took a roundabout, then a traffic light on green, then they sped under a railway bridge, and swept into a right-hand bend.

The bend swung left, and the road became straight and long, lined on either side by terrace houses. Ulrich pointed, finger jabbing at the windscreen: 'There!'

Up ahead, a couple of hundred yards away, the unmistakable dark-blue shape of the prison van.

Harry put his foot down even harder.

Ulrich could feel a tightening sensation in the pit of his stomach; if it was Eilders, then there was a job to be done, and how to do it in front of Harry Jones and a bunch of English prison warders?

'Step on the gas, Harry.'

Jones glanced across, raising an eyebrow.

'Where did you learn your bloody English, Hollywood?'

'Well, as a matter of fact we used to watch gangster films,

you know George Raft and James Cagney, then we used to be criticised in language school for our slang.'

'Bloody good job it wasn't George Formby, or even I couldn't understand you.'

They were gaining on the prison van when a baker's van pulled out of a side street ahead of them, and Jones had to brake hard. He blew hard on the Wolseley's horn, and was rewarded by two fingers poked out from the driver's side in a reverse gesture of the one Winston Churchill was turning into the symbol for Victory.

Ulrich said: 'Rude?'

'Yes,' replied Jones tersely.

Jones tried to pull out to pass, but was forced to swerve back to avoid a bus packed with passengers coming the other way.

There were traffic lights up ahead, and the baker's van slowed to a stop behind the prison vehicle.

Jones said: 'After the lights I'll pull him over when he turns left along the Common.'

'The officer said he wouldn't stop for you, or let you see the prisoner.'

'I'll put the bells on, stop the Wolseley in front of him, stick my warrant card against the windscreen, and if that doesn't convince him, he can have a look at the contents of my magic envelope.'

The lights changed and the unwitting convoy moved up the slight incline which led to a second set of traffic lights facing Clapham Common. Just a few hundred yards now, Ulrich thought.

Jones tried again to pass, to get right behind the prison van, but the bread roundsman was in a belligerent mood. He had had a horn sounded at him, rudely, and after that he was going to do his damndest not to let the Wolseley pass. He closed right up to the prison van leaving no gap.

Jones considered using his alarm on the baker, but dismissed it. He could feel the anger rising in him and tried to suppress it; save that for the German, if it's him. He drummed his fingers impatiently on the steering wheel.

They were a hundred yards from the lights, crawling up the

incline . . . then there was a man, darting across the road to their right. The baker's van braked, and Jones stepped on his to avoid a collision. The man was narrowly missed by a motor-cycle and side-car combination, which swerved violently to avoid him, but he kept on running.

Jones said: 'Bloody fool's asking to get killed.'

Ulrich shouted at the top of his voice: 'Jesus Christ, it's him!'

Jones shoved the Wolseley into first gear, spun the wheel sharp right and tried to turn. He clipped the baker's van, and there was the scream of a horn as a three-ton Army truck coming the other way whooshed past them, rocking the car with its slipstream. The Wolseley stalled.

Ulrich shouted: 'I'll get him.' Then he was out of the car and running.

Jones swore savagely, turned the key and pressed the starter button. The baker's van had moved off and the driver was sounding his horn to alert the drivers of the prison van. Jones got the car started, saw a narrow gap in the oncoming traffic and screeched the Wolseley into a turn. The turning circle was bad, and he mounted the pavement with a loud bump, scraped a lamp-post and came down back into the road. There was the blaring of a horn, a crash of metal, and his car shot forward under the impetus of a rear-end collision.

He didn't even *think* of stopping.

Ahead on the pavement, several hundred yards away, was the running figure, and crossing the road, halfway behind him, Ulrich. The arms of both men were pumping like sprint athletes.

Jones gunned the car forward. The first man disappeared from view. Jones slowed, eyes darting from side to side, trying to pick him up again.

Then Jones saw Ulrich spurt left and disappear from view. It was a side alley. Jones gunned the car, swung out to the right then turned left, sharply, into the alley.

He could see the alley was narrow, and he used the car's wing mirrors as cats' whiskers to judge his width. As the bonnet nosed in the mirrors snapped off with a twang.

Just!

Ahead he could see only Ulrich. Jones realised his hands were glistening with sweat, and he gripped the steering wheel tighter until his knuckles showed white. Ulrich disappeared left again, and Jones followed, but these alleys had not been built for motor cars. As he threw the Wolseley left there was a long, angry scrape of metal, then a loud bang as he clipped a metal dustbin protruding from a back doorway. The dustbin rolled ahead under the impact, then the car hit it again, and it bounced; again, another bounce, and then there was a booming metallic noise. Jones had to keep going, and he struck the dustbin again, but it stuck, jammed into the radiator and metal front bumper bar.

Jones slammed his foot hard down on the accelerator hoping speed and movement would clear the obstacle. There was a spine-scratching scraping sound, and a shower of sparks as metal chafed stones, and the dustbin was pushed protesting along the cobbles.

It felt like driving a bulldozer, when suddenly the car bonnet seemed to lift, and Jones' vision was obscured by a large shape which slammed into the windscreen. The glass became a spiders-web, he was driving blind. He stamped on the brake, there was another scrape of anguished metal, then a loud bang, and the car stopped, throwing his head forward into the glass and his chest into the steering wheel.

Jones opened his eyes and immediately regretted it. The pain was blinding. He put his hand up to his forehead, felt it go wet, and when he brought it down to look at it saw blood. His chest ached like hell. Groggily he squeezed himself out of the car and along past the crumpled bonnet of the Wolseley.

A woman, her hair in curlers, was standing at her backyard door looking at him.

She said: 'Are you all right? You're not supposed to bring motorcars along the entries, you know.'

Jones wiped more blood from his head, it was threatening to get in his eyes.

'Two men, running, which way did they go?'

'The two men . . . ?' She pointed. 'Up there and then across Suvla Street, I think . . . Shall I call the police?'

He staggered past her, trying for a trot at the least: 'I am the bloody police.' He was running like a drunken man. And too old for this game, love.

Ulrich von der Osten wished passionately that the British had issued him with a revolver. Pistols were notoriously in-accurate, but not over short distances if you knew how to use them, and Ulrich did. He had been close enough to put Uwe Eilders on the floor since he'd turned into the alley. But he was unarmed and the man he hated was still alive and running, his lead shortened though not by much. He had known it was Eilders the moment he had seen the man running, so now Ulrich was tireless, indomitable. However long it took he would catch Eilders and kill him. He pounded on, and the alley opened into a street. Eilders ran across it without even checking for traffic, but it was a quiet residential street with just two small children playing on the cobbles who looked up as the man passed.

They were in another alley now, similarly cobbled, and with what looked to be a flat drainage channel, in concrete and set with small grids at intervals, running down the centre of the alley. On either side were brick walls, some crumbling with age, others bowed out as though ready to collapse. Set in the walls every ten yards or so were faded wooden doors which would give access to the backyards of the houses.

Up ahead Ulrich saw a man and a woman, arm in arm, moving aside to let the running man past.

Ulrich shouted: 'Stop him! Stop that man!'

But the couple merely watched in astonishment as Eilders ran by them, making no move to stop him, then gawped at Ulrich as he pounded by.

Ulrich knew that Eilders could not know by whom he was being chased. He had only glanced back, and was surely too far away to identify Ulrich. So he must assume that his pursuer would lose motivation, would tire and give up the

219

chase. And Eilders was not running blind and terrified like a stricken fox before the hounds, he was obviously thinking, keeping away from the main streets where a running man might start a hue and cry. Instead he was keeping to the back alleys and narrow streets, hoping to lose his pursuer in this working-class maze.

But there was no chance of that, none at all. Ulrich intended to stay with him until he closed, or until Eilders dropped from exhaustion.

At first it was hardly noticeable, but the gap between the two men was narrowing. Ulrich felt a surge of savage triumph and he risked his tortured lungs.

'Eilders!'

Eilders half-turned, almost stumbled, then carried on running hard. Ulrich felt the deep anger that had waited years fuelling his breaths. It was just he and Eilders now. Jones was an old man and was far behind. There was no one who could prevent Ulrich from disposing of Eilders when he caught him. He would gain both revenge and the satisfaction of having saved Germany from international calumny due to the actions of a madman.

For a brief moment he thought of Ilse.

'Eilders!' The running man did not turn.

Up ahead two alleys abruptly joined the one down which the two men were running, and Eilders heistated for a fraction of a second, then darted to his right. Ulrich followed and gave an exclamation of triumph. It was a dead end; Eilders had made a mistake. Up ahead was a brick wall with just a wooden door set into it.

He saw Eilders rattling at the door latch furiously.

Ulrich kicked and accelerated. Eilders stepped backwards and leaped for the wall, fingertips grasping for a hold. Ulrich was closing.

Eilders scrabbled for a purchase on the rough brick. Ulrich was ten feet away. He saw two shoes, black and shiny, scraping slowly up the wall.

220

Ulrich dived.

The feet were gone and he crashed heavily into the wall. He cursed: '*Ach du Scheisse.*' He heard a crash of breaking glass and wood. Maybe the fall had injured Eilders.

Ulrich's lungs were on fire, but he stepped back and flung himself for the top of the wall. His fingertips burned as they caught, but he held on. With all the power of his arms, his feet scraping for a foothold, he clawed his way up the wall.

He straddled it with his right leg, eyes searching for Eilders, and seeing nothing. Then Ulrich was over, vaulting to the ground below.

He lost his balance as he landed, and felt the gritty crunch of already broken glass.

Then his head exploded from a blow which shot stars and fireworks in front of his eyes. He tried to get up but something hit him in the kidneys and the pain was so fierce he cried out.

Eilders had stayed, he was unhurt, he simply stood in the lee of the wall and waited for me to come over! Ulrich knew he must get to his feet before Eilders could use the garrotte. Body protesting he tried to rise, feeling the needles of glass penetrating his clothes and skin. Suddenly the sky was black with something descending. He tried to roll away but the baulk of timber caught him on the upper arm, paralysing a nerve and flooding him with pain.

Then he was hit again in the torso, and the blow seared his ribs and knocked the wind out of him with a whoosh. He was disabled and in agony. He had assumed Eilders was either hurt, or if he wasn't that he would run. That assumption might kill him. If only he had a *gun*! His eyes were slits from the pain which screwed his body into a ball, but above him he saw the face of Uwe Eilders.

In the man's eyes was a kind of yellow hate, a violence-lust which chilled Ulrich, cut cold into him through the white-hot pain.

Instinctively he kicked out with his uninjured leg, anything to keep Eilders far enough away so that he could not close in with the garrotte. He put everything he possessed into the kick, but it met only empty space. He tried to raise himself, but then there was the black shape of the timber again and his ribs were hit by an avalanche of hot coals.

He felt light-headed now, his vision was going, he could hardly feel his legs and there was a pounding in his ears.

He felt another blow, but it was dull, as though it came from far away. He seemed to be sliding away from consciousness, yet through it all he was aware of what was happening to him. He was being beaten to death by a psychopath in a London backyard, and there was nothing he could do about it. Soon the garrotte would be about his neck.

His world started to go black. Where, he wondered, was the Welshman?

Jones was lost, and he was hurting.

He staggered into what he thought was the correct alley and saw an old man in shirt-sleeves, collarless, leaning on the wall of his open backyard door. The man eyed him suspiciously. 'Aye, aye, what's all the bother then?'

'Police-officer-two-men-running-this-way. Where'd they go?'

The man took a pinched cigarette from behind one ear; he seemed in no hurry to answer.

'Where?' Jones screamed it hoarsely.

'They turned right at the bottom,' the man said lazily. 'Can't get nowhere, dead end isn't it? Only Mr Spencer's yard that way.'

We've got him! Exultation flooded through the exhaustion. Rat in a trap. He forced himself on.

From the moment the pursuer shouted, Eilders had been in no doubt. The man was Ulrich von der Osten, and one glance had confirmed it. It would have been fantastic had so much not already happened which he would have thought beyond possibility. Now it all fitted. Canaris' traitors the Abwehr were betraying the Reich, working with the British. They

222

had sent probably the one man who hated him more than any other to try and kill him. But, it would be he, Uwe Eilders, who would do the killing.

He swung the stout timber that he had taken from the shattered cold frame, and slammed it with all his strength into von der Osten's legs. The traitor slumped back, almost unconscious, and Eilders threw down the stave and pulled out the length of lavatory chain, forming it into a garrotte. Then he stepped over the prone figure and knelt to do his killing work.

Jones laboured into the dead-end alley only to find it was empty. Then he heard noises from beyond the end wall, dull thuds and a cry of pain.

He ran, the pain in his side lancing into him like a hot poker.

He shouted at the top of his voice: 'Ulrich!'

There was no question of his climbing the wall, he could try all day and never make it. He rattled the latch on the rotten wooden door, violently, shaking it with all his strength, but it held stubbornly.

Then he heard a man's voice: ' 'Ere, look at my bloody cold frame.'

Jones stepped back and charged the door with his shoulder. A vertical panel splintered, but the lock held. He stepped back and charged again.

Eilders knelt over Ulrich with the garrotte. There was a cry from the alley beyond: 'Ulrich!' There would be other policemen, and prison warders, but there was still time to kill the traitor.

There was a shout from behind him: ' 'Ere, look at my bloody cold frame.'

Eilders turned to see a man advancing down the path. He was dressed in trousers over a long-sleeved vest, and he had an empty saucepan raised menacingly in one hand.

Eilders hesitated one second, then got up and darted past the man, who swung at him harmlessly with the saucepan.

He went in through a door which led through a tiny kitchen, into a long hallway, past stairs and to a front door.

Eilders went two more streets before he saw a bicycle leaning against a wall. It was unlocked. He leaped upon it, and cycled away furiously. It was all downhill, literally, down towards Clapham Junction and Battersea.

He had not killed von der Osten, but there was time for that in the future. He was free once more, free to kill the princesses.

The lock snapped on the third charge. The man with the saucepan advanced angrily on the latest intruder, determined that someone would feel the weight of the receptacle for ruining his cold frame.

Jones gasped out: 'Put it down: police officer.'

The man lowered the saucepan. 'Somebody's going to be summonsed for this lot, that's a promise.'

'Go to a telephone kiosk and call for an ambulance . . . now!'

The man hesitated, then turned and ambled back up the path.

Jones knelt over Ulrich and saw the flickering eyelids. 'You OK, mate?'

Ulrich groaned and opened his eyes. 'It was *him*, Harry, Eilders.'

'I know.'

'Christ, I'm sorry, I had him, and then . . . ' Ulrich doubled and groaned again with the pain.

'Shut up and save your breath. Lie still, there's an ambulance on its way.'

Ulrich opened his eyes again and saw Harry's forehead. 'What happened? Eilders?'

'No . . . careless driving.'

In the ambulance they lay on adjoining bunks. They rode in silence for a while, then Jones heard Ulrich's weak voice, and opened his eyes. 'Harry, why don't the British police have guns, like in Germany, France or America? I don't understand it.'

'We don't need them, that's what we say.'

'You're wrong,' Ulrich croaked, 'you do need them, if we'd had one this afternoon Uwe Eilders would be dead.'

Jones decided to say nothing. There was a deal of logic in Ulrich's reasoning.

Chapter Twenty-One

ULRICH WAS wedged into his chair, and tried not to move a muscle. If he shifted an inch, pain shot through his ribs. His arm hurt like hell, his head throbbed, and his legs felt like jelly. There seemed to be no part of his anatomy that did not cry out for relief. The miracle was that the beating had left him with his bones intact, and without concussion or brain damage.

He looked across at Harry Jones. The man was like some picture-book wounded soldier, a white bandage, lint protruding, wrapped completely around his head. But both men's condition went further than the physical. They had had Eilders within their grasp, physically, for the first time, and they had lost him. Jones felt it raw, on the surface, like a razor slash. It was his police force, his assignment, and everyone concerned had ballsed it up, badly.

With Ulrich it went deeper, like a festering wound. With one ounce of care and caution he would not have charged over the wall without checking that Eilders was not waiting for him. Instead he had given Eilders the opportunity to beat him to death and then strangle him, something only a saucepan-wielding Englishman and a breathless Welsh detective had somehow combined to prevent.

The joint mood of the two men in that room overlooking Boadicea and the Thames was sombre, with anger just waiting to surface, waiting for a target on which to vent itself.

It boded ill for the two men who had just come in. It was

none of Ulrich's business, and he knew they had, by their negligence, helped to almost get him killed, but despite that he felt a flicker of compassion. Harry Jones would be merciless.

'You know why you're here.'

The sergeant and the weasel-like detective nodded.

'Good. Then this won't take long.' Jones pointed at Ulrich. 'This officer was almost killed . . . one prison officer was not as lucky. A dangerous murderer is now at liberty, simply because you two both failed to recognise him, and failed to follow procedure.'

Weasel said: 'We followed procedure, I typed the flimsy myself.'

'Funny it didn't reach our office. And how come you didn't recognise him, don't you study your own Wanted posters?'

Weasel coughed uneasily, and the sergeant started to speak.

'Look, Superintendent, we're working all hours God sends up at West End Central, Eric and me . . . '

'Shut up!' Harry Jones' voice was a bark. 'I'm not interested in your excuses, your *reasons*, your tiredness, your overwork, your wife's bloody piles. That prison officer had a wife and three kids. Put that down on your consciences, it's your fault.' Ulrich stared intently at the desk. Jones was crucifying them.

'You two have spent so long in the West End taking backhanders from the villains and free shags from the tarts you've forgotten what a policeman's job is. You're suspended. The Commissioner wants your resignations on his desk by Wednesday. Now get out.'

Weasel turned to go, but the sergeant stood his ground: 'So we're out, are we? Well, let me tell you something, you jumped up bloody Taff. I've got fifteen years in, and no sheep-shagger from the valleys talks to me like that.'

Jones' fist was a blur, and the sergeant went sprawling. 'Get him out of my sight, and enjoy the war both of you, you're going to be seeing a lot of it.'

* * *

227

Jones opened his desk drawer and handed a package to Ulrich, who gingerly ripped off the brown paper and found himself holding a revolver by the barrel. He winced and pointed it to the floor, quickly.

'Don't worry, it's not loaded. Colt .38. Can you use it?'

'Yes, of course.'

'Good.' Jones took out a small box, spilled some bullets out on to the desk and counted six.

'Plus six rounds. I think under the circumstances I won't make you sign for them. But if you lose any, tell me.'

Ulrich stared in astonishment: 'Six? Is that all I get?'

It is one more than most of our infantrymen have for their Lee Enfields at this precise moment, chum, Jones thought. But said: 'If we meet Eilders again it won't be George Raft stuff, Ulrich, six will do.'

Ulrich pulled the bullets across the table with his cupped hand and slid them into his pocket. 'How about you?'

Jones lifted a similar revolver from the recesses of his desk. 'It goes against my better judgements, but . . . '

'Do you have a holster or something similar?'

'I'm afraid not, tuck it in your pocket, load it when you need it, and for God's sake don't shoot yourself with it.' Jones put his own gun back in his drawer and came out with a bottle of Napoleon brandy.

Ulrich's mouth watered. Brandy was the painkiller he needed at that moment. He said: 'I would have thought such a drink was difficult to come by—from what I've seen.'

Jones winked: 'It's a bribe, from a villain up West. It isn't going to get him anywhere, but this time I took it. Because tonight I intend to retire to my less than penthouse apartment with its view of the Kennington Oval turnstiles and get absolutely mortal pissed.' He lowered his eyes: 'Join me if you want.'

There was something about the man, the look in his eyes, the way he held his body, something that said he did not want to spend the evening alone.

It had been a traumatic day and all Ulrich wished to do was lower himself into a soft bed and drink as much of Jones' brandy as necessary to dull the ache in his bones and his heart. 'What about Eilders? Shouldn't we be doing something?'

Jones looked up, a sort of defeat in his eyes. 'Like what? Like for instance what? Patrol the streets, check the bloody files . . . there's *nothing* we can do, every other copper in London's looking for him, and there's bugger-all we can do.'

Ulrich put his hand out and took the bottle. 'Napoleon cognac, eh? Did you know I was a Prussian, Harry?'

Jones shook his head but his look said he didn't care.

'Well, I am, and the Prussians fought Napoleon at Waterloo. It was Blucher's intervention that saved the English.'

Jones looked up, some animation at last in his face. '*British* actually, boyo . . .'

'Yes, of course. So why don't we join forces again, and this time kick the hell out of Napoleon and his brandy?'

Their eyes met properly for the first time, and held each other's gaze. 'A good idea, Ulrich, a very good idea.'

This Waterloo was a push-over. The brandy was an eighth-of-an-inch left in the bottle and a hint of deep brown in the two brandy glasses.

Ulrich felt physically better. He knew he hurt when he moved, something distant seemed to hint at it, but it was very distant. As the evening had turned into the small hours, Jones had ripped away the pretentious bandages, and the six stitches stood out black against the livid cut and surrounding bruise. His tie was on the back of a chair, his shirt tails were out, and he was fulfilling his early pledge. He was getting mortal.

Their conversation had been neutral, friendly, but skirting areas of possible danger or conflict. Harry Jones looked up from his glass. 'Ask you a personal question, don't answer if you don't want?'

'Yes, ask me.'

'If we let you go back to Germany . . . ' he corrected himself quickly . . . '*when* you go back to Germany, will you tell them what you've seen? Will you?'

Ulrich met his gaze, both men were drunk, at that stage when the inhibitions are gone and the embarrassing questions are asked. But this was not two cronies drinking in a bar in Krefeld or a pub in Cardiff, it was two enemies flung together for a brief but common purpose. Ulrich liked the man, but . . . 'Well, what would you do in my position, Harry. Be honest?'

Harry Jones finished his brandy. 'Cough the bloody lot, mate. And so will you.'

Ulrich drank his own brandy. 'But I won't be allowed to go back, will I, despite all your promises. You asked me a question, let me ask you one. Have you orders to kill me, or has someone, when this is over?'

Jones looked genuinely shocked. 'Come off it, man, this isn't Chicago, nor Berlin, we don't do things that way.'

Ulrich shook his head, cynically. 'But the Isle of Man perhaps, that's where you keep your internees, isn't it?'

Jones went red. 'It's not up to me . . . but if you want my opinion I'd send you to Portugal or somewhere for a year, until anything you know is useless, then let you do what you want.'

Ulrich bowed drunkenly. 'Thank you for your compassion.'

Jones pulled out a half empty Scotch bottle from a cupboard and poured a slug into his brandy glass. He turned to Ulrich. 'You know, it's hard to say this, but I like you . . . I wish I didn't but I do . . . it's just Germans, do you see, after Gareth, and what they've been doing . . . ' He drank more Scotch. 'They've raped the whole of bloody Europe, Christ, I mean . . . '

Ulrich drained his own brandy and put his glass out for some Scotch. Jones poured him a generous slug. The Welshman was beginning to sprout a double, and Ulrich closed one eye. He felt utterly weary, heartsick and drunk . . . only the pain had receded.

'What do you do, Harry, when your country does things, things you don't like?'

Harry shook his head.

'Join the other side, forsake everything, your language your family, friends, culture . . . become a traitor? As a matter of fact I don't love the English. The Royal Navy blockade killed two of my cousins . . . they starved to death in 1919 because the Royal Navy wouldn't let food through.'

'Come off it,' Jones drank more Scotch, 'the Great War ended in November 1918.'

'Yes, the war did, but the blockade didn't . . . it was a technicality, but the British said until the peace treaty was signed the blockade remained. They say over a million Germans starved to death.'

The brandy glass Harry Jones was holding snapped under the pressure of his grip and blood dripped from his fingers onto the carpet.

Ulrich took out his handkerchief and bound the Welshman's hand. 'I didn't kill Gareth, Harry and I'm not a Nazi . . . I know you were in the Royal Navy but I don't believe you personally starved any Germans. It's nations, and it is out of our hands.'

'Maybe . . . ' Jones turned away and walked to his bedroom. 'Maybe.'

Ulrich fell asleep on the sofa, and dreamed of Ilse.

Harry Jones dreamed of Gareth, but it was not a good dream.

His son was running with the rugby ball towards the try-line, but suddenly his face turned into that of Adolf Hitler, and the crowd were chanting *'Sieg Heil, Sieg Heil'*. The Welshman began to cry softly in his sleep.

Ulrich was shaking him. 'Telephone, your office.'

It was daylight. Jones got unsteadily to his feet, still fully clothed, and staggered into the lounge to pick up the receiver.

He listened and then said: 'We'll be right in.'

He threw the receiver down and it missed the cradle. Ulrich replaced it. He felt dreadful but Jones looked worse.

'Important?'

'Yes. They're coming to London, both of them. To the

Palace, into the lion's den. He won't have to go to Windsor, they're coming to him.'

'Princess Elizabeth and Margaret?' Ulrich was incredulous.

'Right first time, our precious little princesses are coming to London.'

Chapter Twenty-Two

THE FEELING of exultation was fleeting. Eilders knew that he had only the clothes he wore, no money, and of course no papers of any kind.

He had to find a new place of refuge quickly where he could lie low.

The suitcase was still in the left-luggage office at Charing Cross station. He had kept the ticket stub in his sock, and it had not been found in his initial search by the police. But later he had disposed of it because the risk of keeping it was too great. If they found the stub and retrieved the suitcase, they would discover among other things the illicit address book which he had taken from Lord Blackington's study. After that, very little deduction would be needed as to his identity.

But the addresses in that book could be the key to his salvation. It was clear to Eilders now that the Abwehr had somehow faked the recall message, possibly aided by Lord Blackington, and by now Heydrich must assume Eilders had fallen into enemy hands. Even if he could reach a radio, Heydrich would treat any message as enemy-controlled. There was only one thing to do, and that was to go on . . . kill the princesses. Operation Raven must already have been aborted, but he, Uwe Eilders would make sure that his mission had not been in vain.

The odds were totally against him. Every policeman in London was looking for him, aided by the Abwehr traitor, Ulrich von der Osten.

He pumped harder on the pedals, driving himself on. He could see the park on his left as he headed North towards the bridge that would take him across the Thames.

The police could not know yet that he had stolen a cycle—the street had been deserted when he took it—so they would put any immediate search in a tight circle, based on the speed of a man on foot. He heard a faint but growing clatter of bells, and saw a black police car surge towards him on the opposite side of the road. He tensed but kept on cycling, and the car roared past. Eilders crossed the river and turned right, down the embankment beside the Thames. If only he had the address book, he could go to one of the names in it, get into the house and threaten or blackmail its occupant.

He pulled the cycle into the kerb. It could work, just as when he had had to memorise lines in his days as an actor. You closed your eyes and simply conjured up the page you had been studying . . . when it worked, the lines came up, just as if there were a photograph in your brain. He had scanned several pages of the address book, casual glances, hardly taking it in. But it was a chance. There were few passers-by and little traffic, so no one would think him strange. He leaned forward and put both hands over his eyes. Nothing. Blankness. He concentrated hard. He was in the study, the address book in his hands, flipping through the pages . . . and . . . yes! One address clearly . . . a name . . . he repeated it over and over, then opened his eyes. And if the address proved useless, he would summon another, he could do it now, he knew it.

He started to pedal away, moving instinctively towards the right-hand side of the road. A car horn blared and a man's voice shouted: 'Watch where you're going, mate,' and a small Austin saloon swept by him on the inside.

Eilders checked himself, looked over his shoulder and moved back to the left side of the road. *It was the smell things that caught you out.* He had gone instinctively to ride on the right-hand side of the road as in Germany. Thank God it was only a cycle he was riding. He pedalled slowly, trying to calm himself again; it was nothing, no one would report such a thing, all cyclists took liberties.

234

The address was close by, in Pimlico, and he found the street easily. The houses had large porches supported by tall, circular pillars. Eilders had seen nothing of their like in Germany, and he presumed they must ape some Roman style of architecture.

He parked the cycle against a low brick wall. He realised he must return for it quickly. Once it was reported stolen the police must assume the escapee had taken it, and it would become a focal point of the hunt. Neither did he wish to have it stolen, for he would need it again, and he had a suspicion that the law insisted cycles must be locked or immobilised to prevent their being used by German invaders. The man from whom Eilders stole the cycle had clearly not heeded the warnings, and might be shocked to learn that a German had indeed stolen his machine.

Eilders walked briskly down the street; the British suspected those who walked slowly or slouched. He found the number he wished, and walked up the three steps to the carved front door. He rang the bell.

He had no idea who might open the door, or what he would say when it was opened. But he would concoct a story, and get into the house. If necessary he would push the answerer back into the hall and close the door behind them both, praying that no one in the street saw what happened.

He rang the bell again. He was carried up on a wave of his own daring. So much had happened, he had risked so much, been at the precipice so many times, that he felt as though on a wave of fortune.

He rang the bell again. There was clearly no one in, so he walked back down the steps and retraced his path. Near where the cycle rested was a passageway. The insular British had walled in the narrow gardens, and the houses which backed on to them were screened by a line of trees for the sake of privacy. He felt sure he would not be observed, so he walked along the back of the houses and counted. When he reached the correct house he tried the latch on the back door gate. It opened. He walked up the garden path boldly. He must not look

235

furtive at this stage in case anyone was watching from a back window of the neighbouring houses.

There in the small garden was a shelter made of two curved walls of corrugated iron topped with earth and grassed sods. It was an Anderson shelter for when the bombers came. Leaning against it, hopelessly optimistic, was a black stirrup pump. Eilders thought of Warsaw and Rotterdam. The British would need a little more than makeshift shelters and hand pumps when the Luftwaffe came.

He tried the back door of the house, but it was locked. He quickly took off his jacket and wrapped it around his forearm. Now was the moment. If someone saw him now, his actions were without any other explanation but malicious. The police would be called.

He thrust his protected fist into the lower left-hand pane of glass, one of four set into the upper part of the door. The smash was partially muffled by the coat.

He reached through and turned a key, but the door still would not open. He reached further inside, found a bolt and slipped it. He retrieved his arm carefully and opened the door.

Once inside he stood on the balls of his feet, every muscle tensed, straining to hear a sound from within. There was nothing. He decided to wait thirty minutes; if someone had seen his illegal entry and the police arrived, he would have to try and escape again. If within that time limit there was no activity, he would presume no one had seen him, go out quickly and retrieve the bicycle.

His armpits were black and wet when he took off his jacket. They all believed England was cold and damp. Eilders knew different. In the summer, in the city, it was warm and humid.

Ulrich said: 'I can't believe they can be so stupid. They know Eilders is still at large in London, and yet they let the princesses come here.'

'They're not coming to Lyons Corner House, they're coming to Buckingham Palace. They don't allow casual visitors in there, you know.'

236

Jones' head was aching from too much booze the night before and the effect of his injury—*and* his chest hurt. He felt like a wreck.

'Windsor is a *castle*, a fortress, and it is in a small town: any stranger would stand out straight away. The Palace is only a couple of hundred yards from Victoria Railway station . . . it's madness, madness.'

Jones was getting angry: 'You listen to me, Ulrich, I've been in this job a long time, and I know what I'm talking about. He's up shit creek, back to square one, no papers, no cash, nothing! He knows you're after him . . . what can he do? Where can he go? And he won't know the princesses are coming to the Palace, there isn't going to be an announcement in *The Times* you know . . . strict secrecy all the way.'

'Suppose he found out, I don't know how, but suppose he did?'

'He couldn't get in if he tried from now until 1960.'

Ulrich pulled at his own bandages in annoyance, they seemed to hurt more than the bruises now. Harry Jones was beginning to infuriate him with his complacency. 'You've been saying that all along. He can't do this, it's impossible . . . soon we'll arrest him . . . but he's still free. Every time we think we have him he slips through our fingers. It's been two nights now. Where did he go? He has one set of clothes, no money and a bicycle. Where is he?'

Jones said grimly: 'I don't know, but I'm going to have him, mark my bloody words.'

They lapsed into silence. At last Ulrich said: 'Why *are* they coming to this reception? Why would the King and Queen take that risk, why would Mr Churchill? Why, Harry?'

Harry shrugged his shoulders with affected nonchalance.

'Haven't the faintest idea, mate, I really haven't.'

It was a lie. Harry Jones knew perfectly well why the risk was being taken, and it all had to do with Britain surviving the war and eventually bringing in America on her side. For once America joined in, so Mr Churchill's reasoning went, then Germany's defeat was a foregone conclusion.

But America's ambassador to the Court of St James was one Joseph P. Kennedy, Boston-Irish and no lover of the British. At one time he had actually been put under MI5 surveillance, an extremely unusual act to take against the ambassador of a friendly power. Kennedy always boasted about how he faced facts. The facts as he saw them said that Britain was finished, and he had a lot of evidence to back his case.

Her army had just been defeated in a continental war and her ally France beaten into submission in less than six weeks. Most of the British army's tanks, lorries, guns and heavy equipment had been left in France. Although the country's naval forces were still supreme, the air force was desperately battling to get up to strength before the expected onslaught of the Luftwaffe. And after what the German air force had done in Poland, Belgium, Holland, France and Norway, Joe Kennedy gave the Royal Air Force little chance.

In addition Britain was alone, with no allies, save the far-flung underpopulated countries of the Empire, who could at this stage add little to the struggle. Churchill had said defiantly that Britain would fight on the beaches, the landing grounds, the fields, the streets and the hills, but never surrender. Kennedy doubted if the British would go along with the rhetoric of their prime minister when the invasion actually came, and he had no doubt it would. It was time, Kennedy believed, for America to realise the inevitable, that Britain would either sue for peace or be occupied, perhaps both.

President Roosevelt should cease his cosy relationship with Churchill and prepare to deal with the new leader of Europe, the Germany of Adolf Hitler. Already, Joe Kennedy whispered it in court circles, the little princesses had been evacuated to Canada, and the King, Queen and government—Churchill too—would follow.

It was dangerous defeatism on the part of perhaps Britain's only ally, if an ally solely in the passive sense. America was sending guns, ships and food. It was working out phoney deals involving Caribbean naval bases to get past Congress the acts necessary to ship warlike goods to Britain.

If the poisoned word of Kennedy began to be listened to, if Roosevelt was ever persuaded that Britain was finished, her resolution gone, defeat inevitable, then those supplies would dry up.

So Mr Churchill had proposed a show of defiance and the King had readily accepted. There would be a reception at Buckingham Palace for every ambassador still resident at the Court of St James. The power, pomp and historical ritual of the monarchy would be unleashed. Richer, more powerful men then Joseph P. Kennedy had wilted before it. The friends and neutrals alike (and no doubt the enemies too when the diplomatic wires hummed) would learn that the royal family was going nowhere. That the King and Queen and their beloved children were still in the capital. That Britain was as resolute at the top as it was all the way down to the base of its masses of soldiers, sailors, airmen, wives and workers who had responded so heartfeltly to Churchill's bulldog 'never surrender' speech.

The message would be rammed home forcefully to the American ambassador: the royal family do not quit and neither does the British nation. Whatever his personal prejudices he could hardly fail to communicate the spirit of defiance to Washington, and if he failed to do so, the American intelligence services would discover it themselves from other neutral sources.

In the midst of the sceptred isle's darkest hour, there would be pomp, ceremony and the majesty and continuity of the English throne.

Mr Churchill would present himself late at the reception, and in a private conversation, add the grittier parts of the message. Britain would not capitulate like Belgium, Denmark or France. If the Germans did come they would be met by fire and steel and the Channel would flow red with their blood.

If it came to the worst there would be no Wehrmacht marches of triumph, like that down an unscathed Champs Elysées. If they entered London it would be over a carpet of their own feldgrau, and they would occupy a city of smouldering ruins. A mighty and historical nation would die fighting and clawing to the last, and the victor would inherit a wasteland.

Would America, with all its historical ties with Britain, wish to see that?

So the US must take sides now! That would be Churchill's message to Kennedy, using the footballing parlance old Joe used on his own sons: get on the winning team.

Churchill, the King and Queen and their advisors knew the risks. The assassin was still free and was in London.

The King agreed that the risk to his daughters meant less than Britain's survival against Nazi Germany—survival that might hinge on continued American shipments and her early entry into the war.

Superintendent Harry Jones was summoned to Whitehall and apprised of the situation and the reasons behind it. He felt flattered that he had been told, but alarmed at the responsibilities involved.

He certainly didn't think Ulrich von der Osten had to be privy to the reasons of state behind an apparently incomprehensible decision.

He sneaked a look at the German. Ulrich was going back through the files once again. That didn't mean of course, Harry conceded to himself, that the Jerry wouldn't be able to fathom it out for himself.

The house was extremely narrow, but was on three levels. The ground floor consisted of a kitchen, a dining room and a small hall which led to the front door and the stairs. The kitchen had a gas stove, plenty of expensive looking pots and pans, cutlery and cut glass wine goblets. It looked as though the occupant was something of a bon viveur; the kitchen cupboards were full of food (another one with black market contacts, thought Eilders) and there were even several bottles of French wine.

He climbed the carpeted stairs to the first floor, which consisted of a long through sitting-room, carpeted luxuriously. In the section that overlooked the street was a living area furnished with a leather chesterfield, two leather armchairs, occasional tables, a bookcase with locked window doors, and a radio. A black telephone rested on an antique card table.

In the bookcase were rows of leather-bound books, many classics, including Stendhal, Victor Hugo, Dickens, Shakespeare; and some books on antiques. The other half of the room was clearly a place for work. There was a roll-top desk, and a separate small inlaid writing table with pens and ink-bottles in a fixture. The whole room was decorated in dark green flock wallpaper, below a deep cream ceiling, and the walls were adorned with hunting prints and several old maps in frames, which seemed genuine. There was a collection of framed Victorian postcards, and, almost out of place, a pencil sketch of a nude man.

Beneath it, resting against the base of the wall was yet another hunting print. Eilders smiled. If he needed confirmation of the man's predilections that was it. If visitors were not deemed 'sympathetic' the nude would be removed and hidden, and replaced by the hunting print.

Now he wanted evidence. The roll-top desk was locked, but he upturned several Chinese vases on a window shelf and found the key amid a welter of paper-clips, pencils and theatre ticket stubs. He opened the desk and rooted through it. There were invoices for furniture, bills, antiques catalogues, several insurance policies. Then, wrapped in an elastic band, a bundle of envelopes smelling of lavender. He opened one, the fading postmark reading 'Les Issambres, Var, France, May, 1938'.

He read it quickly, and it was enough. Julian was rather too explicit, there was enough in this one letter alone to send him and the man David Chetwynd to prison. Rummaging further through the desk, Eilders came upon a thin, soft-backed address book. It was almost a replica of the one he had discovered in Blackington's study.

Chetwynd's current lover was Julian Topliss, who was studying art in Cambridge. But there were other friends, including the late Lord Blackington, a man called Colin Davidson, who was, if Eilders could deduce properly, an officer in His Majesty's Navy, Alastair Newman, a clerk in the Ministry of Works, and Ronald Brown.

Eilders was particularly interested in Ronald Brown.

Eilders checked the two bedrooms and then took a long, slow bath. Tucked into the edges of the bathroom mirror was a faded snapshot of two men, one much younger than the other. They were both in tennis dress, holding rackets and squinting into the sun. Mr Chetwynd and friend. Eilders dressed and pocketed the photograph. Then he cooked himself some food, drank a little wine, and settled down to wait.

It was around 8 p.m. when the front door opened, and Eilders heard the man climb the stairs and then open the door into the sitting-room.

The man started with shock when he saw Eilders lying on the chesterfield dressed in clothes he had taken from the bedroom wardrobe.

'Who the hell are you? Get out of my house before I call the police.'

'Sit down, Mr Chetwynd.'

'I will not sit down, I shall call the police immediately.' He moved towards the telephone.

'If you call the police I shall show them Julian's letters . . . and the picture of you together. Do you realise what happens to queers like you in prison? They bugger you for breakfast.'

Chetwynd sat down heavily in one of the armchairs. 'A dirty blackmailer. Which stone did you crawl from under?'

Eilders ignored him: 'I want to stay here for a few days, then a little money and I'll be gone. I'm a deserter. I agree with the Oxford Union, I have no wish to fight for King and Country.'

'You can't stay . . . you can't!' Chetwynd got up, face indignant and red, his hand moving along the mantelshelf to a heavy figurine. Wielded properly it would break a skull, and Eilders knew what the man was thinking.

He said: 'Lay one finger on it, and I'll take that finger and snap it, then each of the others, in turn and slowly. I can do it, and I will, believe me.'

242

Chetwynd winced at the thought, and any thought of resistance crumpled. He sat down again.

'Do you have a domestic?'

The man's eyes shifted; 'No, no one . . . '

'You're lying . . . the beds were made. I don't believe you did it, and there is no dust, the place is spotless.'

'Just an old woman, she comes in once a week. She came this morning, so she's not due for another week.' Eilders believed him.

'I want you to invite a friend.'

'A friend . . . ? Look I don't understand, what is this? I'll give you money, but don't involve my friends, not Julian, I beg you.'

'Not Julian, I want you to invite Ronald.'

'Why?'

'I want to talk to him . . . and you, of course.'

'It's impossible. I can't telephone him. They're not allowed to take calls.'

'Write a letter, you have stamps in the desk. We can go out together and post it later when it gets dark. He will receive it first post tomorrow and he can come here tomorrow night.'

'Please don't involve Ronald. He's only a servant, he has no money.'

'Do it!'

Chetwynd looked into Eilders' eyes, and they said, killer, maniac. Chetwynd was terrified, bemused, mystified. Why was this happening to him, and what? He had been blackmailed before once, but the man had just taken his money and gone.

Chetwynd wrote the letter.

Ronald was an older man, thin, cadaverous-looking, with wispy hair the colour of nicotine and skeletal hands. Eilders was introduced as Simon, 'a friend', and Ronald arched his eyebrows. Clearly he thought Chetwynd was being unfaithful to Julian, and that suited Eilders, though he had never thought he looked homosexual.

243

The man drank wine, talked of art, music, and antiques, and Eilders was, despite himself, impressed. The English were known to be philistines, yet these two homosexuals, one pushing sixty years old, were clearly lovers of the finer things of life, although only Chetwynd could actually indulge his passions while Ronald talked of them. For despite his aristocratic manner and his languid charm, the upper-class accent and affected sophistication, Ronald was a servant.

It was a phenomenon Eilders had read about, and only once glimpsed in childhood. A ruffian lad in the street had gone off into 'service', to be a lowly servant in some far-distant country house. A year later he returned to see his parents and the difference in him was striking. His accent had changed, as though he were aping his masters, and he stood aloof from the other boys. He walked differently, and his mannerisms were those of some Eton schoolboy rather than an East End corner boy.

Eilders had read that the servants of the English became more snobbish than the people for whom they slaved. Politically they supported the status quo that paid them meagre wages and gave them little time off. Their manners were almost fastidious compared with their lords and ladies. The masters and mistresses of the house might get uproariously drunk, belch, vomit and chase each other through the bedrooms, while the male servants vied with each other to see who could drop the least aitches and hold his teacup with the little finger extending at just the right angle. And such lives, with the servants strictly segregated according to sex, often led the males into homosexuality. Thus the man Ronald at sixty. Though he worked in the most royal of palaces, Buckingham Palace, none of the glitter rubbed off on him. He had little money and just a cupboard of a room. Chetwynd on the other hand was the real thing, born into the English upper-middle class and with enough money to indulge his tastes.

The only common denominator was their deviation.

Eilders had brought Ronald there for a purpose. He wanted to know exactly where in Windsor Castle the princesses were.

244

It would have to be done subtly, without alarming Ronald, for he could not kill him. A missing Palace servant might set alarm bells ringing in whatever security agency the traitor von der Osten was working.

Chetwynd, of course, he would kill before he vacated the house.

But as the evening went on, and Ronald started on his fifth glass of wine, the servant leaned back and closed his eyes. 'You know I'm absolutely worn out. It's been panic, panic, panic all day long. Whisper it not beyond these four walls but our beloved princesses are moving back for a day or two. We've been dusting rooms and airing sheets, lighting fires . . . my God, the whole place has had a spring clean, and about time too. It's not a fit place for children, mouldy old ruin, the damp plays havoc with my knees.'

Eilders had to conceal the look of surprise on his face. 'The princesses . . . I thought they were "at a house somewhere in the country"?' He gave a self-mocking smile at the official-ese.

'Windsor my pet, guarded by half the British army. But we have an oh so grand reception planned for next Thursday. All the ambassadors in London will be there in their finery, the King and Queen dressed to the nines, the princesses like two little fairies on a Christmas tree, banquet rooms polished, the silver out, cooks working wonders, and nothing but work, work, work for the likes of yours truly.'

A reception. The Palace would be invaded by scores of strangers and the princesses would be there . . . out in the open . . . on show! It was Providence.

For a moment he contemplated killing both men there and then, and taking the servant's place at Buckingham Palace, but he instantly dismissed it as absurd. Ronald was a thin, old, simpering homosexual; no amount of make-up, disguise or play-acting could conceal that. It would have to be another way, for he had the information, the place, and soon the time. There would be another way into Buckingham Palace and he would find it.

The servant left around midnight, and Eilders watched

Chetwynd carefully. The man was clearly intelligent and had seemed to show a flicker of suspicion at Eilders' interest in the forthcoming banquet and reception.

The previous night Eilders had slept lightly in the sitting-room, a chair arranged against the door in case the antique dealer should try and harm him, but nothing had transpired. He knew the man would be too frightened of arrest because of his homosexuality to go to the police, but he did not rule out some attempt at violence when his back was turned. Chetwynd excused himself and went upstairs, and Eilders remained on the chesterfield, thinking of a way to get into Buckingham Palace.

When that was decided he would kill Chetwynd.

The man must have crept in barefoot and been incredibly quiet, but before he lunged he took a sharp intake of breath to fuel his actions, and that saved Eilders' life. He dived to his left and caught a blur of light flash past him. The momentum took Chetwynd over the chesterfield, the antique cutlass still in his hand. Clearly he had intended to push the blade right through Eilders. A split-second later and he would have succeeded.

Eilders rolled up and onto his feet, quickly, legs apart, balancing himself for the attack that would come.

Chetwynd had regained his balance and was standing breathing heavily, the blade held out in front of him. Eilders silently cursed himself. The cutlass had hung on a wall beside the stairs, and he should have removed it, it was so obviously a deadly weapon.

He said: 'You fool. I'll have to kill you now.'

'Oh no my friend, oh no . . . not at all, *I* kill *you*.' Possession of the cutlass had given the man tremendous confidence, but it was ill-founded. 'You are a deserter, you broke into my house, you threatened me with violence, theft, I defended myself and you died. I am a respectable man with contacts and no one will blame me.'

Eilders kept his eye on the blade. The first rule of knife-

246

fighting was never to take your eyes off the blade, and the cutlass was simply a long knife. He did not speak.

Chetwynd's eyes were afire with righteous indignation. 'Did you really think I'd let you blackmail me? Julian, Ronald, any of us . . . and just what was your interest in Buckingham Palace, my dirty friend . . . ?' He advanced with the cutlass. 'I can use this, you know. I fence, yes even a *queer* like me can use a sword . . . how brave do you feel now . . . *blackmailer*?'

Eilders stepped backwards, carefully. Then the blade tip moved like lightning and he flung himself to one side. The sword's tip cut his shirt, and he felt a sting and the hint of blood. It had only nicked him but by God it must be sharp.

He was being forced backwards, back into the office corner of the room, and Chetwynd was advancing, concentrating now, face set, waiting for the right moment to impale Eilders on the blade.

Eilders felt behind him and steadied himself on the writing desk. Out of the corner of his eye he glimpsed one of the Chinese vases within reach. He grabbed and threw.

Chetwynd ducked, the vase missed, but the man was off balance.

Eilders darted forward inside the sword arm, Chetwynd lunged quickly but without thought. He would have done better to try a downward slashing stroke, but it was too late, and the blade swished harmlessly past Eilders' body.

He had the man's sword arm in a second, and locked it in a merciless grip, forcing it back against its joint. Chetwynd screamed and Eilders hit him with his free hand. The screaming stopped. Chetwynd was making a choking sound. Eilders forced the arm until it was on the point of snapping at the elbow joint and the man was groaning and choking in pain and fear, then Eilders changed his mind. He lifted the sword arm until the hilt of the cutlass was above Chetwynd's head, the blade's sharp point an inch from his belly. The antique dealer brought up his other arm, gripping at the cutlass handle, trying to resist the downward pressure.

He knew what was happening and strained every middle-aged sinew to try and prevent it.

Eilders began to push downwards, and felt the tip of the blade make contact with the man's stomach. Chetwynd was weeping silently.

Eilders pushed harder, quickly, and the blade went in with a squashy sound. He thrust again, using the man's own arms as the killing lever.

Chetwynd's face began to contort, his eyeballs stood out. His mouth was wide open but no sound came from it, just a kind of gurgle. Then blood.

Eilders pushed again, enjoying it, watching the old queer dying slowly. The blade met some resistance, Eilders pushed again, in a short, sharp stroke, and the resistance seemed to disappear, and blood gushed in a torrent from Chetwynd's mouth.

Eilders released his grip and stepped back. Transfixed by his own blade, a look of absolute horror on his face, Chetwynd sank slowly to his knees, eyes still wide open. He toppled to one side and lay there for a full minute as Eilders watched, fascinated, then the eyes glazed over and lost focus.

Eilders laughed, knelt down and closed the man's eyes.

Chapter Twenty-Three

WINSTON CHURCHILL said: 'Outline your plans, Superintendent.'

Jones cleared his throat. He was nervous, understandably so, but he and Ulrich had been over it a million times and it was as foolproof as they could make it.

'Our . . . my . . . assessment, Prime Minister, first of all, is that the German agent cannot be expected to have knowledge of the fact that their Highnesses will be at Buckingham Palace. That is our first line of defence.'

The prime minister glowered: 'And if that *first line* fails?'

'Physical security, sir. The Palace will be surrounded by soldiers at ten-yard intervals for twelve hours before their Highnesses arrive, and for the whole period of their stay. Their convoy from Windsor will consist of armour-plated vehicles with windows that will withstand a rifle shot. The route will be decided upon at the last minute. Each soldier outside the Palace must be personally vouched for by an officer before he goes on duty—that is to avoid impersonation, sir.'

Churchill nodded. The nod said: Go on.

'A similar plan applies to the Palace staff who absolutely must be on duty. To avoid any chance of a bogus invitation being printed, each card contains an easily identifiable mark in the right-hand corner . . . we check that mark against the proclaimed identity of each ambassador who comes through the gate.

'If the marks do not tally with the name, entry is refused and the man interrogated.'

'What if the German agent chose to impersonate one of the ambassadors, *and* had the correct card?' Churchill sipped at his brandy and Harry Jones dearly wished he too could have a glass.

'We've thought of that, Prime Minister. Each embassy, with the exception of the United States, for reasons which I'm sure you'll understand, sir, has been asked for and has furnished an up-to-date photograph of its ambassador. That will be at the gate of the Palace. Von der Osten and I will both have copies, so that each man can be checked as he comes in. It helps us, sir, that most of the ambassadors are known to each other, so if any imposter did get through he would be instantly recognised as such by his diplomatic colleagues. I gather it is something of a small world. To sum up, Prime Minister: he cannot know; if he knows, he must realise there is no way he can even try to gain entry; if he is foolish enough to try then we shall arrest him.'

'The chauffeurs, Mr Jones . . . Miss Agatha Christie has made me paranoid about chauffeurs.'

Jones allowed himself a smile. 'I beg your pardon, Prime Minister, I overlooked mentioning that. The embassies all have to supply up-to-date pictures of the chauffeurs who will be on duty on that day. If the man calls in sick, is suddenly taken ill, whatever event, the embassy must call us and we lay on a Ministry of Works driver. Any chauffeur whose face and name does not match our list goes no further than the Palace gates, whatever embarrassment that causes to his ambassador.'

Harry Jones warmed to his theme: 'Once inside the Palace the chauffeurs will be guarded by men of the Coates Mission. They will be provided with food which they will eat under supervision, and they will be escorted to and from the lavatory facilities.'

'You seem to have thought of everything, Mr Jones.'

Jones exhaled breath. 'I hope so, Prime Minister.'

'You will of course be present at the reception.'

'Yes sir, myself and Colonel von der Osten. We will be armed in the eventuality that . . . '

'No!' Churchill's voice was suddenly a whiplash; gone was the sleepy, deceptive calm of before.

'You shall be armed, Superintendent, the German shall not.'

'Sir, Colonel von der Osten has been entrusted with every part of this up to now, if the German agent does get in, and von der Osten spots him, he *must* be armed, sir.'

'A fine state of affairs, don't you think? To protect their Highnesses from a German agent we give another German agent a revolver and put him close to their royal personages—a man sent to us by the Reich's Fuehrer himself! I consented to this man's entry into Britain because I dare not spurn any chance of catching this madman. But suppose it is all some elaborate plan, a double-cross from the Machiavellian mind of the German Chancellor himself, to get Herr von der Osten close to their Highnesses so that he could kill them. Have you considered that?'

Jones was staggered. He had certainly not considered that, and said so. But Ulrich, an assassin? It was unthinkable. Surely?

'Sir . . . we have to trust Colonel von der Osten, we *have* to . . . I think I would trust him with my life.'

Churchill glowered. 'Very noble of you, Superintendent. They say that if you lived with the devil for a week you would find good qualities in him. However it is not your life with which we would have to trust him, it is lives far more important than either of ours.'

'Prime Minister, I'm pleading. Let us both be armed. It can't happen, nothing can . . . but if it did . . . ?'

'My last word, Mr Jones. Good day and good luck and God speed.'

The prime minister crumpled his face into that well-worn mask. The interview was over.

Eilders found four telephone directories in the house, and they covered the whole of the London area. He went through them and began to write down addresses. He noted ten, concluding that was the number he could usefully cover in one day.

He and the late Mr Chetwynd were of similar height, indeed he had already worn the man's clothes, but the antique dealer had had a certain middle-aged flabbiness on his hips and a slack paunch, allowed for by his tailor. When Eilders put on one of the man's pin-striped suits he decided to allow for the difference by padding with folded newspapers. He had darkened his blond hair with applications of Cherry Blossom black shoe polish. The bowler was really a size too small, but Eilders jammed it on.

With a rolled umbrella gripped in one hand he surveyed himself in the bedroom wardrobe's full-length mirror. He was an English gentleman, above suspicion.

The first three addresses were all in Belgravia; to reach them he passed close to the home of the late Lord Blackington. At each address he presented himself to the receptionist and told her he was enquiring about the possibilities of emigration or investment when the hostilities ended. As the women checked diaries, made appointments at some future date for him, or simply answered questions or produced brochures and mimeographed sheets, Eilders observed carefully the large colour portraits of the men who stared down from the walls of the reception area.

The first three excellencies were clearly unsuitable, far too old and far too fat.

The fourth and fifth were also impossible, and the sixth had a duelling scar which cut from eye to chin. Eilders cursed under his breath. There had to be one! Just one, that is all it would need.

By now he was in North London, not a natural embassy area. The district was tatty, down-at-heel, the road insignificant. But, so, he had to agree, was the country which placed its ambassador here.

The receptionist was middle-aged, very plain and very English. As Eilders went through his routine, he noticed with quickening interest that the area on the wall behind her desk, the usual site for the hanging of the ambassador's portrait, was empty. But the square was distinctly outlined by its lighter shade. The portrait could only recently have been removed.

He enquired politely if the ambassador's picture had hung there.

'The *old* one did . . . ' the woman said, with a significant pull to her facial expressions, 'the new one hasn't had his painted yet. He only presented his credentials ten days ago.'

'A new man, eh?'

'You see, the *government* changed,' said the woman, with that unique British look of xenophobic disapproval. 'So they booted out the old man—a lovely chap he was.' She leaned forward conspiratorially. 'The new ambassador is the nephew of the latest president. Between you and me I'll bet he's not much over thirty . . . thirty, can you imagine? An ambassador. It's ludicrous, he'll be the laughing stock of London.'

Eilders had deliberately made himself look older, and the woman felt some kinship of age. 'He's just a kid, really.'

Eilders tut-tutted in sympathy, then said: 'I wouldn't have thought that this was a popular posting, what with the war and all.'

The woman pursed her lips in an expression of moral distaste: 'It wouldn't be for a *family* man, but Señor Alvarez is a bachelor, and you know what London's like these days, some of the goings-on: personally I blame the foreigners, city's full of them.'

Eilders agreed that London's moral decline was definitely the fault of the foreigners.

The woman was enjoying this, betraying her employer. 'If he spent as much time on embassy business as he did on . . . well . . . do I have to spell it out?'

'Nod as good as a wink?' Eilders said.

'Precisely.'

Eilders made an arrangement to see the ambassador the next morning. If he was as young as the woman suspected, he might be only five or six years older than Eilders. That would certainly help if everything else fitted.

As he turned to leave the woman said hastily: 'Here, you won't go telling him, what I said I mean? After all we're both English, aren't we, blood's thicker than water?'

'Not a word.'

She was shielding her mouth with her hand: 'If I were you I wouldn't bother going to that swamp. They support the Nazis you know, they say the president has a picture of Hitler on his wall.'

Eilders shook his head in sorrow. 'Well, I never.'

Ulrich handed Harry Jones the gun and pushed his six rounds of ammunition across the desk. His face was a mask of contempt. 'They don't trust me. *You* don't trust me.'

Harry took the gun and put it in his drawer. 'Look mate, it's got bugger-all to do with me, I've told you that.'

'Has it? And if Eilders gets into the Palace, and if I see him, what am I supposed to do?'

Jones struck the table in annoyance. He was trying to remember that Ulrich von der Osten was a German, the same nationality as the man they were hunting, a temporary friend but a permanent enemy. He liked the bloke but it changed nothing, nothing at all. 'Listen, Ulrich, would your people trust me? Would they? Me with a revolver in a room with Hitler and Goebbels and that mob? Come off it.'

'Was this your idea?'

'I'm just obeying orders, mate, just obeying orders.'

'That's what everyone in Europe is saying, in Germany, here, no one thinks for themselves any more.'

'And just why are you in London, Ulrich? I'll tell you, because *you* are obeying orders, so get off that bloody pedestal.'

Harry Jones pretended to read some papers.

'Well . . . ' Ulrich said at last, breaking the silence, 'you haven't answered my question, what do I do if Eilders gets into the Palace and I spot him?'

'Call for me,' said Jones sharply.

'Very well, I shall. But last time I seem to remember you were a little far behind the race.'

There was the problem of the map. Like every other valued item it was in the suitcase at the left-luggage office at Charing Cross. Eilders could conjure up an address he had previously committed to memory, but he knew it was beyond him to reproduce in his mind a whole floor layout plan of Buckingham Palace.

He remembered a boast Mr Archer had once made to show what a free and democratic country Britain was. The man had said that no foreign spies need go around looking for secret documents as everything they wanted to know about the British Army and Royal Navy could be read in the local library.

Eilders wondered if that applied to Buckingham Palace. He hunted through the house until he discovered a ticket issued by London County Council which enabled Mr Chetwynd, so the ticket boasted, to take out two non-fiction books from the Pimlico library. The card was under a vase, dirty and dog-eared. Eilders hoped Mr Chetwynd had not used it for a while.

The library was warm, smelled of furniture polish and was very quiet. A large sign on the wall cautioned: *Silence*. He searched the shelves, and within minutes found exactly what he was looking for, a large square volume with both text and photographs, and best of all a three-dimensional layout plan.

A spinstery woman, dusty as the shelves and with brown warts on her face, took the ticket, inserted a slip which she extracted from inside the book, and put the ticket in a wooden rack. She seemed to approve of the choice of book, for she gave Eilders what he assumed must be a rare smile.

That evening he read for several hours, going over and over the text. He wanted to know Buckingham Palace as though he had lived in it all his life.

He learned that the Palace had only become one when King George the Fourth used it, that it had taken its name from the original owner the Duke of Buckingham. Eilders knew the British monarchy was lavish with money but he was staggered when he learned what had been spent on restoring the Palace in 1825, a quarter of a million pounds sterling! Eilders translated that into Reichmarks and allowed for the inflation of money in 115 years . . . by 1940 standards it was an incredible sum.

The Palace layout itself was relatively simple. It was a three-storey rectangular building, built around an open courtyard, with vast areas of gardens, trees and a lake to the rear, most of it enclosed by high brick walls topped with barbed wire. The exception to that was the east side of the Palace, the 'public' side where Kings and Queens took the homage of their people at coronations and royal weddings. There stood railings, broken only by three gates. It was through the flanking gates that visitors arrived, were checked by policemen and allowed through. That was the face of the Palace that was to have been assaulted by Student's men in Operation Raven.

Inside, the three floors were connected by staircases and lifts. The plan obligingly indicated that some were for the exclusive use of the royal family themselves. Eilders read on into the night.

The princesses had quarters on the second floor of the Palace on the east side—and that is where he must eventually make his way.

On the west wing of the first floor was a state dining room. The servant Ronald had said there was to be a banquet, and undoubtedly it would be held in that dining room.

That meant, Eilders knew, that he had to get from just that floor to the next. But the book was specific: no one who did not serve or work with the royal family at close quarters was allowed to ascend to the second floor.

He went over the layout plan again in detail, noting every room and its use—specifically the location of the Palace's own police station and its guard detachment—and memorising it. He sucked at a pencil with which he had been making notes.

First he had to get in; the plan for that was well-advanced. Then he had to escape detection long enough to get from the first floor to the second—if his assumption about the banquet venue proved correct—or from the ground floor if it was not.

Then he must somehow get past the armed bodyguards who must surely be in attendance on the princesses.

He began to go over the diagram yet again, and by the time his eyes closed involuntarily he felt he knew Buckingham Palace better than the King of England himself.

Ulrich was definitely puzzled. 'Mossbross, Harry? Where is this place, and why do we have to go there.'

Harry Jones shook his head. 'It is not a place, it's an institution. We are going to Moss Brothers: in English "brothers" is shortened to Bros when it's on a shop sign or something, hence Moss *Bros,* known to one and all as Mossbross. Are you with me up to now?'

'No.'

'Well, we need monkey suits for the Palace . . .'

'*Monkey* suits? I . . .'

'Morning suits, dress wear, formal clobber, tails, top-hats, the whole lot. I don't have any and I don't suppose you brought any with you, so we go to Moss *Brothers* of Covent Garden, who for the outlay of a couple of pounds will hire to us all the items we need.'

'The Moss Brothers will hire us formal clothes . . . now I understand.'

Harry Jones winked. 'Well, I'm not sure that the brothers will be in personal attendance. Anyway, it will look good on your expenses when you get back to Berlin. "Hire of dress suit for Buckingham Palace reception—£2." '

'And when *will* I get back to Berlin—1953?' Ulrich couldn't take the thing as lightly as Harry Jones seemed to.

'Ulrich, in the first lot, my Dad used to say, "Don't worry lad, it'll all be over by Christmas". Who the hell knows.'

At Moss Bros. the man who was measuring Ulrich asked

him which side he dressed. Even Ulrich's knowledge of colloquial English didn't encompass that.

Jones explained and Ulrich had the decency to blush a little.

As soon as His Excellency Señor Jorge Alvarez rose from his chair to shake hands, Eilders realised that the man would be satisfactory. Not perfect, that was too much to hope for, but satisfactory.

Alvarez was a shade taller than himself, but Eilders saw a flash of shiny black boot, like that of a Spanish flamenco dancer, and the heel seemed very high. The man had a goatee beard, which presented little problem, and his hair was thick, dark and heavily greased.

Eilders judged the man to be five or six years older than himself, and his nose was somewhat more aquiline, although the effect was dampened by fleshy cheeks and mouth. The eye colour was different too, but there was nothing Eilders could do about that.

The figure was too full for such a young man, but in disguise you could always add weight—taking it off was the problem. Beneath the man's eyes were dark patches, probably testifying to his sampling of wartime London's rather free morals in comparison with the rigid Puritan double standards of the country the ambassador had so recently left.

Eilders felt he could do it. He would have to find a way of avoiding the embassy staff. Even though they had known the man for just a few weeks, they would surely spot an impostor. Most chauffeur-driven limousines were not fitted with an interior rear-view mirror for the driver, to avoid him observing the rear compartment. Thus, Eilders concluded, he must get to the ambassador's bedroom, then from the bedroom to the car without confronting the embassy staff. At that point the chauffeur who would already be at the wheel must get a glimpse of him, but it would be fleeting and sideways on. He would then have little conversation, avoiding possibly revealing himself as an impostor. He would have the correct credentials, and entry into the Palace should then be a formality. From what the receptionist had told Eilders, His Excellency Señor Alvarez had attended no receptions since his arrival, with the exception of presenting his credentials. So most of the other ambassadors would take him at face value.

King George would be about the only person who had met the ambassador, but Eilders hardly thought the King would recognise the difference: the man had a little more pressing matter on his mind, and it was well-known that the English couldn't tell one foreigner from another.

Señor Alvarez' country was a poor land-locked jungle state in South America, whose people lived on maize, and where the life expectancy for a male was forty. The country's constitution was modelled on that of Fascist Italy and its Grand Council. Following the recent *coup*, the new president had sent a telegram of congratulations to the Fuehrer on his military successes in Europe. But the country remained neutral —thank God.

Eilders lied fluently to the ambassador for fifteen minutes, and agreed to make a further appointment with a commercial attaché for discussions on investing £50,000 in jungle farming projects. The ambassador's mouth seemed to water at the prospect, and Eilders realised quickly that whatever money went into that poor, benighted country, large slices of it would be passed around among the ruling junta and their cronies.

On his way home he called in at a small joke and toy shop in a street off York Way, a stone's throw from the mainline railway stations at St Pancras and King's Cross. He bought several items that cost a total of nineteen shillings and sixpence. He paid with a one pound note belonging to the late Mr Chetwynd, and very much genuine legal tender. The shopkeeper made a good-natured enquiry about what Eilders intended using the items for, and he told the man he was going to a fancy-dress party.

Which, Eilders reflected, was not so very far from the truth.

In the afternoon he rested. The telephone rang twice, long,

259

seemingly unending rings, but eventually, neglected, the telephone fell silent. Eilders thought it might be the young man Julian. He hoped he was still out of London, too far away to cause any problems that day.

Once, someone knocked at the door. Eilders peered suspiciously through a chink in the lace curtains of the sitting-room window. It was a man in a white smock and a little peaked cap.

Eilders felt his heart miss a beat. Was the visitor some kind of official? Then with relief he saw parked in the road a cart to which a horse was harnessed. On the cart was a mound of empty crates and a few bottles of milk. In England, as in no other country that Eilders knew of, milk was brought to the door without payment, and then once a week or once a fortnight, the man would come to collect his money. This was a respectable neighbourhood, and if an occupant was not at home, the milkman would collect double the following week.

The man knocked again, then got in his cart and went further down the street. Eilders relaxed.

In the early evening he packed his joke-shop items in a holdall, and took a length of washing-line he had discovered beneath the kitchen sink. He cut off a length of the line, and carefully made two knots. He would have preferred wire, but there was none in the house.

He felt it safe to use the bicycle. It would not be possible to circulate a cycle's description like one would a car's. You could stop everyone on a cycle during the first minutes of hue and cry, but not days later, there were simply too many people cycling. The bike was a popular make, and with a man on it pedalling, it would be beyond suspicion.

Eilders bathed, dressed in casual clothes taken from Chetwynd's wardrobe—he included a trilby hat—ate some tinned food, put his holdall on the back of the cycle and left the house by the back way.

As he left he noticed that familiar though faint sensation prickling at his nostrils. Chetwynd's corpse was beginning to putrefy.

* * *

260

The embassy was two semi-detached houses made into one, the embassy proper on one side, the ambassador's residence on the other.

Eilders was sweating when he arrived, and his muscles ached. It was a long ride, and a lot of it uphill. The street was pitch black and deserted. Perhaps there had been rumours that tonight the German bombers really would come.

He quickly pushed the cycle up the driveway that fed the ambassador's residence, and into the rhododendron bushes where he hid the machine. He waited, letting his knotted muscles relax and his skin dry in the cool night air. His watch said 11.35 p.m. He could hear the distant sound of a gramophone, but no live human noises. He took his holdall, came out of the bushes and walked up the drive, keeping in the dark shadow of the shrubbery all the way. A small brick wall with an inset door blocked access to the rear of the house. The door was locked, but Eilders scaled the small wall easily, landing crouched on the balls of his feet.

The noise of his fall on the gravel seemed deafening.

He stood for a few seconds. Surely if there were a dog it would have barked by now, or attacked him if it was a guard dog.

He carefully skirted some metal dustbins, and came to a small set of steps with an iron railing, leading to a porch and door. He climbed the steps silently and tried the door, but it was locked.

The sound of the gramophone was louder. It was a warm night, and someone in the residence must have left a window open. With a sense almost of detachment, Eilders noticed that it was opera, a male tenor in full voice.

He slid along the wall with his back to it, and up to a darkened bay window. Beyond it he could see a pool of orange light flooding out, illuminating a small rockery. The gramophone was in that room, and Eilders could now hear, as a backdrop, that the tenor had some amateur accompaniment— or opposition.

Eilders came up to the edge of the window sill, and looked in at an angle. It was a bedroom, fully-lit but with no sign of anyone in it. He risked a wider look.

A dinner suit was draped across the bed, and two shoes highly polished sat neatly to attention at the foot of the bed. The ambassador had a late-night appointment. Another problem. By the side of the bed, a wind-up gramophone on which the opera played. Eilders heard a loud splash, and His Excellency Señor Jorge Alvarez strained for a note he had no hope of reaching.

Eilders hauled himself quickly into the room, put down the holdall and took out the knotted rope. The tenor and the ambassador gave voice in uneasy tandem towards the opera's climax.

Eilders skirted a cane table on which stood half-empty bottles of liquor. He pushed open the bathroom door. The aria reached its peak, but now the gramophone tenor sang without amateur competition.

Chapter Twenty-Four

IT WAS 1.15 a.m. and Harry Jones went over the details of the next day's reception again.

The princesses would leave Windsor at 9 a.m. The car in which they travelled would have armoured body panels and bullet-proofed glass. In front of and behind the car would come two lorries, three-tonners, packed with armed Coates Mission men. There would be an armed motor-cycle escort and an armoured car at the front and rear of the whole convoy, which had orders to stop for nothing. The route would be decided on and communicated to the drivers at the last possible moment.

Once at the Palace the princesses would be accompanied by their personal detectives to their rooms on the second floor. The ambassadors would begin to arrive fifteen minutes before noon. The two flanking entrance gates at the front of the Palace would be used for arriving cars, many of which would, presumably, turn up at the same time. Each gate would be manned by one unarmed palace policeman, several armed Coates Mission men, and either Harry Jones or Ulrich von der Osten. Jones would take the left or south gate, Ulrich the right or north gate.

Each ambassador would be required to hand his invitation through the window of his car, and this would be checked against a list held by the palace policeman. The ambassador's identity would then be checked against the submitted photograph from his embassy. A similar check would be made against the submitted picture of the chauffeur. Once satisfied

263

that neither man was an impostor, a Coates Mission man would mount the vehicle's running board and guide the driver across the Palace forecourt and through the entrance arch on the left of the east wing, an entrance which led to a courtyard quadrangle within. The car would be signalled to stop against the interior of the south wing. There a palace official would greet each ambassador and escort him across the interior courtyard.

The meteorological office had forecast a warm day with clear skies, but in the event of rain the ambassadors would be lead instead down the grand corridor into the Grand Hall.

Eventually each ambassador would mount the eight carpeted steps of the Grand Entrance Hall, heralded by a fanfare blown by trumpeters from the Household Cavalry, then to be greeted by His Majesty King George the Sixth, Queen Elizabeth, and the princesses Elizabeth and Margaret. The King would greet each man by name, a personal touch bound to impress. The King did not have a magic memory, the trick was a palace one. Each ambassador was assigned a number. As the palace official ushered the man into the entrance hall, leaving him to cross the carpet and mount the stairs, he had already consulted his list, and passed on the relevant number to an aide who would precede the ambassador and whisper the number to an equerry. The equerry would simply whisper the name against the number into the King's ear. It had been tried before on similar occasions and worked without a hitch.

After paying his respects, each ambassador would then be led discreetly to the 1844 room. It was so called because Czar Nicholas the First of Russia had occupied the room in that year while on a visit to England. It was often used for small luncheon parties, and it was there that ambassadors came to present their credentials. Here the men would be served cocktails, dry sherry and other apéritifs, and offered canapés by liveried palace servants in powdered wigs, buckled shoes and knee breeches.

After each guest had been individually greeted, a process estimated at forty-five minutes, the royal family would then join their guests in the 1844 room. A supply of orange squash would be on hand for the little princesses.

The time allowed for mingling with the ambassadors was thirty minutes, then at one o'clock if everything was on schedule—and Buckingham Palace could usually run these events to the minute—the guests would be led to the state dining room on the first floor. This room was magnificent. The ceiling was carved and inlaid with deep recessed bowls. Cut-glass chandeliers caught and reflected the candlelight onto the large oil portraits of former monarchs that peered down at the guests from their golden frames.

But it was the table itself that was the *pièce de résistance*. It had been extended to its full length, an incredible eighty-one feet, fifteen more than the length of a cricket pitch. The deeply-polished table was eight feet across and set with sterling silver plates and cutlery; lustrous Waterford crystal glasses would take the fine vintage wines to be served.

At 1.15 precisely the servants in their red tunics would serve luncheon. When the port was being served, Queen Elizabeth would retire, and the princesses return to their room for tea.

Her Majesty would wait in the White Drawing Room where the King and Ambassador Kennedy of the United States would join her fifteen minutes later. There the three would be served coffee and would make conversation.

In two corners of the White Drawing Room are identical china cabinets made of ebony. Above each is a mirror. One cabinet conceals a secret door, which at the press of a secret button swings back to give access to another private room. At a roughly pre-arranged moment the Queen would take her leave of Ambassador Kennedy, press the button, and to Kennedy's amazement disappear through the secret door. From that door, a second or two later, would emerge Prime Minister Churchill.

Then Mr Kennedy would get what his own countrymen would call the hard sell: the blood, fire and resolution of the British premier and his monarch.

* * *

265

The rest of the ambassadors, meanwhile, would be taken on a guided tour of the Palace, and then escorted back to their cars. The chauffeurs would be required to stay with their vehicles the whole time. They would get tea and sandwiches, and any of them who wished to visit the lavatory would be taken to and fro by a Coates Mission soldier.

Among the royal detectives, the equerries, the palace officials and policemen, the flunkies and the soldiers, two extra guests, suitable attired, would circulate. Harry Jones and Ulrich von der Osten.

They would watch the guests at dinner from a position at the rear of the state dining room, and would follow at a discreet distance when the princesses were taken by their detectives back to the private quarters. After that the job was done.

And anyway, it was all covered. Surely? Jones rubbed his eyes wearily, stretched his arms. The left one felt like a lump of lead. He felt sure he'd slept on it the night before. 'Anything else?'

Ulrich yawned. 'Only the food—I mean, if somehow he got to the food and poisoned it. But you say there's an armed guard on the kitchens.'

'All night, and the staff have been personally vetted and vouched for. The meals are going to be cooked in batches of five by separate chefs, so he wouldn't know what to poison if he did get in there. The girls have a different, less rich menu . . . I've got the chefs to prepare three lots, and we decide which lot goes out. I trust bloody no one.'

'I think you've read Machiavelli.'

'Shakespeare's my limit, mate.' They lapsed into silence.

It was a strange moment. Each knew that tomorrow meant everything, and that if they failed . . . well, it was simply unthinkable. For a brief second each caught the other looking at him, and they both looked away sheepishly.

Harry suddenly remembered what the prime minister had said. Tomorrow he was going to take a German intelligence agent into Buckingham Palace and stand him within thirty feet of the King of England.

Harry felt his heart miss a beat—suppose it *was* some awful plot. Could Ulrich be an assassin? In any case, he was a German, and Harry Jones intended watching him like a hawk. Suppose Eilders was just a decoy, the false duck to get them all running around London like blue-arsed flies, while all the time, Ulrich was planning . . .

'What?' He realised that Ulrich was talking to him.

'I asked if you were all right, you look pale.'

'Yes, I'm fine . . . fine.' Jones lay down on his camp bed, and Ulrich tried to make himself comfortable on the other.

It didn't matter, Harry Jones thought, Eilders can't get in . . . *can't* . . . and if it *is* Ulrich, may God forbid it, he'd shoot the bugger himself. He thanked God for Churchill's wisdom in ensuring Ulrich did not have a gun himself.

Ulrich closed his eyes and experienced a sensation like that of peering into a vast, bottomless pit. They had either thought of everything, or nothing. Eilders was out there somewhere, waiting. He could not know what tomorrow would bring to the Palace, and if he did there was nothing he could do to harm the princesses. A German agent could not get into Buckingham Palace, it was impossible.

Unless . . . Ulrich smiled in the darkness . . . unless your name was Ulrich von der Osten. He felt the pit begin to swallow him. He dreamed of Eilders wearing a crown. Every time Ulrich reached for his revolver there was just an empty holster. Eilders was laughing.

The train carrying Julian Topliss was extremely late getting into Liverpool Street station. It had taken four hours from Cambridge, which was crazy.

He was worn out because he had had to stand the whole way, but worse, he was worried.

David had missed two arranged telephone calls, and when Julian had tried to call him, the telephone had not been answered at home or the shop. He had called mutual friends, but no one had seen David in his usual haunts.

The taxi from Liverpool Street crawled through the blackout, and it was the early hours before Julian could let himself into the Pimlico house. He switched on the hall light and immediately noticed a vile smell. He went upstairs and checked the bedrooms. In the sitting-room he noticed a large dark stain on the carpet, as though someone had spilled red wine. He went down to the kitchen and saw a plate with the remains of some tinned meat on it. That wasn't causing the smell, which was now strong and awful. He went into the kitchen-dining room and switched on the light. Under the table was a bundle, like dirty washing only it was the wrong shape, too long. He knelt down and looked. The bundle had a head.

Julian screamed and carried on screaming. When he finally stopped, got his breath and calmed down, he forced himself to pull back the sheet and look at the face. He felt faint and had to sit down before the nausea and faintness passed.

Eventually he went to the telephone and called the police. Before they arrived, and hating himself for his callousness, he went to the writing desk and found his letters. He flushed them down the lavatory.

The invitation was in a dressing-table drawer, and Eilders noted the location of the reception and luncheon. The ambassador's morning suit and sash were in the wardrobe, and when Eilders tried them on, it was obvious that with some discreet padding they would pass. The dinner suit still lay on the bed, and Eilders worried about the appointment the ambassador would no longer keep, that night or any future night. But no one knocked on the door, there was no commotion, so he assumed it had been an assignation with a woman and she would simply assume her lover had failed to appear.

Eilders closed the window and drew the curtains. With the bedroom door locked he played a little opera before climbing into the ambassador's bed and sleeping soundly.

*　*　*

Harry Jones awoke to the persistent ringing, and groped a hand upwards to his desk to shut off the alarm clock. The ringing continued, and he sat bolt upright and grabbed the telephone. He grunted, listened, grunted a little more and replaced the receiver.

Ulrich was stretching himself awake awkwardly on his camp bed. Jones swung his feet to the floor and rested his chin on cupped hands. His eyes said he had only slept as daylight came. Ulrich said: 'What was the call—urgent?'

'I dunno really, some old queer was murdered in Pimlico last night. It's near the Palace so a mate of mine gave me a bell. Few suits missing, money, stuff like that.'

'How was he killed?'

'A big stab wound, probably a sword or something, he was an antique dealer, had one or two on his walls. The queer's boyfriend found him in the early hours, been dead a few days the doc thinks.'

Ulrich was looking alarmed: 'Maybe Eilders hid there, blackmailed the man because he was a homosexual, stole his money and clothes and killed him . . . and then he left last night . . . *why* last night?'

Harry was pulling on his shirt, and said with exasperation: 'Hold your horses a minute, son. There's no evidence it's Eilders, and no evidence that *whoever* it was moved last night, the boyfriend just happened to come home last night. Chummy could have broken in, killed the queer, nicked his gear and moved out days ago.'

'But Pimlico . . . God he's so close to the Palace he could fire a shot into the grounds . . . My God, Harry, suppose he is hiding somewhere, in an attic, on a roof, with a rifle with a lens . . .'

'Calm down. There is nowhere but nowhere in the Palace that is overlooked, I promise you, that was worked out years before you and I came on the scene. The only place he could use a rifle is from the grounds, and apart from the fact that the perimeter is guarded, the grounds themselves will be swarming with men.'

Ulrich left the office to wash, soaking his face in a cold

269

basinful of water. It was only 7.45 but already it was warm.

Harry Jones was more worried than he'd let on. There was evidence that someone had been living in the house for a few days, eating the food and sleeping in the sitting-room.

But there was worse. His contact had not rung him out of friendship, it was because of an address book that had been found in the dead man's house. Among his friends, it seemed, was the late Lord Blackington, who had been killed by the Belgravia Murderer. Which—though the policeman who telephoned Jones did not know it—was Uwe Eilders, German agent. It could have been a coincidence, but if it wasn't it could spell danger.

He went back in his head over all the arrangements. If Eilders had left his safe house the previous night there was no time for him to try some clever ruse. If he did know the princesses were at the Palace and was trying to get in, it would have to be by bluff or brute force.

Ulrich came back in, face serious. He said: 'Harry, I accept that this Pimlico murder is almost certainly nothing for us to worry about, but I want to ask you for a favour, it will involve breaking the rules a little.'

'Ask, it's a free country.'

'Give me my gun back . . . just for today.'

'No!' The Welshman lit a cigarette and coughed vigorously, thumping himself on the chest. 'You can forget that.'

'Please! If he gets into the Palace, and I'm unarmed, what can I do? What? Please Harry, break the rules for once.'

Jones calmed his laboured breathing and looked Ulrich straight in the eye. 'No. And if I so much as see you sniff at a firearm you'll be under arrest.'

Harry Jones drove them to the Palace, a journey of less than a mile. Ulrich said sharply as the car cruised past St James's Park: 'How did you know that murder victim was a homosexual? Was he on your files for committing some offence?'

Jones shook his head and tossed a half-finished cigarette butt towards the park: 'They found some letters from the lad who called the police. Letters and photographs tucked under a cushion on the sofa . . . Very naughty according to my oppo. The lad should have done a bit of tidying up before we arrived.'

'And will he be prosecuted?'

'Very likely.'

'And that's British justice? His lover is murdered, he does the right thing and tells the police, and it is *he* who ends up in a courtroom?'

Jones swung the car right towards the Victoria monument. The met. men were right, the sky was clear blue, and it was very warm, set for a glorious day. 'Ulrich my lad, in this country arse-banditry is illegal.'

Ulrich laughed bitterly. 'What a lovely phrase . . . murder is illegal too, but I think you find it easier to apprehend homosexuals than murderers. Perhaps you English are a lot of hypocrites.'

Jones contrived to look hurt. Ulrich had called him an Englishman.

Chapter Twenty-Five

FROM THE bed, through the half-open curtains, Eilders could see the sky, a brilliant, cloudless blue. He rose and went into the bathroom. Señor Alvarez was lying beneath the cold, green water, and Eilders gave him only a glance before washing carefully and shaving with caution. He did not want to cut himself: he needed the skin silk smooth so that the false beard would adhere properly. He found several glass bottles containing various—to Eilders' nose—unwholesome scents. He chose one and sprayed it on himself liberally.

Wearing the late ambassador's bathrobe he went back into the bedroom and started to prepare. After this, of course, it became a matter of chance, of luck, bluff, and the vigilance or lack of it on the part of others. If he failed today, then it was all over. Even if he succeeded he knew that his chances of survival were slim.

There was a gentle knocking on the door. He kept his voice low: '*Sí?*'

'*Desayuño,* Your Excellency.'

In Spanish he said: 'Leave it outside the door, I am still dressing.'

The woman called compliance. Before she could leave he called: 'I have a guest. Please ensure that the car is brought to the side door of the embassy for when we wish to leave. And kindly do not make up my room until I have returned from the reception.'

He heard the slight, significant pause before the woman

replied: 'Yes, Your Excellency, I shall tell the driver, and inform the maids.'

The woman would be disconcerted. She was a native of the ambassador's country, a strict Catholic. It would be one thing to her for a man to whore discreetly in his native land, but for him to bring his *puta* to the embassy in a foreign land was another.

He heard her footsteps moving away, waited, then opened the door and took in the tray. It was covered in a white cloth, and under that, a pot of delicious-smelling real coffee and a plate of hot rolls with a dish of butter. He ate hungrily.

He replaced the tray in the corridor, then went back to the bathroom to take a long careful look at the dead man in the bath. Eilders sat at the bedroom's dressing table and began to make his disguise. Using a child's crayon he added dark smudges beneath his cheeks. With wetted cotton wool he padded his cheeks and lower gums, giving his jaw and face the extra fleshy pronouncement of Señor Alvarez.

He had removed the ambassador's rings shortly before he had killed him, in case rigor mortis prevented him doing it later. He managed to get two onto the larger fingers of his hands, but several were too large. Alvarez obviously had fleshier fingers, and Eilders was forced to discard the extra rings. It was a detail that he hoped no one he met would know the ambassador well enough to notice.

He took a jar of pomade, unscrewed the lid and greased his hair until it shone, then he combed it carefully in the ambassador's style. He took the joke-shop beard, trimmed it carefully, removing the sidewhiskers, leaving only a goatee.

With the adhesive he had purchased from the same shop he stuck on the beard and smoothed it down carefully, searching for any beads of excess glue. He leaned back and surveyed himself in the mirror. It was good: no one casting him a casual glance would suspect. If the ambassador had been in London such a short time, and if he had spent most of that on business other than diplomatic, few could know him.

The embassy staff were the only danger. If he was seen up

close, they must surely suspect. But the plan was for the car to come up to the driveway at the side of the embassy, where a door existed for deliveries, commercial travellers and the like. Eilders had seen it on his first visit. When he had had his interview with the ambassador, he had observed that a long corridor led from the man's office to a small vestibule, off which stood the tradesman's entrance. If Eilders had judged the geography of the house correctly, the bedroom in which he sat was directly adjacent to the office.

When the woman called to tell him the car had arrived, he need only move a few paces from his bedroom, past the office, then along the corridor to the vestibule. If he went to the front of the embassy, as would be normal, it would mean passing administrative offices and walking past the receptionist with whom he had had the conversation.

There was no reason—surely—for him to encounter anyone on the route he planned to take. Once again, chance, luck, fortune.

He dressed in the morning suit, padding the empty areas with pillow slips and some shirts and underwear he found in the drawers. He slipped into the blue sash with its star at the centre, some obscure South American order of chivalry. The rope garrotte was in the bag, and Eilders pushed it into his sock, and hid the bag under the bed. Then he locked the bathroom door and hid the key under the carpet, just in case the maid did come in to clean. He was ready.

At eleven o'clock there was a knock on the door. 'Your car is at the side door, Your Excellency.'

'Thank you. We shall be out in one minute.' He waited until her footsteps moved away, then opened the door.

He turned right, through a swing door, there on the right was the ambassador's office. The corridor stretched ahead, and he could see the vestibule, the sunlight streaming through the different coloured panes of glass, making a technicolour display on the tiles. He walked without haste, ambassadors did not scurry. He could see now the dim outline of the black Rolls-Royce through the semi-opaque glass.

Almost there. A door adjacent to the vestibule opened and a

274

woman came out. Eilders' whole body stiffened and he had to force himself to keep on walking. She was locking the door behind her; small, dark-skinned, she turned. She was in maid's uniform.

She saw him . . . and stepped back . . . *lowering her eyes!*

'*Buenos dias,* Your Excellency.'

'*Buenos dias.*' She would be a maid, a cleaning woman, or some minion. She had probably never set eyes on him before, and she was looking respectfully at the floor.

He was past!

The vestibule door opened, the Rolls-Royce a few feet ahead, the chauffeur looking back, moving to get out of the car, presumably to open the door for the ambassador, but Eilders was a pace away, the door open and in. The driver said: 'Begging your pardon, Mr Ambassador, I didn't see you come out.'

'Do not worry.' Eilders sat back in the seat, in shadow.

'Am I to wait for . . . the other person, Mr Ambassador?'

Of course! He had told the woman there would be two, she had told the chauffeur . . . Damn!

'No . . . she is unwell. Please proceed.'

The chauffeur touched his peaked cap, and put the Rolls-Royce automatic gear shift into drive.

Ulrich was beginning to feel more confident. Most of the ambassadors were in, and every one tallied with his picture. Ulrich knew Eilders, and if he was a foot from that man he would recognise him, whatever disguise he used.

Jones felt a similar surge of confidence. He had Eilders' picture pinned up in the gatehouse, and studied it every time a car came through. He was convinced the German had not got past him. They were getting paranoid; the man was probably starving to death out in the open somewhere.

He cleared two more cars, lit yet another cigarette, and looked up as he heard a screech of tyres as a Rolls-Royce made a sharp turn off the Victoria monument and pulled up sharply in front of the palm of the palace policeman. And who might this be, Harry Jones thought, the ambassador for Chicago?

The Rolls-Royce came along the bottom of Trafalgar Square, under Admiralty Arch and into the Mall where the trees were in full blossom. Ahead lay Buckingham Palace, the Royal Standard hanging limply from the flagpole.

Eilders' nerves had vanished now, and his mind was clear. Ahead lay the enemy's fortress and within it the children of its King. As they got closer he could see a queue of limousines at both Palace entrances. The later they went in, the more relaxed the security check would be: that was logical.

He leaned forward and tapped on the glass partition. The driver put a hand over his shoulder and slid the partition back.

'Yes, Mr Ambassador?'

'Don't join the queue. Go up Constitution Hill and up Park Lane. Perhaps by the time we get back they will have cleared these cars, I don't want to be gawped at by onlookers.'

'Yes, Mr Ambassador.'

The chauffeur really couldn't understand it. Normally the ambassador was a chatty cove, but this morning there was hardly a peep out of him. Bringing the Rolls up to the trades-man's entrance, he'd never done that before, then he's supposed to have some fancy piece with him, and he bloody leaves her in the embassy. He's got a nerve.

Now he makes me take a tour of London, and risks being late for the King of England.

At last the car came down Constitution Hill and towards the Victoria Monument. Eilders glanced over towards the north gate. A man in civilian dress, formal wear, was coming out of a gatehouse. There was something familiar about his stance, the way he walked.

Eilders went cold. It was Ulrich von der Osten. The car was coming round the monument now . . . Eilders shouted: 'This entrance, *this* one!'

The chauffeur swung the wheel of the Rolls, making the

276

tyres squeal, almost sacrilege in such a car, and brought the car to a sharp stop at the feet of a policeman with outstretched palm barring entrance to the south gate.

The chauffeur thought: The ambassador's like a different man today.

Eilders lowered the window and handed his invitation to the policeman's immaculate white gloves.

'Won't keep you a moment, sir.'

Jones checked the invitation and ticked the name off the list. He picked up the two recent photographs of Señor Jorge Alvarez and his driver, and took another glance at the picture of Uwe Eilders.

Harry Jones came out of the box and first took a good, long look at the chauffeur, who grinned self-consciously. That was all in order, and Jones slipped the picture beneath the other.

He moved to the passenger door of the car. The ambassador was sitting on the far side of the vehicle. The window was open and scent wafted out into the hot day. Jones wrinkled his nose, it smelled like a bloody Belgian brothel.

He peered in, trying to adjust his eyes from the bright sunshine to the semi-darkness.

'Yes?' The ambassador inclined his head in query.

'Won't be a moment, sir. Just routine.' Jones glanced at the picture, and sunlight caught the glossy surface and flashed into his eyes. He squinted at it. It was hot now, and he was tired, he felt he just wanted to sit down for a long time. He discovered his eyes were closed, and opened them again.

The ambassador said with a hint of impatience: 'Is there some problem, Officer, I am late as it is, must you delay me further?'

The accent was Latin, the tones calm and measured. It was not the nervous, fanatical voice of a Nazi assassin, it was that of a diplomat, polite but assured.

Something was triggered in Harry Jones, something unconscious and probably unavoidable after half a lifetime as

277

an English policeman. It was an instinctive respect for authority and breeding, station and wealth, a respect bred from the English class system which recruited its policemen from the lowest layer.

He took another quick look at the photograph. No problem there. Typical bearded, dago queer who smells like a flaming woman.

Jones felt a momentary twinge in his chest.

'My invitation, Officer.'

'Yes, sir.' He handed it back through the open car window.

A Coates Mission man came up at the wave of a hand, jumped on the running board and spoke to the driver. The car moved off. Jones went back to the gatehouse and sat down on the camp stool. He didn't like the heat, wasn't used to it, he felt damp and weary. Then there was the business of too little exercise, not enough fresh air, and too many cigarettes and greasy canteen dinners. Slowly his breath started to come back, and he made a vow.

Tonight he would get a good, long sleep. Bugger the princesses, bugger Eilders, bugger Ulrich, bugger the whole of the British Empire. A good, long sleep, and not in any camp bed either.

The car went out of sunlight, into shade, and quickly back into sunlight again. It rolled to a stop and the soldier jumped off the running board. The passenger door was opened by a man dressed like something from a Restoration comedy, then a morning suit with a tiny man inside it stepped forward, and a voice said in honeyed tones: 'Good morning, Mr Ambassador, welcome to Buckingham Palace.'

Eilders crossed the carpet and mounted the eight steps, the fanfare ringing in his ears.

The King of England was in naval uniform, and said: 'Good morning, Señor Alvarez, such a short time since presenting your credentials.'

'An honour once again, Your Majesty.' He bowed stiffly from the waist and took the proffered hand. The grip was soft, almost unmanly, but Eilders realised that a King must shake many hands in a year, and if he gripped each of them, his own hand would be pulp. Queen Elizabeth put out her hand, and Eilders took it and bowed.

Then he was before them. The little princesses. He felt a sensation like nothing he had ever experienced, almost an intoxication of joy. Against all the odds, hampered by traitors, he had made his way into Buckingham Palace. In a few short hours he would become the greatest hero in German history, eclipsing Frederick the Great and Bismarck.

Princess Elizabeth said: 'Good morning, Mr Ambassador,' in a firm voice for a girl, and then Princess Margaret said her line in a reedy voice.

Eilders bowed, and took the soft hands quickly. Then an official led him away to the 1844 room.

Jones joined Ulrich at the entrance to the Grand Hall. Both men showed their special passes complete with photographs to the guardsmen on the door, and were admitted. Ulrich said: 'What held you up?'

Jones patted his chest: 'A bit of a turn, I came over strange, nothing to worry about.' Jones was sweating heavily.

Ulrich said: 'He was not in the ones I checked, chauffeurs or ambassadors, I am absolutely certain.'

'Mine neither, nothing remotely resembling Eilders. All invitations in order, every one tallying with his picture.'

'Was there anything from the perimeter?'

'Nothing since midnight when some idiot full of champagne tried to climb the wall for a bet. He's swopped his suite at the Ritz for a cosy little cell. He's the Honourable someone-or-other, nothing to worry about.'

Ulrich mopped his brow with a handkerchief. It was very hot, and one associated London with fogs, not heatwaves.

Jones took a short breath, finding it was easier to speak that way: 'Right, Ulrich my boy. They're in the 1844 room now, with guards outside, personal detectives inside. We take station just inside, and no further. We stick out like a couple of sore bloody thumbs anyway, so we've got to be as inconspicuous as possible. The Palace was very definite on that. They don't want the ambassadors getting wind that we've got a panic on.'

'But if we move among the ambassadors we can be absolutely sure . . . '

'No . . . for God's sake will you do as you're told . . . ' Harry Jones felt another burst of irrational irritability; they seemed to be more frequent as the days went on. 'I'm in charge of this show, not you, and this isn't some mayoral fucking reception in Yorkshire, it is the King of England in there, and if we've been told to stay at the door, that's what we do.'

'OK, Harry, calm down.'

The Welshman looked terrible, he was perspiring heavily, and his face looked damp and unhealthy. 'My bloody nerves are all shot with this damn business.'

'Well, don't worry. Eilders hasn't got in, we're pretty sure of that. And we're around, so if he had got in he couldn't get far. Right?'

Jones nodded: 'Right.'

'And very soon I'll be able to book my hotel in the Isle of Man.' He winked, trying to lighten the mood.

Harry Jones forced a smile and grabbed a breath: 'Boyo, they'll send you to the Isle of Man over my dead body.'

'I'll hold you to that . . . Superintendent.'

Together they walked to the 1844 room, the Colt feeling like a ton weight in Jones' waistband.

Their Majesties had been well briefed. Some ambassadors received more attention than others. Joseph Kennedy, of course, but he would get the full treatment later, including the charm of the former Lady Elizabeth Bowes-Lyon, now Queen, whose radiant smile and genuine warmth had made her such a popular monarch.

But especially the ambassadors from Japan, Spain, Turkey, Greece and Yugoslavia, all for strategic reasons. Each country was neutral, and Britain wished them, for the time being at least, to remain so. In Japan's case Britain had no wish for that country to try and expand her Empire further than China, attacking Hong Kong, rubber-producing Malaya and the Dutch East Indies, while she thought Britain was prostrate and unable to respond.

Neither did Britain wish civil-war-ravaged Spain, led by the Fascist general Francisco Franco y Bahamonde, to throw in its lot with the Axis and either attack the British base at Gibraltar or allow passage for German troops to carry out such an attack. If Gibraltar fell, Britain's Mediterranean position could become untenable.

Britain knew that Germany had ambitions in the Balkans, and that a tripartite front of Yugoslavia and old enemies Greece and Turkey, might deter her. The three must be made to understand that although Germany looked like a victor now, time would change that. The King and Queen of England were soiling their hands with the dirty business of politics. Both realised that their survival as monarchs and individuals, and the survival of the nation they ruled might depend on it.

Jones needed to lean back against the wall for support. He was exhausted. Ulrich kept his eyes roving over the mass of heads, searching for the glimpse of a face, a profile, anything that might be Uwe Eilders.

When luncheon was announced, Jones and Ulrich moved out into the corridor, standing way back while the royal family and ambassadors filed out. Ulrich kept looking, but it was an impossible task. It was a sea of heads and faces, constantly moving, shifting, one face blotting out another, and, anyway, he knew he would find nothing. Eilders was not in the palace. He and Jones had checked them all, and everyone was clear. He trusted himself and he trusted Jones. *Did he?* The policeman had been wrong too often, he was too complacent, too slow-witted . . . but surely this time?

It was simple enough to check a face against a photograph.

The Welsh policeman looked to be on the point of exhaustion, that was the problem. He looked ghastly, his face grey and pasty.

Ulrich scanned once more the disappearing heads. Damn it man, Eilders is not here, he could not know, and if he knew, he could not get in. Stop suspecting Jones, doubting everyone, imagining the worst. He tried to reassure himself, but there was this constant nagging doubt which fluttered his stomach with unease. And he tried to maintain his vigilance.

No one knew Ambassador Alvarez, that was certain. At lunch Eilders had the Portuguese Ambassador to his left, the Finnish Ambassador to his right. Each chatted cheerfully in English and no one seemed other than convinced he was Señor Alvarez.

There had been only one moment of fright at the reception earlier when the Ambassador for Paraguay had taken his hand, congratulated him, and passed on felicitations to Alvarez' uncle, the new president. Eilders had replied in kind, and there was no hint of suspicion in the Paraguayan's eyes.

But the danger was acute. At the end of the room he could see two men, one of them quite clearly Ulrich von der Osten. The man was too far away to identify Eilders in his disguise, but Eilders knew he must make sure the distance between them remained.

Eilders had been informed that after the lunch he and the other ambassadors would be taken on a tour of the Palace. It was then that he would make his break, get to the princesses's quarters and kill them.

He had no doubt whatsoever that he would do it.

Ulrich nudged Jones, whose eyes were closed. 'They're leaving.' The two men exited from the state dining room by a side door, and followed thirty yards behind as the girls were led to their own rooms by their personal detectives. As they climbed the stairs the Welshman was panting badly, and had to stop to catch his breath on two occasions. His colour was now definitely worrying Ulrich: it seemed to have gone from paste to something darker and more sinister.

The princesses went in a door, and it was closed behind them. A few seconds later it opened again and a detective came out. 'Superintendent Jones?' He nodded.

'They're in now. We'll take it.'

'Well, thank God for that.'

'Thanks for the cover. Much ado about nothing, eh?'

'Seems like it. It's all yours now, anyway.'

Eilders watched the girls leave the table early as he sipped at a vintage port. From the very beginning he realised that had he a pistol he could have shot the girls down before anyone could have moved a finger to prevent it. But he did not have a pistol, and if he had, the risk of bringing it into Buckingham Palace was too great.

He wished to do it his way, and could afford to wait.

He sipped again at the port. It was excellent.

It was hot in the courtyard, but after the stale, musty air of the Palace, the air outside was positively alpine.

Jones said: 'What I need now is a fag.' He patted his pockets and swore.

'Damn, got a ciggie, mate?'

Ulrich shook his head: 'Why not forget the cigarettes for a while? They're not doing you any good. Go and see a doctor, you look ghastly.' Jones felt worse than ghastly. He lied: 'I feel great, marvellous, especially now this has been sorted out. What I need now is a good long drag on a Senior Service followed by a touch of the Rip van Winkles.'

Ulrich shook his head. 'It's your life.' He still had that feeling, almost a presence, a shadow of doom over the sunny day.

'Come on man, cheer up, we've done it. They'll be back at Windsor tonight. Tomorrow we can start tracking down this bastard again. He's got to be in deep trouble now. This was

283

his only chance, and he's blown it. Come on, I'm going to cadge a fag off one of the drivers.'

They started off across the courtyard, Jones' chest feeling as though it was in a vice. He made a promise to himself. This was his last cigarette, definitely. He was giving them up, straight after this one, just like he'd promised Gareth. He'd been sticking to it as well, until this bloody load of trouble landed on his desk.

The ambassadors were split into three parties and Eilders' group was led back to the ground floor and the Belgian suite. Eilders decided he would leave the group, somehow, when it reached the first floor. Then there was only one flight of stairs between himself and the princesses. He could not do it now, there was simply no opportunity. And the ambassador for Spain had his arm around Eilders' shoulders, telling him a risqué anecdote about Herr Joachim von Ribbentrop.

Jones accepted a cigarette from a big red-faced chauffeur who stood talking and smoking with a driver built like an under-nourished whippet. Red-face struck a match, lit the cigarette for Jones and said: 'No grub for the likes of us, then?'

Harry Jones took a long, delicious drag of cool smoke, feeling better the moment it touched his lungs.

'Bugger all to do with me, mate, I'm a copper.'

Red-face put his hands up. 'Fair cop, I'll come quietly.' He and Whippet laughed.

Ulrich had sat down on the running board of the nearest Rolls-Royce, leaning his head back against the warm metal bodywork, eyes closed.

Whippet said: 'That's right, I remember you, you're the one who gave me and the boss the once over at the gate.'

Jones took another short puff: 'Oh aye, I remember you too, you drove in like you was Malcolm Campbell.'

The disembodied voices seemed to drift into space for Ulrich.

'Aye,' Jones added, 'thought for a minute you were going to carry on right through the Palace.'

All three laughed. Jones felt positively jovial now. Nerves, that's all it had been, nerves and tiredness.

It was Ulrich who felt weary now, weary, heartsick and homesick. He was tired of Jones and his bad jokes and forced joviality, his see-saw moods that careered between anger, irritability, and matey back-slapping and folk wisdom. He was sick of England, the stupid confusing language, the bad food and the absurd anti-German prejudice. He felt a physical hunger for Germany, for cool forests and cold foamy beer, for the richness of the language, the sparkle of the Wannsee, Ilse lying out on the grass . . .

' . . . not guilty, Officer, on my life. Bloody guv'nor wasn't it? He made me drive up Park Lane *twice*, just because there was a queue at the gates. We're bloody nearly late, I'm halfway past your entrance and he's shouting, "Thees entrance, thees entrance" . . . '

Red-face laughed at his mate's impersonation.

'I mean blimey O'Reilly, only two choices, what difference it make?'

Everyone laughed, and Jones felt another twinge.

Ulrich opened his eyes.

Jones said: 'I remember him, right ponce, stunk like a Belgian whorehouse, aye . . . ' he suddenly remembered, 'moaning about *me* making him late, and he had you poncing up Park Lane with him; dago . . . what a smell.'

Whippet winked, delighted to be able to dish dirt on his employer: 'He's been in a few whorehouses between you and me, and they ain't in bloody Belgium.' He winked again. 'Know what I mean? Been out on the razzle-dazzle every night since he got here, and that's not so long ago. Had a tart in the embassy last night, straight up, Rolls at the side of the house this morning . . . prying eyes . . . then he leaves her in his flaming boo-doar . . . he's got a nerve.'

Ulrich got up from the running board, he felt terribly frightened.

He said to the whippet-like driver: 'He made himself deliberately late, you say, and then he chose the entrance manned by my colleague?'

Whippet shrugged: 'Par for the course this morning. Been acting like a different man ever since he got in the car.'

Ulrich grabbed Whippet by the shoulders. '*A different man?*'

'It's only a figure of speech, mate; look, who is he?' He looked appealingly at Jones. 'Tell him to get his hands off me.'

'Come on, Ulrich, for Christ's sake.'

Ulrich released him. 'You say he's been acting strangely? That he insisted the car was brought to the side entrance of the embassy?'

'So what, he obviously had some tart in his bedroom he didn't want the staff to see.'

'But she *didn't* come out with him?'

Whippet shrugged. 'No . . . she was . . . unwell . . .that's it, unwell, that's what he said.'

'And if he came down Constitution Hill he had time to take a look at the other entrance, the one manned by me?'

Whippet was looking bemused. 'I suppose so . . . look what is this, Agatha flamin' Christie?'

'Did you get a good look at his face? Are you sure it *was* the ambassador?'

'Of course it was him. Blimey, I mean who else would it be?'

'Is there a mirror in the interior of your car? Did you observe him closely?'

'No . . . look I'm getting fed up with this . . . there's no mirror, but it was *him*, I tell you.'

Ulrich whipped round on Harry Jones. 'Harry, you checked him, are *you* sure?'

Jones was white, breathing heavily. 'Christ, mate, of course I'm sure . . . I looked right into the car, I had the photograph, I mean it was gloomy in the car . . . he was in a hurry . . . his face matched the picture . . . '

Ulrich interrupted him: 'He was in a *hurry*!? He asked the chauffeur to take him up Park Lane *twice*, he was deliberately making himself late, if he had been in a hurry he could have joined the queue.' He turned on Whippet. 'Which embassy—quickly!'

'Look, mate, I don't want to get into any trouble, I've shot my mouth off a bit.'

'Tell me!'

Whippet told him.

'Name?'

'Alvarez.'

Ulrich turned and grabbed Jones by the arm, the Welshman looked unbelievably old and tired. 'Come on, Harry, let's get into the Palace, we've got to check him.'

Harry Jones was mumbling, half to himself, it was difficult to make out the words: 'Can't be him . . . impossible . . . checked the picture . . . can't . . . '

Ulrich shook him hard, real anger in his eyes. 'Can't! Impossible! Nothing has been impossible for him since the start. You were so sure, you British, weren't you, so bloody sure. He was a foreigner and he couldn't beat you. But he did, every time, and there is a trail of bodies behind him, maids, landladies, factory girls, newsagents, queers . . . all because you thought it wasn't possible. Give me the gun, Harry!'

The two chauffeurs were moving away now, frightened. They didn't know what was going on, and they didn't want to.

'No, damn it . . . no!'

Ulrich softened his voice: 'We've got to check this Alvarez quickly. Maybe it is all a mistake, but we have no time to waste. You are tired, Harry, tired and sick. Give me the gun, *please*.' There were tears of frustration in Ulrich's eyes.

Harry Jones snapped his head up, suddenly alert and composed. 'I'm *still* in charge. If it *is* him, we'll both get him. Come on.'

Both men ran across the courtyard beneath the hot afternoon sun.

Chapter Twenty-Six

THE GROUP of ambassadors that included Eilders was in the throne room on the first floor, crowded around the two thrones, one for the King of England, the other for his Queen.

Eilders edged to the back of the room where two liveried servants stood staring blankly into the middle distance. 'I must use the lavatory. I feel unwell.'

One statue moved. 'Come this way, sir.' Even the palace servants had strict instructions that no one was to move around unaccompanied.

Eilders followed the servant out into the corridor. It was incredible, but there was no sign of a uniformed armed guard. They turned a corner and the servant opened a door and led Eilders across a long, empty room with furniture covered in dust sheets, until they reached a further door.

Through it was a line of wash-basins, a mirror and some towels marked with the royal crest on rollers, and three cubicles.

The servant pointed: 'You will find facilities in there, sir.' The man then signed his death warrant: 'I shall remain here, sir, and escort you back to the throne room.'

'Of course.' Eilders went into the cubicle, made suitable sounds of nausea, and took the garrotte from his stocking.

When Eilders came out of the cubicle he could see the distaste on the servant's face. 'I'm ready.'

'Very well, sir.'

The servant turned his back. Eilders killed him, amazed at how the man fought futilely for life.

Had the servant left him there, the man might have lived. In the event it would help, for he would take the man's ridiculous garb and use it to get to the next floor. He stripped off his own clothes, then those of the dead servant. Eilders wiped the mass of grease from his hair and jammed the powdered wig onto his head. He ripped off the beard with an agonising tug that made his eyes water. He began to pull on the knee-breeches and the ridiculous jacket.

One floor above. Just one.

It was a party trick but it worked. Queen Elizabeth paid a polite farewell to Ambassador Kennedy, then stepped over to one of the china cabinets and pressed the concealed switch. Kennedy watched in amazement as it swung back to reveal a door that the Queen then opened. Seconds later, Prime Minister Churchill appeared. He bowed: 'Your Majesty.'

'Prime Minister. You have met Ambassador Kennedy?'

Churchill took the American's outstretched hand. The two men hated the sight of one another. 'Indeed, Your Majesty. A great pleasure, Mr Ambassador.'

'Likewise, Prime Minister.'

Five minutes later the King withdrew to the next room, and Mr Churchill began to tell Mr Kennedy exactly why Germany could not win this war, and why her army would never land on Britain's shores.

In the throne room next door, Ulrich von der Osten of the German Abwehr addressed a group of ambassadors. Harry Jones was simply unable to speak. 'Señor Alvarez? Will he identify himself please?'

The ambassadors looked around them. One said: 'Well he *was* here, I was talking to him.'

A man in livery moved from the door, coughed politely, his hand in front of his mouth, and whispered something to Ulrich.

Ulrich said: 'Show me. Quickly!' He and the servant rushed from the room, Jones following slowly.

Eilders put the garrotte up his sleeve and left the washroom, walking slowly for he had no wish to draw attention to himself. Before he reached the stairs he saw a man in a lounge suit coming down, a sheaf of papers under his arm. Eilders held his breath, but the man walked off in the opposite direction with hardly a glance at Eilders.

He came to the stairs and climbed them. Everywhere was deserted. Eilders could not realise that normally these corridors would be bustling, but that the majority of the palace staff—those, in fact, who were not absolutely essential to the function—had left the Palace for the day. It had been done in the interests of security, and by cruel irony it was working the opposite way.

At the top of the stairs he turned right, came to the end of another corridor and turned right again. If he was correct he was just fifty feet from the princesses' room.

Yes! There, feet apart like an English civilian policeman, a man in a lounge suit standing outside a door as though on guard.

Eilders walked boldly down the corridor. The servant's garb was ill-fitting and hastily-donned. Up close it would survive no scrutiny.

He was forty feet from the man now. Thirty. Twenty. The man had seen him and turned to look. Fifteen feet. 'Yes?' Ten feet.

The man was looking the arrival up and down, something suspicious beginning to register in his face. Five feet. Suspicion came alive.

The man's hand darted inside his jacket.

The body was sprawled out in its underclothes, face dreadfully contorted, and the servant with Ulrich took one look, heaved, stopped himself, then vomited.

290

Ulrich took the man's grey face in his hands.

'Where are the princesses' quarters, tell me, quickly?'

The man clenched his teeth shut, fighting nausea, and shook his head. 'I can't tell you . . . not allowed.'

'Look . . . look at that . . . ' he forced the servant's face around to look at the bulging eyes of the corpse. 'It's vital you tell me. Their Highnesses' lives are in danger.' The man pulled his face away from the dreadful sight, and told Ulrich what he wished to know.

At that point Harry Jones came in the door, heaving for breath. He got a glimpse of the body and tried to say something, but Ulrich and lack of breath cut him short.

'It's Eilders. He's dressed as a servant, heading for the princesses' quarters on the floor above.'

He ran, half-dragging, half-pushing Jones, until they reached the stairs, and Harry Jones leaned for support against a banister.

'Give me the gun, I'll go on alone.'

Jones shook his head, and started to take the stairs, each one an Everest. Suddenly he gave a cry of agony, clutched his chest with both hands, his face contorted, and collapsed.

He'd rolled two steps before Ulrich stopped him. He pulled Jones face-upwards and loosened the man's tie. The Welshman tried to speak but there was no sound, only a series of bubbles from saliva that drooled from his mouth. Ulrich hesitated. There was a whiplash pistol shot from very close. Ulrich pushed aside Jones' coat and tugged at the handle of the Colt, tearing it free from the man's waistband.

The Welshman's eyes were wide open, staring, terrified.

Ulrich checked the chamber of the revolver. Fully loaded.

Harry Jones made a gurgling noise, and his head flopped to one side.

Ulrich ran as he had never run.

The gun was half out of the detective's shoulder holster, the butt in his grip, when Eilders leapt. He caught the man in the face, jerking his head back, chopping for the gun arm.

291

The pistol dropped to the carpet, and the detective punched at Eilders, but missed.

Eilders brought his knee up into the man's groin. There was a sigh of agony, then he was on him, thumbs gouging into the neck pressure points. The detective crumpled, Eilders stepped back to avoid him, and picked up the gun from the carpet.

The door opened, a man.

'Keith, crikey, what's the . . . Jesus . . . '

He saw Eilders and was going for his gun.

Eilders shot him once in the chest and the man went back into the door jamb with a sickening crack as his head hit the wood. Eilders went in through the open door.

The two girls were sitting side by side on a sofa. Both had teacups in their hands, their faces registering the shock of the commotion and the shot.

Princess Elizabeth said severely: 'Who are you? How dare you burst in here? What have you done?'

She saw the gun in Eilders' hand and he saw her grit her teeth. Suddenly she hurled the teacup at him. It was a brave and utterly futile gesture. The fragile cup missed him and shattered against the wall.

Princess Margaret looked on the point of tears, her lips trembling.

Eilders put the gun down on the small table next to him and took out the garrotte. The younger girl did not know what was happening, but she began to cry.

Ulrich turned into the east wing and immediately saw the crumpled bodies fifty feet away. He heard a small crash like breaking glass. He ran faster, lungs heaving, cocking the hammer on the revolver as he ran.

Eilders felt giddy with the power of it. Now was the moment. He moved a step forward. 'Do you realise who I am?'

'You're a parachutist,' Princess Elizabeth said gravely. 'You've come to harm us and you'll be punished.'

Eilders smiled. Then, from the depths of his nightmares, came *that* voice.

'Eilders!'

He turned, the garrotte held in both hands. Ulrich was framed in the doorway, a pistol held out before him.

Eilders' gun was on the table. He screamed: 'Traitor!' And freed one hand and dived for the gun. Two bangs and flashes of flame.

Eilders' chest erupted in little gouts of blood, and he pitched backwards into the table.

The ludicrous powdered wig flew off. He lay very still.

Both girls were white, shocked and quiet.

Ulrich kneeled over the body, feeling for the pulse. Uwe Eilders was quite dead. It was over now. He put the warm gun down on Eilders' body and sat down heavily on the carpet, drained, incapable of movement.

He heard a small voice and looked up. It was Princess Elizabeth. Her voice was quavering but she said: 'He was a German parachutist, wasn't he? Like they had in Holland? He was going to harm us.'

Ulrich looked at the daughter of his enemy's King.

He said: 'Yes, Your Highness, he was a German. One kind.'

Then to the girls' astonishment he put his head in both hands and began to cry.

Epilogue

With refined cruelty, they did not even let him attend Harry Jones' funeral. Within an hour Ulrich von der Osten had been served with an internment order, and was put on a night train to Liverpool handcuffed to a military policeman in a reserved first class compartment. At Liverpool's Lime Street station an army truck met them and drove them to the docks. As the steamer approached the Isle of Man in sheeting rain, Ulrich realised the Welshman had been right. They had sent Ulrich to the Isle of Man over Jones' dead body.

The corpse of Uwe Eilders was hastily taken from the Palace to Horseferry Road mortuary, where it was placed in a bath of preserving liquid until someone high up made up his mind what to do with it.

The next day the editors of all Fleet Street newspapers and senior officials of the BBC were called to a top security briefing at Number Ten, Downing Street, where they were addressed personally by the Prime Minister. They were advised that a member of the Buckingham Palace staff believed to have Nazi sympathies, had made a bungled physical assault on the King. In the scuffle, two royal detectives had been accidentally killed by the discharge of one of their pistols. The editors were urged that in the interests of national security, the matter should go unreported. The editors did their patriotic duty and complied with the 'request'.

Special Branch officers went to the home of Señor Jorge Alvarez and were reluctantly admitted to his quarters by suspicious staff. A corpse was removed under a sheet. The staff assumed that corpse was of a woman. They were later told Señor Alvarez had succumbed to a heart attack following the Buckingham Palace reception. They linked the two events and assumed the promiscuous young ambassador had killed his girlfriend in a crime passionelle, then killed himself.

The British ambassador in Lisbon took morning tea with the Swiss ambassador, who later took lunch with the German ambassador. The enigmatic message: 'The bird is dead' was sent to Berlin.

The Fuehrer was informed.

He was pleased, and decided that now the princesses were safe, it was time to deliver a speech. He told a packed audience of the Reichstag, sitting in the Kroll Opera House on 19th July, 1940: 'It almost causes me pain to think that I should have been selected by Fate to deal the final blow to the structure which these men have already set tottering . . . Mr Churchill ought perhaps, for once, to believe me when I prophesy that a great Empire will be destroyed—an Empire which it was never my intention to destroy or even harm.

'In this hour I feel it to be my duty before my own conscience to appeal once more to reason and common sense in Great Britain as much as elsewhere. I consider myself in a position to make this appeal, since I am not the vanquished begging favours, but the victor speaking in the name of reason.

'I can see no reason why this war should go on.'

In Britain the speech was greeted with stony official silence. Adolf Hitler was not greatly surprised. Three days earlier he had given the go-ahead for Operation Sea Lion, the invasion of Great Britain.

If the British had made some response to his speech, perhaps he would have reconsidered. Now however the war must take its course. Goering's Luftwaffe could be let loose on the British to destroy the Royal Air Force as a prerequisite for invasion.

Of course, the Fuehrer completely forgot about a certain Colonel Ulrich von der Osten.

*   *   *

296

On a bleak January day, with the sea mist settled like a damp shroud on the seafront of Douglas, Isle of Man, Ulrich was playing chess with an Italian chef from Glasgow. The man had left Bologna aged seven, and could still not come to terms with the fact that his adopted country had put him behind barbed wire on an island in the Irish Sea.

A guard told Ulrich he was wanted at the camp office. There, a nondescript man with a briefcase and Whitehall clothes and manners told Ulrich that the British government were prepared to offer him a concession. If Ulrich signed a binding agreement that he would not attempt to return to Germany, and not communicate to anyone anything of what he had witnessed, then he would be allowed to spend the remainder of the war in Mexico.

Ulrich agreed without hesitation, signed the document, and in two hours the Isle of Man was a receding brown stone set in a frothy emerald sea as the Sunderland flying boat rose and banked towards England.

He had lied. And lied without compunction. The British had cheated him. His reward for saving the lives of their little princesses was handcuffs and internment.

He did not know what diplomatic pressure had been exerted, but he intended to go to Mexico, then make his way from there to the United States.

German liners still plied a regular service between New York in neutral America, and home.

One day he would make sure the truth was known.

When his ship docked at Acapulco, he did not leave as he should have, but booked onward passage to Long Beach, the port of Los Angeles. The fact that he did not disembark was noted by agents of the Mexican secret service, who telegraphed the information to their big brothers at the Federal Bureau of Investigation in Washington.

In turn, and in accordance with a recent and strictly unofficial agreement, the FBI told MI6's outfit in New York, British Security Co-ordination. Two men were detailed to wait for the boat when it docked at Long Beach, and to follow Ulrich von der Osten, who now had false papers provided by the British in the name of Don Julio Lopez Lido.

Ulrich spotted the two men when he left the ship, and they followed him to a hotel in downtown Los Angeles close to Union Station.

Ulrich checked at the train station, and discovered that the Super Chief was leaving for New York the following day. He booked a compartment.

He noted that one of the men who had been following him went to the pigeon-hole and spoke earnestly with the reservations clerk.

They would almost certainly board the train the next day and travel with him all the way to New York, or they would prevent him boarding, perhaps by arresting him, although he knew he had committed no offence. So he packed his suitcase, paid his hotel bill, left the hotel by a side door and caught a bus to Pasadena.

When the Super Chief pulled in on its first stop out of Los Angeles the next morning Ulrich boarded, made some apologies and took up his compartment. His two tails were still standing at Union Station wondering why he had not boarded the train.

Once in his compartment Ulrich wrote two long letters to Ilse, put them in envelopes and addressed them to his own house at Wannsee. Any secret service could intercept mail, but they could not check every mail-box in a country the size of the United States, and mail between America and Germany flowed unhindered.

He called the coloured attendant and asked if the letters could be posted by the man at Albuquerque, New Mexico, the train's next stop. The attendant said there would be no problem, and gratefully pocketed the two dollars.

Ulrich sat back and took a bottle of brandy from his bag. He added a little iced water from the silver thermos provided courtesy of the Santa Fe railroad, and took a long drink. The desert scenery was amazing.

Two more men were waiting at New York. Ulrich took a taxi to a tourist hotel the cabby recommended, the Taft on 7th Avenue at 50th Street in the midtown district close to Times Square. It was big, over a thousand rooms, and there was no problem getting in. In his room Ulrich wrote another letter to Ilse, almost a duplicate of the others.

He did not think the American secret services would harm him; his country and theirs were not at war. But he did not give such qualms to the British. If he did have an 'accident' he wanted on record what had taken place during those summer days of 1940. He found a post office and mailed the letter.

One hour later it was being studied by the FBI and was eventually handed to MI6's BSC. An urgent coded message was sent to London.

The matter was taken to the highest level and the reply was precise and unequivocal.

On 17th March, 1941, Ulrich von der Osten booked passage on a German liner sailing to Bremerhaven from the Hudson Pier the following night.

That evening he planned to eat at Child's, a popular eaterie just a stroll away on Times Square. Then he planned to take a taxi, go to Harlem and listen to some coloured jazz.

When he left the Hotel Taft a yellow cab with its lights and hire sign off, but with its engine idling, pulled out from the kerb as Ulrich began to cross the street.

The driver gunned the engine, smoke burned from the screeching tyres, and the bonnet of the taxi struck Ulrich square in the back.

He was dead by the time he rolled up onto the bonnet and off again into the gutter, his spine shattered. No one got the number of the cab.

The corpse of Uwe Eilders was taken from its bath of preserving liquid ten days later, put into a closed van and driven to Cambridge.

There it was dressed in a suit in which money, small

299

personal possessions, cinema ticket stubs, cloakroom tickets and a set of identity papers in the name of Jan Villen Ter Braak, had been placed.

In the last days of March he was dumped in an empty air-raid shelter, a suitcase radio captured from another agent placed beside his body.

In the early hours of 1st April a call was made to Cambridge police by an anonymous man. As a result police officers went to the air-raid shelter and found the body of 'Jan Villen Ter Braak', a man registered at a fictitious address in the town. The police took one look at the gunshot wounds and the radio and called Special Branch, who went back up to Cambridge to collect their body. It was April Fool's Day. Eilders' body was quickly cremated at Golders Green cemetery, an ironic touch bearing in mind that the Golders Green crematorium held many Jewish funeral ceremonies.

Thanks to carefully-placed whispers, the word began to get out. A German agent shot himself in Cambridge because he couldn't escape the spycatchers.

London liked that, and the April Fool's Day touch. It wouldn't be unnoticed when it filtered back to Berlin.

Pour encourager les autres.

At 9.30 on the morning of 27th May, 1942, two Czechs called Kubis and Gabčik, members of a parachute mission from England called the 'Anthropoids' waited with sub-machine guns and grenades on a hairpin bend in the Prague suburb of Holesovice. Two other gunmen were in position at different points of the bend.

They were waiting to kill Reinhard Heydrich.

One hour later a girl called Rela Fafek, Gabčik's girlfriend, was in her own car approaching the bend. She wore a hat, which was the signal that some way behind her, the chauffeur-driven Mercedes carrying the Reichsprotektor of Bohemia and Moravia was unescorted.

Minutes later another man with a mirror signalled that the Mercedes was approaching. As the car slowed and rounded the bend, Gabčik stepped out and pulled the trigger of his Sten gun. It jammed. He was immediately shot by both Heydrich and his chauffeur. Kubis threw a grenade which exploded, injuring himself and Heydrich. The Reichsprotektor managed to stagger a few feet and then collapsed.

The injured Kubis escaped with the others.

On 4th June Heydrich died from gangrene caused when pieces of his uniform lodged in the wound.

The Germans took a terrible revenge. Over ten thousand Czechs were arrested and a thousand executed. At the small mining village of Lidice, which the Germans erroneously thought had sheltered the assassins, all males between sixteen and seventy were shot. The women and children were deported to extermination camps. The village itself was demolished by explosive and fire, and later levelled by bulldozer so that no trace of it remained.

Someone betrayed the Anthropoids. Cornered in the crypt of a Greek Orthodox church in Prague's old town, down to their last few bullets, Kubis was killed by a grenade, another man took poison and then shot himself, and then the remaining men shot each other until the final man shot himself.

Heydrich's death was an outright political assassination of the type the British had never before indulged in, and never did again, with the exception of a half-hearted and clumsily executed attempt on the life of Rommel.

The official reason for Heydrich's killing was his increasing brutality and efficiency against the Czech resistance. But everyone knew the Czech resistance was totally unimportant. No one chose to launch assassination attempts against German leaders in Yugoslavia later in the war, or in France, whose resistance movements were far more vital.

Did the British know it was Heydrich who had broken the rules of war and launched Operation Raven which so nearly killed their beloved princesses? Did Heydrich pay with his life for the madness of Uwe Eilders?

* * *

301

It was night, and so the bombers were British. Tomorrow the Americans would come and pound the ashes.

By the lights of the Berlin fires that reflected off the waters of the Wannsee, Ilse re-read the letters. She had not read the letters for six months, but today the official from the Foreign Ministry had come and told her of the Red Cross message. Ulrich von der Osten, under an assumed identity, had been killed in a New York traffic accident . . . two years ago!

The state of war between the two countries, the false identity, all had delayed the news of his death being passed to Germany.

Coldly she re-read the letters. They had murdered him, killed him after all he had done, simply so that he could never speak of what he had seen. Germany had washed its hands of him and the British and Americans had closed his mouth for ever. But she knew, she had the letters.

She wheeled herself across to the window, where the hot winds off the lake smelled of smoke, and wafted the curtains and her hair.

She watched Berlin's agony and vowed. One day the world would know.

Only three of the principals involved in that shattering day at Buckingham Palace are still alive. They are the King's widow, Queen Elizabeth, now titled the Queen Mother, Princess Elizabeth, now Queen of England, and Princess Margaret.

In the words of newspaper reporters, none of them are available for comment.